LETHAL

THE DISCIPLES SERIES – BOOK ONE

USA TODAY BESTSELLING AUTHOR
CASSANDRA ROBBINS

Copyright © 2019
ISBN: 9781090805263

LETHAL by Cassandra Robbins
All rights reserved. No part of this book may be reproduced, distributed, or scanned in any manner without written permission of the author, except in the need of quotes for reviews only.

This book is a work of fiction. The names, characters, and establishments are the product of the author's imagination or are used to provide authenticity and are used fictitiously. Any resemblance to any person, living or dead, is purely coincidental.

Edited: Nikki Busch Editing
Cover Design: Michele Catalano Creative
Formatting: Elaine York, Allusion Publishing
www.allusionpublishing.com
Cover Photo: Wander Aguiar Photography
Cover Model: Roddy

LETHAL

THE DISCIPLES SERIES - BOOK ONE

DISCIPLES

ONE

EVE - Present

"**H**oly shit, they're coming." *Strike that—he's coming!* "Where the fuck is Benny?"

The dust cloud is so thick it's almost suffocating. I close my eyes against the dirt to keep them clear.

"Never mind." My voice is loud over the rumble and screeching of their iron horses. "Get to my dad before they do."

The dark-haired boy named Santiago nods. His big brown eyes hold terror. He should be scared. Hell is about to burn us open. A small twist of guilt wraps around what's left of my questionable conscience as I look at the dirty ten-year-old who happened to have the bad luck of working in my booth today.

"Go."

He bolts under the counter and takes off like the boogeyman is after him. And maybe he is, or at least after me. I watch as dirt puffs up while he runs toward my trailer. My eyes scope the neon lights, the Ferris wheel, and the Tilt-a-Whirl. The rides still move; people are still laughing even though bad men are coming. Pushing open the counter on the side of my stand, I ignore the couple whining about the darts that I've dropped on the plywood floor.

LETHAL

"What the hell? I paid you ten dollars. Where do you think you're going?" the stupid guy sneers.

The girl covers her nose, dust swirling and dancing around us as the motorcycles spin and skid in the parking lot.

"You two need to get out of here. Shit is going down." I reach for my knife taped under the wooden counter, grab my backpack, and almost laugh at the horror on these two idiots' faces. Truth be told, they are probably my age. But I feel ancient compared to them.

The guy slams his fist on the counter causing the girlfriend to gasp and jump. "This is unbelievable. I've heard you guys are scum, but you can't steal my money and leave. I'll call the cops, bitch." His light brown hair is gelled back and he's wearing skinny jeans. That fact alone should make me let the motorcycle club take him out. I heave the backpack over my shoulder and start to walk across the loud carnival area.

"Hey! You can't do this, blondie," the douche screams at me.

"I don't have time for this," I yell over my shoulder. "Get away from here. Trust me, that's worth the ten dollars you gave me." My hands clench at my sides as I watch the girl wisely pull the guy away. He's still bitching about not being able to win a disgusting, moldy stuffed animal from China.

"Fucking pathetic." I run across the long field checking behind me as I go.

"Benny... please be in the trailer, *please*."

The sun is lowering and heavy metal music blares out of the speakers. I know in my heart Benny's gone and more than likely not coming back. Same way I know this betrayal will be the final straw for me. As I exhale, the taste of dirt lingers in my mouth. My mind scrambles with all my options, but with my dad and his lack of mobility... I'll have to take responsibility for Benny's actions. They're coming, and the only person I give two shits about in this fucked-up world is my dad.

Pushing my long hair behind my shoulders, I wish I had something better on. But who am I kidding? The bikers want their money. I could be wearing a ball gown, and unless it's covered in diamonds, it's not going to do me any good. Though I don't know how much Benny owes them, I only have about $500 stashed away, and I can only pray it's not as bad as I think. Tucking my head down, I run to my trailer. I don't even get the door open when a tan tattooed hand grabs me and jerks me inside so violently my teeth chatter.

Blinking, I try to adjust my eyes to the dark cave-like feel of our trailer. The sound of wheezing comes from the corner and my eyes bolt to my father. His once-strong frame, now shriveled and weak, is slumped over in a sad excuse for a wheelchair. Another tattooed monster stands next to him.

"Jesus Christ! He can't breathe without his oxygen." I go to move toward him, but that tattooed hand is still wrapped around my arm. I twist back and forth, then stop as I realize it's pointless. What I need to do is think and assess the situation. My dad's oxygen mask is still on, but his skin is sweaty and pale, with an almost gray, waxy look. My tears burn as I watch my sweet father take small hissing breaths.

"Please." I look around for the first time since I was jerked into the trailer and I'm stunned. It's been completely ripped apart. They've torn off cabinets, thrown the microwave and TV on the floor, and split open all the furniture. That means our piece of shit couch and chair, along with Benny's and my mattresses in the corner, are trashed. Feathers dance around causing me to shiver at how serious this is.

"Where's Benny?" His voice is deep and gravelly and I instantly search for the leader. A shudder goes up my spine. I'd know that voice anywhere. After all, its haunted me for two years.

"Or better yet, where's Paul?" I can't place that voice.

I glance around for poor Santiago. I don't see him, but there are a lot of big bikers in my small trailer.

"My father needs his oxygen," I plead.

"Where's your junkie brother? You want oxygen for your old man, you better talk fast."

I search the room for that voice.

I shake my head. "I don't know." It's the truth, but they'll never believe that.

Then I see him, like a fucking immortal. He's almost too beautiful to be real. I take a step back, tilt my head up, and realize that I'm fucked. There will be no negotiating. There will be no mercy. It's all right there in his pretty green eyes.

Unless my brother, *the junkie*, miraculously walks through this door, I'm not going to live to be a day over eighteen. Happy Fucking Birthday to me.

TWO

EVE - Two years earlier

"Just let me handle this, all right?" I look over at my brother's current girlfriend Marina and make a necessary decision. "Actually, wait here. I'm only running in for a couple things."

Her carrot-red hair that always reminds me of Pippi Longstocking, bounces back and forth. It's one of the few books I've read, so whenever I see her, I almost look around for the pet monkey. Marina is like the adult version of Pippi, meaning she has the bright orange hair, lots of freckles, and big boobs. I guess that's why men like her. Because her personality and face are lacking. But hey, that's my opinion.

We're parked in a Walmart parking lot. Her stocky, freckled legs are on display in her ratty denim miniskirt. Of course, she sports a wife beater with no bra. At first, I thought I could use her as a decoy but her nonstop bitching about my brother and their sex life or lack of one is making me want to gag and reconsider.

She opens her door to my dad's piece of shit Ford pickup. "No way. I'm supposed to babysit you." She squirms as she tries to wiggle her skirt down.

I roll my eyes as I exit the truck too. "What do you want in here? And nothing fancy. We're running late."

LETHAL

The sun is out and I lift my face to its wonderful soothing warmth. With my eyes closed, I chant in my head for her to say nothing.

Instead I hear, "I need mascara and some lipstick. Red and maybe some nail polish to go with the lipstick."

I eye her and smile. "Absolutely. You know what to do."

She snorts as we enter the large store, a blast of cold air making my skin pebble. I rub my hands up and down my tan thighs, ignoring all the leering looks we get. Men are gross. All they do is stare and maybe because they think I'm trash, they think they can disrespect me with their disgusting mouths.

I sigh as I hear a catcall and a "hey baby come sit on my face." This is why I hate growing up. It was so much easier to steal as a dirty-blond-haired girl than as a pretty blond woman. And as much as I try not to be, I am. I look like my dead mother. Tall, blond, and thin. Blue eyes, long legs, such a fucking drag.

Marina swishes her ass so much she actually bumps into me.

"Jesus Christ. Pull it together," I snap. "I'm going to go get my shit. You just... I don't know... browse." I wave my hand at the magazine section.

"Don't forget my stuff." She's not even looking at me, her eyes glued on a creep sitting at a table stuffing his face with a Subway sandwich.

I take off down the aisle quickly taking in the cameras located inside the store. I have my large purse and I don't like to brag, but I'm kind of a master at this shoplifting thing. In a flash, I have all my stuff. Balloons, tampons, Neosporin for my dad's elbow. I throw in a couple CoverGirl LashBlast Volume mascaras and some hideous red lipstick. If I was nice, I would tell her she should never wear red lipstick. But I'm not and Marina's a stupid slut so *whatever*. My handsome brother is way too good for her—or at least he used to be. Benny looks a lot like me but taller. Although lately he's been losing weight and his pretty skin is breaking out.

As I walk over to the electronics section, my skin pebbles again with excitement. I stand and watch a couple kids argue about which is better X box or PlayStation. Rolling my neck, I notice two blue-colored shirts behind a white counter. And halleluiah, they have girls in them. Both are engrossed in their phones, not caring at all what people are doing. The store is enormous, but this section always has more traffic. I glance at the smartphone section and sure enough, a small guard is looking at me. This is why I wanted Marina. Even with her homely face, her tits could have been useful. I smile at him and he immediately looks away.

Smirking, I don't hesitate and grab a display phone then turn and walk away along with my giant tampon collection. Got to love tampons. They make even the biggest, scariest guys look away. I bring the phone to my ear—and this is my favorite part—I start talking to my pretend boyfriend. We're fighting, so of course my voice is loud. The more I talk, the less people have interest in anything but what I'm telling him. *Easy peasy lemon squeezy.*

As if I own the place, I walk straight for the nice little Hispanic man. He smiles kindly at me as I sit down my giant box of tampons and start to get tears in my eyes as I pretend to hang up on my pretend boyfriend. Shaking my long hair I drop the phone in my bag and sniffle up into his concerned eyes.

He clears his voice. "That will be fifteen dollars and forty-five cents, and are you okay?"

"Yes, I guess. Guy problems."

He nods. "Well, I have a daughter around your age. You need to dump him and concentrate on school."

I nod and mumble, "You're probably right." Brazenly I open my bag and grab my wallet, handing him a twenty. He gives me my change.

"You take care." His kind smile should make me feel bad. It doesn't. I smile sweetly at him. It's almost too easy. That charge I need not even coming anymore. *How is that possible?* Maybe I've gotten so jaded that at sixteen, nothing makes me excited. That would be depressing.

After I stop to retrieve Marina from the creeper, who wants her number, I pull her along and together we approach the exit. At last, I feel a twinge of adrenaline because if the smartphone has a security tag, this will be when the alarm goes off.

A couple of guys walk out right before us and it's almost like I'm blessed. The alarm goes off and I have to bite my lip not to smile. Because as soon as I get close I go off too, but the guard is bringing the boys in thinking it's them.

Marina and I keep talking and exit the store. Warm air hits me as we make our way to the truck.

"Did you get my stuff?" Her dilated eyes make me think she and the creeper might have smoked something.

Again, I wonder why my brother keeps her around. I start the truck.

"Yeah, I got your lipstick and some mascara. We need to hurry. I want to reinforce my balloons. Last night I gave away way too much shit."

She nods but is clearly in another world. I reach over and roll down my window and turn up the radio.

We hit traffic. Of course we do—we're in LA—and a drive that should have taken fifteen minutes takes forty-five. So, I'm sweaty and pissed that I can't change my balloons. There's not enough time since the lights and music are already on when we arrive. The carnival is almost ready to open. I park the truck next to my trailer and slap at Marina to wake up. Whatever she took was definitely not an upper.

"Here." I toss the mascara and ugly lipstick at her.

"I'm late and I need to change. I'd say thanks for coming with me but..." I raise my eyebrow at her.

"What?" she snips, reaching for the visor and checking herself in the mirror.

"O-kaay, I'm out." I grab my purse and swing open our trailer door. A cloud of smoke hits me. On our ugly green and brown couch sit my brother and Paul. Or Pauly the prick—that's what I like to call him.

"Jesus." I wave my hand in front of my face. Deep wheezing coughs bring my attention to the back of the trailer where my dad sits on the edge of his bed.

"Daddy? You okay?" I maneuver my way through the pile of dirty clothes and stand in front of him. His head hangs down and he is clutching a lit cigarette as he coughs and hisses his way through his latest bout.

"Daddy?" My voice sounds small and frightened because I am. My dad is sick. His lungs are black and he's slowly suffocating with emphysema. But do you think he would stop smoking for a second? No.

For a moment, he looks up at me with bloodshot eyes and smiles. "Don't give me crap, Baby Girl. I need one today." He stands his full height and I almost burst into tears at my tall handsome father, not even fifty yet getting ready to die.

"I understand. Are they… are they still coming?"

I go to sit on the bed as he grabs his leather jacket. It's hot out but he seems to get the chills. I know it's because he gets fevers. But today he needs to look strong. He would rather die than show any weakness to the head of the Disciples, the MC that basically runs this area. Since we are only passing through, my dad and Benny usually buy a bunch of weed, meth, and whatever else is popular and sell it to the locals who come to the carnival. He's been doing it for about five years, and it seems to be working for us and the club. Easy money on both sides.

I bite my bottom lip.

"Evie." He reaches under his dirty mattress, bringing out his six-shooter.

"I want you to stay in your booth tonight. Don't go wandering around while they're here. I know Blade is trustworthy but the others I can't be sure of." He brings the cancer stick to his pale lips and inhales as if it's his lover.

Unable to watch him without crying, I stand. "Whatever you want, Daddy. I need to get ready."

I walk back out to the main room where Marina is straddling Benny. He seems to be fingering her as Pauly the prick watches, his gaze odd and disturbing.

"God." I pretend I don't see it or hear it even when her moans get louder.

The hacking and gasps from my dad's room are what I focus on. I grab a clean top and my bag and run into the bathroom flipping Paul off as I go.

The bathroom light buzzes and the ugly fluorescent glow fills the small space. I dig in the bag, pull out some deodorant, face wash, and face cream. I keep everything with me. You never know who might jack you. After I scrub my face and moisturize it, I slather on some bright pink lip gloss and use my bag as a shield as I walk out hearing Marina's loud obnoxious groans along with Paul's sick grunting. I might throw up.

This can't truly be my life, can it? I wish for the millionth time things were different, starting with my mom dying of an accidental drug overdose when I was twelve. She had sent me to the store for milk. When I got back, I found her staring blankly at the TV.

My dad never got over it. Truthfully none of us did. I mean, how do you move on after that? My dad's grief was real. And suddenly I was alone. It was like I lost everyone that day. Even Benny... instead of watching TV with me or working in the booth, he was busy trying to find a girlfriend or doing drugs.

"Oh yeah, I'm gonna come, Benny." Marina's loud declaration snaps me back to my life.

"For fuck's sake, do it and shut up," I shout over her. Wasn't she complaining about her sex life not two hours ago? I slam the door, thankful I have somewhere to go.

The ground trembles slightly before the loud rumble of bikes fills the air. And I can't help but hesitate. Maybe if I tie my shoe long enough, I can see these guys. A quick peek wouldn't hurt anybody. After all, these guys are treated like gods in this area. No man, in my opinion, is that great. But women lose their shit over the MC. So, the president of the Disciples is supposed to be hot? Like *superhot*, and his vice president and a couple other guys who ride with him are rumored to have giant penises and rock star good looks.

Squinting at the sun, which looks like a big orange ball making its descent, I twist my long hair into a ponytail. This is dumb—I'm late and my dad doesn't want me around bikers.

I take off and head for my booth, hoping I don't regret not changing into pants. My daisy dukes are fine right now, but later I might get cold. I usually take a bathroom break and change if that happens. But tonight might be different because of the bikers.

I'm almost ready to open when Pedro walks toward me carrying a Big Gulp, his old darkened face covered mostly by his black cowboy hat. He opens the counter and drags the weathered aluminum chair over, grunting as he plops into it. I frown at the groaning of my chair. His large beer belly hangs out of his red T-shirt.

"Really? I get you tonight?" I say, unable to help but smile. Pedro is ridiculous.

"Yep." He looks down at his old dusty cowboy boots, takes a sip of his drink, and promptly passes out.

"Fantastic." I sigh, catching the Big Gulp before it falls. I'd say from the smell of it it's half rum and half Coke. His loud snoring almost becomes an attraction in itself. It's busy tonight, so eventually I tune him out and focus on my business. Ninety percent of my customers have sucked at darts. So unlike last night, I haven't given anything more than a handful of junk and a frog and a bear out. Rolling my neck, I almost grab Pedro's drink I'm so freaking thirsty. This is stupid. These motorcycle thugs have to be gone. It's been hours.

I'm about to bring out my "Be back in twenty" sign. I like to lay it on Pedro's belly.

"Your brother said we can play for free." I stiffen and feel a tingle start in my belly and travel to my core. I don't turn around and face the smoky, gravelly voice. Instead I lean over, my hand reaching for my knife. After all, you never can be too safe.

"Sweet Jesus, fuck yeah, I think I can see your pussy if I try."

I swing around and stare at the pig who dares disrespect me. Instead of a biker, I see a preppy boy with his hands up, almost scared at my venom.

"Sooory, I had no idea. I thought you were, you know…" He looks around as if the men standing next to him will help.

"I mean, I heard that some of the girls here like to…"

I spit at him.

"Obviously not you." He backs away, knocking into a giant of a man. His height alone would scare the shit out of you.

"You got a foul mouth for such a little punk." The biker pushes the coward and I want to laugh. The piece of shit looks like he might have pissed his pants.

"Look, I don't want any trouble." Then he runs.

My eyes instantly go to the man and the giant by his side. "Thank you. I had it under control, but still, thanks." I smile up at him.

"I hate pansy-ass shits like him." My heart is pounding, my chest almost too tight to breathe. I simply stare because this guy is not superhot—this guy is a fucking Greek god.

"I'm closed. And I'm never free." I glare and suck in much-needed oxygen. If I don't pass out, I will have a heart-to-heart with Benny. He can't be promising free shit at my booth.

He stands there with his arms crossed, nothing but his vest and his beautiful abs on display. *Jesus*, this guy has the most perfect body I've ever seen. And even though I'm sixteen, I have seen plenty of couples having sex. The carnival kind of asks for it. Then add my dad and brother selling drugs. Yeah, I've seen naked bodies. But I can honestly say this guy makes me have butterflies and I don't *ever* have butterflies in my stomach.

He reaches into his jeans pocket and my eyes follow. Now I can see his abs flex and that V that all the girls always talk about. He pulls out a pack of cigarettes and lights up. Full lips wrap around the end. Adrenaline rushes through me and my skin heats.

He cocks his head and smiles, and I see his eyes.

Time literally stops. The noises, the screams and laughter, the rides—everything stops as I stand mesmerized by the greenest eyes I've ever seen. Like green, green. Not hazel, not bluish green. I'm talking *green* with long dark lashes that make them seriously pop. His face is tan and he has stubble—not a beard like his buddies. *He's a blond.* For some reason I had visualized a dark-haired monster. Instead I stare at a tall blond-haired, green-eyed, almost too pretty to be believed biker god. One arm is covered in tattoos and on his chest he seems to have wings with a knife completing the image of a cross, I think. I can't fully see in this light.

"What's your name, beautiful?" That snaps me out of the creepy staring fest I'm having with him and his tattoos.

"Eve." *Why the hell would I tell him my name?*

His eyes travel over my face, hair, and body as he smokes.

"Yeah, it fits you." His voice is like seriously heaven. Gravelly and… well I've never heard a voice like his. I place one foot, clad in a dirty Converse sneaker, over my other foot. As I meet his scorching stare, presence, whatever, this guy oozes self-confidence. And, for the first time in my life, I fall. Hard. This guy could make me feel things.

"How old are you, Angel?" He leans his strong arms on my counter. Another biker leans his ass on my counter and I shoot him a glare.

He chuckles. "This one's wild, Blade. I'd be careful if I was you."

Blade, I guess that's his name, stares at me and my cheeks burn.

"Answer me." It's soft, but I jump at the command and take a step back, then straighten reaching for my knife. I don't care how gorgeous this man is. I will never be intimidated.

I bring my knife down with a thud. "I'm nineteen." If I thought my dramatics would impress him and his friend I'm sorely disappointed. They both look surprised at first then burst into laughter.

"Christ, Prez. she's got a thing for blades too." The dark-haired cute friend stands up. "I'm gonna go get my cork sucked by that redhead."

Blade nods, his pretty eyes watering at laughing so hard. I jerk my knife back and gasp when my wrist is painfully grabbed by long tan fingers. My knife easily falls with a clank. Frantically, I look around, but all I see are bikers. God, how many guys does he have with him? A loud snore comes from Pedro. I don't even bother trying to get help from him.

"Let's try this again, Angel. How. Old. Are. You?" His face is so close I can smell him and God, he smells fucking amazing. Like smoke and spice.

"I'm sixteen." That does the trick. He releases me like I have the plague.

His nostrils flare for one moment and he steps back. "Do you know who I am?"

"Yes."

He nods. "Good. Now wipe that schoolgirl crush off that pretty face. I'm a bad guy, Angel." His guys snicker and catcall.

He ignores them zeroing in on me and my harsh breathing. "You're young, so I'm going to give you a pass. But if you ever pull a blade on me again, I'll pull your pants down and blister your ass." He turns and walks away, his posse following. I don't know how long I stand there. It could have been five minutes or twenty. But suddenly a gentle hand pulls me into the cold aluminum seat. I look at Pedro, his eyes full of worry.

"You stay away from that boy, Eve. Everything he said was true. He is bad—bad to the core. Now he showed you mercy tonight, but don't ever pull a blade on the Blade again. How do you think he got his name? How do you think he became president of one of the strongest MCs on the West Coast?" He reaches for his Big Gulp and takes a long sip.

When he removes his hat, it reveals an old, weathered face painted in terror. "Why don't we close early tonight? Soon we will be far away from this place and the Disciples."

I stand and rub my arms, suddenly cold. "Yes, soon we'll be gone." I should be happy about that. Instead I can't help but feel cheated. Like I was teased with a really good piece of candy only to have it taken away from me.

My eyes narrow on Pedro. "I thought you were passed out?" Retwisting my hair, I put it up with a pencil since my rubber band seems to be gone. "And the night's barely ten. I'm not closing." I tuck the sign away.

Pedro sighs and the loud sounds of the club's engines firing up drown out all other sound. I hold my chin high, wondering why I'm sad that a monster is leaving.

THREE

BLADE/JASON - Present

To say I have no patience right now would be an understatement. I'm fucking pissed and tired. And here I stand in this tiny shithole, looking at a man who needs to be put out of his misery. Yeah, I'm two seconds away from doing James Smith a favor and blowing his head off. The fucking guy deserves more than dying in a chair knowing his son is a thief and a junkie. And his daughter is going to be my whore to pay their debt.

"James? Out of regard for you, man, I'm gonna give you some air." I nod at Ryder my enforcer and brother, not by blood—by respect. He's got my back, and I respect the fuck out of him. He leans down. The dude is pushing six foot six, so this tiny box of metal they call a home barely holds him. The air stinks of stale cigarettes. Not to mention half of us have been on our bikes the better part of the day. We smell of pussy, BO, and booze.

When we hear the small sizzle of oxygen releasing, the blond girl held by Axel, my VP, sags with relief. I almost laugh. She can't be that naïve to not know what's coming.

James Smith sits, wheezing and choking in oxygen, his hands shaking as if he's trying to will himself to stand up. But life isn't fair and his body is too weak to even try.

"Rest, man. I'm gonna ask you one time since I already asked your baby girl. *Where is Benny*? Where is that piece of shit Paul? And where the fuck are my money and drugs?"

The girl hisses and struggles, again pointless. Axel is a foot taller. All she's doing is wearing herself out. She's got a fire, this one. I warned her I was bad years ago. I guess some people hit the shit lottery.

"We don't know. He doesn't know. Please don't hurt him." Her voice quivers. I know because the trailer is silent save for James gasping and the small hiss of the oxygen machine. All my guys are probably waiting for me to lose my shit. After all, I am the president of the Disciples. We don't take kindly to bitches with mouths.

It's an image I need. I don't actually abuse women and I don't tolerate my brothers to either. But we come from a long line of sexists. I know a lot of guys join so they can get pussy. It's an ongoing struggle and making sure your guys are in it for the right reason is another headache. It was a whole lot easier when there were fifty of us, rather than three hundred plus now. We've become the biggest 1 percent in the area all because of our drugs, or let me rephrase, *my drug* that Doc and I perfected years ago. It's made the club strong and wealthy. But with all that comes a fucking mess to keep together. So, I don't need shit today. I especially don't need punks like Paul and Benny stealing from me and being dumb enough to think they can get away with it.

I turn and face the beauty. She's even more striking than two years ago, and she haunted me then. Her blond hair is longer, wilder, almost beckoning me to put my hands in it. She's golden and tan, with legs that look like they won't end. But her fucking baby blues are what pull my soul to hers. It's all there, everything I crave in those ocean blues. It's her innocence. Almost like an aphrodisiac making my cock stiffen as I drop my gaze to her pouty red lips. She's definitely screwed unless her old man comes through for her.

"Eve," he rasps, causing me to reluctantly turn toward him.

"Let her go. And I'll give you the deed to all the rides that I own," he wheezes out.

I look around this shithole too small for all of us.

"James, I don't want the last of your buckets of deaths. Hell, you only have two left. Your son and his partner owe me ten grand." I crouch down so as to be on his level. I need him to see I'm serious. "Do you have that money?"

He gasps for air then shakes his head no. His once handsome face is shriveled. I don't think he's much past fifty. Tears fall down his eyes as he weeps in his chair.

"James... don't make me take your baby girl. You know what we do to our bitches. I need you to tell me where your son is for her sake."

The girl is sobbing and screaming that I'm a monster.

"Shut her up," I grumble at Axel, who pulls her to his chest, his tattooed hand squeezing her neck until her eyes bug out. But her insane screaming and name calling have stopped. My eyes turn back to James, his whole body stiff.

I lean forward. "You don't know where he is, do you?"

His yellow-stained hand grasps my forearm. It's weak but I admire it anyway.

"And you don't have my money, do you?"

His eyes are red and leak water, but his raspy "No" makes me believe him.

Unfortunately, it also sucks for his daughter.

"Ryder?" My eyes stay on James. "Brand her. She's mine now. Your debt is paid. If your junkie son shows his face, you be sure to tell him his sister paid his debt."

The gasping and wheezing are brutal and again I feel like I should do the man a favor and put him down. I mean, that's what I would do in his situation. He's probably been living for Eve anyway.

"What the fuck do you think you're doing?" Her high-pitched screams bring a smile to my face. Such a badass. Her long legs kick out and I hear Ox curse as he doubles over holding his nuts.

"Give her to me, Axel." And like the king I am, I can't help but feel a possessiveness as soon as her statuesque form fills my arms. My nose breathes her in and she stiffens. She smells like coconut. And I take my tongue and lick her cheek all the way to her neck.

My guys laugh and James wheezes.

Christ, if the man doesn't have a heart attack, I'll do him a favor and leave him a pistol. At least he can take himself out. Die with a little dignity.

Ryder grabs her right wrist as she fights, making my cock swell with her labored breath on my chin.

Edge has his lighter out. Heating the Disciples logo. The cross with angel wings running parallel through it. This particular brand is about the size of a quarter. Some of our old brands are huge, but most of us prefer tattooing rather than that. For one, it hurts like a bitch. I watch as the branding iron glistens a bright orange in the dark and dusty trailer.

"I... please... don't... you can't do this." She whimpers and twists.

I pull her tighter, my lips at her ear. "Stop struggling, Angel. If you fight it, it'll burn your whole wrist."

She's terrified, and her body starts to shake. She nods her head and licks her puffy lips. "I'll behave. I promise. You... you don't have to do this."

"Fuck, Angel, thinking of my mark on you does something to me," I growl into her ear. Her breathing is about as shallow as poor James's.

She screams in terror as Ryder grabs for her wrist again and turns it over.

"Stop." I command and feel her slump against me. Ryder's curious eyes dart to mine.

"Not her wrist. Here." I hold her chin and her long graceful neck is on display. "I want her. She's mine."

If all my brothers are shocked, they do a decent job of not showing it.

"Blade, you claiming her?"

Fuck, what am I doing? I don't even know this bitch. And here I am claiming her, which I've never done *ever*.

"Do it." I wrap my hand tight in her long, silky hair. It's like spun gold around my tan fingers.

Her beautiful eyes are closed as she silently weeps.

"Be brave, baby. Trust me, you'll be happy to have my mark." My eyes meet Ryder's, his dark eyes questioning. He must be satisfied because we brand her right under her ear. The smell of burning flesh fills the small space.

She hisses but stays still. A wave of admiration for this woman flows through me. I've seen most bikers need a bottle of tequila before they get their brand. Even then, they usually howl like a fucking girl.

But not this girl. I turn her around. Her limp body fits into my arms. All I want to do is hold her.

What the hell is wrong with me? Her hands cling to my cut as I cradle her head in my chest. Shuffling and murmurs of approval come from my men.

I look into James's eyes. He seems calmer, knows I gave his daughter my special mark. The mark of my woman. She won't be the club's whore.

Lifting her into my arms, I frown at how light she is and how much emotion this woman brings out of me. The burn is already puckering and angry and needs to be tended. I'll have someone take a look when I get us back to the clubhouse.

It's been a long, shitty day. I walk out holding her. It's dark and the night air's cooler. Her eyes open and she reaches for her neck.

"Don't," I command. She obeys and drops her hand.

"I can't leave my father." She starts to struggle. "Please, he will die without me." I get to my bike and let her slender body slide down mine.

"No, someone will take care of him. Or maybe now that you're gone he can go in peace. That"—I nod in the direction of her trailer—"wasn't living." I take off my jacket and slip it on her. She must be cold because she says nothing. Her mind's going a mile a minute. I can hear her head dissect my words, knowing I'm right.

"Eve?" Her eyes pop to mine. "Where's Paul's trailer?"

"Second one to the right."

I nod at Axel and Ox. Her eyes dart after them as they approach Paul's trailer. "But he's gone—has been for a couple of days." The hatred that oozes out of her voice makes me pause.

"Did he hurt you?" I was getting ready to forget about all this shit. I have the girl and way too many other things to deal with. But something in her tone makes me want to hunt him and kill him.

"Did he?" I lift her chin with my fingers. I need to see her eyes.

"No. No one hurts me. I told you, I can take care of myself. But he hurt others and he was... not right. Not to mention he—"

"Jesus." Paul's trailer door pounds open with so much force the small glass window in the door shatters.

"Holy Christ." Axel and Ox stumble out the back of the trailer, the smell of death traveling like the grim reaper himself.

My arm goes around Eve as I move in front of her. "Stay." She doesn't move, her eyes huge. I see Edge move to her right.

"The motherfucker's dead. And from the looks and smell of him I'd say by a couple days." Ox spits on the dirt. Eve gags. My eyes search her pale face.

"Ox, get this place closed down." I look around at the carnival—it's in full swing. Thankfully the funhouse is in front of Paul's trailer, pumping out Guns N' Roses' "Sweet Child O' Mine."

"With this stench, people are gonna call the cops." I step into the putrid trailer with Axel.

"Edge, stay with Eve." I look over my shoulder at her. Her long golden hair blows in the wind.

She shakes her head, backing up like she's getting ready to bolt.

"I... I can't leave. Wait... Paul's dead? I need to talk to the police. You can't take me—it's called kidnapping." She looks fragile, her arms wrapped around her as she shivers in the night. My head is starting to pound. She's right, though we need to get the hell out of here. But first, I want to make sure this piece of shit is actually Paul.

"Edge, fucking hold her." She goes to run, but he grabs her and muffles her screams with his hand.

"Let's get this over with." Entering the trailer, I notice the fluorescent light is on. I don't know what I was expecting but not Paul sitting on the couch, his head bashed in with what looks like someone took a baseball bat to him.

"I take it there are no drugs or money?" I glance at Axel.

He shakes his head. "I bet Benny did it. He wanted the drugs and the money and didn't want to share." He shakes his dark head. "Fuck, he stinks, huh? I haven't smelled this harsh of a stench since Afghanistan."

My eyes scan the trailer. Everything is in order. Whoever killed Paul knew him. Axel's probably right about Benny.

I nod. "Put James someplace where he can get some care. I'll pay for it."

I jump down the steps, slamming the door after Axel. With the window broken, he'll be found soon. We need to haul ass.

He grins at me, his head shaking, a big-ass stupid smile across his face.

"What?" I snap.

"Nothing. You're full of surprises tonight. First claiming Eve.

Now I'm getting James Smith care. You sure you didn't taste that pussy a couple years ago?"

"Fuck you." Not bothering to say more, I jerk a screaming Eve into my arms and give her a hard shake. Her head snaps back and our eyes lock.

"You're an insane maniac. I'll scream, and then I'll turn your whole crew in. You... you criminal." She pants and her eyes sparkle with blue fire. Again, my cock hardens, and if we didn't need to get the hell out of here, I would have her kneel and shove it down her throat. With all my brothers watching. Because as much as I admire her fire, she needs to learn her place.

"Listen to me, Angel." I squeeze her bicep tight and she cries out in pain.

"You ever disrespect me or threaten me again, and I'll take your father out to the desert and shoot him in the head."

Her big, innocent eyes widen. "What is wrong with you?"

"Nothing is wrong with me. I'm in control and you will either please me or I'll give you to my club. So instead of hating me, I'd get to loving me. Unless you like ten to fifteen guys fucking you a night.

"That... you don't really allow that, do you?"

"Sass me again in public and you'll find out." Her pale face actually gets paler.

"Blade... I don't... that is I haven't... oh God." She leans in the other direction and pukes in the dirt. It splatters all over since the dirt is dry.

"Goddammit." I roll my eyes and hold her hair, wondering why I claimed this foul-mouthed gypsy. Sure, she's the most beautiful woman I've ever seen, but big deal. Sometimes a warm mouth and hot hole are all a man needs. This woman is trouble. Still I find myself rubbing her back.

She sways as she raises her head, exhaustion and pain stamped all over her pretty face. Suddenly I'm as tired as she is.

I've been on the road most of the day, and the two weeks I was in Orange County dismantling an MC that claimed they were the Disciples was a fucking mess. Not to mention they had about twenty good men who actually thought they were a part of us. I had to vet and haze them. All I want is a hot shower, a beer, and Crystal's warm mouth on my cock. Not this wildcat spitting venom and vengeance. Christ, she'd probably try to bite my dick off if I shoved it down her throat. I adjust myself because the visual of Eve's lips on my rod is hot.

"Just shut up and obey. You don't have to worry about your father. I'm going to have him put in a place to take care of him. Maybe if you're a good girl, I'll take you to visit him." I dangle the carrot and know I've won. Her whole face lights up. She looks at me for a way too brief second like I'm her hero, not scum.

"I... you would get him medical treatment?" Her lips quiver and I almost lean over and capture them.

"Because that's what he needs." Her hands reach for me. "With proper care he could live for so much longer." Her voice is hopeful and so naïve. James is dying, but if it makes Eve chill the fuck out thinking that I'm helping him, I'll take it.

"Good. So, you're coming of your own free will?"

She hesitates. "No, I mean I'm doing this for my father. Otherwise being your whore would be the last thing I'd do."

I chuckle. "Relax. You might like it and I don't force women. I have plenty more willing to take your place. The last thing I like is a frigid bitch."

She gasps. "So, if I say no, I don't have to fuck you?" Her gaze is wary.

I snort as I sit on my bike.

"And no one but you can touch me?" She's sucking on her puffy bottom lip again and I almost smile as I can hear her thoughts race in her head.

"Nope. You're mine. I'm the only one who can touch you. That's why I marked you. Now get the fuck on the back of my bike."

This time she doesn't hesitate and wraps her long legs around mine. Her arms snake around my stomach tightly. I wonder if I haven't made a huge mistake bringing her.

FOUR

EVE

I hold on tight. My body follows every move Blade makes. He leans forward; I lean with him.

This isn't the first time I've been on a bike. My dad and Benny had one, and I used to love to ride with them. There's something wild and free about a motorcycle—an adrenaline rush that someone like me needs. And this guy can handle a bike. His strong legs grip it like it's his lover, and my body tingles uncomfortably.

I don't consider myself a normal girl. Meaning, I'm not a slut. All the girls and women I've been around were sluts. I used to blush hearing the women who ran the ticket booth talk about how wet they would get or all the dirty things they liked to do. It never appealed to me. Also, Benny and my dad made it clear that I was to be left alone. Only one man ever tried to do anything with me. That was Paul.

He cornered me once and shoved his rancid tongue in my mouth. Then his hands went straight to my crotch. But I took care of him. I moaned like I liked it, then kneed him in the balls. As he cried like a bitch, I took out my knife and told him if he ever dared touch me again, I'd cut off his penis.

I hug Blade tighter, rubbing my face on the back of his soft leather vest—or what the club calls a *cut*. One large warm hand wraps around my locked cold ones. I don't care about leaving the carnival. It was time. I'm happy Paul is dead. It might make me crazy, but some people need to be put down and Paul was one of them. I breathe in Blade's scent and close my eyes. The wind kisses my face and I hold on to this man. Although he acts as if he doesn't want me, I think he does—all men do. He might play king, but he's still a man. Blade's promised to get my dad real medical help, like put him in a place with nurses, and maybe he'll get better. I always have guilt thinking of my wonderful father suffering because we are so poor. It's why I was trying to save. It was why I let Benny talk me into coming back to this area for the drugs. The plan was sell the drugs, give the Disciples their cut, and use the rest for Dad.

As I look out at the inky blackness of the road, it's not cold, but I shiver. *Frigid!* That's what he called me. My mind whirls. I guess I should be pissed. But he's right: I am. I'm completely satisfied with having no sex. My finger works just fine. And living with my dad and brother makes that difficult anyway.

This guy is hot. Like movie star hot. I bet he's nasty too. He looks it. The bike slows down to a low rumble as we stop at a red light.

"You okay?" He gives me his perfect profile.

"Um... Yeah. I love riding." I yell the last part as his whole crew rumbles up next to him. The road trembles. The bikes seem to heat up the pavement, the vibrations going straight to my sensitive core. "God," I whisper, clenching my knees tighter on his ass and thighs.

His big warm hand reaches back and rubs my thigh. "Angel, unless you're going to unzip my pants and jerk me off, you're going to have to raise your hands."

Heat floods my cheeks. I raise my hands up to his chest.

"Sorry."

He grabs one and brings it back to the hardness between his legs, using my hand to do a couple of rough rubs, then places it back with the other as he shifts and we take off.

He wants me, and for some reason that makes me breathless. One more turn and all I see is blackness. The smell of citrus envelops me. Up ahead is a large long house with a shitload of bikes parked out front. It's still pretty dark, but loud music thumps out and screams along with laughter inside.

I stay quiet. Again, I need him to keep his word. As soon as he turns off his bike, the large door opens and the whole yard lights up. It must have a motion detector. A couple of bikers come out as the others arrive. Curious looks are thrown my way, but nobody approaches me. I realize I'm still clutching Blade and reluctantly let go. He gives my thigh a slap and scoops me off his bike. I nearly sink to the ground, which would suck because it's all gravel. As I try to steady myself, he holds me and laces his fingers with mine, laughing as we walk toward the house and the obnoxious music.

Everyone in the large living room stops as we enter. Blade doesn't seem fazed, yet I can't help but cringe and stare at his back. His cut has the large logo of the cross and wings along with numerous patches. We walk up the stairs and I risk a quick glance downward and wish I hadn't. What was I thinking? These people are a group, a family. I'm a carnival rat, a gypsy, and I don't belong. Never have. The women seem to sense it.

Well, it's not like I have a choice, so until I can somehow support my father and pay off my brother's debt, I'm kind of stuck here. As we reach the top of the stairs, the talking starts again. My throat is on fire where he branded me and I swallow. *Wait a fucking minute.* This son of a bitch branded me like I'm cattle. Or a piece of meat, like he owns me. What the hell am I thinking?

"What, babe?" His voice sounds tired as he opens the last door on this floor—it's black and thick.

"You branded me!" I almost stutter. I wave my hand at my neck, positive it looks as bad as it feels. "It fucking hurts."

He pulls me in, flips on the light, and grabs my chin. I try to jerk away but his grip is like a pit bull's.

I'm panting because... well, I don't know why. This guy does this to me. He makes me breathless, gives me false hope. Deceives me with his incredible looks. I mean how can anyone who looks like him be bad, right?

Also, I like the way he smells. Clean even though he's covered in dirt and grime. Spicy, smoky. *God, I'm losing it.* My face burns. Either that or I have a fever. I have to stop myself from bursting into tears. And I never cry. Well, almost never.

He sighs, like I exhaust him. "Go take a shower."

I lick my dry, parched lips nervously as I glance around this room. It's the biggest bedroom I've seen in my whole life. Huge in fact—probably the size of two trailers. The walls are the color of putty and huge, thick-glassed windows face what I assume is the backyard.

His bed is giant-sized with some sort of comforter that makes me want to steal it. And holy shit, I snort in fascination at the hideous art or whatever this is called.

On top of his bed is a huge wooden-framed *velvet* painting of a naked redhead sitting on an old Harley Davidson, her wild red hair and large breasts on display. Her private area is thankfully concealed by the seat.

I swirl around to face him, but he is texting on his phone. I continue to look at his walls. Turning to the one closest to me, I notice it has a bunch of old black-and-white photos of Harleys and a poster of another redhead. This one is in panties and what looks like Blade's cut on her. Her fake boobs are spilling out. It's signed,

To Blade,
I love you today, I love you tomorrow,
I love you forever
Crystal

My eyes snap to his. "Are you married?"

"Go take a shower. Last time I say it." He raises a brow at me.

"Fine, I need to get away from all this anyway." I point at the picture. I can't help but take a quick glance at the rest of his room. He has a pool table. *A pool table*. And a huge black couch that looks so comfortable I want to curl up like a cat and never leave.

I don't have time to see more as I lock myself in his bathroom, turn on the light, and almost snort. It's big of course, but it has a massive Jacuzzi big enough to hold at least three people. "Typical," I mumble. He probably has threesomes in here.

Oh my God, is that what he wants me for? To share me with his wife, the redhead? Didn't he say he had someone who takes care of him? It must be the redhead.

Turning on his glass-encased shower, I look enviously at the tub. I have never actually taken a bath. Living in a trailer, I took showers in what consisted of a small box with lukewarm water.

I barely have my filthy clothes off when I realize I have no fresh panties. I can't stand the idea of putting anything dirty on after being able to take what looks like the most amazing shower. But I also can't go without panties. Grabbing the black thong, I bring it into the shower with me. I'll hand wash it. The thong is a tiny bit of material and it'll dry fast. I don't wear thongs to be sexy. I wear them because they are the easiest thing to steal. Half the time, I simply wad them in my hand and walk out of the store. Steam billows out of the shower. I'm so used to having to wait for hot water that I almost burn myself testing it. Obviously he has good plumbing. Whatever, he's a thug, a drug dealer. So, this is the nicest place I've ever been in. Doesn't mean I'm impressed or anything.

Complete bliss takes over my body and I sigh. The hot water pelts down on me, and even my throbbing wound can't make me not enjoy this. The delicious water caresses my skin. It feels so clean. Maybe this place has a different water source. The faucet is a giant circle spouting water that looks like rain. Touching the rock walls that tile his shower, I turn to let the hot water pelt my back. I mean, there's no other way to describe it. Each tile is blueish gray, like rocks in a cave or something. I close my eyes and enjoy this moment because this could all go away so fast.

Reaching for some shampoo, I see that he has only AXE shampoo for men sitting in the large hollowed-out space of the rock wall. This spot could hold all kinds of things: shower gels, nice shampoos, high-end conditioners. I love all that stuff. It's my go-to shoplifting priority.

I pick up a green bar of soap and smell it: Irish Spring. That's weird. He can't be married. There is nothing at all that indicates a woman lives in his room. Except that it's super clean. Housework was never my strong suit, and since my dad and Benny were pigs, I got sick of being their maid.

Benny. My heart does a painful thud as I think about my brother. I blame that freak Paul for everything. Benny never would have ended up hooked on drugs if Paul hadn't arrived on the scene.

I turn off the shower, reluctantly step out, and wrap myself in a black fluffy towel. Yeah, he can't be married. What woman would allow black towels? Unless he shares another room with her? Or maybe a house? Who cares. I wince as I gently pat my wound dry. It feels bad. And that reminds me that I hate him. He's the enemy; he took me away. Although as I look around, it's starting to feel like he rescued me and that's not an option.

FIVE

BLADE/JASON

She peeks her head out of the bathroom door, her hair brushed off her face, steam billowing around her like fog.

"Um… do you have a T-shirt I could borrow? My clothes are dirty."

She's truly beautiful. I've seen a lot of women in my life and none compare to her.

"Here." I pull open a drawer and toss her a white cotton tee. It falls a few feet shy of her feet.

Her eyes dart to it like she's trying to be a Jedi knight and have the force bring it to her.

Jesus, she's eighteen and has been a carnival rat since the day she was born. Her shy and innocent act is getting on my nerves. I'm used to women prancing around naked. So her death grip on the towel like it's a protective blanket is a bit ridiculous.

I almost tell her that she can stare at the T-shirt all night and it's not going to get any closer, but she straightens her shoulders, steps out, and in one graceful swoop, picks it up. I watch fascinated at how her body movements are a thing of beauty. The more I see her move, the more it becomes a thing for me. The black towel hangs low against the creamy skin of her back. Not one tattoo is on this body. I almost feel guilty for putting my mark on her. *Almost.*

My hand itches to reach out and jerk that towel free. I can't remember the last time I've been with a woman who has no tattoos. I decide right now that she will never get one. I want to see my tatted hands against her porcelain skin.

The slam of the door pulls me out of it. I blame all these spur-of-the-moment decisions on lack of sleep.

The door opens and she glides out wearing my T-shirt. Her wet long hair hangs down her back and I have to grit my teeth. Full breasts, with tight nipples, make my dick start to wake up. I almost throw her onto the bed.

Clearing my throat, I reach for a pack of smokes. "Tomorrow I'll have one of the girls take you shopping. Get some clothes and any other girly shit you need." I light up watching her eyes get big.

"What?" I pull a long drag of nicotine into my lungs.

"I... um, well if you trust me I..."

"I don't. I'll have an old lady take you."

Her eyes widen and she glances around the room. I admire her as I smoke. She moves to the large part of my room. I had a half wall erected in my bedroom, so if I want to watch TV, I can.

She looks up at the ceiling and all around. Her gaze stops on my refrigerator.

"Eve?" She jumps and looks over at me.

"Are you hungry? I can have Amy make you some food. Or there's food in the fridge if you want it. I'm going to take a shower."

She nods but her focus is on the contents of my fridge. As she leans into it, the light illuminates her entire silhouette and I make myself breathe. What the hell is going on with me? I'm acting like a fucking teenager. She pulls out a yogurt, checks the date on the top, then grabs two bottles of water.

I figure she's fine and step into the bathroom to take my own shower, wondering if I should have Crystal come suck me off. But my head is filled with a blond eating yogurt, not Crystal.

Tomorrow will be busy, and in the morning, I'll have one of the girls take care of me.

Opening the door, I expect to see Eve sleeping in my bed. I brought some Neosporin and Advil to help her sleep and intended to give them to her.

"Eve?" A wave of panic fills me. Where the hell is she? Even with my mark, she may be vulnerable. A lot of the guys are new and might not know she's mine.

"Eve?" I stop when I see her curled up like a kitten cradling a bottle of water on my black leather couch, the first empty water bottle on the floor next to her.

"Christ." I run my hands through my hair and reach down to pick her up. She moans and I can't help but stick my nose in her hair and breathe in everything that is this girl.

Putting her on my bed, I squeeze out a large amount of ointment and slather it on her neck using a gentle touch. The angry burn is already calming down. Her eyes slowly, almost sadly open and I hand her the Advil and her water. In her half state of sleep, I like her a lot better. She's warm, smells good, looks fucking sexy, and listens.

She plops back down and snuggles into my pillow. The T-shirt she wears has ridden up and her long legs, ass, and black thong are on display for my eyes to feast on. I allow myself a moment to let this day sink in.

When she shivers, I pull the sheet and down comforter over her.

Again, I wonder if I should call Crystal and rub my face with my hands. Instead I slide into my big bed and reach for Eve. She murmurs something about loving pillows, then sighs. Her soft, minty breath lulls me to sleep.

Warm, vanilla or is it coconut? I'm at a beach and I have the most beautiful pair of blue eyes blinking at me. Her ruby lips move when she laughs and I reach for them. "I love you." She smiles at me. My eyes blink open. *What the hell?* I'm spooning Eve and the hard-on I was having in the dream is in full force. My nose goes into her neck and my hands caress her breasts. Why am I dreaming about this girl? And why am I dreaming that she loves me? For a moment, I stop caressing her. My brain is still waking up, yet I know I need to be careful with this one. I have some strange need, a connection with her. But I don't plan on falling in love. I have way too much shit in my life. A woman is not something on my radar.

Admittedly, I loved sleeping with her and haven't slept that soundly in years. I don't let women into my room. In the beginning, I let Crystal stay a couple of times. As soon as I became president, I slept alone. That way nobody gets confused. But since Eve has no idea about what happens in my MC, she won't know how by claiming her last night, I have basically decided she's going to be my old lady, sort of. That means I can fuck and be with whoever I want, but she's getting a job she knows nothing about. I scrub my hands up and down my face. Why did I do this? The sight of her lithe, glorious form and the sound of her even, peaceful breathing compels me to turn her on her back.

This. This is why I did it. She is the most stunning woman I have ever seen. And I want her.

My hand caresses her stomach. She's too thin—her tiny waist gives her curves, but a few pounds would help. Suddenly I want to give her food, clothes, anything she wants. Her eyes blink open, and long, sooty lashes reveal crystal blue eyes. She stretches, a small smile on her lips, and bolts up pulling the sheet with her.

"What are you doing?" She looks at me like I'm insane.

"I was getting ready to taste you." I take the sheet away.

"But... I mean maybe we could." Her eyes dart around the room landing on the poster of Crystal. "I don't think your wife would like me sleeping with her man." Her cheeks turn pink.

"Well, then it's a good thing I'm not married." I reach for her and she cringes.

"What the fuck is wrong with you? I'm not going to hurt you." *What's the deal with this one?*

"You said you hate… well, frigid girls." She whispers the word "frigid." I pull back to look at her, truly look at her. She's terrified. Her chin is held high, but her lip is quivering. Christ, she's probably been used and discarded. I need to get up. I have a ton of things to take care of today.

"Eve? You need to talk to me. I basically bought you. You get it? I'm not going to force you. But you're mine and we'll be fucking. So, if you have some dark secret you want to tell me, fine. Otherwise be ready tonight."

The door to my bedroom bangs as I swing my legs over and grab my smokes. I light one up. "In a minute," I yell, and she jumps.

Standing up, I watch her eyes trail over my body closing when they come to my hard cock. For some reason, this pisses me off. No woman doesn't want my cock. It's fucking thick.

"Open your eyes, Angel." I wrap a hand around it jerking it for her. Her eyes don't blink as she watches my hand go up and down. Almost like she's never seen a man do this before.

Her breath is harsh and her hands are fisting the white sheets.

I take a drag and allow the smoke to fill my lungs, my hand still jacking myself off.

"Give me your hand, baby." It's a command and it jerks her eyes to mine. She wets her lips and slowly gets to her knees moving toward me. My cock jerks in excitement at her obeying me. She might be a badass, but I'm going to train her to be my badass.

"Blade." Her voice is raspy and her eyes show confusion. She's like a scared virgin, and I don't have time for this. Taking one more drag, I lean over and snub the cancer stick out, then grab her hand and place it on my dick. She jumps at the first contact, her breaths coming in small and short. Gently I guide her hand up and down my thick cock, which grows even longer and thicker as she takes over and does it by herself.

"Yeah, that's it, baby. See how good you're making me feel?" Her blue eyes pop up to mine as if she's not used to compliments. I take her other hand and bring her index finger to my mouth. "You keep stroking my cock and I'll suck on this."

She cocks her head and her golden waterfall of hair falls over her shoulder as her eyes fall to her hand jerking me off. Then I hear her moan as my tongue and teeth suck and swirl on her finger. "Look at me, Angel." Her eyes blink to mine. She obeys so perfectly and for one split moment, I see my future. She must see or feel it too because she hisses and pulls her finger out and her hand away.

"Who hurt you?" My voice is harsh as I breathe through my nose trying not to throw her on the bed and fuck her. "I need to know this before we begin."

She slowly shakes her head. "Everyone. No one. At least not what you're thinking."

There's pounding on my door again. "Prez... I know you're busy but you're twenty minutes late," Ryder's voice booms.

"I'm coming." My eyes never leave her face. I see the relief that I'm not going to touch her. Her whole body slumps back. I don't need this shit. Clearly she's got sexual issues.

I pull on my jeans and a black T-shirt.

"I'll have one of the old ladies come by and take you shopping. Get your hair done, nails, buy a bunch of clothes. You're not leaving, so get a variety of things."

She nods as I pull on my black biker boots. "And Eve?" She looks at me.

"Tonight, I'm gonna fuck you. Prepare for it."

I pull out my wallet and count out a couple grand. "Here. This will get you started." She takes it. Again, her eyes are huge like she's never seen or held that much money. I don't know, but I'm late as fuck, so I'll have to psychoanalyze her later. Raking my hand through my hair, I brush my teeth and take a piss before I open the door to a smiling Ryder.

"Christ." Walking past him, I slam the door and take the steps two at a time. Ryder's large frame is right behind me.

"I had a dream, Prez."

I march toward the far room where we hold our meetings.

"Good for you, man." I know what kind of dream he's talking about. Ryder dreams shit that strangely seems to come true. For years we gave him grief about it. Until he actually dreamed that the wife of one of our brothers had breast cancer. It turns out she did, and he saved her life. After that we still tease him, but when he says he had *one* of his dreams we all listen.

I sigh. "Dude, we're late as shit. Can it wait?"

He smiles and claps my shoulder. "You made the right choice. You and Eve are destined."

My hand is on the doorknob. "You know you sound insane, right? Unless you dream about something bad, or something important, let's not talk about it, okay?"

"Had to tell you. I didn't want you to mess this up." He grins like he's a genius.

"If we're destined, it won't matter what I do." I open the door and all my brothers stand.

Holding my hands up, I say, "Sorry, long night. Axel get me up to speed on what's been going on. Can I get some breakfast?" I sit at the head of the long wooden table. Edge calls for my breakfast and I turn my attention to listening to all the shit that went down since I was gone.

"Some punk kids got a hold of our drug and tried to copy it. They failed and a couple kids OD'd."

I look at Axel. "Did they die?"

"One did. The DEA decided to stop by and say hi. They know it's not ours, but if they can put us down they will." He leans back and lights a cigarette.

"How much did they want this time?"

"Ten grand and a friendly reminder that they are watching us."

"Where's Doc?"

"He's dealing with shit with Sandy again. Said he'll be here tonight," Ox chimes in as he takes a sip of beer. I cock my brow at him.

"You're not the only one who had a long night," he mumbles.

Shaking my head, I look at my brothers. And I mean that literally. All of us served together or grew up together. All of us would lay down our lives for each other. "We're getting too big. I want to pull back on our supply right now."

"That's a lot of money to lose," Axel says.

"Better that than jail. What did you do about these punks ripping us off?"

"I personally took care of it. We won't be hearing about them anymore." Ryder sips his coffee and smokes. None of us need the money. We've all invested heavily in legitimate businesses and houses. I look around. Everyone looks tired. This burning the candle at both ends catches up with even the best of us. The only one who seems rested is Ryder.

"Good." A light knock alerts us that my breakfast has arrived. Amy walks in carrying mine and a bunch of donuts for the guys.

"Thanks, Amy." She nods and efficiently places my plate in front of me. Her father has been with the Disciples from the start. He was with my grandfather in Vietnam. We pay her a shitload of money. Not because she demands it, but because she works her ass off and the clubhouse would not survive without her. At fifty, she's never left or hooked up with any of the guys. She seems happy being alone. She rules the clubhouse with a tight fist. Our food is amazing and my room is so clean you could eat off the floor.

"So, Eve needs clothes. Which one of you wants to volunteer their woman to help her?" Shoveling in a mouthful of scrambled eggs, I glance around the table.

"I called Dolly," Edge informs me.

I raise an eyebrow. "Really?"

"What, you don't want her to do it?"

"No, I think she's perfect. Thought you weren't talking anymore."

"Well, I'm not. I did it for you." He looks down at his phone.

I grab a slice of toast. "So, she's here now?" He nods not looking up from his phone and I shake my head at his stupidity. If he loved her so much, he should have kept his dick in his pants. That's all Dolly ever required. But we are who we are and it's not like any of us are saints.

"I'll be back." I walk into the main room where the bar and a couple of pool tables are set up. A bunch of my guys are drinking and playing poker. They stand when I enter.

Sitting in the corner is Dolly on her phone. We call her that because she literally looks like a porcelain doll. Her dad was my dad's VP, so we kind of grew up together.

"Hey you."

Her big brown eyes blink up at me. "Hey you, I hear you got yourself an ole lady?"

I laugh. "I don't know what I got. Listen, I gave her a handful of cash. If you need more, let me know?"

She stands, and I can't help but smile. Dolly is all of five foot two and maybe one hundred pounds. Her dad bought her a hair salon when she graduated from cosmetology school. At first, it was a place for us to launder money. But she's an excellent stylist and the salon has taken off.

"Oh, don't you worry. I'll take good care of her. When we come back tonight, you won't recognize her." She tosses her phone in her bag. "How's Crystal taking it?" She looks around unable to hide her smirk.

"Haven't told her yet." Rubbing the back of my neck, I add, "She's gonna be pissed. What else is new."

Dolly stares at me. Crystal was the one with her mouth wrapped around Edge's cock. So there's no love lost between them.

"Should I go get her?" She looks around, wrinkling her nose in distaste.

"Yeah, she's in my room."

"Great." Nodding at me, she cocks her head. "Are you okay? You're acting weird."

I run my hands through my hair. She's right; I'm off. I have no idea what I'm getting myself into with this girl.

"Keep an eye on her, Dolly. Like she's not one of us, and I have no idea what she's gonna do. Actually, the more you can find out the better."

She throws her bag over her shoulder, heading for the stairs. "Perfect, so you want me to spy, babysit, and be her stylist. Wow… you are going to owe me."

"I want a full report," I call up to her.

"Yes, Boss." She disappears, and my phone starts ringing. Crystal's big breasts pop up. I push decline. She's the last thing I want to deal with right now. My mind drifts to upstairs and Dolly getting to spend the day with Eve. They're like night and day. Eve tall and golden, Dolly petite and dark-haired. But if anyone can get into Eve's head, it will be Dolly.

"Prez?" I turn to Edge who's holding a cell phone for me. "It's Devin."

I sigh, walking back into the conference room, thoughts of my Angel on hold as I try to contain what seems like a million fires.

SIX

EVE

Someone is tapping on the door. I assume it's the old lady to take me shopping. I clutch the money Blade handed me this morning to my chest. This is the most money I've held in my whole life. And I'm a bit resentful at having to waste it on trivial things like clothes. If I can distract this woman, maybe I can steal most of the stuff and keep the cash.

After Blade left, I took another long, hot shower. His little display this morning made me realize that I'm totally fucked and I might as well wrap my head around it: I'm basically his whore. I hate my junkie brother. He left my dad and me knowing that I would have to pay his debt. That's something I'll never forgive. I'm alone and I will survive. With that in mind, I take apart Blade's room. Unfortunately, besides some condoms, a couple guns, and a knife, his room is boring and super clean. I don't even find a journal or anything that could help me know more about him. I guess he likes motorcycles and redheads with big fake boobs. I'm neither, so my days here are probably numbered unless I can pull off a miracle and make this man keep me. If he's telling me the truth and he did get my dad into a place that will help him, I'll gladly trade my virginity for that.

Someone knocks on the door again and I quickly move to open it. A small, dark-haired pixie girl stands in front of me holding her cell phone.

"Oh... I see now." She waves her hand at me and grins. "All making sense." She chuckles as she gives me a once-over. "So, I'm Dolly, your new stylist-best friend." She shoves her hand at me.

I blink at her. "Wow, when Blade said old lady, I thought he meant like a real... old lady."

Shit this isn't going to work. This girl looks on her game. How am I going to shoplift with her around?

She laughs. "Come on, beautiful. Let's get you some clothes, haircut, waxing, nails, and whatever else we have time for."

"Um, okay." She nods like all this is completely normal. I push my hair over my shoulder. For some reason, I don't want her seeing my brand. It still stings, but I found some Advil and Neosporin in the bathroom. The pain is almost gone.

We walk down the stairs and she stops for a moment then huffs by the redheaded guy from last night. I think I heard his name is Edge? Flame? Whatever. All these guys have fucked-up names.

"Dolly? Can I have a minute?" His muscled arm reaches for her, his voice sounding desperate.

She swirls on him. "Get your filthy hands off me. I'm not one of the whores who have to do what you say. Fuck off, Edge." She grabs my arm, pulling me out the door and into her little black sports car. I look back and he stands on the porch, staring at her.

"Is that your boyfriend?" I mean it's apparent something's going on.

She starts her car and honks her horn then flips him off as she presses on the accelerator. In the morning light, this place looks enormous. Tons of bikes and trucks are parked everywhere. Gravel leads up to the main house, but there might be some grass in the back.

"Not anymore." She steers down the long driveway where tons of trees shade and protect the area.

"Who owns this place?" I look at her. She's got a huge scowl on her face and her index finger is angrily tapping the steering wheel.

"Jason. His grandfather bought it in the sixties, gave it to his son Bobby, and then Bobby died, so it's Jason's and the stupid club's." She reaches into her bag for a cigarette. I think I literally might be the only nonsmoker in this compound.

"Who's Jason?" I continue looking around, trying to pinpoint landmarks in case I need them.

"Oh, right... sorry." She sighs, shaking her head. "Jason is Blade. I forget you're new."

"Oh." That's all I say because for some strange reason, hearing Jason rather than Blade humanizes him. And I don't want to think of him in any other way than a healthcare provider for my dad. Dolly peels out onto the pavement and we're speeding toward town.

"I think..." She glances over at me. "Yeah, let's go to my salon first. After that, we'll get lunch and shop." I don't respond—she's not asking me a question. She swerves into an alley and parks her car. A big pink and turquoise sign that says "Dolly's Doll Shop" greets us.

The door is pink and the building itself is turquoise and gold. She unlocks the door.

"We don't open until eleven a.m." I look around and it's fabulous. My eyes greedily take in her turquoise and gold lounging sofas and white walls. There's even a chandelier in the middle of the store, the crystals casting rainbows all around.

"Here, sit. Let me take a look at you." I drop into a chair and cringe at my appearance. My hair is insane and with Blade's T-shirt and my jean shorts, I couldn't look any more like white trash if I tried.

She looks at me in the mirror and I slump down. Her attractive body and sophisticated hair make me want to run out the door. But I won't; I'll play the game.

"Eve?" Her voice is gentle.

"Yeah?"

"Have you ever had your hair styled?" Her pretty brown eyes hold no judgment. If anything, they're filled with compassion and that's worse.

"Um, yeah just the other day. That's why it's so silky." I rub my fingers on the dry ends.

"You know, Eve, I'm not the enemy. As a matter of fact, I like you. You're gorgeous and you have spunk. Unfortunately, that is a deadly combination at the club." She pulls my hair off my face and the brand shows its ugly redness.

"Holy shit." Her small pixie head is so close I feel her breath.

"I heard that he marked you. I had no idea he did it here. Lucky bitch. I had to get mine here." She shows me her wrist.

"Yeah, I'm lucky all right. My dad is dying, my brother is a thief and a junkie, and I'm living with one of the deadliest MCs. I'd say I'm totally charmed."

She shrugs. "Well, at least he claimed you. That's why we need you up to par. Have you heard about Crystal?" She spits the name out as she takes off her tiny camouflage jacket revealing arms covered in tattoos.

"Is she the naked redhead on Blade's wall?"

"Yep." She drapes a smock over me. "Let's get your hair first then I'll wax you."

My eyes snap to hers. "Wait... what? No waxing." I frown as I look at the door opening. A guy and a girl are entering carrying coffee and bagels.

"Hey guys." Dolly hugs the guy carrying the coffee. "Doug and Jenny this is Eve."

Both are dressed in black and, of course, covered in tattoos. Jenny has purple hair down to her waist, and Doug has pitch-black hair cut close on the sides and long on the top. Skintight jeans and biker boots complete his look. He's like a cross between biker and rockabilly.

"Well, what do we have here?" Doug comes up close, his cologne so thick I have to lean back.

"Relax, Dougie, she belongs to Blade." Dolly pats his cheek.

He pouts. "Fucking Blade. He gets everyone. It's bad enough that he's yummy, but does he always get everything?"

"It's one of the perks of being king." Jenny flops into the chair to my left swiveling to look at me.

"How old are you?"

"I'm eighteen," I respond, not bothering to look at their faces. I can hear Doug whistling.

"Blade never likes them young. If anything he usually goes older. You must be special." She gets up and walks toward the back. Suddenly music blasts on making me jump. My brain is spinning, trying to figure out if these people are friendly or not.

"Come on, beautiful, let's get your hair washed." Dolly leads me to the washing section. A couple of bikers stop by but go straight to the back. Closing my eyes, I sit back and let her massage my scalp.

"Oh my God," I moan. "I don't think I've ever felt anything this good."

She smiles. "Enjoy it, Eve." So I do. I let her have carte blanche with me. The only time I ever get my hair cut is when I can't stand it. And I always go to Supercuts. Dolly happily chit chats with Doug and Jenny, trying to include me. But I'm the most relaxed I've ever been and almost asleep. When she starts the blow dryer, I jump.

"You okay?" She blows the warm air on my face getting rid of all the little hair clippings stuck there.

"I guess. I'm not used to this although I love it." Glancing at my reflection, I grin. Even with my hair wet, the cut looks amazing.

"Wait until we shop and get makeup." She turns to Doug and squeals, "How many appointments do you have today? How much fun would you have doing her makeover with me?" She waggles her eyebrows at him.

"My eleven a.m. canceled, so as long as we are back at two p.m. I'd love it." He scans my face. "How much money do we get to work with?" He rubs his hands with glee and I notice a diamond stud in his nose.

"Blade said whatever she needs." Both of them start laughing. I slink into the chair. Now I have two of them to deal with. It was bad enough when only Dolly was keeping a hawkeye on me. Doug seems ten times worse.

"If you're not with Edge, who are you with?" I ask, trying to distract them.

"Aaand on that note, come get me when you guys are ready." Doug spins around toward the reception desk.

Dolly sighs. "My dad used to be Blade's dad's VP, so I have been in the club since birth. But, I'm not with any of the guys." She sniffs and pushes her shoulders back. "I'm done with those types of men. They think they own you, but God forbid they be faithful to you." Her blow drying becomes aggressive.

"Sorry, it's none of my business."

She looks like she's going to cry. *Great just great*.

"Sorry, Dolly. Men are pigs."

She laughs. "You're a little young to think that. At your age I was boy crazy."

I shrug. "Not me. I couldn't care less. Actually, if I could support my dad, I don't think I would ever be with anyone."

She stops the blow dryer. "Um... does Blade know you hate men? I mean are you into women?"

My whole face heats. I glance around only to see a curious Doug staring at me.

"I'm not into girls," I snip. "But I don't need a man to make me feel whole."

Doug slithers over to Dolly and they both look at me.

"Okay, enough." I go to stand up. They both push me back down.

"Why are you blushing, Eve? If I didn't know better I would think you're a virgin." Doug leans into my face.

I push at him. "It's none of your business. I need some air. All this sharing is not my thing." I try to get up again only to have Doug circle me.

"Holy shit! She is. Oh my God, I'm in love with you." He leans forward caging me in.

"What is wrong with you?" I push at him again. I hate people getting in my space.

Somehow my relaxing morning has gone to shit. And I'm starting to dislike Dolly and despise Doug.

"Doug." Dolly hits his chest. "Let Eve breathe. Sweetheart, are you a virgin?" Her big brown eyes almost glow with excitement. She whirls and grabs Doug's arm. "She is. Do you realize? I mean Blade is going to freak. Oh. My. God. I almost wish I could tell him." She claps her hands.

"Look, I don't need this." My face is literally on fire. The last thing I want is for Dolly to tell Blade that I'm a virgin. I mean he's gonna find out, but not through her.

She reaches over and hugs me. If I was mortified earlier, it seems this morning can keep getting worse.

"I am in awe of you. Don't worry. I've got your back." She grabs the blow dryer again.

I don't say anything because I'm pretty sure if I did, I would burst into tears. I'm Blade's property, a debt, and everyone knows it. *Think about Dad*, I chant in my brain. But what if he's a liar? What if he uses me as his whore and gets tired of me? He'll stop paying for my dad. No, I don't think so. I sit up straight, If I know one thing, I know that men are ruled by their dicks. All I have to do is get Blade, Jason, whoever the fuck he is to fall for me and I'm golden. This is why I need to stay on my toes. Every chance I get, I need to tuck away money. I'll never be at any man or woman's mercy.

"Listen, tonight"—Dolly snaps me back to her—"the Disciples are having a big welcome back party. Everyone will be there. That means all the club sluts, so I need you to trust me and do what I say. I know exactly what Blade likes."

Cautiously I look at her. "What does that mean?"

"Oh." She waves the hair dryer. "I haven't fucked Blade. He's like my brother… Ewww." She shudders dramatically.

"Whatever." I hold up my hand to stop her from saying more. "I give up. I don't know anybody but you so… sure why not trust you." I look at her in the mirror.

"Good, now let's get you waxed and then I'll finish your hair. Then we will tackle shopping."

"What are you waxing? Because I like my eyebrows."

Doug gasps. "Bite your tongue, we would never wax these." He rubs his hand over my eyebrows.

I look at them and shake my head because I'm not stupid—they're talking about waxing my girl parts, but I want to see their faces when I say no.

"No."

She pulls me up and I lean forward. My hair is like a different girl's. She took off a couple of inches. It's still at the middle of my back, but I have layers now, so it falls around my face. It's so clean and shiny-looking I almost smile. Almost, because she is pulling my hand.

I jerk away. "Look, I have no intention of allowing you to wax my vagina," I whisper, glancing around to make sure no one is around. An old lady sits in Jenny's chair. She doesn't look up from her magazine, but by her tight mouth I can tell she heard me.

"Knock it off. Stop being a baby. You have to." Dolly pulls me into the back. I see a small kitchen with a table and adorable bistro chairs. Coffee hits my nose and I wish I could have one.

"In here. It'll take a minute." She drags me past the kitchen and the amazing aroma of coffee and into a small, dark room. After she flips on the light, I blink at the Pepto-Bismol–pink walls that nearly blind me. A huge mirror hangs on the wall and a table stands in the corner. And that's about it besides a small cart that holds the wax.

"Why? Seriously, is he not going to fuck me if I have hair?" This is crazy. She's acting like I'm committing a sin by not skipping in here.

Marina used to try to persuade me to get waxed. I always said no. I mean, it has to hurt. Putting hot wax anywhere near my vagina does not seem like fun.

"It's part of the Disciples thing. All the women have to be bare."

"Wait. What?"

She rolls her neck. "I know. It started years ago. Like before it was *in* to get waxed. The old timers shaved their women's pussies. Now it's tradition, but at least you can get waxed rather than have Blade shave you. Or is that what you want?"

I stumble back hitting the closed door. "What the fuck? Is that true?"

She nods. "Yep."

I watch as she stirs what looks like dark green slime.

"I use the very best wax. Don't worry—you won't even feel it." She snickers.

"I hate all of you. This is so weird. They're like cavemen." I'm rambling but nervous.

I jerk my shorts off along with my panties, climb up on the table, and close my eyes. When she spreads the warm wax on me, I jump a little. It doesn't hurt, though it feels warm. Then she rips—and I mean *rips*—off a patch of my skin. At least that's what it feels like.

I nearly jump off the table. "Are you insane? You said it doesn't hurt! That hurt." I'm glaring at her and she's smiling. "God, you're like a mean little elf."

She giggles. "Come on, you're a toughie." She spreads the wax and swipes again. "And you're blond. You should see when I have to have Doug do me. So not fair being dark and hairy."

"Okay, please just stop." I cover my eyes as she continues to rip. After what seems like an hour but is probably ten minutes she stops and sprays some kind of shit she says calms the redness, and I'm back in her chair where she's finishing my hair.

"Perfect. Let's get you everything you need." She applies some red lipstick and grabs her purse.

"You ready, Doug?"

"I was born ready." He sashays out of the kitchen carrying the best saddlebag I've ever seen.

"So, it's already almost noon. Since she literally needs everything, we need to do the mall." Dolly is checking to make sure she has all she needs for our excursion.

The mall. I cringe. I've never felt comfortable going to the mall. The one time I went with Marina, it seemed like everyone was staring at us.

"God, if only we had time, we could take her to Fred Segal," Doug grumbles.

"Jesus Christ, you two. Take her to the mall. I'll do your two p.m. appointment. But for the love of God… go." Jenny pulls open the door, swinging her arm like a traffic guard.

Both Dolly and Doug look at her and start laughing as they grab for me. "Bye, sourpuss, be back later." Doug throws her a kiss.

We all pile into Dolly's black sports car. I offer to sit in the back because Doug is taller. They argue and laugh the entire way. I almost wish sourpuss Jenny had offered to take me. Something tells me she wouldn't care if I ripped off the whole mall.

"Valet it." Doug waves at the guys.

"Um… so I love your bag." I eye his saddlebag. "I think that's the first thing I need: a bag, a wallet." I try to sound casual; a huge bag is necessary.

"Bloomingdales it is." He jumps out, pulling the seat up so I can get out. It's sunny out. I love LA. We spent a lot of brutal winters in the Midwest the last couple years. It was so much cheaper, so when Benny said it was time to make our way to the West again. I was thrilled. I hate the cold.

Dolly and Doug breeze through the glass doors, and I hang back already self-conscious. At least my hair looks awesome even if I'm in a T-shirt and shorts. The bag and shoes section is right at the spot where we entered.

My eyes trail over all the gorgeous purses. So many bags, all different colors. For once in my life, I want to be able to walk into a store like this and not worry about money. Walk in and buy whatever I want. Of course, I would steal something. I mean, you have to stay sharp.

I walk up to a huge black leather bag and nearly drool. It's fabulous. I check the price tag and nearly throw it. "Holy shit," I mumble.

Doug takes it out of my hand. "I know, but it's a Marc Jacobs bag, so it's pricey. How much did Blade give you?"

"Not that much," I almost scream.

Dolly takes the bag from Doug. "Do you love it?" She arches a finely plucked brow at me.

"Who wouldn't, but that's an insane amount to charge for a bag." I think about my huge ten-dollar bag at my trailer. I got it at Target and it could hold a shitload of cargo.

"Let's get it for her. I'll make Blade give me the money. After all, he is the king and she's now his queen."

I stiffen. "No, no, no I have a certain amount I can spend and this bag costs more than what I have."

And there is no way in hell I'm spending most of it anyway, I want to add. "I want something like Doug's," I say, eyeing his bag.

"Sorry, my love. Got it in West Hollywood. Besides, you love this one. I think Dolly's right—nothing but the best for our queen. Now what kind of wallet do you want? We can stick with Marc Jacobs or maybe.... oh yes, look at this one—it's fitting." He smirks as he points at a large black wallet with a gold skull on it.

I hold up my hands. "Guys, they are incredible, but I can't afford it." I turn away only to have Doug jerk me back. Both he and Dolly look me in the eye. I don't know who to focus on, so I dart back and forth.

"First, Blade has never claimed a woman." Dolly holds up a finger. "Second, you are a virgin." She leans in with big eyes. "So, don't sell yourself short. He has a shitload of money. We are going to get this bag. Pick out a wallet, and let's move on to shoes."

I stare at her, then Doug. "Who are you people?"

"Friends," they both say, then start giggling. I roll my eyes and point to a black wallet that has the same logo as my bag. *My bag*. Holy God, I can't even comprehend having anything this nice. If anyone tries to jack it from me they will definitely regret it. I need to get another knife. I'm startled when Dolly hands me the bag and wallet. I slowly drape the black leather bag around my shoulder. My hand caresses the leather. "Wow, it's so soft."

"Italian leather." Doug snorts.

I reach into my pocket and discreetly pull out my precious wad of cash Blade gave me and unzip my new wallet. It has the most wonderful smell ever. Actually, Blade kind of smells a little like this leather. Looking around, I notice the store is fairly empty, which makes me breathe easier as I shove the hundreds into my new wallet and slide it into my bag.

"Okay, let's do this." I'm ready. I have a killer bag and I'm ready to tackle the mall.

We get shoes, makeup, bras, panties. Clothes, so many clothes. I manage to steal a ton of lipsticks and panties and some face cream. By the end of our shopping trip, I'm kicking myself for not tackling the mall before this. So much easier to steal from, nobody actually watches, and as long as you take shit that doesn't have alarms, you can walk out with anything. We pile into Dolly's car with all my bags from Bloomingdales, Victoria's Secret, Topshop, Kiehl's, and so on. I had to spend most of the money, but I think I still have four or five hundred left. I'll find a hiding spot and start saving. Which means I need to be able to get out of the compound.

"Hey, do you think Blade would let me get a job?" I lean in the middle of the seats so I can talk.

Doug and Dolly are smoking.

"I guess. Discuss it with Blade." She guns through a questionable yellow light.

"Well, is he reliable? Like if he says he'll do something, does he?" I look at my nails.

"Are you kidding? If Blade says he'll do it, it's done. He doesn't lie. He doesn't have to."

She looks at me through the mirror. I flop back against the hot leather seat and close my eyes. Everything is going too fast. Yesterday I was in my crappy trailer worrying about everything. Today I'm sitting in a sports car with way too many clothes and a $3,000 bag.

I rub my temple and try to tune out Dolly and Doug's incessant chatter. If only they would turn some music on. Who doesn't listen to music when they drive?

Dark thoughts take hold. Visions of my dad and how desperately frail he looked. A broken man. He was good, loving, kind. He deserved more. And maybe just maybe I can give him that. For once he can be comfortable, have clean sheets. Jesus, oxygen that doesn't make his nose bleed would be a relief. Dolly said Blade doesn't lie, so I have to trust that. I can do this—be whatever Blade wants me to be as long as my dad doesn't suffer. He's all I have left.

I'm jolted out of my morbid thoughts by Dolly's loud curse as she peels into the alleyway by the salon. She jumps out. "I'll see you guys inside. I'm gonna pee myself."

Doug laughs as he lets me out and reaches for my bag.

"Hey." I push at him. "What are you doing?" My eyes dart around the parking lot.

"Just seeing how good you truly are. I get it. I used to have the same problem. But eventually everyone gets caught." His brown eyes find mine then dip to my bag. Reaching into his bag, he hands me a brand new iPhone.

"I used to be you. But you need to be smart. Don't try and fuck Blade over because you can't. He's like some kind of genius or something. He will find out all your stuff and you'll be screwed."

"Um..." I don't know how to respond to this guy. His brown eyes seem way too smart for his age.

"And this is a gift from me and Dolly. We already programmed our numbers. If you need me anytime, I want you to know I'll answer."

I take the box and frown. "Thank you, but I can't..." I hand the phone back.

"I told you, Eve. I was you. Take the phone." I cock my head to get a good look at him and he's actually letting me see him: his insecurities, his pain.

I shake my head. "Why would you guys do this?" Emotion hits me, whether I like it or not, and my eyes swim with tears. I've lost count of how many iphones I've stolen, but this is my very first gift in years.

"Because you need a phone. And sometimes giving someone a totally unexpected and unwanted gift makes them feel good." He takes my hand and places the phone in it.

"I care." He motions toward the door. Dolly is almost skipping toward the car.

"Dolly cares, and in this world, having a couple of people who care makes all the difference."

"I feel like I should pay you guys something," I say, reaching for my wallet.

He stops me. "Someday, when I need it. One of those days when you look at me and see I could use a gift. Do it then." He looks over my head at Dolly. "Sorry, I gave it to her already." He winks at us and walks through the back door of the salon, his boots crunching on the gravel. I look down at my new phone and over at Dolly.

"I... I'm so not used to this."

She laughs. "Come on. It's gonna take us awhile to get back with traffic." I settle myself in the recently vacated front seat, which is still hot from Doug's presence.

Unable to look at her, I stare at the white apple logo on the box. Opening it up, I glide my fingers over the silver.

"Thank you." It's comes out raspy with the lump in my throat.

"He told you we already put our numbers in, right?" She smiles as she glances over then back at the road.

"He did." I grab the *oh shit* handle on top of the door as she cuts someone off to merge onto the freeway. I stare at her but she doesn't even look fazed at all the honking. Taking a breath, I recross my legs and let go of the death grip as the whole day starts to take its toll. Rubbing my forehead, I remind myself that I'm going to be Blade's whore so there is no way I should have any guilt about spending his money. But now I'm not so sure. Dolly and Doug are actually cool. I've never had any friends. I had my dad and Benny... until I didn't. I never went to school because we traveled all over the United States. What little education I got was from my mom before she died and my dad when he had time.

"Every girl needs a phone. And don't worry. I'll make sure Jason pays for the service." She lights a cigarette and zips down our windows. The warm air caresses my cheeks.

She still doesn't have the radio on and I hate silence, so I fill the empty space with my voice. "What's the deal with Doug?"

She inhales and blows out the window. "You know, shit family, drugs, and being poor. I met him in cosmetology school and we got close. He acts crazy, but deep inside, Doug is one of the saddest, most loyal guys I know."

I glance at her. "He hides it well."

She nods. "He does, and he's getting better, but sometimes he can... well, get really dark." She shakes her head as if trying to erase whatever image passed through it. "Then again, who doesn't have dark moments? He also was my biggest supporter when I was with Edge and he helped me get through the break-up without taking a bottle of pills."

"Wow, that's awful." I glance at my bag, then out the window at the traffic.

"Yeah, love fucking hurts. And being in love with one of the Disciples is like being in a relationship with a rock star or athlete."

Admiring my nails, which are painted a pretty pink, I wonder if that is what my life will soon be like.

"You look hot by the way." She tosses out her cigarette on the freeway.

"Thanks. It was all you guys." Looking down at my sheer pale pink T-shirt and black skinny jeans, I give her a small smile.

"That's not true. We helped, but you definitely have your own style." She eyes me, zips up the windows, and turns on the air.

"I'm obsessed with those boots. I'm going to get me a pair tomorrow."

I smile. "Yeah, they are pretty fabulous. And they were on sale." We both laugh. They were $500 on sale. But they are what I've always dreamed of having. Black high-heeled lace-up boots. Awesome.

"So, Eve, I'm not staying tonight. I want to give you a heads-up on what to expect and how to deal with Crystal the bitch." She zooms down the off ramp exit and stops at a light.

"Crystal has been around for years. She's a whore and a bitch. That being said, she thinks she's Blade's old lady, so she's going to freak out about you." Her small bow-shaped lips can't help but smile.

"You are everything she's not and that is why you are perfect for Blade. But if she gets nasty, don't be afraid to tell Blade or one of his guys. They are all loyal and they will protect you." She sighs. "I hate to say this because I hate him, but go to Edge if Blade is not available. He will protect you. He owes me that at least."

I snort. "Why would she hate me? He's got her stupid poster hanging in his room."

We speed down a country-like street. I see a couple riding their horses. Looking back, I say, "Did you see that?"

She looks in the rearview mirror. "What, horses? Girl, we're in the equestrian area. You are going to see horses all the time."

I shake my head. "I don't understand. Where are we?" Looking around at the grassy park we're passing, kids play in the field and sure enough, another guy on a horse approaches.

She chuckles. "I know it's crazy, huh? Blade's Grandfather bought his land when he got out of Vietnam and it's been passed down. This area of Burbank has huge lots, so there are a lot of horses."

"And they don't get upset about the Disciples being here?"

"Nope, like I said we've had the land for sixty-plus years and the guys are good around here. Now in Hemet, that's a different story." She does a sharp turn into the gravelly road headed toward the compound.

"Oh great, I can already smell the smoke. They're starting early."

"So... What do I do? I mean this is a party, right?" I look around at the tall trees and lush lawn, biting my lip.

She snorts. "Oh, it's a party all right."

We stay silent as I lean forward to take in the sight. There are hundreds of motorcycles. A huge fire pit is going, and the music's so loud I can hear the beat in my chest and I haven't opened Dolly's door yet. But what's more alarming is the hundreds of people. Girls wearing leather skirts, pants, and vests. Others in dresses that a stripper would wear. And the place is filled with so many beards and tattoos.

"Jesus," I whisper, looking at my new outfit. I guess I should have picked more black. A lot of these girls are wearing black. A loud scream comes from the porch. A biker is carrying a girl with nothing on but a G-string. He screams like Tarzan.

"Christ, nothing changes," Dolly mutters as she slams her car into park. "Come on." Reluctantly I open the door, reaching for all my bags. I flip my hair out of my face only to look over at most everyone staring at me.

"Shoulders back, head up," Dolly says under her breath. I'm not sure if she's saying it to me or herself. Doesn't matter; we both do it. Axel, at least I think it's Axel, reaches for my bags.

"Thanks."

He nods, giving me a once-over, then flashes Dolly a smile that would bring any woman to her knees.

"You did good, Doll. Blade will be pleased." He looks at me again. Axel is the one who held me last night. Only now can I get a good look at him. Meaning he must be one of the guys that all the carnival girls gossiped about. With his dark hair and blue eyes, he is definitely hot in a pretty boy way—well, besides his tattoos.

"You okay?" He glares at me.

"Yes, I'm fine." Caught looking at him, I'm aggravated.

He guides us through the large farm-style house. I try to look around, but it's filled with bikers, so all I see are beards and tits.

He stops at a double door, knocks, and lets us in. Taking the rest of the bags from Dolly, he leaves us in a large room with tons of bad art and maps, along with a long, rectangular wooden table and a bunch of chairs. The walls are brown with the Disciples logo everywhere. Dolly flops onto one of the chairs crossing her legs. I stand on the side slightly shell-shocked. I had no idea this MC was this big.

"How many guys are in the Disciples?" I whisper.

"I don't know. A lot. Why are we whispering?"

All of a sudden nervous, I throw her a dirty look. He's coming. I can sense him. It's weird but my body seems to always tingle when he is near. Sure enough, the door swings open and there he is—a bottle of Jack Daniels in one hand and an arm around the redhead from the poster with the other. Staggering, I almost collapse into the chair but somehow manage to stay standing. Behind him are Edge and Axel.

Dolly jumps to her feet and grabs my hand. I almost laugh because with my heels and all the giant guys in the room, her petite form is so not threating—it's comical. But I'm grateful to have her, so I squeeze her hand.

Blade stops and slowly, his green eyes pursue me from the top of my head to my shoes, lingering on my mouth and breasts.

Crystal snuggles into his chest. Her dyed red hair is awful and might give Marina a run for the money. With all the pancake makeup she has on, she could use a shower and I'd love to tell her so. And then he smiles, and I stop breathing for a second because Blade has the whitest, straightest teeth I've ever seen. It's almost unfair. No one should have that kind of smile.

"Dolly, you are amazing." His eyes don't leave mine.

"Angel, why don't you go to our room. I'll be up later." I stand frozen. Of all the things I thought he was going to say, that wasn't one of them.

"Umm." I struggle to breathe and move.

He lets go of the redhead and sets the booze on the table. "You can let go of her, Dolly." He takes my hand away and tilts my chin up. Like a soft breeze, he brushes my lips to his.

"Go upstairs." It's a command and it jerks me out of my daze. My legs tremble and I'm confused at the feelings this man brings out in me.

I turn to Dolly and nod then manage to get myself to move.

SEVEN

BLADE/JASON

I watch her go. There is something about the way Eve moves that I like. With a sigh, I remove Crystal's claws from my arm.

"I need to talk to Dolly."

Her brown eyes squint at me as if she wants to argue. Instead she pastes on a plastic smile and swishes out. Crystal's walk does nothing for me. As she huffs and shuts the door, I turn to Dolly.

"What happened today? Did you get her everything?"

She looks over my shoulder at Edge and then Axel. I glance at them.

"What? Is there some big secret?"

"Actually yes. Yes, there is and I would like to speak with you privately." She plants her hands on her small hips and tilts her cute pixie head up at me.

My guys snort. "Okay, you heard our princess. She needs a word in private." Axel pushes off the wall and leaves, whereas Edge drags his feet, still mumbling as he shuts the door.

I drop into my chair and put my booted feet on the table, interlacing my fingers over my abdomen.

"Spit it out and hand me the Jack. I barely got a sip."

LETHAL

She flounces into a chair next to me and thuds the bottle hard on the table.

I raise an eyebrow. "Speak. I'm losing patience."

"Why would you bring her here? Buy her all that stuff, *brand her*?" Her arms are animated and her face is turning red. Dolly always reminds me of the bad Smurfette when she gets fired up. "Only to keep fucking Crystal?" she spits out.

I reach for the bottle of Jack, unscrew the lid, and take a long, deep sip. That first burn makes me warm and happy for a moment.

"Dolly, I don't even know that chick. She's fucking beautiful and her dad is a good man who is dying. So rather than have to put a bullet in his head in front of her, I claimed her." I take another drag from the bottle. I said these same words not an hour ago to a crying Crystal. The more I say them, the easier it is to believe them. Not that I owe Crystal an explanation. I've been honest with her from day one. But women are fucking crazy. They only hear what they want.

Dolly jumps up and starts to pace. The Bud Light sign flickers behind her. "You are so full of shit, Jason. I've known you for a long time. If you thought Eve was only beautiful, you would have given her to someone else. You claimed her! And she's too good for you." She slaps one of my boots off the table.

"Christ." I lean my head back and gaze up at the yellowish ceiling. "I swear to God, I don't need this tonight. What happened to make you fall in love with her?" I snap.

"A lot of things. She's smart even though she barely knows how to read."

I wince dropping my other boot to floor with a thud. "What?" I don't know why my heart is beating fast. I barely know this girl, but school came easy for me. Reading is one of my guilty pleasures that I still allow myself. It keeps me human when this life wants to kill it out of me. If she can't read, I need to teach her.

Dolly holds up her hands. "She can read. But I don't think she ever went to school. She's never had any friends, and she's a fucking virgin, Blade!" She must not have wanted to say that because her red cheeks instantly go pale.

The silence in the room is broken only by the buzzing from the trashy beer signs that litter the walls.

I scrub my hands over my face, then start laughing. "She's a fucking carnival rat. A gypsy. If you believe that she's a virgin, well then you got played."

She flops back into the chair and crosses her legs.

"Here." Shaking my head, I hand her the Jack Daniels bottle.

She takes a swig then shudders. "God, I hate that shit." But she takes a breath. "Fine, whatever, you will find out either way. It still doesn't excuse you from removing her chance at having us as a family. You need to kick that ugly bitch Crystal to the curb." She crosses her arms.

"I know how crazy Crystal can be and I know that Edge fucked up. But she deserves more than getting kicked to the curb."

"No, she doesn't." Her face is completely deadpan.

I can't help but grin. "Whatever, Dolly, you are not my mother and if I want to fuck a ton of women and keep Eve in my bed every night it's no business of yours."

"But..."

"I'm done. What else?"

"She's a klepto."

"A what?" Again, silence besides the buzzing.

"A kleptomaniac. You know, someone who has to steal. Even if they have..." I cut her off.

"I know what a fucking klepto is, Dolly." I lean back. *What the fuck?* "How do you know? I mean you've only just met her for fuck's sake."

"Oh stop. You're insulting me," she snaps and takes another swig. This time her shudder is almost nonexistent.

Suddenly it's hard not to laugh. "So, you're telling me that in the five hours you've spent with Eve, she has confessed to

LETHAL

being an eighteen-year-old virgin who can barely read and she's a kleptomaniac?" This time I do laugh. "Well, I see why you wanted Edge out of the room."

"Whatever, Blade. You are going to be sorry."

"I'm already sorry! I woke up sorry." She slinks into the chair and I feel guilty for screaming at her. It's like yelling at your sister.

"Hey Prez, we have a situation." Ox sticks his head in. It's got to be bad if he's not knocking.

"What?" I snap, a slither of unease going up my spine. My hand goes for my blade in my boot.

"It's your... it's Eve." I'm out the door in seconds, Dolly trailing behind us.

"What happened?" My heart pounds in my temples, the adrenaline like a drug filling my veins.

"Well, this." He pushes open the kitchen door. Eve stands in the middle of the room, her honey hair cascading over her shoulders. Her face has never looked more beautiful. Unfortunately, she holds a giant butcher knife on Edge, Axel, and a bleeding Dewey.

Badass rings in my head. My primal urge to mate with her almost distracts me from the scene in front of me.

"What the fuck is going on in here?"

She whirls to me, her hand steady as she hisses, "This pig tried to kiss me," and points to Dewey. His father, Gunner, is one of the old timers. Dewey's a prospect, clearly drunk and in need of stiches if his bleeding stomach feels as bad as it looks.

"She stabbed me," he wails, clutching his stomach.

"Wow, Eve, I had no idea you were so good with a knife," Dolly chimes in from behind me.

"Angel." I hold my hands up. "Put the knife down, baby. Nobody is going to hurt you."

"Really? I can't even walk down the hallway without your guys saying gross things. And this guy tried to kiss me and rubbed his disgusting dick on me." She points the sharp knife at Dewey, who backs into Edge.

"Hey Eve?" Dolly chimes in over my shoulder. "Can you go ahead and slice off Edge's penis? He's used it enough."

I turn and give her an eye. She shrugs. "Just saying."

"Fuck you, Dolly." Edge throws his hands up and stomps out.

"Not gonna happen, *ever again*," she sings after him.

I sigh and rub the back of my neck looking at Axel who stands with his arms crossed, his face twisted in concern.

"Well… I have to get up early, and you seem to have your hands full. So, I'm gonna bounce." Dolly's smiling face makes me grit my teeth. "And Eve? Welcome to the family." She slams the door as she leaves.

"Dewey?" He looks up, his face full of pain and remorse.

"Did you touch what's mine?" I love Dewey… have a huge soft spot for him. But he can't touch my woman. I don't care if he is slightly on the dull side of normal.

"I didn't know. You have to believe me. I thought you were with Crystal," he wails again and holds up a bloody hand at Eve. "And she's so beautiful, she smells good and—"

"She's mine, Dewey. You fucked up. But you're bleeding all over Amy's kitchen. I guess we should find someone to stitch you up. Is Doc here yet?" My gaze shifts to Axel who stares at Eve almost baffled.

"I don't know. I've been making sure Dewey didn't get sliced up more from your wildcat."

I turn to Eve. "For fuck's sake, put the knife down. I promise you're safe, and I'm gonna take care of this shit *now*." I grab her wrist and twist slightly watching the large knife clank to the floor. I pull her head tight to my chest holding her still.

"I seem to remember warning you what I would do if you ever pulled a knife on me again." She tries to move. But I squeeze her tight feeling her breasts on my chest.

"I didn't pull a knife on you—I pulled it on him." We both glance at a distressed and bleeding Dewey.

"Christ, he's slow, Eve." Her eyes grow huge and before she can talk, I add, "He should know better. I agree."

I glance at Axel, who raises a dark eyebrow at me. "Dewey, I want to see you tomorrow morning."

"Sure thing, Prez. And I'm sorry. I just wanted a pretty girl."

I nod. "Go with Axel, and see if Doc is here. He'll stitch you up."

"That's it? I thought you said no one would touch me but you?" she taunts, her eyes shooting blue daggers at me.

"I think you stabbing him in the gut is enough since he didn't hurt you." I take her arm and drag her to the front door, ignoring the stunned faces as we all pass by. AC/DC is blasting and it's not quite dark yet. The large bonfire and the drinking and debauchery have begun. I shake my head at Crystal who starts to come over. She stops but glares at me. What is with the women in my life tonight?

"Can I have everyone's attention?" I yell over the music and laughter. The crowd turns. Loud shouting and laughing at Dewey continues. I hold up my hand.

"I know I just got back and a lot of you might not have heard, but this"—I drag a squirming Eve in front of me—"*is mine!*" The music has been turned down, and the loud spitting fire and shuffling feet are all I hear as my guys and the women nod.

"Good, carry on."

A loud cheer goes up and everyone starts to move forward to meet her.

"What the fuck?" As she leans back against my chest, I wrap my hands around her small waist. I can't help myself so I bury my nose in her neck.

"Happy? I just made you my queen." She sucks in some air and her beautiful blue eyes are the size of saucers. Ryder is at our side, his hands making sure nobody gets too close as Eve shoots everyone a frown.

"You okay? I should have been there. I'm sorry." Ryder looks at me.

"Please." She rolls her eyes. "I can take care of myself," she mumbles.

I laugh. "You might change your mind tonight." She glares up at me.

I spot Doc over by a lemon tree checking Dewey out. He nods at me.

"Let's go, Angel." She sighs as if it's an inconvenience.

My lips twitch. "Such a little badass," I say, squeezing her hand. "But I'm the only one allowed to play with knives, little girl." I lace our fingers together, grab a bottle of Jameson, and drag her to our room.

Our room.

Jesus, if my father and brother can see me now, I'm sure they're rolling over in their graves.

I bang open the door and she goes straight to the bathroom. I hear the shower turn on.

I crack open the bottle of Irish whiskey, light up, and look out at my backyard, which is illuminated with stupid lights that some of the wives thought would look festive. Another bonfire and a bunch of bikers drinking and laughing. I glance over at the pool and sure enough, about fifteen couples are in it. I take a drag and make a mental note to have it cleaned tomorrow.

The shower turns off and I hear the door open. Without turning around, I still sense her anxiety. Christ, maybe Dolly's right and she is a virgin. Not that it makes a difference. I'm gonna fuck her regardless, but it makes things messy. Last thing I want is to be her first. Truthfully, I like older, experienced women who have no expectations of me other than getting each other off and leaving. A virgin complicates things. I take another long drag and turn to look at her as I put out my cigarette. She's standing in one of my T-shirts, her long tan legs glistening as if she put lotion on them.

Her face is rosy from the heat of the shower and she literally glows. Inhaling, I smile as her coconut smell fills my nostrils. She gazes down at her feet, then straight up at me. A charge goes through me as I look into her ocean-blue eyes.

"Come here."

She swallows and moves forward a couple steps then takes a deep breath. It pushes her breasts out and my eyes can't help but drop to her nipples. Suddenly, I want this woman more than I've ever wanted anything. She stops about an arm's length away and blinks up at me.

"Closer."

One more step and I feel her body temperature seep into me. Reaching for her neck and hair, I pull her into my arms. Her soft breath is slightly ragged.

"You scared, Angel?" She shakes her head no.

"No?"

"No," she whispers.

"You a virgin, baby?" Her eyes are huge as she slowly shakes her head no. I run my nose against her cheek. Breathing her in, I'm so hard my pants hurt.

"Unbutton me." She blinks, but her eyes remain focused on my mouth. I almost say it again, but she gracefully reaches for the button and pops it open.

"Zipper."

She bites her bottom lip and I lean my head back so I don't grab her head and force her to her knees. I can't remember a time I've felt this possessive, almost primal about a girl. It's like I can barely hold myself back. My zipper slides down and she pushes my jeans down without me telling her to.

Again, she swallows her nervousness, making me want her more. I reach for the bottom of my T-shirt and lift it over her head. Her hair spills over her shoulders and breasts like a waterfall of golden honey.

"I'm going to drink you. Suck you and fuck you."

She holds her breath as though getting ready to jump into a pool. I kick off my boots then step out of my jeans.

"Exhale, Angel. I'm still gonna fuck you even if you pass out."

That snaps her into breathing. She squints as if she's thinking about running. Her eyes roam over my body and I can't help but chuckle. Dolly may be right. Eve is scared. She may actually be a virgin. But she lied to me so I'm going to treat her like a woman. I pick her up, and her legs wrap around me as I walk us to the bed, both of us falling onto the downy softness. Pinning her hands on top of her head, I bite her puffy bottom lip. As she gasps, I lick and suck that juicy lip and leave it with a pop. My hand cups her full breast; my rough thumb rubs her incredible dusty rose nipple.

"Jesus Christ, I've seen a lot of tits but these are by far the best. Look at these fucking nipples." I groan as I latch on to the other one and suck it hard. A moan comes out of her. And she clutches the comforter as her eyes flutter shut. Her breathing is coming in short hisses.

"Are they sensitive?" I lightly bite one.

"So sensitive."

I spread my large, tan, tattooed hand across her flat stomach. Her golden skin is creamy and silky. Roughly I rub my hand up and down her breast and on her stomach till she whimpers.

"You're flawless," I growl and take her mouth. My tongue seeking hers, I barely let her breathe. The need to almost steal her very breath tempts me.

"Spread your legs, Angel."

She's panting, but so am I. I'm not one for denying myself pleasure and this girl gives me pleasure unlike anyone else.

Her head turns into the pillow as she obeys. My blood is pounding and I almost lift her legs wider and sink my leaking cock into her pretty pink pussy. Instead, I pinch her nipples and make my way in between her legs. I stand up and grab her as though she weighs nothing then kneel on my carpet inhaling her pussy.

"Christ, you smell good. Has anyone ever eaten your cunt before?"

Throwing a hand over her eyes, she shakes her head no.

I smile. "That's a lot of noes out of you. Let's see if I can't get some yeses." I want to gently kiss this fucking pussy. But her little clit is glistening pink and her folds tempt me. I spread them open wider and attack. I eat her like I haven't had pussy in years. I lick her sweet nub so hard she's twisting and jerking on my brown comforter, which is getting quite the wet spot already.

"Oh my God... I think..."

"Let me hear it, baby. When I fuck you, eat you, you can be as loud as you want when you come." I add my middle finger inside her. She lifts her hips to my face as her body starts to quiver. I go up and deep and feel that rough spot that sends her over. Her clit pulses and her pussy clenches my finger like a vise that doesn't want to let go. When I pump her some more and my finger goes deep, she yells out.

There it is—I feel it. *She lied*. She is a god damn virgin. I want to be pissed, but instead I'm possessed. Beyond caring, I need my throbbing cock inside her. Even if I go slow, it's gonna hurt. "Wrap your legs around me, Angel and if you want to scream, I'll take it."

Her eyes are heavy and I don't stop. I ease my thick cock into her slick wetness. Only the tip—I rub her swollen clit with my precum and her wetness and we both groan.

"Shit." My back and neck are covered with sweat. I have a thick cock. It's overaverage in size, but the thickness is what takes getting used to. I push in a little farther and she's so tight and small, I groan with pure pleasure. My balls tighten and I can't wait.

She's mine.

All mine.

As I plunge into her, she freezes, tightens, and that barrier is gone. I will never feel anything like it again. It ripped and so did something inside me. I cover her scream with my lips. Kissing her, soothing her as I hold still letting her adjust. I wipe her hair off her forehead with my hand.

"Did you think I wouldn't know?" I look at her eyes filled with tears, but they don't spill.

"That really hurt. Hurry up and get done, please."

I grab her chin. "The first time sucks, and I'm thick, but you'll adjust. I feel you already taking me."

Pulling out, I slide slowly into her again, watching her as she bites on her bottom lip.

"I only like your mouth. This burns," she hisses.

"Kiss me—you'll love this cock soon enough." I lift her ass so I can get in as deep as I can. Christ, I want to crawl inside her. I start to thrust still holding back so that I don't hurt her any more than I already have.

"Jesus Christ, you're tight and untouched." I rock inside her. "Do you feel me? I'm inside you. You're mine, baby," I groan into her ear.

My body is so alive. Her wet pussy allows me to go deeper and her elevated breathing tells me that the worst is over for her. As she digs her nails into my back, I lean down and suck her neck. Head spinning, I let go, knowing she has to be sore. My release spills out of me like a fucking volcano exploding with ecstasy. The vibrations go all the way to my toes. My body jerks and I collapse still pulsing inside her.

"Fuck." I roll to my right so she can breathe and I can catch my breath. I throw my arm over her stomach as I try to focus.

Maybe it was because she was so tight and hot from being a virgin, but I have never had such intense sex like that. Needing her, I pull her on top of me. She lays her head on my chest and sighs.

"Let's get cleaned up," I whisper as I caress her silky back.

"Hmmm?" Her hand reaches for my neck as she snuggles into me more. And I tighten my arm around her. My body is alive, wanting back inside her. My dick hardens needing her pussy as if it's a tempting drug. She's done so I breathe in her scent instead.

"In a minute, K?" Her even breathing and limp body feel so good. Like she was made for me; her body fits mine. I need to get up, so I roll her over, watching as she curls up in the comforter. Grabbing my phone, I make sure there are no urgent messages. Nothing but drunken hate messages from Crystal. Dolly's right—I need to deal with her.

I want Eve. Instinctively, I knew it as soon as I entered her father's shitty trailer two days ago. I plug my phone into my charger on my nightstand, lock our door, turn off the lights, and slide back into my bed next to my warm girl. I pull her back into my arms and close my eyes, sleep easily coming.

EIGHT

EVE

"Eve." The gruff, husky voice comes from somewhere above me. With a thud, something lands on my legs as I blink awake. There's a box on my lap. Groggy, I sit up.

"God." I rub my eyes. "I slept. It must be this bed." Seriously I've slept better in the last two days than I ever have. I reach my hands up to the ceiling and stretch and everything comes roaring back like a giant wave crashing onto me. There's a good chance my face is beet red. Grabbing the comforter, I pull it to my chest. I smell us and sex.

Groaning, I bite my lip in embarrassment. Images of last night flood me and I want to pull the comforter over my head. But I'm an adult, so I need to look at him.

Jesus, he is literally a Greek god with a giant cock, *unfortunately*.

And he is staring at me, his frown making my heart thud at what a hot bad boy he is. I need to pull it together. Next thing I know, I'll be liking him or something. He clenches an unlit cigarette between his full lips.

"I need you to get up and take this immediately. I'm assuming you're not on birth control?"

I edge away until my back hits the bed frame and look down at the box he threw at me. A morning-after pill, *perfect*.

I can't help but laugh. "Feeling guilty? Sorry to disappoint you, but I'm religious and if God wants us to have a baby well... I guess it's his will." I smile sweetly at him. His jaw starts to twitch as I cock my head watching the play of emotions on his pretty face. Maybe his teeth will rip the end of his cigarette like a lion attached to its victim. He slowly brings his lighter up and the quick flick fills the silence. It's impossible to keep from smirking at him. What an arrogant ass. I almost want to say, *When you play you pay*, but he might strangle me. Why chance it? I don't know him *that* well.

He runs a hand through his honey-wheat hair. "I never *do not* wear a condom. Last night was... unexpected. Take the pill, or I will shove it down your throat."

Throwing the sheet off me, I stand. His eyes travel my whole body and his fists clench. I smile again as the sun fills the room, and I wonder what time it is.

"I guess you should have thought of that before you ripped me open. I have no idea why all the girls are panting after you like bitches in heat. That thing is horrible." I wave my hand at his crotch. His eyes narrow, and I think I hear his teeth grind but can't be sure since I'm almost in the bathroom. His black boot stops me from slamming the door and he shoves the Plan-B box onto his large sink.

He nods at it. "Take it—then I'm taking you to get on birth control," he snarls.

Again, my lips twitch. After last night and the pain of his giant cock, this is almost payback. Almost!

"No. We don't need to get me birth control. I have no intention of having sex with you ever again. Once was enough." I snort and point at his penis. "Problem solved." I flash him a big smile.

Okay, I'm making this way worse than it was. Yes, he has a ridiculous penis but I came harder than I ever imagined with his mouth and fingers. I shiver at what his tongue felt like licking my clit.

"You can't be that ignorant. You have to know the first time hurts. I'm ripping open your hymen." He looks at me like I might be dumb. And for some reason, I hate that. Holding my head high, I turn on the shower and step in not even caring if it's ice cold. Thankfully it's warm and then hot and I try to pretend he's gone. Enjoying my new shower gel and shampoo, I take my time. I'm amazed that I'm not that sore. I mean, I'm sore but still, if he wanted to do that thing with his tongue on my clit, I wouldn't say no. I don't have a chance to think about it longer because Blade turns off the water and drags me out.

"Are you insane?" I push my wet hair back trying to wring it out. "I need a towel." He blocks me and I want to stomp my foot.

He grabs the box, rips it open, and shoves the pill at me.

"Stop it." I twist and realize he isn't joking and will force that pill down my throat if I don't take it.

"I don't need the pill," I yell at him as I slap his hand away. "I can't get pregnant, you asshole. Although you can take me to a clinic so I can see if I'm crawling with the clap from your dirty dick." He takes a step back, obviously not expecting that.

"What the fuck are you rambling about? You're young and healthy. You can get pregnant." He hands me the white pill.

I hand it back. "You take it. *I cant*. When I was twelve I got appendicitis. By the time my junkie mother took me to the hospital, it had burst. The bacteria got into my fallopian tubes." I'm yelling, but he's finally listening. "The doctor who did the surgery said I'm sterile. So you see, you need that pill more than me." I brush past him, hot tears threatening to fall. I never think about this because it's something that was taken from me, and much like my whole life, I hate feeling like a victim. But every once in a while...

Strong, warm hands pull me into his delicious-smelling T-shirt. Downy, spice, and a touch of smoke. It's Blade and it's starting to become familiar.

"I'm sorry. I am an asshole." He strokes my hair.

I shake my head. "It's not a big deal." My traitorous voice cracks.

He sighs. "Such a badass." That's all he says and it's perfect. He's not trying to say it's okay or that it sucks; he's holding me tight and letting my truth come out. The tears that I've been holding for years, days, my whole life, finally spill over. And I cry, giant gasps of sadness. Sadness about my dad, mom, Benny, and the truth that I'm never going to be a mom.

He lifts me up and takes me to the mess of the bed. Blurry eyed I blink as he pulls his shirt off. His warm hands caress my cheeks. His lips kiss my tears that won't stop. It's like once the dam broke, I'm undone.

"Kiss me. Just be with me." His warm tongue twists around mine. His hand cups my chin, his eyes roam my face. I grab at his shoulders as I seek his mouth, my core instantly becoming wet and slick. My body shivers as I quiver and pure need takes over.

I want him. I'm somewhat shocked at this. He licks my tears and I moan as his large hand moves to my breast, his lips following. As my nipples strain toward him, he grips my breast and massages it. His mouth is on mine as I open for his tongue. I pull at his hair and he bites my lip.

"I'm going to teach you everything I like." His tongue licks my ear down to my neck as he sucks on me.

"Blade." I drop my hands to the sheet as I push my head back giving him full access to my neck.

"Fuck, baby you like it, don't you?"

There's no need to answer because his thumb is dipping inside me and rubbing my clit. My eyes fly open as I look down at my legs spread open and his tattooed arm and fingers fucking me.

"Oh my God." I'm bucking into his hand. He takes two fingers and thrusts them inside me as I hear myself saying, "Yes."

Dragging them out, he rubs them roughly on my clit and I have to let go of the sheet as I grasp his muscled biceps. I'm whimpering. My core pulses as my hand grabs his strong wrist, and I don't know if I'm trying to stop him or encourage him.

"That's it, Angel. Open up those baby blues and let me see you come." My eyes fly to his dark green ones as my body jerks and I blink as dark spots dance in front of my eyes, the pleasure so intense I might scream.

"Fuck yeah... look at me." His gaze lands on me as I quiver and clench, his stilled fingers on my swollen clit.

"Eyes on me. I want to see you when I fuck you." I blink again as he takes his hand away and unbuttons his pants. He's not wearing underwear and his thick cock strains toward me. I want to back away but he is stroking himself. I lick my lip at the engorged pink mushroom head. I almost reach to touch it, but he shakes his head no. His hands pull me to the edge and he positions himself at my pussy.

"Eyes on me," he grunts as he slowly pushes into me. I tighten and he groans.

"So tight. Angel, relax and I swear I'll make you see stars." I look into his eyes and relax as he thrusts into me. It stings slightly, but then he pulls out and thrusts again and I reach for his shoulders, anything, because he makes me feel full, whole. I can only hold on as he opens me wider.

"That's it. Fuck, you are going to be my downfall." He groans as his eyes stay focused on mine.

"Talk to me. I can feel you leaking all over my balls. You love my cock, don't you?" I'm climbing, reaching for what seems like could be my own downfall. My stomach is clenched as he hits that perfect spot that makes me see spots again.

"Tell me." He grabs under my knees and lifts my ass so he's even deeper.

LETHAL

"Yes," I pant and go over as wave after wave of pleasure pulses through me.

"That's my girl. Milk the come out of me." He is rough as he pounds into me and I whimper.

"Blade, I think I'm coming again." This time, I lean up and wrap my arms around him as I jerk and come on his thick cock, barely registering his release. All I hear is my name and his beautiful body jerking and filling me up.

"Jesus Christ." He thrusts inside me one more time and pulls out. Both of us sound like we ran a marathon.

"I have stuff that needs to get done." He grabs me and kisses my swollen lips. Pulling up his pants in one quick jerk, it's only now I realize he didn't even completely undress. He throws his T-shirt into his hamper and reaches into his drawer for a clean one.

"I'll be back later and we'll go out with everyone." His eyes rake over me.

I sit up. "But... what am I supposed to do all day?" He grabs his phone and cigarettes, getting to the door in three strides.

"I don't know. Go lie out at the pool. Just don't swim in it. I need to make sure it's been cleaned."

"Um, okay. I think I did get a bikini. I don't know how to swim, so no worry about me getting in." Flopping back on the bed, I move slightly and notice the bottom sheet is stained with dried blood.

"Wait, you don't know how to swim?" He takes a step toward me.

"No." I look out the window, then back at his frowning face. "Stop looking at me like that. I moved around my whole life. It's not like we had one in the backyard." Getting up, I pull the sheet with me.

"Eve, I don't want you by the pool if you can't swim."

I roll my eyes. "Do you have fresh sheets? These are ruined." I look at the blood. Blade glances down at them.

"Leave it. Amy will take care of it."

"No." I straighten my shoulders back. "I would rather do it," I say, tucking the edge of the sheet under my armpit.

Someone pounds on the door. "Prez, we're ready when you are." I think its Ryder's voice.

"Minute." He searches my face and must not see what he wants because he starts to rub his face with his hands. "I need a shower. How am I going to concentrate with the smell of your pussy on me?"

"What?" I whisper, horrified. I don't know how he manages to make me blush, but it seems constant with him.

He laughs and I stare mesmerized at his tan face and blond hair. His eyes are such a gorgeous green it's almost unfair. Glancing down, I study the pink polish on my toenails.

"Just don't stab anyone and be safe." He reaches for the back of my neck bringing me to him.

"The sheets are in the cabinet over by the pool table, along with extra towels. And I'll teach you to swim—it's easy." He turns and leaves me. I sink to the edge of the bed and look at the mess on the sheet. Thank God I didn't bleed on the comforter—I like how soft it is. Pulling my legs up, I look around. It's so quiet now. With Blade gone he seems to have sucked out all the energy and taken it with him. I can't decide if I should move to his clean side and try to go back to sleep or get up. It looks like a beautiful day, if the bright sun in the room is any indication. I can't help but stare at the redhead hanging not ten feet away. Would he be mad if I took her down? I mean for fuck's sake if I'm expected to live here with him, her fake boobs and stupid red hair are the last thing I want to gaze upon.

"You know what? I'm going to sunbathe." I nod, jumping up and searching through the numerous bags from yesterday. I'm almost ready to give up when I stifle back a scream. A middle-aged dark-haired woman is standing in front of me staring down at my clothes.

"Holy shit, you scared me." I look at the door. Does she not feel the need to knock?

"I'm Amy. Let's take off all the tags and I'll wash and press everything." Her matter-of-fact attitude throws me for a second. She turns and looks at the bed.

I jump up. "I'll take care of it." My face heats.

"Don't be absurd. And don't be ashamed." She starts stripping the bed sheets with so much authority I back up and let her move. She's tall and thin and seems to be in charge.

"I... well thank you." Clearing my throat, I realize I'm wrapped in a sheet. "I'm going to hop in the shower." She ignores me as she continues to clean up his room, dumping the ashtrays, spraying the bed with Lysol. Scurrying into the bathroom, I stuff the sheet into a hamper and start the water. After a quick rinse off, I peek out the door. The room is spotless. The bed is made with navy sheets and a navy comforter. Big white throw pillows are on it along with my bikini. I still smell the lemon Lysol—when I spotted the can earlier, it said it's fresh and kills germs. I make a mental note to remember that. I reach for my cherry red string bikini, slip it on, and pull on a sundress that we found at Forever 21.

Before I venture out, I need to find a perfect spot to hide my cash. I twirl around. His room would be the best place, but with Amy cleaning it every day, putting it under the mattress won't work. I glance up at the hideous velvet painting. Standing on the bed, I lift it up. It's freaking huge but it's perfect. I stash my rolled-up cash behind it and jump down, straighten the bed, and look for Amy. I find her in the large kitchen drinking coffee. There are a couple bikers getting breakfast but they don't even look at me.

"Hi, I'm Eve." I hold out my hand to her. She raises a nonexistent eyebrow at me.

"Sweetheart, let's get this straight right away. I'm thrilled you are the one. You don't need to be shy. Now sit and let me get you some breakfast." She indicates for me to use one of the stainless steel barstools. I plop down on the barstool and look around. This is the first time I've been in here in the daylight. The cheerful yellow walls are a welcome change considering the rest of the house sports a lot of brown and black. It has a row of pretty windows along with shiny appliances.

"I think this is my favorite place in this house." Resting my chin on my hand, I look at her.

"That's because this is my domain." She waves her hand toward the rest of the house.

"I painted, designed, and order everything in this kitchen, so next time you want to stab someone, do it in another area of the house." She cracks a couple of eggs in a pan. The sizzling butter along with the smell of coffee makes my stomach growl.

"So, what am I supposed to do? I'm used to working." I twirl on the barstool.

"Well, today I would relax by the pool. I hear he's taking you tonight." Her voice laced with disapproval.

I stop twirling. "Is that bad?"

She hands me a fork and napkin, then places an omelet in front of me. I lean forward to look at it. "Is that broccoli?"

She washes her hands and turns. "Yep, Jason likes to eat healthy, so you will too."

I want to argue, but since I've never had anything like this before, I take a small bite.

A burst of butter and fluffy egg melts in my mouth and makes me look up at her.

"This is delicious." I swallow. "If this is healthy then I want it every day." I pluck a large piece of broccoli and nibble on it. "This"—I point at my plate so that I don't talk with food in my mouth—"this omelet is a whole lot different from the ones I've had at IHOP." I smile at her.

She cocks her head. "I'm going to the store. Is there anything you need or like?"

I take a sip of the coffee and groan at the fresh bitter flavor.

"Eve?" I open my eyes and see Amy smiling at me. "Anything?"

"No, this is the best breakfast I've ever had. I completely trust you." She seems to like that answer.

"I'll turn on some music out by the pool. Jason wants me to remind you not to go in the water." She grabs her purse and list and is out the door before I can say something I might regret.

Does he think I'm stupid? God, he does. He insinuated it earlier when I was terrified of his penis. Picking up my plate, I wash it. My eyes take in Amy's kitchen. She wasn't kidding when she said everything is perfect. It literally shines in here. Even the large glass window is spotless—there's not a speck of dirt on it. I can see all the way to the end of the grass yard and where the gravel starts toward the front. Looking down at my hands, I use the pink sponge to wash my plate. I've never been ashamed of myself or where I came from. Maybe because everyone I was around came from the same place. But with Blade, he has this way of making me feel inferior or dumb. I mean, I know he's older and obviously smart, but I'm smart too. Just because I didn't go to school doesn't mean I don't have what it takes to survive.

Turning off the water, I spin around trying to find something to dry my hands on. My eyes land on two perfectly folded floral dish towels. Biting my lip, I dry my hands on my cheap dress rather than messing anything up. I open the sliding glass doors and step out into the beautiful sunny day. As I gaze up at the blue skies for a second, I let all my crap go and make my way toward the pool. With a deep breath, I smell flowers and chlorine. Strangely enough I love it. I'm so caught up in my shit I almost scream. A couple is passed out on a couple of lounge chairs to my right. The bright sun looks like it's burning them up. But hey, it's none of my business. I grab a lounge chair with a striped red pillow and drag it to the other side. Wishing I had thought to bring a towel, I look down at the pale blue water of the pool and hope Blade follows through and teaches me how to swim. The water looks refreshing. I pull off my dress, settle back into the cushions, and try to relax, listening to the pop music Amy turned on for me.

"God." My hands slap the cushions as I shoot the couple a dirty look. I can't relax with them there. I need to think about what has happened to me, create a new plan. Also, they're going to be in a world of pain if they stay out here much longer.

I get up and walk over to them. The woman seems smart enough to turn her face into the cushion so only her legs and arms are red. The man on the other hand...

"Excuse me." I kick at him. He's fat and his beard is huge. Sprawled out on his back, he snores loudly, reminding me of Pedro. His black T-shirt and leather cut seem to be inviting the sun to bake him. Shaking my head, I acknowledge I need to get another knife. These guys can't be trusted.

"Hey." I kick at the lounge chair again. Nothing but another loud snore. I look at the woman. Much like the guy, she's heavy and her dress is not covering much.

"Hello?" I give her a little shake. She groans and flops to her stomach almost rolling off the lounger. The sun makes her blink and curse as she sits up.

"Who the fuck are you?" she snarls as she covers her eyes.

I don't answer her but point at her man or whatever he is to her. "He's getting burned to a crisp." Walking back to my lounge chair. I hear her scream at the man. He stands up, tells her to fuck off, and throws himself fully clothed into the pool.

A bunch of water splashes me as I gasp at the coldness. He comes up for air and looks at the woman. "Bitch, if you ever scream at me again, it will be your last breath." I stare, my mouth hanging open.

"She was only waking you up because you were getting sunburned." I have no idea why I'm engaging except that he looks like the meanest man alive and I feel sorry for the woman.

"You talking to me?" He heaves himself out of the pool, his ugly red face dripping with water. He looks like one of the guys from ZZ Top except that he's fat.

"You see this?" He points to a patch. "I'll put you both in your grave."

"Dozer? That's Blade's girl." The woman I just stuck up for pets his wet arm. He looks at her then me, his beady eyes taking in my body. His disgusting perusal makes me feel violated and dirty.

"He needs to put a leash and muzzle on you. I'm gonna have words with him. A woman needs to know her place." He grabs the woman who gazes up at him like he's a god rather than the fat serial killer he looks like. "Drop down and blow me." She instantly drops; her knees crack as they hit the concrete.

"Are you kidding me?" I jump up and back away. She ignores me and unzips him taking out his soft, disgusting penis.

"You people are insane." In a flash, I'm running back to the house. His laughter trails after me. I don't even stop when Edge asks me if I'm all right and keep running until I'm in my room, locking the door. My heart races, and I run into the bathroom and lock that door too. Gulping the air, I choke on it. I have to get control of myself, can't let these guys scare me. But they do—they are not nice. And my fantasy that I'm getting a better life has slapped me in the face.

There's a knock on the door, and I clutch the sink, my breathing more rapid. "Eve? You okay?" I look around the bathroom. *Hide.* I open the shower door and curl up in the corner. Memories of my mom telling me to hide as a child threaten to come out. Closing my eyes, I will them away—I never want them to come out. *"Go under the sink Evie. Mommy needs to talk to this guy for a bit."*

"But why, Mommy? I hate that guy. He smells."

"Go and don't tell Daddy." She pushes me into the small moldy-smelling cabinet as I wait for her to do what she has to do to get that bag of white powder. I hate that white powder. I

wait, crying, surrounded by the bottles of cleaning supplies we never use.

"Eve? What the fuck, Angel?" I open my eyes to see Blade's handsome face with Edge behind him. Both of them frown as I crouch even farther into the dark cave-like feel of the shower.

"What happened?" He looks at Edge, his voice harsh.

"I don't know. She ran up the stairs as if someone was chasing her." Edge looks at me with pity, and *that* I won't allow. I reach for the built-in stone chair as I stand.

"I'm fine." Both of their heads swing back to me.

Blade runs a hand through his hair. "Go see if you can figure this out. I need to talk to Eve." I should be scared. His eyes look fierce. Instead my heart starts beating normally again. Edge backs out of the bathroom and I look into Blade's green eyes. He holds out his hand. I don't take it and try to mold myself into the stone.

"Fine." He steps into the shower and grabs me. "What happened?"

I should tell him. But what do I say? A really mean man, one of your guys, made his girlfriend give him a blowjob because she tried to get him out of the sun?

"I..." I lick my lips. "I don't fit in here."

His eyes narrow. "You don't have a choice."

I cringe. "Maybe we can keep track. You know, like you let me go in a year." It's stupid and I can't believe I said it.

He backs up and crosses his arms. With his boots and clothes on he looks huge in here.

"So… how are you planning on paying over ten grand?"

"I gave you my virginity—shouldn't that be worth something?"

He looks like I slapped him. "You want to be a whore? Fine, I'll treat you like my whore."

A cough behind us makes us turn. "Um, Prez. Dozer wants a word with you." Edge looks almost sorry for me. God, can my life be any more fucked up? Blade stares at me. I shift uncomfortably beneath his penetrating gaze. He sneers as if he finds me lacking, then pushes open the heavy glass door of the shower leaving me clutching the cold stone wall.

NINE

BLADE/JASON

"Maybe Eve should stay put tonight." Axel signals for another beer.

I lean my head back on the red leather booth, wondering if he's right. The conversation we had earlier is still too fresh. I shouldn't be arguing, engaging with this girl. We're not a couple, yet the more I'm around her, the more the lines are blurred. The asshole inside me is tempted to have her show up so I can fuck her in the corner since she's willing to be a whore. But I won't. I rub my face and look at the stripper in front of us. The music is thumping as Deedee slides into splits. She smiles and slowly pulls her silver G-string to the side allowing us prime view of her waxed pussy.

"Fuck." I slam my whiskey, ignoring Deedee.

I rub my forehead. "Let's see, in the last forty-eight hours…"

I tick off her transgressions starting with my thumb. "She's stabbed Dewey, causing him pain and humiliation." Then my index. "Gotten in a fight with Dozer trying to defend his old lady." Raising my next finger, I add, "and she's a klepto according to Dolly." I reach for my whiskey. "Why wouldn't I want her with me tonight?"

"Nice, a klepto." He nods. "Don't forget she likes to play with knives." His sarcasm is thick.

I look past Deedee's spread legs to the door. We're at the Pussycat, taking over the VIP section as if we're royalty. My eyes are like radar, taking in the night crowd that's filing in. It's Saturday and this club is one of my favorites. It makes a lot of money and it's classy for a strip club. The girls are beautiful and the clientele wealthy. Axel and I own it and our manager, Derrick, is a partner too. We gave it a facelift a year ago and it's paid off hugely. The dive it used to be is transformed into the trendy place for millennials to bring their bosses, wives, girlfriends. The Disciples don't usually hang out here—it scares the suits. But I needed to get the hell away from everything, meaning the blonde in my bedroom. So here I sit, drinking whiskey with Axel. The whole upstairs is closed tonight for us. A group of about five girls are pouting and flashing the bouncer. Cricket, one of my guys, gives the bouncer the okay and the girls climb the stairs. All of them are wearing dresses that barely cover anything and too much makeup and hairspray.

"Text Edge to keep her in my room tonight. Tell him to make Dewey stand guard as part of his punishment."

Axel raises a brow, but he pulls out his phone. The girls make it up the stairs and I stand.

"I need to walk around. Where's Derrick? The lights are too bright on the stage."

He looks up from his phone at the stage then back to his phone. I know he's getting ready to lecture me about why men like us don't have girlfriends. I don't want to hear it, especially since I can't seem to get Eve off my mind.

"You want a private dance later?" Deedee twirls in front of me. "Please, Blade, I'll make it worth your while."

She pushes her large fake breasts out. Her long blond hair swings past her ass. It's dyed blue on the ends. She wraps a tan leg around the pole. I've fucked her a couple of times. But she started to get clingy and I've avoided her since.

"Not tonight, darlin'." I give her ass a playful swat as I rush down the stairs and through the office door. Only to be greeted by Ox's white ass thrusting into Lindsey. She's bent over the manager's desk moaning like a porn star.

"Christ. Where the fuck is Derrick?"

Lindsey smiles at me. Ox doesn't even lose his stride and keeps fucking her. "Bar," he grunts out.

"Finish up." Shaking my head, I walk to the long black bar with fluorescent pink lights illuminating it. We're full nude so we can't sell alcohol, but we do. You have to have the right connections and money.

Derrick, my manager and partner, is instructing a girl on how to use the computer. He's in his mid-forties and used to be a professional wrestler. You would never know it looking at him now. He wears nothing but Tom Ford suits and designer shoes. But he runs this place with no tolerance for any bullshit. He also brings in a ton of business, making way more than he ever did in wrestling. Plus, he's someone outside of the club we can trust.

"The lights are too bright," I tell him. He looks over at me and rolls his eyes.

"No shit. My office is occupied." I sweep the room and can't help but smile. The red walls along with the massive number of lights and lasers make the dark stage seem like a show rather than a strip club. The booths and tables along with the chairs around the stage allow for everyone to have an optimal visual of the girls.

"He's done." I watch as Ox exits the office, his face flushed. Lindsey says something to him as she walks toward the dressing rooms.

Derrick eyes me. "You okay?"

"Lot of shit happening lately," I yell.

He pulls out a bottle of Macallan Fine Oak and pours me a full glass.

"It's hard to be king."

I grin. "That it is." Taking the glass, I head back up to the VIP area, which is now packed with bikers. The three poles are being used by different strippers.

My phone vibrates.

Edge: She's not happy

Me: I don't care

I shove my phone back in my pocket as I look down, slumping back into the booth with Axel. Ryder is sitting next to him, a shot in his hand.

"Everything okay?" Ryder's brown eyes sweep my face.

"Yes," I snap.

"I heard about what happened with Dozer. He's getting old and mean in his old age." Ryder smiles at Roxy who slithers up to us.

"Who's gonna be my lucky guy tonight?" She licks her glossy red lips for effect.

"Well, that depends on what you're feeling like, baby." Ryder grins as he scoots his six-foot-six frame out of the booth.

Axel takes a sip of his beer. His passive-aggressive quiet disapproval is getting on my nerves.

"What?"

He sighs. "Blade, when you became president, you knew that having a wife or kids was not in the cards. Look at your dad and mom. Look at everyone who has a wife. You know they will use it against you."

I laugh. "I think you're jumping the gun."

"Am I?"

"I'm not marrying Eve, and she can't have kids so it's perfect," I growl and shake my head. "Ryder told you his dream?"

"No. I'm not blind, man. This one is different. You look at her different." He picks at the label on his beer.

"Just be careful. You're putting a big X on her and she doesn't know the game."

I close my eyes. He's right. I know he's right. I take a huge gulp of the Macallan. "God that's good whiskey. I need to ride, get out of town. Plan on Hemet tomorrow." Women are everywhere. I often wonder what attracts them to us. Most of the guys treat them like shit.

"I'm restless. I should take Daisy in the office."

He smirks. "Just be sure and get her name right when you come."

"You're making too big a deal of Eve. She has a tight pussy and that's it. Don't get confused." I sneer into my glass. The numbing effects of the booze make me aggressive.

"Hey Ryder." I motion with my fingers. "Tell Daisy to meet me in the office."

He looks over, his eyebrow raised then he mimes that he can't hear me. Then back to fondling Roxy.

"Dick," I yell.

He gives me a thumbs-up. "Doing it for your future, Prez."

"Whatever. I'm satisfied with my whiskey." My eyes drift down to the stage in time to see Crystal dance. As I watch her strip, I feel nothing. Her glittered body moves gracefully, but all I see is Eve swooping down in my black towel picking up my T-shirt. Her long, silky legs glisten with small drops of water. I've never been someone who noticed movements in a woman. Maybe it's because when I was a kid, my dad was dragging me and my brother Chuck to strip clubs. But with Eve, she has a walk, a way she moves that reminds me of a ballerina.

"Prez. Hey man, you okay?" I'm jolted back to Lana Del Rey's sultry voice. Crystal slinks around the pole to "West Coast" and I have to blink to get rid of my visions of long honey-blond hair instead of harlot red.

Axel shakes his head at me. "Maybe you should slow down if you're gonna be in any condition to ride tomorrow." I look up at the lasers and deep red moving spotlights and grin at him.

"I'm fucked, Axel."

He frowns and nods, bringing his beer to his lips. The music and booze take over my mind and I lean my head back. This time I don't fight it. Letting my eyes close, I see her swaying in front of me, her head thrown back as she laughs and dances only for me.

"Blade, brother? You want to take off? Or you want to sleep off the hangover with your woman?" I crack my eyes open to Axel and Ryder standing over me. I sit up and rub my hair and scalp before I focus on where we are.

"Derrick told me to tell you to fuck off and make sure we tip the cleaning crew." Axel grins as he twists the top off a beer.

Leaning back on Derrick's deep leather couch, I look at my guys. They both look a hell of a lot better than I feel. Maybe I should go back to the compound and crawl into bed with Eve. My cock likes the idea.

"Jesus, what time did I pass out?" I look around the dark office. The air conditioner clicks on, blowing cool air in the room.

"Beer, Prez?" I never drink while I'm on my bike, but this morning I might have to make an exception.

I look around at the large gray safe sitting to my left. "Open the safe. I need a line if I'm gonna ride." They both grin. Ryder punches in the code and we stare at all the goodies Derrick keeps in there.

"Fuck, this is why this guy is our partner." Axel exhales.

I grunt, taking in the cash, guns, and whatever kind of drug you want. Along with bottles of Dom, Cristal, and other pricey shit. A bunch of passports and drivers' licenses sit stacked in the corner.

"Toss me some coke." I motion to Axel who has his nose stuck in the safe like it's a refrigerator and he can't wait to make himself something to eat. He tosses me a bag and I take Derrick's envelope opener and bring the white powder to my nose.

"Yeah." My eyes sting as the coke makes its way into my system. "All right, let's do this. I'm gonna piss and let's get the fuck out of here." I swing open the black door and the smell of alcohol hits me as I walk to use the john.

"Tomas," I yell over the music he's playing as he scrubs the bar mats. He looks over at me and turns down the music.

"Make sure you use bleach. If a cop stopped in right now, it would be an expensive bribe."

He looks around the large dark club, the only light from the open back door.

"*Sí.*"

I nod, banging open the door. I piss, splash some water on my face, then take the stairs two at a time to see the damage in the VIP section. Numerous bikers lay buck naked with girls draped over them. Cricket and Dillon are in the corner fucking a girl, their exclamations of "fuck yeah" echoing in the room. I shake my head, thankful I passed out. The thought of waking up next to a naked girl I don't know is completely unappealing.

"I'm riding out to Hemet. Cricket, when you're done, take the guys and girls out of here. Tip the shit out of the poor assholes who clean this place up, and call me later."

He doesn't stop thrusting, but he does respond, "On it, Prez."

I pull out my phone and scroll through my messages before I take the stairs. It's only seven so Eve probably won't be up, but I call her cell using the number Dolly gave me anyway. It rings and goes to voice mail, which pisses me off. I tend to get aggressive on coke, and as I've grown older, I rarely use it. The blood pumps in my temples as I run a hand through my hair and call again. It goes straight to voice mail. I take a breath and call Dewey.

On the fourth ring, "Yellow."

"Took you long enough," I say.

"Prez?"

I sigh. "Yes, Dewey, it's me. You taking care of my Angel?" When I realize what I've said, I almost bite my tongue.

"I'm watching her, Prez. Don't you worry about anything. I've got it under control."

"Where are you? You sound like you're in a tunnel." I walk outside to the sun where it's warm enough for me not to worry about a jacket. I light up a cigarette trying to get the dumpster smell out of my nose. The alleyway is littered with broken-down cardboard boxes. Squinting at the people walking by with coffee, I grit my teeth. Maybe I shouldn't have done that bump. I'm aggravated with everyone.

"Just outside your door."

"Listen." I inhale, the nicotine giving me a moment of calm. "I need you to wake up Eve. I need her."

I hear him shuffling around then a loud shriek.

"Get the fuck out, you perv. I swear to God, I'll cut off your penis this time." I hold the phone away. Axel laughs behind me and I turn.

"I guess I should have told him to knock."

More screaming. Poor Dewey is trying to apologize and tell her it's me. "Tell him to fuck off," she yells. I raise an eyebrow as Axel chuckles.

"Wildcat." He shakes his head, stretches, and smashes his beer bottle at the wall. I frown and wonder if he snorted the same coke. He's looking a little crazy.

My boots crunch as I walk through the shattered glass over to the street area. "Dewey?"

"Prez." He's panting. "I'm scared of her. She's... not happy, and she told me to tell you to fu—"

"I know, I heard. When she's calmed down, tell her I'll be back in a couple of days and to turn her phone on. I want to be able to get ahold of her at all times. Got that, Dewey?"

"Yeah, I got it. I hope she forgives me. She's so great." He sighs and I can almost see his sad face.

"Just don't go into my room without her permission. I'm counting on you to take care of my girl."

Axel snorts, and I flip him off. "Don't forget, Dewey, I want her phone on at all times." I push end and flick my cigarette at the dumpster.

"Let's do this."

TEN

EVE

He didn't come home last night. I shouldn't care, but I do. "Asshole."

Dewey woke me fifteen minutes ago and now I'm pacing. Nothing like opening your eyes to an unfamiliar face and having a phone shoved at you.

A small knock jerks my eyes to the door. "Unbelievable."

"Um… Eve? Blade wanted me to—"

I rip the door open and Dewey jumps back, his hand instinctively protecting his wound.

"Why are you here? I thought I took care of you."

His eyes are bugging out of his head. His dark hair is buzzed and he looks young—my age. Blade said he was slow. That might work to my advantage.

"Umm…" He looks at his boots as I roll my eyes. "Blade, that is Prez, is gone." He licks his lips.

"No shit."

He winces, and I feel a pang of guilt. It's as though I've kicked a puppy.

I take a breath and twist my long hair on top of my head securing it with a rubber band.

"He told me to tell you to turn on your phone."

I snort in disgust. "I'm shutting the door. You tell your Prez, if he wants to talk to me he can come home. Otherwise I'm busy."

"Wait." He puts his hand out. "I have something else to tell you and you're making me forget it. You talk too fast." He stares down at his feet again.

"God." I look up at the ceiling. "I'm such a bitch," I mumble then hold my hands out in a calming gesture. "Take your time, Dewey. What else did Blade want me to know?" This poor guy is a bit slow.

"Oh." His face lights up. "He said he will be back in a couple days and I am supposed to watch over you." He's so proud I almost smile.

"I don't understand." I lean on the door and Dewey's eyes follow my every move. "Why do I need you to watch me?"

"Because you are the Prez's girl and he must think I'm the most trustworthy."

This time I do laugh. "Wow, I feel so special." He cocks his head confused again.

"Never mind. You got a car, Dewey?"

"No."

Shit, I was hoping to get some more supplies. Maybe have him stop by the carnival to see what's going on and if my dad has been taken care of.

"I have a Harley." He smiles. He's not ugly if you don't notice the faraway look in his eyes.

"Even better. Listen, I'm going to get ready and I need you to help me run some errands."

I shut the door on his surprised face. I'm in and out of the shower, makeup on, and in a new pair of black jeans and a tight charcoal T-shirt in under fifteen minutes.

I swing open the door with my brightest smile and stop when I'm greeted by Edge not Dewey. My bag slides to the floor.

"Where's Dewey?"

"What are you doing?" His penetrating blue eyes make me feel guilty.

"I'm going shopping." I arch my eyebrows at him.

"No, you're not." He crosses his arms and suddenly I see why Dolly was with this guy. With his auburn hair and his huge arms tatted up, the guy is hot.

"Why? What am I supposed to do?"

He sighs. "Hold on." I watch as he pulls out his phone. I turn toward the window watching two guys clean the pool.

"She wants to go shopping again. She wants Dewey to take her on his bike."

I look over at him and shoot him a glare. Uh-huh... I'll tell her." He hangs up.

"Turn on your phone if you ever want to leave this room." He points at my phone on the dresser and walks out.

"Jesus, is everyone an ass?" I mumble as I power up my new phone. It starts ringing immediately. I almost don't answer but the only person I'm hurting is myself.

"Hello."

"Angel." I shiver as his gravelly voice seeps into my skin. And just like that he makes me forget that he didn't come home last night. That I never thought I would want sex and yet all I've been thinking about is how good he made me feel.

"Yes," I breathe out.

"You are not allowed to go on anyone's bike but mine," he says, his voice a low rumble. "If you can't follow the simple rules, Eve, I will have you locked in and you'll stay there until I come home."

That snaps me out of his sexiness. "Well, what exactly do you want me to do? I'm not used to not working. Also, I need to make sure my father is okay." I hear him inhale on a cigarette.

"Well, I guess we both need to work on trust. I trust you to behave while I work, and you trust me to take care of your father."

"Why didn't you come home last night?" I sound crazy, especially since I don't actually like him.

"Why?"

"What do you mean?" I start pacing. I can't be locked in this room for days—I'll go insane.

"What difference does it make to you? You're mine. That's all you need to know." His deep voice turns me on. God, if I'm not careful, I'm gonna start thinking he's a good guy instead of the ruthless man who had Ryder turn off my dad's oxygen.

"Please, tell me I'm not a prisoner. I promise to be good." I stop and stare at the skanky picture of Crystal and stick my tongue out at it.

"You're welcome to go shopping with Edge in a *car*. And Eve?"

"Yeah?"

"I want your phone on at all times."

I roll my eyes. "Sounds perfect. Should I call you Prez? Master?"

"No, I want you to call me Jason."

Silence. My heart is pounding as excitement snakes down to my belly.

"And when I get back, I'll take you to see your dad. Be good, baby." I hear the line go dead before I can respond.

"Shit." I close my eyes taking in deep breaths. I look up to see Edge watching me.

"You okay?" His lips twitch as my face starts to burn. I'm sure I'm flushed.

"I'm fine," I snap. "Do you guys go and take off all the time?"

He looks around the room bored. "Do you want me to take you somewhere?"

"No, I thought Dewey was my guy?" Hopefully I don't sound obvious.

"Sorry, Wildcat, if you want out, you go with me. You want to stay here, Dewey is fine." He turns to leave.

"Fine, I guess I'll go to the pool." I shut the door and think for a second. I can't shoplift with Edge spying on me. Dewey was perfect but that seems to not be happening. I tap my new boot on the floor. *Fuck it,* at least I'll have a killer tan if all I do is sit by the pool and swim until Jason comes back.

"Jason." I say his name out loud and I like it. I grab my bikini and change. In all honesty, if I'm going to sunbathe every day, I will need another bathing suit. I toss some sunscreen into my bag and open my door, half excepting to see Edge. I'm alone. Clutching my bag close, I head down the steps. I'm barely outside when I'm joined by Edge.

"Now what? I thought you said this is Dewey's turf?" I look around but it's only us. I roll my eyes and go straight to my side of the pool and drop onto the cushioned lounger. A huge stainless grill, which wasn't there yesterday, has appeared in the corner.

"Dewey's busy today. I decided to join you." Edge saunters over dressed in torn jeans, his vest, and boots.

I shade my eyes. "Really? Nice bathing suit." I can't help it— Edge is being absurd.

He lies back on the lounger next to me and throws one of his tatted arms over his eyes.

"Pretend I'm not here," he grunts.

I scoot back and close my eyes. "That shouldn't be hard," I snip. The day is beautiful: sunny but not scorching. The warmth sinks into my skin and I sit up to spray on some sunscreen.

Standing, I observe Edge. He's definitely hot, no doubt about it. Auburn hair, freckles but still tans. Tall, not as tall as Jason or Ryder, but tall.

"How old are you?" He drops his arm and opens one eye.

"Why?"

I shrug. "Curious."

"Twenty-eight." He closes his eyes again but puts a muscled arm behind his head.

"So, you fucked around on Dolly, huh?" I smirk as he instantly sits up.

"What did she tell you?" He looks tortured, almost sad at the mention of her.

"Just that loving a Disciple was like loving a rock star."

Again his eyes change and he looks almost dazed at the pool. "She's not cut out for this kind of life." He reaches into his back pocket for his pack of cigarettes and lights up. "Very few are." He looks at me as I spray the sunscreen all over my shoulders and arms.

"I guess." I put my sunglasses back on. "I mean, she's sweet and beautiful. If I was a guy, I'd want her." Lifting the frames, I wink at him.

He snorts. "Wanting her is not the problem."

"What is it then?" I lean back so that I can see his face.

Guilt is eating this guy up. He takes a huge inhale and lets it out slowly. "You need to be able to put up with a lot of shit, be able to support this kind of life…" He shakes his head. "Few women can live like this"—he gestures all around, his cigarette hanging out of his mouth—"and be happy."

"Because you guys can't keep your dicks in your pants?"

He lays back. "Yeah, maybe. I was young and high. Trust me, if I could take it back, I would. It's… to be a partner you have to look the other way or join in."

That stops me and I set down my can of sunscreen. "Well, I think if you truly love someone, you have their back no matter what."

Flicking his cigarette on the concrete, he looks at me. "You might be one of the few. I guess we'll see." He stares up at the sky. "Dolly was not." He closes his eyes.

"So—"

"I'm done talking."

I can't help but smile. These guys act so tough, but the right woman can bring them to their knees. This is new to me seeing as I have never given this much thought. I never thought I would want someone. Not that I want Jason... but what would it be like to be his? Today, when he said I was his... *my* whole body got hot. What would it feel like to have him look at me like Edge looks at Dolly?

God, I'm losing it. I have to stay sharp. No man is ever going to be all that. All they do is lie and disappoint you. I need to stop daydreaming and start planning. My dad needs me, not Jason.

ELEVEN

BLADE/JASON

It feels good to ride. Once we got the hell out of traffic, we were able to stretch our legs. There is nothing like the numbing vibration of a bike working at its best out in the middle of nowhere.

I can't help but smirk. Eve's tight pussy might be better, but other than that I can't think of one thing I enjoy more. As we all rumble into town, I notice a new donut shop opening up and wonder if Eve likes sweets. Shaking my head, I practically slap myself. I need to cut this shit out. I can't believe how much my thoughts have swayed already to her today. It's bothering me because I don't do this. Like never. I fuck and leave. It's the way I am. Taking a deep breath, I assure myself it's only that she's new and innocent. It's not like I'm going to fall in love with this one. I don't fall in love, and I'm not even sure I'm capable of it. With the need to ride and clear my head satisfied, now I want to take a hot shower. I stink of stale booze, dirt, and sweat. It got hot riding on the black pavement. Parking our bikes, we go straight for the main house. Three women stoned out of their minds look up and smile at me and my posse.

"Where's Doc?" I ask the one who at least is able to stand.

"Umm... I think he's cooking." Her glassy eyes tell me they've been sampling my drug. Gritting my teeth, I head upstairs barking out an order to find Doc and Sandy. I enter my bedroom and look around. It's ingrained in me. I learned real quick when I was in the SEALS never to trust anyone besides my brothers. And never enter a room unaware. Stripping off my leather jacket, cut, and T-shirt, I pick up my phone and pull up my tracker on Eve's phone. Even as I do this I know I shouldn't, but it's almost as if I've been possessed and can't stop myself. The little red dot shows her location at the compound and I have to force myself not to text Edge to confirm. Tossing the phone on the bed, I strip and get into the shower ignoring my tight balls and rock-hard erection. I need to deal with Doc and our "product" and get back to LA so that I can fuck Eve out of my system. Or not. I mean, she's mine. I bought her. Why not keep her, and I won't have to worry about any crazy chicks anymore. Someone knocks on the door as I'm pulling on a pair of clean jeans.

"Enter," I bellow, aggravated at my thoughts.

Sandy opens the door and I almost roll my eyes. She's using again, which would explain Doc's absence.

"Blade, Axel said you wanted to see me?" She averts her eyes.

"Yeah... how are things doing here?"

She shrugs, her long, greasy hair looking darker than it actually is. "Oh... you know, been helping Doc take care of business."

I snort. "Sandy, cut the shit. You're using. Where's Doc?" Her haunted brown eyes look up at me, and a wave of compassion fills me.

"I... all I was doing was sampling a new drug he's been working on. I haven't used up until today." And there goes my compassion. Nothing like trying to talk to a junkie. They'll swear they're clean even if you catch them with a needle in their arm.

"Where's Doc?" I say, pulling on a faded gray Van Halen T-shirt.

"I think he's at the lab." She leans against the wall. Jesus she's so fucked up, she's literally falling asleep on her feet. When I grab her arm, her eyes pop open as I propel her down the stairs with me and plant her ass on the couch with the other junkies.

"Blade," she mumbles as she cowers with a girl who looks at me, terrified. Christ, what do they think? I'm going to hit them?

"I don't have time for this shit." Walking into the hallway, I bang on Axel's door.

"Come on, man. Time to roll."

Axel opens his door, pulling up his pants. Candy sits up from the bed. She leans on her elbows, her large fake breasts still wet where Axel's jizz is dripping down to her stomach.

"You need a release, Blade?" Her pointy red nails trail down her stomach as she spreads her legs.

"No," I snap, and they stare at me wide-eyed. I turn and walk outside leaving the door open to get some fresh air in the stagnant house. I light a cigarette and breathe the nicotine in deeply. Rolling my neck, I hear it crack.

"You okay, man?" Axel walks out putting on his sunglasses.

Ignoring the question, I say, "Where the fuck is everyone?"

He stands there, looking at me.

"Jesus, Axel, I'm tired and hungover." I rub the back of my neck completely regretting my decision to ride out here.

"See, this"—he points at me—"this is what I was talking about last night."

Flicking my cigarette, I straddle my bike. "Axel, just because I have no desire to fuck Candy with your load dripping down her tits does not have anything to do with Eve."

"Since when haven't you wanted to fuck Candy with or without his love cultures on her?" Ox says from behind me.

Sitting on my bike, I'm ready to go off on both of them.

Axel interrupts my rant with, "I guess it's Ginger's birthday. Most of the guys are at the club celebrating," a shitty, knowing smile on his face. I shake my head and start up my bike and peel out. Their bikes rumble behind me as we twist around the bend and over a dirt road to our lab. The smell of chemicals wafts through the air about a half mile before I even pull up.

"What the fuck?" Ox coughs into his cut.

"Christ, Axel call Ryder and get his ass over here." I pound on the door. "Doc?" Silence and plastic bottles are strewn across the ground along with a lot of fast food trash.

"Fuck, it's hot as shit out here." I step back and break open the door, shaking my head at how easy that was.

"What the hell?" Axel steps in and kicks at a couple of Disciples who are passed out on the floor.

"They dead?" I plow through the garbage in search of Doc. The kitchen is where the lab is. Doc has three stoves on and numerous things are cooking in pots. The chemical stench is so heavy it makes my heart pound and throat raw simply from standing in the room. I turn off the burners and open up some windows as I turn to the sound of the back door opening. Doc walks in and freezes.

"Axel? Talk to me." My eyes never leave Doc. He looks like shit. The other night at the party, I saw him all of a minute as he patched up poor Dewey. Now that he's standing next to me, his sallow skin and his already thin body make it look as though he's ready to collapse.

"They're alive. I've got Ryder coming with a truck to take them to the ER."

"We need to get the fuck out of here. Anyone else?"

Doc stares then starts crying and sinks to his knees.

"Christ." I reach for him and drag him out of the kitchen, tossing him in the dirt as I head back in to check the bedrooms.

Axel meets me in the hall as we check the rooms. "What the fuck happened?" His eyes are glassy as I'm sure mine are too.

"Light this place on fire. I'm done with this shit."

He nods. "I'll try and save as much as I can. This is definitely going to cause a big problem."

I look around at the house that no one should ever set foot in and I'm fucking done.

"Prez? Doc's not doing well," Ox yells as he comes around the corner.

"Stay with Axel," I grunt, spitting all the shitty chemicals out of my mouth.

Ryder has arrived and stands with Doc, who is puking, and the two other Disciples, both prospects. They seem brain dead as they convulse and stare.

"Get them out of my sight." I look at Ryder.

"We take them to the hospital, there'll be a lot of questions," he announces the truth.

I look around. The sun's still bright and it's hot. Maybe I'm not in the mood to deal with bodies or maybe I don't want to kill my childhood friend.

Grabbing Doc by the head, I ask, "You want to die? I need to know, brother. I'll put you down, or I can drop your shit ass off at the hospital. What's it gonna be?"

His brown eyes look wild and his skin is covered in a cold sweat. "Hospital, you dick. You know I won't talk." I shove his sorry ass away. "Load him up. Who did you call to help us clean this shit up?"

Ryder stares down at Doc then grabs him and tosses him in the back with the other two. They all groan as if their bones hurt, but that's the first response I hear from the two prospects so that's positive for them.

"George and Mickey are on their way," Ryder says. "If it was anyone other than Doc..." He lets it go at that. I nod as he climbs in the pickup truck and takes off toward town. Axel and Ox come out carrying plastic bags full of what I assume are drugs. This is serious and is going to cost a fortune in bribes. Along with the very real fact that the two prospects could talk. I almost text Ryder and tell him to get rid of them, but at this point, the whole lab is getting destroyed. As long as there's no evidence, I guess it's their word against ours. And I have guys who can take them out if need be.

I look around at the puffs of dirt coming closer. Mickey and George are the best at cleaning up—it's why I keep them here.

"You get it all? We need everything. I'm not about to let Doc bring us down any more than he already has."

"We got as much as we could find. It looks like he's been living here."

I light up a cigarette and hand it to Axel. He takes it and his eyes search the shithole lab. "Jesus Christ, had we not come today..."

"Burn it—make sure there's nothing left." The loud thunder of bikes explodes as I stop Ox from entering again, his eyes wild and breathing harsh. "Get some air, man. Let Mickey and George check it out."

"Prez." George gets off his bike. "Jesus, what the fuck has Doc been cooking?" He pulls his shirt up to cover his mouth and nose.

"You tell me. Why do I show up and no one but sluts and junkies are at the house? Then I find two prospects OD'd and Doc ready to blow himself up."

George drops his shirt, and fear enters his eyes. He's been with the club for five years and also served in the military, but this is a major fuckup.

He swallows and looks at Ox, who is panting like a dog with rabies, and Axel. His calmness always unnerves people.

"I was here four days ago. Doc was here with the prospects and Sandy."

Mickey walks up. "I was here two days ago. Everything was normal."

I look at Mickey, a six-foot-four bear of a man. "Go and take care of the fire department and police. Give them what they want until this place is gone." He rubs his head. Fuck, whatever he was cooking is strong. "Where is Sandy? This must have just gone down."

"No shit, it just went down. Otherwise they'd be dead."

I spit out the fumes.

Mickey gets on his bike. "I'll take care of it."

I turn to George. "Go in and make one final sweep then light this bitch up."

"Got it, Prez."

Ox paces back and forth, his fist clenching as dirt follows him.

"Take it easy, Ox." The force of my voice makes his head snap in my direction.

"We light this place up, we're fucked." He spits and a small amount stays on his chin. "Do you know how much money we're going to lose?"

"I do. We'll deal with that later." My phone vibrates. It's a text from Ryder with a thumbs-up: code for he dropped them off and is on his way back. This is how we've all stayed alive. We're a team. Not for the first time do I hate that we're too big. It makes us sloppy.

George runs out. "It's clean. Fuck, that kitchen was not like that days ago." His eyes water.

"Burn it down." I watch as Axel, George, and a screaming Ox throw lit T-shirts in the house and on the porch. The garbage lights up like a bonfire and flames continue to crawl up the columns and the dry wooden door.

Almost mesmerized, we all straddle our bikes as we start our iron horses up. I go first and my men follow. We're not that far when the explosion sends the heat flowing past us. Reflected in the mirror on my bike, flames and sparks cover the landscape, making me feel as though I'm in a *Mad Max* movie. The end of the world is coming.

A bloodcurdling scream blasts around us and I know it's Ox letting out his demons. Colors and heat: that's what I feel. That and my ears are ringing, and for a moment, I'm confused as to where I am.

"Jesus Christ." I turn to watch the billowing black smoke fill the sky. The massive amount of ashes causes me to move forward and my chest actually aches.

"I guess we'll see how good our bribe money is. That's a lot of smoke." Axel rubs a hand through his sweaty hair.

"We stay until we're sure everything is gone."

"Or until we hear sirens." Axel stares at me deadpan. His confidence in us getting out of this unscathed seems pretty negative.

I grin. "Or that." The longer it burns, the lighter my chest gets, and I'm feeling better already.

"Should we do something about Ox?" George interrupts Axel and me.

"Nah, let him rage," I say, barely glancing at the wild beast that is Ox. He's doing donuts in the dirt with his Harley, which is impressive in itself. The amount of dust kicking up around us is somewhat welcome. Better dust than chemical smoke. I look down at my phone and calculate that if we're lucky, the lab will explode again and we can get the fuck out of town.

"We head back to LA at night. Hopefully no one saw us when we came in this morning. Besides the junkies, we should be fine." Axel nods.

"We're fucked. I have no idea if Doc is in any condition to start over anytime soon." My head is already pounding. "Round up the guys and bring them to the clubhouse."

George nods and takes one more inhale, snuffing it out but putting it in his back pocket. "I'll have them there."

I don't watch him leave. I stare at the shithole that made us rich burn to the ground. "Call it in, man, and let's go to the clubhouse. I want to be back in LA tonight." I start my bike and hear my brothers follow.

TWELVE

BLADE/JASON

I don't know if I've ever wanted a shower as much as I do right now. We just pulled into LA and it's two in the morning. The lights are on and the front door swings open. Pete and Edge stand and wait for us to enter. Axel says nothing and goes straight upstairs. Not that I blame him. After we called the fire in, it has been nothing but one fucked-up thing after another.

"I'm going to bed. I want all my officers here at ten a.m.," I say gruffly to Edge who hands me a bottle of Jack. Grateful, I grab it and guzzle at once. For a split second, the spicy, stinging warmth actually gets rid of the chemical taste that no amount of water seems to remove. The stench seems attached to my throat, and I want to drink the whole bottle. Instead I take one more swig and decide to go to my room and let the shower and Eve rid me of the last twelve hours of hell.

"You need anything else, Prez?" Edge is on alert. I'm sure he's heard everything.

"No, I'm going to bed. Don't disturb me unless someone's dead."

Ryder enters along with Ox who promptly demands a woman and booze. I climb the stairs two at a time, turning at the top.

"Edge?"

"Yeah, Blade?"

"Everything go okay today?"

He nods. "Yeah, she spent a couple of hours at the pool then helped Amy in the kitchen." I frown. For some reason I don't like her working at all. Brushing aside my caveman thoughts, I nod at him and stand at my door. She'd know to lock it, right? I reach into my pocket for the key. It opens right up, and my hands clench. I'll discuss this with her in the morning. Again, I don't trust anyone but my brothers. Even with them, I would expect her to lock the door. Entering, I take in the darkness although she seems to like the curtains open and the moonlight spills inside. *What the fuck?* The first thing I do is shut them—I can't stand them open—and force myself to walk past her. I stink and if I get too close, I'll want to touch her.

I start the shower and besides my cut, I throw every single article of clothing away. When I enter my blue rock shower, I turn the water so hot it scorches my back and allows my tense muscles to relax. My mind replays the day; I can't seem to turn it off. Closing my eyes, I see the faces of my members concerned about what exactly the loss of our lab means. I lower my head and let the water massage my neck as I go over the night. Half the guys were drunk and high or both and I'm sure some guys will show up at the LA compound tomorrow. Most of them have jobs and families in Hemet, so they'll stay, but the younger ones couldn't wait to pack up.

Maybe I'll take Eve to my private house, keep her away from all this crap getting ready to go down. My eyes pop open—I have never let any woman besides my mother walk into that house. That's the house I use when I want to forget, feel normal, be normal. Reaching for my soap, I hesitate. The hole that holds my shampoo and soap is now filled with different bottles of what seem to be shampoos, conditioners, shower gels, girl's shaving cream, and a pink razor. I pick up a tube that says cleansing mask. My AXE shampoo is in the back and I have no idea where my bar of Irish Spring went. Instead there's a green bar that says Dove on it.

"Christ." I pick up the soap and smell it. It has a fruity kind of smell. Whatever—I need soap so I use it to lather my filthy body. I do this twice and wash my hair. All I want is Eve and my bed. Stepping out, I wrap a towel around my waist and grab my toothbrush. After what seems like ten minutes, I can do no more to rid my mouth of the chemicals and smoke. I shut the light off and toss my towel on the floor. I'm tired, fucking exhausted, and instead of climbing into my comfortable bed, I stare down at golden wild hair on a dark pillow. Light and dark... her ripe puffy lips are slightly parted as her chest rises softly. She's so exquisite it's almost startling. She sleeps in one of my T-shirts and my whole body tightens. The need to sink into this woman and claim her is overwhelming.

I sit down and peel the sheet off her and she rolls over toward my already hard cock. I reach for her, and she blinks her eyes open. Long lashes flutter as she sleepily smiles. My rough hand caresses her soft cheek.

"Angel." She looks at me and I lean down and take her lips. It's soft and slow, almost sensual in a way I've never experienced. My tongue finds hers as we both groan. I lower my body onto hers and the day is gone: the fire, the drugs, all gone.

I pull back almost startled. My eyes search her face in the darkness. The moonlight peeks through a slit in the curtains, and I kiss her again because I can't stop drinking in her sweetness. Her tongue touches mine as we both deepen it.

"Eve." I trail my tongue to her long neck and pull the T-shirt off her.

"Lift up, baby." It comes out as a growl. She shudders as she raises her hips, and I slip her panties off. Her body shines in the tiny stream of remaining light, which reveals a tease of her tan line.

"You're beautiful." She exhales and licks her swollen lips.

"I have to eat your pussy." I lean down as I spread her legs and dive into her honey core. She's slick and wet and her clit gets plump as I suck on it. My stomach tightens as her body arches into my mouth and I add a finger deep inside her. Her body starts to jerk and I lay my hand on her stomach to keep her still as she moans her pleasure into the dark room.

One more suck and rub with my finger and her sex grabs my finger and pulls it in, pulsing and clenching. A surge of glory comes over me, which is stupid because I'm acting like this is the first woman I've made come. Far from it, but this is the first woman I want to make come over and over. She's screaming my name and my balls tighten. *My name.* Not Blade, not Prez; she's screaming Jason and that about makes me jet off like a fucking punk. I climb back over her, my hands touching her full breasts. Wish I could suck on her nipples, but if I don't bury my cock inside her now, I might go crazy. My frantic brain has channeled everything into how good she feels. I reach for my cock and rub her swollen, slick clit with the tip and she moans loudly. I can't wait any longer... can't remember a time I wanted a woman more.

As I thrust into her, those silken walls are still so tight they grip me. Each time I bury myself deeper, she moves with me until the room is filled with our bodies smacking and my muscles tightening.

"Fuck, I'm close. Touch yourself, Angel."

"What?" Her voice is breathy and I don't have time to explain, teach—all that can come later. I reach down and rub her clit hard as my thick cock thrusts into her and her pussy pulsates on its way to a climax.

"Oh my God... Jason... I'm coming." Her fingernails dig into my back as she scratches her nails all the way down toward my ass. The sting burns and I fucking love it. I let my body be fulfilled in a way that I've never done before. And when I come, I call out her name and can't stop. She reaches up to kiss me as my orgasm rocks me all the way to my toes. I don't say anything; I don't even pull out, yet I pull her onto me and let my breath calm and my mind go blank.

THIRTEEN

EVE

I smell smoke, leather, and fresh clean something. Whatever it is, I love it and need to sink deeper into it. I open my eyes and the smell I was dreaming about is actually Jason's neck and chest. Not moving, I'm frozen. What the hell is happening to me? My cheeks burn and my mouth parts so that I can let some much-needed air into my lungs. The room is dark save for the slit in the curtain allowing one bright line of sunlight on the edge of the bed. I know I'm an innocent when it comes to sex, but what the hell? I want to groan and bury my head in his neck yet I'm mortified. What I'm doing with Jason is way too intense, too connected and I can't have that. I slowly move back, but his arm tightens around me, almost like he doesn't want me to move.

Warning bells are going off loud and clear. I need to put distance between us or I'm going to start falling for this man, god… Whatever he is, I'm out of my league. Sitting up, I look at him. He must be a heavy sleeper or he's exhausted. My gentle movements make him stir and that's about it. When I sit up quickly, all he does is move his arm under his head allowing me the ability to admire his bicep and tattoos. They're beautiful. Most are black, but then there will be a splash of color like my favorite red rose, which seems to be bleeding blood and tears. They do something to me. Tempted to reach out and trace them with my fingers and tongue, I hungrily let my eyes take in his tan chest. So hot. He's perfect. Power radiates off him, and it's no wonder why every woman wants him. I get up to use the bathroom, my mind doing a one-eighty. *I mean, why the fuck not?* He wants me—that much is obvious, I reason. If I could actually do the unobtainable and make this man fall at my feet, I could be safe.

The key to this plan is making him love me while I only like him. Flushing the toilet, I reach to wash my hands and look at myself in the large mirror. I have never once cared about the way I look. In a way, it was a big problem as I got older. But as I stare at my reflection, I hear myself whispering, "Thank you, Mama," because for the first time, I'm grateful I inherited her big blue eyes, high cheekbones, and puffy lips. I remember crying when my breasts started to grow. My poor dad looked almost helpless then told me to be grateful that I inherited my mother's body. That's all he said, and I stopped crying. I turn around and assess my reflection from behind. Long, thin legs—that's good. My butt looks a little small, but hey, no one's perfect. I smile at my tan lines. Actually, sunbathing for two days has already lightened my hair. If I keep at it, I'll be a light blond. Reaching for my new sparkly pink toothbrush, I quickly brush my teeth, my mind scheming at how to get the hot god in the other room to keep me. It can't be that hard, right?

I'm so engrossed in my thoughts I nearly scream when large tan hands snake around my waist pulling me back against his hard chest. He buries his head in my neck and my heart starts beating like a drum.

"You smell good," he says, and I almost choke on the toothpaste in my mouth. I lean over to spit and his large, hard dick lines up at my ass. Quickly, I straighten. He looks up into the mirror and for one heart-stopping moment, the world is gone. All I see are his green eyes gazing at me as if I'm special.

"Jason." My voice sounds raspy or maybe hoarse. His eyes narrow and change as if a curtain has closed over them. I look away then, wanting whatever we shared to come back. But it's gone, the spell broken. His warm lips are at my neck sucking and licking, and I find myself staring at us in the mirror. His hands massage my full breasts.

"Christ, look at you. Look at these fucking tits." He squeezes them and I can't help but groan as he pinches my nipples taut and hard.

"God." My voice sounds like someone else's as one hand jerks me tightly back into his warm arms. I watch his tattooed hand slide down my flat stomach to my sex and I feel everything: his chest, his breath, his lips.

"Open," he commands, and I gaze at him in the mirror. Those pretty eyes of his are mesmerizing. My legs spread open and his fingers glide right inside. In the back of my mind, I wonder if I should be embarrassed at how wet I get. But he groans and says, "God, I love that you are dripping for me. Watch me, Angel. Watch how fast I make you come." And I do. His one hand that was playing with my breast is gone and holding my leg up so I have a direct view of my pink, wet pussy. His other hand rubs my clit roughly.

"Oh God," I hiss at the sight of his fingers, covered in my slick wetness, rubbing my clit. I grab and latch onto his arms.

"Please... I can't." My cheeks and lips are red.

"You're doing it, baby."

As my body convulses, a burst of white light blinds me for a second. I latch onto his arms. "Jesus," I pant.

He spins me around and the hand he used to rub my clit is on my neck, bringing me closer. He's aggressive; whereas, last night he was gentle. Lifting me up, he dumps me on the sink and impales me with his thick cock before I can recover.

"Don't ever tell me you can't come," he snarls into my mouth and I wonder what the hell is happening to us as I attack his mouth with mine. The craving is there, and I want him more than I care to admit.

"Jesus, Angel... I can't get enough of this fucking cunt." Somehow his nasty words suit him and I open my legs wider feeling so complete, safe, wanted.

"Yeah, that's it." He leans me back onto the cool mirror and grabs my legs so that we can both watch his long, thick cock go in and out of me.

"Take your finger, baby, and rub that swollen clit. Rub it hard and come on my cock before I fill you up with my glue." I hesitate.

"Take your finger and touch yourself. I need to see you, feel you." His eyes lock with mine and it's there again—only us and he's inside me and I want to please him like I've never wanted to please anyone in my life.

I reach toward my clit. "Use two fingers," he commands and I do. "Angel... talk to me. Tell me how much you love my cock and your fingers getting you off."

"I... I love it." I rub hard. His thick cock picks up speed and I'm gone, orbiting into bliss.

"Fuck yeah, Angel." His body jerks deep into me. I don't know how long we stay joined, both of our eyes locked on to each other's as we try to steady our breaths. Jason slowly pulls out and my sex latches onto him as he goes.

We smile at each other and it's as though I'm floating as I watch him gently lower me and start the shower. I sink to the toilet seat wondering how I'm still alive.

"What are you thinking about?"

I look over at him, his gorgeous body making me lick my lips. "I was thinking I had no idea it would feel like that." Instantly, I regret what I said.

He cocks his head and motions for me to get into the shower with him.

The water pelts down on us and he tilts my head. "I like that you are mine, and I like that you are untouched. I've fucked hundreds of women and I've never had this with anyone." I blink the water out of my eyes. I'm happy, warm, and fuzzy—such an alien feeling for me. And no doubt, I'm smiling again.

Then he grabs my chin roughly. "If I ever catch you fucking someone else, I'll kill you."

At first, I think I misunderstood him. But his green eyes are not blinking and a shiver of excitement fills me. Holy shit, he's telling the truth. He would kill me. And all the warm fuzzy feelings I was having double. Because if he would kill me for touching another man. Wow... that definitely sounds promising. He lets me go and reaches for the soap and I swallow as I do nothing but watch him soap his perfect body. As he turns his back on me to rinse, I finally move. Grabbing one of my new shower gels, I squirt some into my hands and lather up. The energy is charged and I can sense him start to pull away.

"I have a busy day. What are you planning on doing?" His broad shoulders block the water and his gaze stays on my face instead of my soapy hands that have started to wash my body with vanilla bubbles.

"Um... I kind of need another bathing suit or maybe I'll help Amy in the kitchen."

He shakes his head. "No. No helping Amy anymore. I'll have Dewey take you to the mall. I need a new pair of sunglasses anyway. I'll leave some money on the dresser." He reaches for my open mouth because did he just allow me out... with Dewey?

"Be good, Eve, and we'll see where this goes." He brushes my lips with his. And I stand up on my tiptoes to deepen it.

"I have to go, babe. I've got shit going on." He pulls back and steps out and I instantly miss him. Quickly I finish washing myself. My body feels so different. My muscles are sore and my vagina is somewhat throbbing and tender. I smile and start to hum then stop and turn off the shower.

What is wrong with me? I don't hum and I don't smile. I jerk one of his ugly black towels from the rack and dry myself off. I wish I could buy some pretty towels, maybe even a shelf to hold some of my stuff. This bathroom is so clean but completely bare. He doesn't even have a hamper in here. I need to pull myself together. We're not a couple *yet*. Throwing my wet hair up in a messy bun, I moisturize my face and put on some pink shimmering lip gloss. I'm tan and after hours of awesome sex, my cheeks are nice and rosy. I slip into a pink summer dress with crisscrossed straps and buttons going all the way down. I almost skip over to the dresser, and sure enough, he left me—holy shit—he left me $500.

I look around like someone might be watching me. All I see is the ugly Crystal picture with her ugly tits. As I grab a pair of white Converse sneakers, someone knocks on the door. This time, it actually is Dewey. With a look of determination on his sweet face, he wears a white T-shirt and his prospect badge is proudly displayed on the front of his cut. I'm starting to realize that these patches mean stuff. I'll have to ask Jason because some are ugly. I smile at Dewey who instantly smiles back.

"Are you ready?" he asks.

"I was born ready." I laugh at myself, and he looks confused. "Whatever… let's hit it. Maybe we can go through McDonald's drive-through and get a sausage biscuit and some hash browns, huh?"

"I was told to take you to the mall and back to Blade." He walks ahead, keys in his hand, as we descend the stairs. It's crowded—tons of new faces swarm the downstairs. On instinct, I move closer to Dewey as a bunch of bearded guys stop and start the usual degrading banter. This time I think someone says he wants to claim my ass.

Then silence, like all I hear are chairs and feet on the wood floor. And I know he's behind me. I can feel him.

"This"—Blade reaches for me as I see Edge and Axel from the corner of my eyes—"is mine." He turns my neck, and murmurs of "shit" and "we didn't know" fill the room. "She wears my mark and the only one who claims her ass or anything else on her is me." He growls as I look up at his pretty face except his eyes are serious and, same as in the shower, I sense his power. He's the real deal. Anyone touches me, they would die and I don't know if it would be quick. He laces my cold fingers with his strong, warm ones and escorts me to the front porch. He takes in my dress with one sweep then looks at my face.

"You okay?" He rubs his hands up and down my arms.

"Yes." I breathe out, leaning closer to him and swallowing as I hear the music and loud chatter of bikes and laughter. "What's happening? Is it a holiday?" I look around outside. Something has happened and it can't be good.

"Dewey?"

"I'm here, Blade." Despite his gentle face, he tries to look mean.

"You take care of my Angel." He looks at my lips and, as if he can't help himself, he pulls me in for a searing kiss. I close my eyes and feel the sun beat down on us as I kiss him back.

"Prez." Axel's voice breaks us apart. "The guys are ready."

"Watch her." He stares at Dewey then turns and walks inside. I face the bikers outside and almost smile at their stunned faces. Most are men but a few women are talking and smoking and looking at me.

Dewey takes my arm and opens the door to a black Chevy Tahoe. One older-looking woman walks over to me wearing a cut that says *Property of Titan*. "I'm Bella." She holds out her hand.

I smile and shake it. "I'm Eve."

She eyes me up and down. "Pretty little thing, aren't you? I heard all the rumors. I've been around this club for twenty-five years. You let me know if you need help."

Her soft, brown eyes seem sincere and I almost say I'll be fine. Instead I say, "I will, and I have a lot of questions. If you have time, I'd love to pick your brain."

She stares at me and smiles. "You'll do fine." She pats me on my shoulder and walks back to the group of bikers. An older, short man with a pot belly drapes an arm around her.

"I guess that's Titan?" I say, hopping into the soft leather seat. I inhale the new car smell—it's almost erotic. I've never smelled it before and now that I have, I never want to get out.

Dewey looks over at me then at the group smoking.

"Nah, that's his best friend Bobby. Titan's an officer. He used to be high up, but he crashed his bike ten years ago, so he's been in a wheelchair ever since." My eyes dart out the window as we pull out. Bella stands and smokes, laughing at something Bobby said.

"But her vest said property of Titan. I'm confused."

Dewey starts to fidget, rubbing one hand on his dark jeans then the other. "Um... well Titan can't, you know, anymore..." His eyes get big.

"So?" I snap.

"So, he lets Bobby take care of Bella." I look over at him. His cheeks are pink.

"Wait, Titan let's his best friend fuck his wife?"

"Yep, I mean he's always there watching."

"*What?*"

"Eve." He grips the steering wheel tight. "It's not unusual to share your woman with the... you know, guys."

I open my mouth then close it. Pinching my nose, I say, "So that's why you thought you could touch me? Because everyone has what? An orgy?" My voice is getting high-pitched.

He looks over at me and shifts uncomfortably in his seat. "Don't get all fired up. Blade ain't gonna share you." He looks back at the road.

I cross my arms and have that weird tightening, aggravation, something I've never felt before. "So he's shared his other girlfriends?"

Dewey grins and turns on the radio. KROQ blasts out of the speakers.

I reach over and try to figure out which one is the off button. "I asked you a question."

He sighs. "Blade ain't never had a steady girl before."

I turn toward him, but the seat belt locks up. "I thought Crystal was his girlfriend."

"Um… well you should ask Blade about—"

"Dewey," I yell, causing him to flinch.

"No… she thinks she is but he has never been exclusive with her or anyone. Well, besides you." I lean back, horrified and happy. I'm horrified that I'm happy. Jesus!

"Crystal sleeps with everyone. I guess she thought that would make Blade jealous." He shrugs.

I look out the window and spy the golden arches. Grabbing Dewey's arm, I say, "Oh my God… Thank God. I'm starving. Pull into Mickey D's."

"But Blade said…"

"I'm starving. You don't want me to tell him you didn't take care of me, do you?" I bat my lashes at him. He frowns, looking confused.

"Turn, Dewey."

I actually have to make Dewey go in. Geez, you would think I was asking him to rob a bank or something with the way his dark eyes dart around.

When I'm on my second sausage biscuit, I notice Dewey staring at me.

Sighing I put down my biscuit and fold my hands in my lap. "What?"

"I have never seen a girl eat so much." He says this like I'm a freak.

"Oh." I shrug and dive back into my breakfast. "My metabolism is incredibly fast. I can eat anything." I smile and he frowns. Poor Dewey. Guess I'm ruining all his fantasies about me.

"So, how's your stomach? Is it healing okay?" I'm talking with my mouth full, so I slow down slightly.

He stiffens and looks around the air-conditioned McDonald's. "Fine. Doc stitched me up. You ready to go?" He stands, shoulders slumped.

"Yeah." I shove the last bite into my mouth and ball up the yellow paper to throw it away. I love McDonald's. That greasy smell comforts a person. The brownish red tiles on the floor always remind me of happy times with my mom.

Shaking off any memories that might distract me, I blink as my eyes adjust to the sunny day. "Now, Dewey, when we get to the mall, I need you to follow my lead." I wave my hand in front of his face as he beeps the truck open. "Hello… are you listening? I have a certain way I like to shop—"

"You talk too much and too fast for me," he mumbles, and again there's a little tug at my conscience.

Taking a breath, I jump in and sit back. "Don't worry about anything." I smile at him. "It will be super fast, in and out, and back to the compound." No lie—I knew Dewey would be perfect for me. Meaning, he is tall and sweet-looking even with his cut. I pretend he needs sunglasses. We try on so many that I confuse the guy behind the counter. He doesn't even notice when I slip the black mirrored Ray-Ban Aviators into my leather bag as Dewey continues to harass the guy for me. I actually pay for mine, so I don't feel like a completely bad person.

I run inside Macy's—they're having a sale—and pull out about fifteen different bikinis to try on. Inevitably if you try enough on, you can always find one that has a broken alarm. A couple of nice hard slams on a plastic chair and the bulky plastic tag will usually fall off. Today must be my lucky day. When I pick up a metallic-gold bikini, the tag falls off on my first try. I take a breath and wait to see if anyone comments on the noise. All I hear are other people talking and trying on clothes. So I try on around five more, but my luck has run out and none budge. Whatever, the gold one will look fantastic with my hair and tan. I pick up a black one with pink cherries on it and smile. Jason will love it.

"That will be eighty-nine dollars and ninety cents," the older woman at the cash register says, her eyes darting to Dewey.

"I thought this was on sale."

"It is." She stares at us. "Do you want it?"

I smile. "Of course I want it." And pushing aside the gold $250 bikini in the bottom of my bag, I grab my wallet and pay. This may go down as my best day ever!

FOURTEEN

BLADE/JASON

I'm staring at the clock. The rusty Coca-Cola clock still keeps such perfect time I want to take out my gun and shoot it.

"Prez? Does that sound good?" Axel has been going on and on about different locations for the new lab and I'm tired. In the last week, I've averaged about two to three hours a night. You don't get to where I am by not being a workaholic, but this has been a shitstorm that keeps on coming. Every day I'm dealing with different gang members, other bikers. The cops. You name it and in the last week, I've dealt with it. When I do climb up the steps and into my large bed, I can't help but pull Eve to me and fuck her then pass out and repeat. She's been with me two weeks, and I haven't lost interest the way I thought would. If anything, she has become a necessity. A reason for me to get up and go to bed because she will be there. Like now, I'd rather be with her than here in the main room, with music playing and half my guys well on their way to being drunk already.

"Axel, if we can get land cheap and out of the way, the cops will look the other direction. Chatsworth is perfect. It's closer and we can make more runs. That said, we're established in Hemet and if we can ever get the cops paid off, I think we should try to rebuild. A lot of our guys have families there." My boots are on the table and I push back, balancing on the back legs of my chair.

Axel rubs the back of his neck. "I don't know... I think it's weird we haven't heard from the Feds yet."

I snort and drop my legs to the hardwood floor. The metal chair to clanks. "Give them time. I'm sure they're still trying to find anything to tie us to the fire."

He nods and stretches. I stand and dismiss everyone until tomorrow when it starts all over again.

"Hey, Prez. Amy wants to know if you want to have dinner with Eve." Ryder reads a text from his phone. Axel and Edge look over at me.

"You're not going to join us tonight?" He arches a dark eyebrow at me.

The sad thing is I would love to have dinner brought up to my room with Eve, which causes me to frown and shake my head. "Tell Amy I have some phone calls to make. I'll take it in here." I glance at Ryder who looks disappointed. Then I turn to Edge and Axel. "And yes, I plan on getting fucked up with you guys tonight."

Edge smiles as if he's relieved and quietly leaves with Ryder who is grumbling about having to keep an eye on me.

"You hungry?" I look at Axel who's lighting a joint.

"Nah, I think I'll join the boys. You should think about mixing it up tonight, man. Maybe get your cork sucked by someone besides Eve tonight."

I nod. He's right. The fact that I would rather spend time upstairs than with my brothers makes me aware I'm getting in over my head. And for what? A mouth is a mouth. If you close your eyes, it can belong to whoever you want. My phone vibrates as if we are so in tune she felt me pulling back and has to reel me back in. My balls tighten and I shift uncomfortably with the knowledge that I grow hard at the sound of my phone ringing.

She's upstairs—I could go to her and fuck her before the night starts.

"Angel."

Axel inhales and his eyes narrow as he watches me like I'm something he can't understand.

"Jason... I was hoping you were almost done." Her voice does something to me—it's gravelly... sexy.

I turn and look out the window. It's dark and I wish... fuck I don't know what I wish. "Go to bed and I'll be there soon."

Silence. I can feel her wanting me to say something else. It's fucked because I never have cared enough to wonder what anyone thought but me and my brothers. So, when Eve gets silent it makes me crazy. I *do* want to know what bothers her, what she needs, likes.

"Spit it out, Eve," I say, getting madder by the second.

She huffs and her voice changes, and I almost grin. "Why am I never allowed downstairs when there are parties going on?"

"Because I said so. Unless you want to see something you might not like, I'd heed my command and stay upstairs." I hang up and look at a frowning Axel. Holding up a finger, I grumble, "Don't say a word."

He chuckles. "Jesus, man... I'm glad I'm not you." As he opens the door to leave, Amy arrives with my dinner.

"Here." She hands me my plate filled with grilled salmon, a large kale salad, along with sweet potatoes and creamy spinach.

"Thanks, Amy." I rub my head, needing sleep and the gypsy upstairs not a party. But I'm the president so I don't exactly have a choice.

She sniffs and I can tell she's pissed I'm not with Eve.

"Amy?" She looks at me as she reaches the door.

"Don't get too attached to her. She's temporary. Men like me don't do relationships. I have a whole houseful of men and women who have to come first." I don't know if I'm reminding Amy or myself.

She stiffens. "Keep lying to yourself, Jason. You're crazy about her and she is your future." She opens the door and walks out.

"Fuck." I almost throw a beer bottle but instead pick up my fork to eat. The small buzzing of the beer signs and the beat of music coming from outside the door make me more tired. I finish my dinner and lean back and close my eyes for a second. Warm hands are massaging my neck and caressing my chest. For a split second, I think it's Eve, but this woman's smell is all wrong, so I grab the hand as it starts to trail to places it shouldn't.

"Crystal, not tonight," I grumble and sit up. She leans forward, shoving her breasts in my face.

"It's been a long time. I miss you," she coos. I look at the door and wonder how I didn't hear her come in.

I stand up and reach for a bottle of Wild Turkey. Opening it, I take a long swig. The spicy whiskey burns all the way down to my stomach.

"Sit." I motion with my head. She does and her black skirt rides up as she crosses her tan legs. I take a seat next to her.

"We go back a long time. You were Chuck's girl and that's probably how it should have stayed." Her eyes tear up at the mention of my brother. She looks years past her age: sun, smoking, and too many men and alcohol have not been kind to her. Suddenly I'm comparing my Angel to her. Eve's dewy fresh skin that glows while Crystal looks like she needs a shower and a hose to take her makeup off, revealing every large pore and wrinkle. She's only thirty-two, but she already frequents the plastic surgeon's office for Botox and fillers. Her hair is too red and damaged, her breasts too big, and her smell is all wrong. I wake up every morning to golden sun-kissed tresses that smell like coconut and feel like silk when I wrap them around my hands or neck.

"Blade, why do you always hurt me?" It's an honest question, so I give her an honest answer.

"You were never mine. I was young and grieving. But come on, Crystal, I've never lied to you."

She looks at me and at her legs. "So you're that attached to this *girl*?" She sneers "girl" and my patience starts to fade.

"It's not your business. Be smart, Crystal. Stay away from her."

She stands and reaches for the bottle of Wild Turkey and takes a sip. Like the pro she is, she doesn't even shudder. "You always come back. I've put too much time and energy into you, Blade. Yes, Chuck was my first, but you will be my last."

I stare at her, then start to laugh. "Perfect." Taking the bottle from her, I drink from it.

"But stay away from Eve. I'll let you know if I require you." Her eyes narrow and she reaches for me, but I'm done. Have been for a while. Crystal was easy and for the most part knew her place. I'm not programmed to be monogamous. It's not my life or future to be with one woman. I can't imagine anything more hypocritical being who I am. It's why I don't ever want kids. Axel is right—as soon as I was kinged, I gave up my personal life. I watched my dad trot whore after whore in front of my mother. Hell, when Chuck and I were little, we had to call some of them Auntie whoever. So, I should just unzip my jeans and let her suck me off. But instead, I take her hand and guide her out of my conference room and into the loud party.

The door to my room is locked. At first my drunk ass can't figure out why I can't get in. My whole body is pushing at the strong wooden door. Eve is inside—she's my goal. At last, I take a step back and realize she has locked me out. I know I got after her about leaving the door unlocked, but now that I can't get in, I wish I hadn't.

"You okay, Prez?" Edge is behind me. He sways, not in any better shape than me but willing to help.

"I'm fine," I say, wondering if she magically changed the locks because my key does not fit. I blink—how did I get this fucked up? The blond-haired blue-eyed siren sleeping in my bed is the reason. I needed to prove to myself that I was still me. That I could drink everyone under the table. That I could fuck two girls and not blink an eye. The only thing is that I couldn't. I tried, but my dick wouldn't cooperate. I saw her blue eyes everywhere, so in the end I growled at anyone who dared to get close to me.

"Fuck this." I pound on the door and I can't be sure, but I think I hear, "Go fuck yourself."

I look at Edge who is smiling and swaying as he types on his phone. "Wildcat, that's what you got, man. You're smart, Blade." He pats my back and I frown as I watch three of him walk down the hall.

I try the door again. Nothing. So I pound. Two prospects poke their heads out to see what's going on.

"Go away," I command and try my key again. This time I get it and I stumble into the darkness. I kick off my boots, pull off my shirt, and fall right into bed. She doesn't move. In fact I don't hear her breathe until I reach for her and pull her into my arms. Her sweet breath tickles my chest and I smile because nothing this whole day has felt this good. Then I pass out.

I roll over and all I feel is empty, nothing. Blinking, I sit up. The room is dark since the curtains are still closed, but sunlight spills from underneath them.

"Angel?" I look toward the bathroom and see the door is open and dark. Unease fills me, starting in my head and ending at the bottom of my stomach. I bolt up and open the curtains to look down at the pool. It's empty. The clean turquoise water winks and glistens up at me. I look down at myself; I'm barefoot and shirtless and still wearing my jeans from yesterday. I reach into my back pocket for my phone and cigarettes and sit on the edge of the bed, light up, and turn on my stalker tracker to locate Eve.

The red light blinks and says she's here. I inhale my cig and look around. Flashes of last night's bad decisions make me squint and look at the red dot again. Something's wrong—I can feel it. I push on Eve's name and instantly swing my head at the phone lying not three feet away from me, vibrating.

"God damn it." I grab a black T-shirt before I explode out of my room.

"Ryder, Edge," I bellow as I enter the kitchen where numerous Disciples sit respectfully drinking coffee. Amy looks up from her cooking and for a second, I see her lips twist up in a grin. Then it's gone, making me question if I'm still drunk. I grab a mug.

"Where is she?" I'm not fucking around. The unease has turned into full-blown irrational behavior.

"I have no idea what you are referring to. Which slut are you talking about?" She wipes her hands on her apron and looks me straight in the eyes. I take a step back. Amy has always been in my corner, a confidante, but this morning she looks at me like I'm a disappointment and I throw the mug across the room. Coffee and ceramic smash into the cherry cabinets and a few guys jump up and look uncertain at my next move. Amy doesn't flinch—she turns off the stove and walks out the door.

"Fuck," I roar and this time the guys do leave as Ryder and Axel run in. Axel wears only his pants and Ryder has his Glock out.

"What?" he yells. I must look crazy because they both take in the empty room and broken cup. Ryder puts his gun in his pants. "Prez, what's going on?" His hands are up like he's trying to calm a wild animal.

"Where's Eve?" I spit out the words. They both look confused.

"She's gone." I run my hands through my hair trying to stop the pounding in my head as I try to think.

"Get Edge." Ryder nods, his face filled with concern, so I ignore him and turn to Axel.

"Get me the digital recordings of the whole compound, starting with last night." I reach into the cabinet and grab another mug. "Tell Amy to come back," I snarl as I pour myself some black coffee.

"Blade?" Axel looks around the room then at me. "What happened?"

I take a sip and swallow. The thick, dark, bitter taste does nothing to improve my mood so I take another. "I woke up and she's gone. If anyone has touched her... hurt her..." I can't finish the sentence because deep down I know if she's gone it's because of me and last night.

"I want her back. I don't care how many men it takes, you get her back," I yell in his face. He stares at me as if I need to be put away.

"I'll find her," he says.

Edge walks in, his hair clearly signaling he also just got up. "The Feds are here."

I literally have to steady myself because are you kidding me? Today? They pick today when I probably need to be sedated? Instead I take a breath. "Tell them I'll be right there and get Amy back. Tell her I'm sorry... and I'll make it worth her while." I'm going to have to eat shit. Doesn't matter if I'm the president—you don't fuck with Amy or her kitchen.

"Did you hear about Eve?" I hiss as I take the stairs two at a time.

"Yes." He looks at me. "And I'm on it."

I don't have time for a shower, so I slather on some deodorant and brush my teeth, then at the last moment grab some Visine.

When I burst open the door to the conference room, two dark suits are talking to each other. One is a tall black guy and the other is a normal-sized Hispanic guy. I almost laugh because this is literally a joke. I can't take them seriously. All my thoughts are consumed with Eve.

"Can I get you guys anything? I'm Jason McCormick." I hold out my hand. They look at my outstretched hand, shake it, then smile and take a seat.

"Actually, if you have some coffee, I'd love it," the Hispanic guy answers.

"I do. How do you take it?" I pull out my phone and text Amy, looking up to see his answer.

"Just black."

"Perfect. I'm assuming that I don't need my lawyer?" I sit on my throne and cross my hands in my lap.

"Jason, I'm Agent Raul Diaz and this is Agent Devon Deckard."

I raise an eyebrow. Devon Deckard *really?* I stay quiet, biting my tongue so as not to make a *Blade Runner* reference.

"We're only here to talk. I'm sure you heard that a house that you own in Hemet burned down?"

I stare at them—both are wearing cheap black suits. "Again, I have texted my lawyer who is on his way. But if we're only having coffee…"

"We're only having coffee, Jason." Deckard smiles, hands outstretched.

Amy barges in carrying two cups of coffee and a glass of water.

"Thank you." She rolls her eyes and leaves. The agents look around the conference room.

"Cool sign." Raul points to the vintage Bud Light sign.

"So." I lean forward and sip. "Why are we having coffee together? Usually I have coffee with Agent Stevens."

Raul sips his coffee. "Well, Agent Stevens is taking some time off. Apparently he can afford it."

I raise my eyebrow at him. "Nice. Good for him."

Agent Deckard clears his voice and opens up a folder spreading out a bunch of eight-by-ten photos of the compound in Hemet: the burned-up lab and Doc and Sandy, along with numerous Disciples.

I look down at the pictures. "Now, see right away this looks like my lawyer should be present." I look over at the door opening. Ryder and Axel enter, showered and appropriately dressed.

"Agents, these are my business partners, Axel and Ryder. This is Agent Deckard and Agent Diaz. We're having coffee."

"Nice." Axel pulls out a chair and crosses his arms.

"Yeah, anyway if we wanted this to be official, you would already be in our office. But since we're new, we wanted to see if what we have is correct."

I lock eyes with Deckard. "O-kay."

"So you grew up here?"

I snort and look at the Coca-Cola clock. "Yes."

"And your father, brother Chuck, and a cousin David McCormick, his girlfriend, and his one-year-old daughter were all in another explosion—one that killed everyone but David?"

Silence. The clock ticking is all I hear.

"That was a sad time for my family. Is something going on with David?"

"We don't know. Just wondering why things seem to blow up so much around you."

I reach into my pants pocket and pull out my smokes. Lighting one up, I say, "Bad luck."

"We see that you were in the military at that time. Navy SEAL?" I inhale deep and the nicotine burns all the way to my lungs. "Yes, we all were." They look at Axel and Ryder.

"Why did you come back? How come you didn't re-enlist?"

My eyes narrow, and I shrug. "My mother needed me. Again, I'm sorry, but this sounds like we're getting away from coffee."

"Okay, Jason, we'll cut through the bullshit." Deckard smiles. "We know who you are. We know how much money you have. How many men follow you. And we know that was your drug lab that burned to the ground." He stops and looks at us.

"We've talked to Doc and Sandy and they're both in rehab, so we thought we might give you some friendly advice." He stands up and throws his card on the table. "We are not Agent Stevens—we can't be bought. Sooner or later, we're going to nail you. Kids are dying. That shit you guys have gotten rich off of goes through my community and quite frankly, I'm sick of it." They both turn to leave and none of us stands. "You might have gotten away this time, but everyone eventually gets caught."

My phone dings and I see it's a text from Edge: *I found her. She's at Dolly's. Do you want me to go get her?*

I can't help but breathe out some air I've been holding since I got up and discovered her gone. I look up at the agents; they're at the door, staring at me.

"Sorry, I have to take this. Nice having coffee with you two."

Deckard takes a step toward me as Raul grabs his arm. The door swings open and my lawyer, Rodney, barges in wearing a three-piece suit.

"What is going on? I want names. This is unbelievable," he lectures as I text Edge.

Me: *No, I'll pick her up myself.*

The door closes as I see my lawyer, who looks almost comical in that he is so perfectly put together, arguing with the agents. I look at Axel.

"Edge found her."

He stares at me, looks down at his hands and back up. "Well, I guess that's good news since we don't have enough shit going on."

"I'm going to shower and go get her. You're in charge."

"You realize you're bordering on addiction with this girl, right?"

I simply look at him. He sighs and picks up his phone. "Jesus, Blade, go get her."

FIFTEEN

EVE

I have made a huge mistake. I stare at Dolly who is pacing back and forth in her adorable high-heeled sandals. When the phone rang and she started telling Jason off, I felt validated, secure that what I was feeling was right and just. In seconds, I've been stripped of that. Her face has gone from angry red to pale and almost eerily quiet. It dawns on me right now that I may be doomed. My only hope is that I didn't get her in trouble. I look down at my tan legs and my dark purple pedicure. Dolly and I came back from the salon a little while ago. I never went to sleep last night. Jason's betrayal was too fresh, too soon. What was I thinking? Obviously I'm nothing to him, and all this playing boyfriend and girlfriend stuff was made up in my stupid head. I became so attached I was starting to forget my plan. I try to swallow as I look around Dolly's domain. It's well... Dolly. The walls are pink and yellow. She must not have much closet space or her love of style and shopping is her main pastime because in the corner, she has three rolling racks with clothes. Dozens of dresses in every color hang on them.

"Oh my God, what have I done?" When I called her at 5:00 a.m. this morning, whispering about what a disgusting pig Jason was and how I needed to get away, I never thought I might be signing not only my death warrant but hers also. I sink back into her white leather couch, lifting one leg up then the other, seeing as I'm stuck to it. The realization that I have completely subjected myself to death makes me sweat. He wouldn't seriously kill me. *He wouldn't, right?* I keep telling myself he wouldn't, but the way Dolly has gone mute on the phone and her pale, sallow face makes me want to throw up.

"Okay, Blade." My eyes snap to hers as she throws her phone on the table.

"Dolly?" My voice sounds almost like a child's: pretty pathetic. Screw this. If he's going to kill me, I refuse to go out whining. She covers her face with her hands, almost as if that will protect her.

"Well, fuck," she screams, and I cringe.

"What did he say?" I'm yelling because she's screaming every curse word imaginable.

Suddenly the small apartment is quiet and we both stare at each other.

"Okay." She looks to be trying to calm herself with her hands, almost like she's strumming a guitar. "So… we're fucked. But"—she stops me with her finger—"Jason is coming to pick you up, so I think that's good." She throws herself next to me on the couch.

"You don't sound convinced."

"He's upset, like super upset. Like so mad I've never heard him like that." She points to her phone and we both look at it like it's a poisonous snake.

"I'm sorry. I should never have called you and made you come get me. He's not mad at you, is he?" I'm trying to sound calm since she is anything but. Her crazy laughter is making me think I might have to shake her.

"The only thing you have going for you is that if he didn't care, he wouldn't be coming to get you. He would have sent one of his guys… so that's good." She's stuttering and it dawns on me that she's terrified.

I take her cold hands in my cold hand. "Don't worry. I'll tell him I made you, that I needed some air. You know, play it off like we we're going shopping." I smile.

She screams and starts pacing again. "Eve." She takes a breath. "*Do not lie*! Please, for your sake. Tell him that you don't appreciate him fucking around on you." She turns and almost spits in my face. "Beg him not to be too hard on you. Remind him you're only eighteen! Fuck... tell him *you love him*! But don't lie." She's breathing heavily and before I can tell her that there is no way in hell I'm saying any of those things, the doorbell buzzes and we both scream.

"Oh God," I whisper. He's going to kill me. He's not a good guy. How did I let incredible sex cloud my judgment? *How, Eve, how?*

Dolly stands, frozen, then pushes her shoulders back and strides to the door and opens it.

My heart leaps and my blood pressure pounds in my ears as he walks in. He's beautiful, majestic, and a monster. Larger than life. His eyes find mine and I know that everything I was scared about isn't half as bad as I had imagined. It's ten times worse maybe even a hundred. Anger, if that even properly describes what is radiating off him, has taken over the small studio. Like a Ziploc bag it suffocates all the air in seconds. I may pass out, except that would be too easy as he jerks me up to his hard body. A small whoosh comes out of my mouth as he drags me toward the door. He doesn't speak or look at Dolly, who stares in horror, her pretty brown eyes the size of saucers. Her eyes bolt from Blade's to Edge who stands with his arms crossed. What is he doing here? Is he here to *kill Dolly*?

"Jason... it's my fault. Dolly didn't do anything," I plead. He shakes me so hard my head falls back.

"Not one fucking word, I swear to God, Eve. Say one more word and I don't care that Dolly and Edge are here. I'll shut you up with my cock, then dump you on the side of the road with a bullet between those baby blues."

Dolly places a hand over her mouth as tears stream down her face. And that's the last I see of her as Edge grabs her and shuts the door.

I'm smart enough to keep quiet as he pulls me over to his bike. He grabs his helmet and dumps it on my head. I think I might have gone into survival mode, or maybe it's that I'm resigned because I can't help but think he wouldn't bother with a helmet if he was going to kill me.

I watch his long, muscular legs grip his Harley and I don't make him wait as I hop on the back. My hands cling to his hard stomach.

He starts the bike and thankfully, I'm ready because he takes off. My legs tighten around his warm thighs and tears sting my eyes. I refuse to cry. My chest burns as I hold it in. We don't go far as he brings the bike into a dark concrete parking garage save for some blinking neon lights. His large Harley rumbles almost as if alive causing the bottom of the garage to vibrate with his rage. He pulls up to the front and drags me off the bike. As he tears off the helmet, I try to blink away any tears and start to shake. He takes my arm as he taps a code into a metal door. A wave of sheer terror snakes up my spine and I have a bad feeling about this. "Jason…"

He either doesn't hear me or doesn't care as he pulls me into a large, dark nightclub. The pulsing music and neon pink and blue lasers zap all over the floor. Smoke, the smell of liquor and sweaty bodies hits my tearstained face and I almost try to talk again. Instead I remain quiet. Something in his presence tells me I need to stay silent. He roughly maneuvers us through the crowd of people dancing and into a corner.

"Blade… my man." A huge black man with a bald head and a diamond in his front tooth smiles at him as he comes out a door that I would never have seen had he not emerged from it.

"Jordan." Jason nods. "I need a room." I inch closer to Jason not caring that he may kill me. The need and feeling that I should be close to him overrides that worry.

I feel the man's stare upon me and I look up.

"Hmm nice, very nice. Are we sharing tonight?" Jason turns and looks at me. His silence makes my eyes pop. He must see fear in my eyes because his full lips smile and he chuckles. "You'd be disappointed with this one."

"If you're unhappy with her, leave her with me. I guarantee I can train her for you." His voice almost purrs.

"How much would you give me for her?" He pulls me in front of him facing the man. I whimper as he pushes my hair off my face. "She's young and beautiful but I bought her for a lot of money... so I'd need you to give me more." Vaguely I realize I'm not breathing, but air is still filling my lungs. The room is blurry and the fear is so painful that if Jason wasn't holding me up I would be on the floor. The large man reaches to touch my cheek and I think I hear Jason hiss. But he allows the man to touch me all over. When his large dark hand goes toward my pussy, Jason snarls, "Enough. How much?"

"I'm sorry," I gasp out. Suddenly his hand is around my neck, silencing me.

"How much?"

The man looks at Jason then me. "Five hundred thousand. I can see her going for maybe a million." He motions for Jason to enter his office.

Sobbing, I cling to him; his gravelly voice is at my ear. "Half a million dollars is a lot of money, Angel. I'll give you a choice: you can go with Jordan and be sold, raped, and broken or you can know who owns you." He lets go of my neck and I scream as he tries to detach me from him. Somehow, he turns me to face him. My nails still dig into his forearms and he grabs my face with both hands.

"*Who. Owns. You?*" His green eyes are fierce and if I hadn't seen firsthand how much of a monster he is I think I'd see remorse.

"You, you own me, Jason." He brings my lips to his.

"You ever pull a stunt like this again, you'll wish…" He stops as his eyes latch onto mine. And I can't stop crying, nor will I let go of his wrists.

"Don't ever make a fool out of me again," he snarls.

The loud beat vibrates through my shaken body. I hiccup and nod. Instead of dragging me, he lifts me up and I bury my face in his neck and breathe in his spicy, smoke-filled skin.

"Blade?" Jordan's voice sounds amused.

"I'm gonna pass. I think I'll keep her." Jason walks out the door. The dark garage makes me wrap my arms tighter around his neck. He doesn't talk to me as he sets me on his bike, gently puts his helmet on me, and opens the visor because with all my crying, I guess I'm fogging it up. He gets on but doesn't start the bike as I collapse on his back, my hands holding on tight. He sits with me clinging to him. His warm hand reaches for mine and I start to cry harder.

"Lower the visor, baby, and hold on." His voice makes me shiver, and after all he did a few minutes ago, I think I may be going crazy. I don't want to be anywhere but with him.

He pulls out, not slow but not fast either. Steady. I close my tired, burning eyes, not needing to see anything. The smell of orange blossoms tells me we're close. I can't remember a time I have cried this much, and I can't seem to stop. He parks his bike and I finally open my eyes only to be greeted with curious faces. Not hostile—almost like they are waiting to see what Blade does. He lifts me from the bike and I take off the helmet and bury my face in his neck again. As he lifts me in his strong arms, I see Axel standing with the door open.

"Welcome home, Eve." His voice is not sympathetic; it's almost laced with humor. And I hold on to Blade's cut.

He takes the stairs two at a time like I'm not even in his arms. Again, the reality that he is bigger and stronger hits me. Once he kicks the door to our room shut, he sits us on one of the chairs and holds me as I cry. His hand strokes my hair and he kisses my temple and forehead. When I can't cry anymore, I look at him. He stares at me, his green eyes filled with wonder and something more. Hunger, need maybe. I don't trust myself to dissect it, but he groans as he pulls me up and I straddle him. The kiss is hard, and I hold on to his shoulders. My body responds to him, burning as if I have a fever. He forces the kiss deeper. Still sensing his anger, I scoot closer. Maybe if I do, he won't ever let me go.

He pulls back and orders me to strip. As he pulls down his pants, his thick cock stands up almost waiting for me. I'm naked in no time, my flimsy T-shirt and shorts easy to get rid of.

"Come here." He watches every move I make. I stop and stand in between his legs. Reaching for my hips, he jerks me on top of him. As he places my legs on either side of him, I grab the top of the chair for balance. He lines us up and lowers me down on him in one rough thrust.

I can't help but groan at how deep he is. He wraps his hand tightly in my hair and brings my face next to his so that he is stealing my breath and giving it back.

"Fuck me, Angel." He holds my hair as I rise up and down on him. I fuck him so hard his nostrils flare. Up and down I pound on him unleashing everything until I see stars. My body jerks, my pussy contracts, and moisture seeps out.

"Fuck yeah... fuck, Eve." He thrusts up into me, coming in a loud, guttural groan. I'm collapsed on him, still connected, and I try to steady my breathing. He doesn't push me away and pulls me to his mouth.

"I have work to do. Go clean yourself." He brushes his lips to mine. I go to lift up but he holds me on top of him.

"You okay, baby?"

I cock my head at his question. "No." I have nothing to lose by being honest.

"You will be." He pulls me off his semihard cock. I try to stand, but everything seems to be shaking. He pulls up his pants before he holds me again.

"Why?" I whisper.

"You're not stupid. This is our life. It's not a fucking fairy tale. I'm dealing with all kinds of bad things. You're mine and I intend on making sure you act like it."

I want to ask him what that means because my heart just skipped a beat. But I'm too raw and tired to do this conversation justice. He starts the shower for me and I watch from the door as he changes his T-shirt. Then he's gone and I'm left with the consequences of my actions. I step into the dark blue rock shower letting the hot water soothe me. I survived and if I can do that today, I can thrive all the rest of my days. I decide right then, right now, that I will stop at nothing to get Jason to love me. I lift my face to the hot water and smile. I'm going to be his queen.

SIXTEEN

BLADE/JASON

"I'm telling you, I'm fine. We need to get another lab going. Sandy is going to be in rehab another three weeks. The time is now." I'm standing in fucking hot Hemet staring at the black pit that used to be my lab and listening to my childhood friend act like what he put us through over the last month is no big deal.

"We need to try and sell this land." Axel interrupts him. The ground still stinks of smoke and chemicals.

"Who's going to buy it?" I light up and shield my eyes as I look around.

"I don't care, Blade. This area is dead to us." Axel removes his cut and tears off his T-shirt. I nod while I watch Doc out of the corner of my eye. He's pacing and mumbling to himself.

He stops and looks at us. "I say we get me a trailer and I'll work out of it for a while. I'm telling you, I'm onto something." He pushes his glasses up on his nose.

I look around. It's hot with nothing but dirt and trash and burned ashes. I'm sick of this day already. Quite frankly, I'm sick of Hemet and Doc. I've been in a foul mood ever since he called and said he was done with rehab and had walked out.

"I'm fine. I had one bad day." He sulks like a teenager, and I wonder if whatever he was working on screwed with his mind because this is not the Doc I grew up with. This guy seems sketchy, guilty, and not for the first time do I wonder if the Feds got to him.

"Doc?" I need his attention. "The only reason you aren't lying in an unmarked grave is because we go way back." I look down at my phone—it's vibrating.

Edge: *Dolly is having a birthday party this weekend. She wants you to bring Eve.*

Pocketing my phone, I take a deep drag and flick my cigarette into the black pit.

"You got some nerve, Jason. I've made us all rich," Doc rambles. He reaches for his cigarettes. His twiggy arms look like he hasn't seen sun in years.

"You're fucking joking, right?" I walk over to him. He stops pacing and looks up. "You cost us hundreds of thousands of dollars. The Feds are on my ass and the two prospects you had helping you cook your shit are in a home because their brains are fucked." I turn away not wanting to be near him. He let Sandy and drugs rule his life.

"Where are you going? I need a trailer," he whines.

I snort. "That drug was as much my creation as yours. Don't think I don't remember how to make it." The threat is real but he doesn't even stop pacing.

"I'm calling Gina and telling her to put the land up for sale. I'll get Jimmy and his crew to clean it up," Axel informs me as he pulls out his phone. He keeps his eyes on Doc as he paces.

"Tell her to push it hard. I want out of here." I move toward my bike.

I've barely seen Eve this week. I've been here for a couple of days and at a club I'm taking over, so I stayed in the office for a few nights on the couch. She's in my blood, and like a thirsty man needs water, I seem to need this girl. So I've made a real effort to distance myself from that. But not today. I'm sick of running from her and what she does to me.

Ryder joked the other morning that I was scared of her. I ignored his jab, but as the day wore on, I wondered if he wasn't right. Am I afraid of the way I feel around Eve?

I don't feel guilty about scaring her when I threatened to sell her. It was needed. If she's going to be in my life, for her safety and my sanity, she needs to be where I can find her at all times. She's young and beautiful, but she is also tough as nails. I can't tolerate her dramatics. My guys will lose all respect and I wouldn't blame them. Threatening to sell her not only scared her, it brought us to a place we have to be.

I know I'm an ass, but watching her cry and knowing she needs my comfort to feel whole turns me on. She's never had that kind of attention, so her whole psyche soaks it up like a sponge absorbs water. She knows the rules and has committed to being mine. I don't feel guilty about keeping her. Each day that I wake up to her sweet-smelling skin I learn a little more about her, even when I try not to. Like how when she smiles big, she has a small dimple on her right cheek. How her blue eyes turn color with her emotions. How she is grateful every day because she chooses to trust that I'm taking care of her father. All of these things are why I had to give myself some space. Jesus, the other night I almost took her out for dinner and a movie. I had to force myself to leave her and go to our local bar where the Disciples hang out. I don't do dates and I can't remember the last time I've gone to the movies—maybe when I was sixteen. The thing is, the more I learn about this stunning gypsy, the more I want her. More than likely she's never even been to a movie. And if she has, it was a long time ago. So I almost did it—almost took her hand and jumped over the cliff. Instead I locked her in my room and ran like a fucking pussy.

I get on my bike and start it up. Doc looks shocked. "What the hell, Blade? What did you decide? Do I get my trailer?"

I don't respond and leave him with Axel. Suddenly I'm through running. Jesus Christ, she's only a girl. But I'm going to teach her to swim today. Then maybe we'll go get pizza and a beer. Fuck, I want to take her to the movies and see her face light up with wonder. I want to kiss her pouty lips and watch the sunset with her. This is why I should head in the other direction. Instead I merge onto the freeway toward LA and Eve.

I find her sitting with Amy and Dewey laughing in the kitchen. Her back is to me, and for a moment, I stop and listen to her giggle at their ridiculous conversation. Amy is trying to convince Dewey that if he wants a girlfriend he needs to be a gentleman. By gentleman she means he needs to take off his cut and wear preppy clothes. If Eve wasn't laughing so hard she was hitting the counter, I would barge in and tell Dewey no woman is worth taking off his cut. But I don't. I watch her hands wave around as she snorts out a laugh about picturing Dewey in skinny jeans and a collared pink shirt. That even makes Amy crack a smile and my heart tightens like someone is squeezing it.

I push off the doorway and walk into the kitchen where everyone turns to stare at me. Eve jumps off the stool and Dewey stops grinning.

Edge is sitting in the corner on his phone. His copper head shakes at my entrance. He's been acting standoffish ever since that day I got Eve back. When I asked him how things went down with Dolly, I got, "I handled it." And he hasn't talked about it since.

I need to talk to him tomorrow about what's going on with him. And I guess the details about the birthday party. I haven't forgiven Dolly for taking Eve's side or all-around betraying me. But Eve is young and likes Dolly, so maybe I'll consider taking her.

"Jason… you're back." Eve exhales and her pretty fingers grip the counter.

"I am." Walking up to her, I sense every eye in the kitchen watching me. Strangely I don't care.

"Go change, Angel. I'm finally going to teach you how to swim."

She bats her long eyelashes at me and I grin as she bounces up and down and throws herself into my arms.

"I'll be right back." She squeals as she runs up the stairs.

"Wow, that sure is nice of you, Prez. She has been wanting to learn for so long." Dewey smiles at me like he is congratulating me on getting engaged or something.

I shrug. "She needs to learn if she is going to continue to… be out there."

I hear Edge chuckle and walk over to get a glass of water. Amy grabs my arm and smiles up at me.

"Jesus." I shake my head at all the happy faces. Even Edge seems pleased.

"I'm going to make sure she's ready. Actually, Amy, can you make us a batch of your famous margaritas?"

"I would love to." Her brown eyes twinkle. Shaking my head, I walk past Edge.

"You coming?"

"Maybe later. I'll let you two get the basics down." Then he's back to his phone, a shitty grin on his face.

"Close off the pool area. Only you three are allowed in," I inform them over my shoulder as I take the stairs and throw open my door. Eve is spraying sunblock on her long thin limbs and I instantly get hard.

"Come and kiss me. I missed you." It comes out way harsher than I meant, but again, I'm struggling with why this particular woman makes me want to throw her on the bed and mate, claim, conquer. She doesn't hesitate and drops the can on our perfectly made bed, wrapping her arms around me. I look down at her— she's blushing and her chest is already flushed with excitement. She wants me and I almost lose sight that I need to teach her to swim. I pull away so I can look at her bathing suit. It's gold and with her golden skin and long blond hair pinned up on the top of her head, she looks almost too beautiful to be real.

"Do you like it?" She puts her hands on her hips and I grit my teeth.

"Yeah, I like it. I'm gonna throw on my trunks. We need to get out of this room if you want to learn to swim."

When she cocks her head, my mark is visible under her ear and I groan—she seems to be focused on what she'd rather do.

"We can fuck later. I promised to teach you to swim weeks ago. Today's the day."

"I'm so excited." She claps her hands and grabs the spray and her big leather bag. I have given up trying to reason with her about her purse, bag, backbreaker. It's the one thing she always keeps close and never leaves anywhere without. As crazy as it sounds, somedays I find myself getting jealous over that bag. The way she loves it and needs it makes me want her to feel that way about me. Kicking off my jeans, I pull up my black board shorts and take off my cut and T-shirt. Her eyes are huge as she stares at my chest and arms. I know she has a thing for my tattoos. She's constantly touching them, asking questions about them. Reaching for her before I stick my throbbing cock into her, I spin her around and slap her ass.

"March. Lesson one: you need to trust me." That stops her and I wrap my arms around her small waist so as not to knock her over. When have I ever felt this light? *Unburdened* comes to mind even if it's only for this afternoon.

"Um... I'm not... I didn't think about that." She stutters, her frown making me want to kiss that small wrinkle between her eyebrows.

"Let me get this straight—you don't trust me?" Somehow this bothers me. It's irrational and not needed, but somewhere deep inside, I never thought she wouldn't trust me.

She stares at me. Her pretty head's probably spinning. "I have problems with that, but if I trust anyone, it's you."

I lift her chin up so that she can see me. "Good. I want your trust."

Her eyes dart around the room. I watch somewhat fascinated that I've been inside her almost every night, took her virginity, and yet she still hesitates to trust me. I'll have to work on that. Because much like all things with her, I need her trust.

I let it go for the moment and take her hand, walking like a regular couple down the stairs, ignoring all the stunned, bearded, tatted-up brothers who are playing pool.

As we walk outside, Amy has turned on the sound system and Frank Sinatra's smooth voice sings "My Way." Amy has a thing for Sinatra. Personally I like the Sid Vicious version, but I bow to Amy and her choices when it comes to the running of the house. I had to apologize three times and swear no matter how frustrated I get, I will never throw anything again in her kitchen. I also had Ryder buy her a gift certificate to a spa day at Burke Williams.

"Okay, Angel, we're going to start by learning how to float. If you can float you can..." Her big blue eyes stare down at the turquoise water.

It's impossible not to grin. She is adorable in her neediness as she holds my hand tighter. "Did you ever see that movie *Jaws*?"

"Of course."

She nods and licks her lips. "It was always on cable when I was a kid."

I start laughing. "Are you worried Jaws is going to come out of the drain?"

Her big eyes pop to mine. "That's crazy, right?"

And I can't help but pull her into my arms and kiss her lips and nose.

"I'll protect you. Now let's do this." As I dive into the pool, knowingly splashing her, she lets out a squeal. She gracefully walks down the steps like a fucking swimsuit model then stops when she's at the last step. I stand up and go to her, my dick completely ready to fuck not teach. I scrub my hands up and down my face and hold my hand out for her. She takes it and I slowly bring her to me. The cool water cascades around us like a caress. Her legs wrap around me as she fits her pussy on top of my cock.

I smile. "Baby, you have to let me breathe."

Her breath is at my ear and its sharp and sweet. My hands travel up her ass to her hair and pull it back. "Look at me, Eve." Her blue eyes lock on mine. "I will not let anything happen to you." Her eyes search my face and she exhales, her whole body relaxing against mine.

"Are you ready to learn how to float? Because if you can float you can save yourself."

"I am." She smiles, showing me that dimple, and I pull her lips to mine. "I want to untie those strings and fuck you in this water." Instead I detach her hands and place them under her. Lifting her up, I say, "Now relax and breathe, and gently become one with the water.

"O-kay, you aren't going to let go, right?" She lifts her head and starts to sink.

"Eve, knock it off. I'll never let you go," I snap.

Her eyes find mine and she slowly relaxes back into the water, her head up and my hands lightly on the small of her back. "Close your eyes." She does and I grin as she starts to float.

"That's good, Angel. You're doing it." My praise makes her lips twitch. "Relax. Forget I'm here."

She exhales. "I can never forget you are here." I lower my hands and watch as her body embraces the water like she was born for it. And my chest almost hurts. I am connected with her and I'm not even inside her. This is not how I should be feeling and I frown at my thoughts.

Someone coughs, causing Eve to pop her eyes open and promptly sink. I reach for her and she wraps her arms around my neck. We both look over at Edge who stands with a pitcher of margaritas and three glasses.

"You guys ready? Amy said enjoy them now." He sets the glasses on the table and pours himself one from the pitcher. I sigh and reluctantly walk us over to the stairs although I should be grateful he's here. Otherwise God only knows what I would have said or done. I motion for Edge to hand me mine. I don't need him seeing my hard-on. Eve is busy making sure her bikini is in place—smart girl—and walks up the steps. As she emerges like a mermaid, her skin glistening as water trails down her toned limbs, I stare. Unfortunately so does Edge.

He averts his eyes as he pours her a drink and hands it to her. "So, can you swim yet?"

"Um... well not yet. I'm learning to float." She reaches for a towel and flops down onto a cushioned seat under the red umbrella. "I did it though, right Jason?"

"Yeah, you did it." I emerge from the pool not caring if he does see my erection. Actually he needs to see it. I pull Eve's chair closer and instead of growling "mine" at my brother, I refill my glass.

Edge shakes his head. "I'm gonna let you two carry on with the lessons." He laughs as he stands, grabs his drink, and heads back toward the house.

Her eyes follow him, and as he turns the corner, she shifts her gaze to me. "Jason, you made him feel like a third wheel. He's sensitive, you know." She shields her eyes so she can see me.

I almost choke on my drink. "Really?"

"Yes. He's in love with Dolly and feels like shit that he cheated on her. He's tortured because he can't give her what she wants." She says all this with her feet tucked under her as she sips her margarita and glares at me like it's my fault Edge couldn't keep his dick in his pants.

"I'm sorry—how do you know this?" I pull the legs of her chair closer to face me.

"You're kidding, right?" She looks at me like I'm clueless. It almost makes me laugh, but she's being serious so I watch as she takes her finger and stirs the icy drink then puts it in her mouth to suck. My cock jerks. "We talk. I mean, besides Dewey and Amy, he's my only friend around here."

"He's not your friend, babe." Gritting my teeth, I try to keep my temper down. "What he and Dolly had was a teenage fling. Then they were basically fuck buddies on and off for years."

She shrugs and looks around the pool area then back at me. "If you say so."

"Eve," I say, unsure why I'm so aggravated all of a sudden. Her eyes narrow on mine, but she's listening.

"Men like us can't get serious with one woman. We aren't programmed to be monogamous."

She looks down at her drink then back up at me. "Maybe you can't be with just one woman, but I watch the way he is with her. He loves her, and I guarantee if he could have a do-over on that night, he would never have allowed your dirty skank of a girlfriend to wrap her disgusting lips around his cock."

"What the fuck? Who the hell are you to judge?" I stand up and pull her out of her chair. "You have no idea what the fuck you're talking about. I never want to hear the word cock come out of this mouth." I grab her chin and rub her full lips with my thumb. "Unless it's to say thank you to me for letting you have *mine*."

I tighten my grip. She jerks her head away, turns, and bolts toward the house. I'm so stunned, I almost can't believe this woman is running from me. She's quick as I lunge at her. The patio chairs tumble to the side and I toss one in the pool trying to grab her.

"Motherfucker... I swear to God, Eve." It falls on deaf ears—she's already opening the sliding glass doors.

I should stop and think instead of chasing after her. She's got some balls thinking she can run away from me. My cock hardens, almost to the point of being painful, as thoughts of throwing her on the bed and showing her who's boss run through my head. I own this wild gypsy. She needs to learn this.

Barreling through the glass patio door, I notice Edge and a couple of other Disciples who were playing pool are now looking at me. Led Zeppelin is screaming and the room stinks of weed already.

"Don't disturb me," I snarl, not caring what they think.

I take the stairs two at a time, gritting my teeth as I see a flash of blond hair and hear the slam of our door. Ryder is smoking and leaning against his door, his brown eyes full of interest as he arches a dark brow.

"You okay there, Prez? You let me know if you need some help." His chuckle is almost my undoing as he slams his door. I stop outside our door and breathe for a second. She has to have locked the door so I already have the key out. To my surprise, it opens right up and as always, I go on alert. She isn't stupid and can't possibly think she's going to win, right? She has to know I can't and will never allow this kind of behavior. Slowly I enter and let my eyes adjust to the darkness. The curtains are closed giving the bedroom a much smaller feel. Maybe it's our crazy chemistry bouncing off the walls, but it's thick and I adjust my cock so it's not throbbing against the Velcro on my board shorts. My eyes scan the room only to land on the bathroom door: it's closed. Breathing heavily, I move toward her like a dog smells a bitch in heat. I try the door, and again, I'm surprised when it opens right up. I look around and don't see her. Flipping on the light, I pull open my shower door and there she is in the corner. I freeze—not because she's afraid. If anything, her eyes hold nothing but defiance. She's angry and if I was a nicer man I would pull her up and kiss away her anger. Like a tornado, she's seething with it. Her harsh breath makes her spectacular tits rise up and down in her gold bikini.

"Stand up," I spit out.

Her eyes narrow as she gracefully stands. "Now come here." Again I watch her, waiting to see some sort of weakness. But she shows me nothing as she holds her shoulders back and head up, stopping right in front of me.

I reach for her silky hair and pull her up and into my chest. Our bodies burn with our heat and I wonder again why I have this crazy attraction to her.

"Are you kidding me? You ran from me?" Our eyes clash and our breathing is harsh.

"Angel, I'm not the one. I'm a bad guy. I told you this years ago. I will not allow this. You will know who owns you and you will obey." Her blue eyes are pooled with tears but she doesn't cower, which makes me almost see red. *What the hell? Why does she push me?*

"You don't get a right to feel anything except what I let you."

"You can't control my mind, *Blade*," she sneers. My eyes sweep her face, taking in her pink cheeks and red swollen lips, sliding to her neck and her rapidly beating heart. Suddenly I push her away.

"So, you're saying that you are done paying your father and brother's debt?" Her face pales instantly and I know I have her again. "Trust me, Eve. The place I have your father at is a fortune. If you're done with me, I'll tell them to dump him in the street and you can pick him up." I grab her arm and pull her into the bedroom. Whimpering, she still holds her head high.

"Watch." I reach for my phone. She grabs my arm.

"Wait... stop. What do you want from me?" she screams. I lower the phone and look at her. If only she would bend to me, I wouldn't have to do this. Christ, all I wanted to do today was teach her to swim and go out to eat.

"I want everything, and if you ever run from me again, I'll make sure it's the last time." I turn away unable to look at her or face all the ugly stuff I've said to her. I rip off my trunks not caring that she can see how much I want her. I need to get the fuck away from her, or I might do something I regret. Reaching for my pants and T-shirt, I take my phone and boots with me and call over my shoulder, "All you have to do is shut up and look good.

Even someone with your limited amount of education can figure that out."

She gasps. It's a cheap shot, but her father and her lack of education are the only things that make my Angel insecure. I push back and lock away the nagging need to go to her and confess that I don't mean it. But I do. She needs to let me control her or she's going to get hurt. Trying to beat her down isn't necessary, but since she still has a fire in her eyes, I haven't succeeded. She has too much power over me already. Slamming our door, I pound on Ryder's door to get ready to ride.

SEVENTEEN

EVE

I'm staring at a shimmering, black mini halter dress. Mini is the key word. Literally when I lift it up I'm wondering if it's going to cover everything. Edge handed me the box this morning with a note. At first, I couldn't help the butterflies in my stomach at the thought that Jason had given me an "I'm sorry" present. What a naïve stupid thought that was. Turns out it was from Dolly with a note:

You're welcome. That's all it said.

I look down at the halter dress and the high-heeled ankle boots and can't help but smile. Dropping my towel, my body still warm from my shower, I start to slather on my cocoa butter cream and slip into a black lace thong so that I can start on my makeup and hair. Of course, my mind wanders to Jason and us. He left two days ago—it's a pattern we have apparently. Anything gets intense and Jason runs. This time he's been gone two days. I roll my eyes at my reflection, aggravated that I can't stop thinking about him. He's a shit and a true manipulator. What he fails to understand is that I'm not stupid. And nobody can make people do what they want better than me. Jason can rage and threaten me, but I see the way he looks at me, and that gives me an edge, however slight that may be. He's fighting his need for me. I have all the confidence that I can still bring him to his knees. Whether he talks about other women, or not being able to have a lasting relationship, I'm not stupid. This man wants me as much as I want him. I have no idea where he is. He's called, I guess to check on me. Yet whenever I ask when he's coming home or what he is doing, he gets quiet and says he's working.

But not tonight. I smirk at my reflection and bite my lower lip. I reach for my vanilla-coconut perfume, spray some on my wrist and breasts, and reach for the scrap of a dress. A shiver of excitement goes up my spine as I get goose bumps. Jason is actually taking me out. Well, Edge is taking me, but Jason will show up eventually. It's Dolly's twenty-eighth birthday and she's having a party at a club in West Hollywood. It's not a club that one of the Disciples owns. When I asked Edge why, he said she'd rather die than give the Disciples any more money. The longer I stay here, the more I'm learning that Jason and the main guys seem to have their hands in all kinds of things. I'm not stupid enough to think all of them are nightclubs. I know Jason has a couple strip clubs and I'm sure he launders money through them. Snapping the halter around my neck, I turn and look at the back of the dress through the mirror. It dips low, like almost seeing my ass low.

"Jesus, Dolly." I snicker as I sit down and pull on the high-heeled ankle boots.

Standing, I straighten my shoulders and take a good look at myself. I have never looked better. Amazing what some makeup, a haircut, and new clothes will do.

Tonight I want to make Jason notice me. I want him, and I won't settle for anyone else. I look over at the picture of Crystal that still hangs in our room and wonder what he'll do if I take it down. What did he ever see in her? She's been creeping around lately. Her dirty looks and snide comments that my days are numbered make me even more determined.

Walking toward the poster, I reach up and lift it off the wall, looking around for a place to put it. I set it down and go to find Dewey. Instead I see Edge as I peek out the door. *Great.*

Sighing, I smile at him and his eyes travel up and down me. "You are not actually thinking about wearing that are you?" Sometimes Edge reminds me a lot of Jason, and not in a good way.

"Yes, I am." I stare at him and wave him in. "Can you help me, please?"

He walks in and looks around. "Eve." He rubs the back of his neck. "Did Dolly send you this dress?"

"Yep." I point to the poster of Crystal on the floor. His eyes look at it then me.

"I need this"—I tap my high-heeled boot at it—"out of here. I'm here more than Jason and I'm sick of looking at her ugly face and flabby tits." Her tits aren't actually flabby because they're fake, but I'm beginning to detest her and say it anyway.

Edge ignores it and goes right back to my outfit. "Look... Eve, Dolly is... Dolly she looks good wearing things like this." His eyes laser onto my legs.

I flutter my long, mascaraed lashes at him. "So what? You're saying I don't?"

"Jason will not want you like this." He looks beyond annoyed.

I clear my throat. "I disagree." Fluffing my hair, I look him straight in the eyes. "Jason is gone all the time. Plus, I can't tell you how many times he's told me that I'm nothing to him."

"Christ." Edge looks up at the ceiling.

"Yes... Christ. That's what I say every time he reminds me that you and basically all the Disciples can never be monogamous." I wave my hands around. "So, I doubt he's going to care what one of his *many women* wears."

"Eve, don't do this tonight." He shakes his head. "Seriously, we've had a shitty week. Please, wear something else."

"Um, no." I walk over to my phone, which is charging, toss it into my black bag, and twirl to face him. "Wait."

His eyes narrow on me as I snap my finger.

"I know, maybe I'll meet a really rich guy and Jason can sell me to him." I smile and do jazz hands at him.

He blows out some air. "If that's the way you want to play it, don't say I didn't warn you." He picks up the poster with one hand and walks out leaving me feeling like maybe I was a bit dramatic.

And did I just act like I actually care about Jason? "Great." I put my hands on my hips, mortified at the hot sting of tears in my eyes.

Shaking my head, I sniff and grab a tissue. "What is wrong with you? Stay on course," I chant to myself as I march into the bathroom to put the final touches on my hair and makeup. I hate that I've become... I don't know, emotional lately. I mean my whole life I made fun of the girls who cried over their boyfriends. Sighing, I close my eyes then open them. God, why won't Jason be like all the other guys: stupid and easy to push around?

"You wouldn't want him if he was normal." I tell my reflection. "Shit." I grip the edge of the sink. What is happening to me? Not only do I want him, but I think this sensation that rips at my heart anytime he smiles at me or ignores me might be...?

I shake my head. "You can't, Eve. You *cannot* fall in love with Jason." He's supposed to fall in love with me, not the other way around. Staring at myself, I try to deny the truth: that I, Eve Smith, might be having strong feelings for the president of one of the most dangerous MCs on the West Coast.

I exhale and breathe in. I can't. He basically kidnapped me and could at any moment discard me. But that doesn't stop the very real fact that I get turned on by his fierceness, his power. Is that love? The sad thing is that this man lights me on fire. He challenges me in a way that makes me want to please him. When he is near me, he makes me feel safe and wanted like I never thought existed. I'm connected to him in a way I never imagined.

I twist open the sparkly pink lip gloss and shimmer up my lips. After one last look, I shut off the bathroom light.

"Let's see if you can ignore me tonight, Jason." I don't even care that I'm talking to myself. It gives me courage. With my bag in hand, I lock the door behind me.

The ride to the club is filled with quiet but obvious disapproval from Edge and pleasant nonstop chatter from Dewey. The valet comes out to open my door and park the Tahoe. I can already hear the music pumping and pulsing inside. Strobe lights dance around as I look over at a patio overflowing with people. Laughter and smoke permeate the air as Edge reaches for my arm. He doesn't get stopped as he nods at the large bouncer dressed in all black. We walk in like we own the place. It's dark in here with twinkling lights all around along with the strobe light and lasers bouncing off the walls and ceiling. The place is packed, wall-to-wall people, most in line for alcohol.

"Where's Dolly?" I yell.

Edge doesn't respond and propels me forward and over to some dark stairs. Fluorescent purple light shines down on us. As the music changes, so does the light. Another bouncer nods at us at the top and opens the red velvet cord to let us enter.

"I guess they know you here." I turn to him.

"Eve, until Blade shows up, I need you to stay with me."

I nod. His eyes are taking in the place and it's clear he's on alert. I guess this is the way they live. This is my first time in a club, so maybe it's normal to be aware of everyone. Jason does the same thing—even walking into our bedroom, he always goes first, his eyes searching.

He guides me through the crowd of people, most of them wearing Disciples cuts but some obviously friends of Dolly's. Many have purple or blue hair. He lets go of me to reach for a woman dressed in a red, skintight slip dress and black pumps with striking red bottoms. She turns and smiles up at him. My heart thuds as I witness their eyes lock. On her head is a tiara with blinking lights that say Birthday Girl.

"Oh my God, he actually let you come?" Dolly detaches herself from Edge and grabs me for a hug.

"Dolly… you look beautiful." Looking at her happy and healthy makes me feel drastically less guilty about last month.

"No, you're striking. Turn around." I laugh feeling like a load I didn't realize I was holding has been taken off my chest. I spin and she reaches for Edge.

"No looking," she snaps and he arches a brow.

"I only have eyes for one woman. I wish to hell she'd trust me on that," he grumbles.

"Eve, you want something to drink?"

I look at them both and it all makes sense. I almost sigh since I'm rooting for them.

"Oh yes." Dolly wiggles her body against his. "Shots, please. Doug and I are drinking Cosmopolitans, so three." She smiles at him and I look away. The hunger in their gazes is too depressing since I haven't seen Jason and he seems determined to keep it that way. Suddenly I'm tired, which is crazy since it's not even ten yet.

Arms wrap around me from behind, I swing around to a smiling Doug who is wearing a dark suit and a blinking tiara.

"Hello beautiful." He dips his nose to my neck.

"Doug… knock it off." Edge's eyes are serious.

Doug laughs then says, "Oh Edge, always a pleasure, and since Blade is stupid enough to let his queen alone, I shall volunteer to babysit her." He winks at Edge.

"Christ, Doug." He rolls his eyes, keeping a firm hand locked on Dolly. "Blade's on his way so keep your hands off. I'll get drinks."

Doug pouts but drops his hands. "Fine, as long as you're getting drinks." He fans himself.

"Let's dance." He grabs my hand propelling me to the center of the room as soon as Edge is at the bar.

"Don't aggravate Edge, please, Doug. He'll take me home and this is the first time I've ever been to a club." I can't help but feel some excitement as I watch people on the dance floor. The exhaustion from earlier disappears as he pulls me onto the lit-up floor. The music is loud and thumping up through the floor. Doug grabs me and starts to grind on me and I instantly turn.

"Behave."

"You need alcohol, baby. Come on, let go, Eve. Let your body move to the beat."

I glance around and watch people of all shapes and colors dance and move. Closing my eyes for a moment, I let myself feel the beat and start to move.

"That's it. I knew you'd be a natural." A smile tugs at my lips. We dance a few moments until I swing into Ryder's huge arms. I almost scream, but his frown tells me I should smile instead.

"Your drink is on the table." He takes my arm and drags me off the floor. I hear Doug yelling at Ryder that he's no fun.

"Eve, sweetheart." Ryder brings me to a booth in the middle where Edge is scowling at me and Dolly is hanging on him. "Here." He hands me a drink that's pink.

"Jason is particular with you... so until he gets here, no more dancing all right?" His kind brown eyes search my face.

"I haven't seen you around much." I sip the drink. "This is delicious by the way."

"Go slow, Eve." He looks down at his phone as the alcohol already warms me. Doug thrusts on the dance floor and laughs at himself.

"Oh yay, you're back." Dolly throws herself at me. "Here." She hands me a shot.

"Yeah... I think you need some water, babe." Edge looks at her.

"Hurray—to us!" She clanks my shot glass. I have no choice but to follow and shoot it. The sting is so strong I visualize fire coming out of my mouth.

LETHAL

"What was that?" I say, fanning my mouth with my hand.

"Mescal, what else?" Like I know what Mescal is.

"Um... Edge, you need to get control. I don't want to deal with a pissed-off Blade," Ryder snaps at him.

"Let's dance." I grab Dolly's hand.

"Fucking great." Ryder hisses behind us as we wiggle up to a happy and sweaty Doug. The music takes over and this time, when Doug grabs me from behind, I lean my head back and sway with him. The song changes and I twirl out of his arms into Dolly who reaches for me to grind on her. I look over at two miserable faces. Edge's hands are clenched and Ryder seems to be looking downstairs.

"Hey, can I dance with you two?" A tall guy with bad hair and stupid-looking hipster clothes tries to dance with us.

"Fuck off, unless you have a death wish," Dolly yells in his face. He backs away, shaking his head.

We both start laughing. "I need to pee. I'll be right back."

"I'll be waiting." She grabs Doug, who was dancing with another girl, and they both start putting on a show. I can't help but giggle at poor Edge's face. I head for the dark door that is marked women when a tattooed hand reaches for me and spins me around.

The man is tall and completely tattooed up to his neck. Instantly, I pull my arm away and decide right then that I have to get myself another knife. Jason keeps me locked up in his compound, and I refuse to be touched by anyone but him.

"You Blade's whore?" His breath stinks of weed and alcohol and I take a step back. Hating that, I look over his shoulder for help. See, this is why I need a knife. I turn, but he grabs me again.

"Are you insane?" I hiss.

"Answer me...You're his, aren't you?" I wrinkle my nose at his ugly face. He's bald and his eyes are dead. They remind me of Pauly the prick's eyes. And suddenly I shudder because he's not alone. Three other tattooed guys are right behind him.

"I'm going to give you a message. You tell him I want my shit. You see, he and I go way back, but business is business." He moves closer.

"If it's business then you should tell him yourself." I turn again and he touches me.

"Holy shit, you are stupid. He'll kill you. Back the fuck off," I scream. They laugh.

"Pretty full of yourself, huh? Listen, princess, you may be gorgeous, but Blade doesn't give two shits about any woman. In fact, since we're in business together, he always shares his whores with me." He trails his dirty fingernails over my throat toward my breast. Then I feel it. Heat, power, a pull. It's him. I know same as I know this pig in front of me might die tonight.

Blade.

He stands like a god of a beast. Magnificent and untamed. My breath stutters in my throat and desire flutters in my core. *What is wrong with me?*

"Darrel." His voice radiates off the walls and all eyes swing to his. Green fire pours out of them as he looks at me. He doesn't have to tell me to go to him. I do. Like a moth goes to a flame, I go to my king.

"Did you touch her?" His voice is eerily calm and I see fear flicker for a second in the other man's eyes.

He chuckles and holds his hands out looking at his buddies for support. "You always share, Blade. This one might be the most beautiful, but pussy is pus—" Jason pulls me behind him. In a blink he has his hand around the bald guy's throat.

Hands pull me back into the crowd and I see Ryder, Edge, and four other Disciples surround Blade. I pull my arm preparing to knee whoever is taking me away from Jason in the nuts.

"Try it, wildcat," he snarls, and I glance up into blue eyes so dark they almost look black. Axel has me and he is furious. "If I were you, I would sit down and shut up, Eve. You've caused enough problems." He moves me to the booth.

"Axel..." I try to pull back. "Jason needs me. Axel what the hell?" He swings toward me.

"Do you think our lives are a fucking joke? This is us. We're not good men, and now you have Blade all screwed in the head. He's changing and that makes him dangerous. Meaning he's not thinking clearly because he has you in his brain." He points to his head. "I can't make him not want you—you're in his blood—but I can keep you safe so he can do what he needs to do."

"This was not my fault. I was on my way to the restroom and that piece of shit grabbed me. Oh, as Blade's whore I'm supposed to tell him that scumbag wants his shit." Suddenly I'm not trying to get away.

"Axel... I don't feel good." He looks at me.

"Christ." He takes me over to the restroom and zooms us in as if it's no big deal that a huge hot biker guy is in the women's room.

"Hey Axel," I hear as I burst into the stall and barely make it to the toilet. I hadn't had any food so all that comes up is my cocktail and shot. I lean my head against the cool metal wall, not even caring that it's probably full of germs. My mouth stops watering as my stomach settles until I hear, "Is she okay?"

"Too much to drink. She's fine, Nicole," Axel snaps.

"She's not pregnant, is she?" And my stomach that was starting to calm starts to knot again as I lean over and retch again.

"Fuck no, and if I hear any rumor that she is, I'll know it was you."

I brace myself and push my hair back. "I'm definitely not pregnant," I snap at both of them as I try to rinse my mouth.

"Phew... That"—she points to the stall I vacated—"reminded me of the early days of my pregnancy." She smiles at me, fluffs her hair in the mirror, and sashays out. I close my eyes. *Nightmare.* When I open them, two sapphire eyes stare at me as if he can read my mind.

"You're not, right?" he demands.

I look at him through the mirror then back at my pale face.

"There is no way I'm pregnant." I roll my eyes and almost tell him that I can't, but why try to convince someone who is suspicious of everybody? "I'm not used to drinking and the excitement—that's all."

"That's good, for your sake." He slowly nods and opens the bathroom door. Two girls giggle as we step out.

"I'm tired," I snap. His threat not only bothers me, but it's none of his business. "I'd like to go home. Or should I wait for Jason?"

"Oh, don't worry. I'm sending you home." He propels me out to the blaring music and neon lights. I barely get to grab my bag before he is urging me down the stairs. I don't even get to say goodbye to anyone. They're all on the dance floor. The laser lights downstairs are going wild with the beat of the music, but now it's making me nauseous. Axel guides me outside and the fresh cool air hits my face like a welcome friend. I take a huge gulp and close my eyes as Axel barks an order. Some guy named Tim apparently will be taking me home. A couple of girls scream and laugh next to me waiting for the valet, their loud, excited voices announcing where they are going next. I feel ancient, and I have to be younger than them. I can't believe that was my first nightclub experience. If I wasn't feeling woozy, I'd be pissed. As it is, I'm somewhat grateful when the door shuts behind me. As I reach over and turn the vents on me, I wonder If I got a bug or something. The last couple of days I've felt crappy. Closing my eyes, I let Tim the prospect drive me home.

EIGHTEEN

BLADE/JASON

The sun is rising as Axel, Ryder, Edge, and I pull up to the house. It's almost startling how quiet and calm it is at 5:00 a.m. All the crap that is strewn around the front yard takes a back burner to the sunrise. Orange, yellow, purple, even blue grace the sky and it seems surreal that less than three hours ago, I was slicing up the fingers on Darrel's right hand. I should have done more, but I didn't want it to be completely obvious that Eve has become my full-blown obsession. I only sliced off the tips to remind him never to touch what belongs to me again. This is what happens when you get too big. The worst people who walk the earth start sniffing around. Unfortunately, they get power and money because they have nothing to lose. When you are raised with absolutely nothing, you learn real quick how to survive.

Since the lab is down, everyone is coming out of the woodwork. I take a drag of my cigarette and continue to watch the sunrise. The light yellow ball slowly rises over the trees. I'm ashamed that it's been years since I actually enjoyed a sunrise.

"I'm going to bed," Ryder grumbles as he passes, boots crunching on the gravel.

Edge looks at us, sighs, and starts toward the Tahoe. "I have something that needs my attention. I'll be back in a few hours."

"Kiss Dolly low for us." Axel chuckles as Edge slams the Tahoe's door and puts it in reverse to maneuver around us.

I inhale and close my eyes. The adrenaline is wearing off and I'm exhausted.

"Prez? How do you want to proceed? This shit that happened tonight is going to continue."

Blinking, I drop my cigarette and snuff it out with my boot. "I know. I'm sick of it, Axel. All this shit that comes with drugs is getting old, man."

Axel's blue eyes are alert. "We need to get out of dealing. All of us have lost the passion for it."

I sniff the cool morning air. "It's not that simple and you know it."

He reaches into his pants pocket and pulls out a joint. Lighting it, he inhales and says, "You think the Feds got to Doc?"

I take the joint from his hand and inhale deeply. "Probably. Either that or they got to Sandy."

He sighs and takes the joint back, raising his hands as if he's stretching. "We're getting too rich and old to go to jail."

I grunt and let the mellowness take over my tense muscles. "I need to talk to Dimitri. If he wants to continue getting anything from us, he needs to get his crew under control."

As the sun spreads her morning shadows, Axel's eyes seem almost black. He nods. "Blade... one more thing." He takes a deep inhale, squints at me, and releases his smoke. "I don't sugarcoat things, don't know how to."

The hair on the back of my neck stands up. "What?" I say, my throat tight.

"Eve was sick tonight." He doesn't look at me but stares out at the horizon.

"So what?"

"She puked her guts out at the club, that's what." He says this so fucking mellow I almost laugh.

"How much did she drink?"

His lips twitch and he looks at me. "Not much." He leaves it all hanging in the air. I almost can see the thought bubble on top of his head like a cartoon saying all kinds of shit that I don't want to know. I shake my head and wonder what kind of shit we're smoking.

"I'm going to bed for a couple of hours." He starts to move past me then stops, looking at his boots. "I hope she's worth it."

Again, I see the words drift away with him with a cartoon pop. *Fuck!* Leave it to Axel to have some crazy shit to smoke. I rub the back of my neck. I'm filthy and won't deal with any of Axel's insinuations. Eve threw up, but it means nothing except that she's a lightweight when it comes to drinking.

After that stuff I smoked, I need a shower and coffee to get my mind functioning. Although I do have a nice numb buzz of bliss all over my body. I swing open the clubhouse front door and almost gag. *Christ*. It smells like dirty feet. Bob is lying on the couch, feet hanging over the edge while he snores so loudly it's amazing someone hasn't thrown him outside. I feel sorry for him. When Amy discovers his smell, he's going to wish someone had put him outside. It's times like this when the clubhouse is still a place where I can feel a sense of pride. For being built in the fifties it's held up amazingly well. The plumbing always needs work, but come on—with the amount of brothers coming in and out this door, the old farm-style house is in good shape. As I take the stairs, I almost hear my father's laugh over by the bar and the sound of him screaming at my brother Chuck. Forcing my mind to understand that it's the weed talking, I move my legs faster as if running away can help. Shit needs to be taken care of. At certain times, I need to be available to talk to some pushers and a couple of our arms dealers.

I stop at my door and let myself calm for a second. My heart races. I can't seem to shake Axel's words.

Sick. Eve was sick. I unlock our door, blinking to let my eyes adjust to the darkness. I grit my teeth. Her smell is everywhere in our room. My cock wants to sink into her silken walls, fuck her until my mind is numb with exhausted satisfaction. Ignoring my addiction, I turn on the shower, strip out of my blood-splattered clothes, and wash quickly.

I throw the towel in the corner and notice a wicker hamper over by the sink. All her creams and perfumes are set nicely over on her side of the sink. I shake my wet head marveling that somehow we have become a couple. "What the fuck?" I look around at my bathroom and it's like a Claritin commercial. You know where the blur is removed and you can see everything clearly? Her hairbrush, makeup, and blow dryer sit in a wicker basket. Both our toothbrushes touch in the brass holder. Rubbing a hand through my hair, I turn off the light and leave. A small groan and a sigh force me to look at her as she turns to her other side. Gritting my teeth, I can tell I'm losing what little motivation I have. Especially as I allow my eyes to feast on her perfect ass almost begging to be touched. *Goddamn it.* My eyes go to the ceiling as I breathe through my nose. Why didn't I jerk myself off in the shower? I'm like an alcoholic who has been white-knuckling it and the body in the bed is my poison. Somehow this wild gypsy has turned my whole world upside down. I pull on my jeans and stand over her, watching her sleep. So warm and delicious. I turn to grab a T-shirt when she kicks down the covers and shows me one long tan leg. My cock is rock hard and getting painful, and I'm losing this battle. Maybe I should wake her up and fuck her—she's mine after all. Also, I cut a scumbag's fingertips off because he dared to touch her. Almost as if she knows I'm in torture, she turns onto her back and blinks her long, sooty lashes open.

"Hey." Her voice is all raspy and sexy with sleep.

"Hey yourself." I sit down and caress her soft skin. "Fuck," I groan as I bend down and claim her soft lips. She moans and opens for me. Our tongues twist and we drink each other in. Fire burns through my veins with her, and it's becoming a serious addiction.

My hand sweeps up to one full breast, her nipple already hard, and I have to taste it.

"I have shit to do, but I can't do anything until I take care of this." I lift my T-shirt off of her and stare at her perfection.

"Look at these nipples." She groans and stretches like a cat. I reach and grab her sides as I lift that ripe tit into my mouth and suck.

"Jason," she growls and I lick her nipple. Everything I need to do can wait. I lost the war; I'm caught in her slumbering web of seduction. I stand up, ripping my T-shirt off and tossing my jeans to the floor. Reaching for her, I roll her onto her stomach and caress her smooth, flawless skin. Nothing but creamy perfection. I lift her up so her ass is in the air and she moans into the mattress.

"Spread your legs." My voice sounds as harsh as my hands are gentle. She maneuvers them open.

"Christ." I caress her ass then line myself onto her wet pussy, rubbing my semen on her cream and thrust in. "Jesus," I grunt out. "Tightest cunt ever, and it's mine." Thrusting my thick cock into her slick walls, I'm almost crazed with her scent and whimpers of "Oh God." I'm close, fuck, I was close the second I buried myself inside her. I dig my fingers into her thin hips and fuck her hard and deep.

Her hands are holding onto the sheet as she rests her head on her forearms, whimpering, "Jason... I'm close... Oh. My. *God I love it...*"

Again, I thrust hard and reach my hand around to rub her swollen nub.

"Yeah... that's it. So wet. You gonna come for me?"

"Uh-huh," she cries out as her pussy contracts. She's so wet it makes it easy to rub her hard and fast.

"Fuck yeah," I grunt my approval as her pussy squeezes and pulses on my dick. I close my eyes for a second, my release so massive I see spots. I think I call her name. All I know is my cock is jerking into her hot core and I'm weightless, peaceful.

She slumps down. Her lips are open as she catches her breath, but her mouth is smiling. I want to drop onto the bed, pull her into my arms, and go to sleep with her. But that will have to come later. Reluctantly I pull out and she moans her disapproval.

"I have to go take care of stuff. Trust me, all I want to do is spend the day in bed with you." I slap her ass. She squeals and turns over. We both slowly smile.

"Jason." She licks her lips, her eyes huge. "I think I'm…" Cocking my head, I force myself to look away. Whatever she wants to tell me is not something that should be said right now. I back away and rub my hands through my hair as I go into the bathroom. I run the hot water and splash some on my face as I catch my reflection and freeze. The face that stares back at me is different and it's in my eyes. They look alive, the haunted look gone. Dropping my head, I try to focus on what I need to get done rather than the gypsy in my bed. Reaching for a washcloth, I warm it up. I find her lying on our bed propped up on two pillows, legs crossed, one foot bouncing up and down. My heart tightens at her complete look of happiness. *Christ*!

"Spread your legs." She doesn't hesitate. Reaching down, I gently wipe away our sex. She inhales and our eyes lock as we stare at each other. She's the one who breaks the connection by scooting back.

"Thanks." She reaches for the sheet. "Jason?"

I pull open my dresser drawer and slip on another black T-shirt. "What?"

"I need a blade."

I stop reaching for my pants to look at her. She's serious as she stares me straight in the eyes and I can't help but laugh and lift my hands. "I'm right here." She rolls her eyes, but her lips twitch into a smile.

"Seriously."

"Seriously." I pull on my jeans. "Why do you need a knife? I'll always protect you."

She shrugs and picks at the satin edge of our sheet. "I've always had one. It wasn't until I got with you and I've lived... like this."

I reach for my pack of cancer sticks and light up. As I inhale, my eyes sweep her. My cock hardens.

"You unhappy, Angel?"

She drops the sheet and crawls to the end of the bed. When she wraps her arms around my neck, I force myself to breathe. Her full tits and hard nipples rub against me.

"Truth?" Her voice is velvet soft. I should say no. Instead, like an asshole, I nod.

"You make me happy. I think... I think I might be falling for you," she whispers the last part, her sweet lips almost touching mine. I'm trying to get my numb brain to work. Her words stop time, and my mind goes to that dream I had the first night I took her. *I love you* she had said in that dream. Suddenly I feel caged, hot, like I stayed out in the sun too long. I pull back and her arms drop to her sides. Our room needs air, the scent of us making me confused. The lines are being crossed. I turn toward the door. "I'll see about getting you one of my blades."

"Jason, wait..." I look back and she reaches for me like a golden goddess wanting the unthinkable. She must see it in my eyes because she shrugs, says, "Nothing," and slides back under the covers.

I'm an asshole. Rubbing my hands over my face, I glance up at the ceiling. "Look, Eve... maybe if I'm not completely wiped out tonight, we can go check on your father."

As soon as the words are out, I regret it because she's in my arms in a second, her sweet lips all over my face.

"Eve." Pulling her off me, I add, "I said *maybe*." I can't help the grin that creeps out. She jumps back into my arms. The fact that I'm enjoying this alerts my fuzzy brain that I'm definitely in too deep with her.

"I got to go, babe." She rubs her nose on mine and my heart speeds up. Unable to stop myself, I take her lips for a slow burn of a kiss and force myself to walk out.

The day drags on and when my mind clears around noon, I can't stop thinking about her. The way she can be shy and fierce all at once. She is by far the most independent woman I've ever known. Yet there is a real need to nurture her and if I were a nicer man, I'd let her go. She's getting attached and I'm... I'm the president of a one-percenter motorcycle club. This thing we've got going is for regular people, not fucked-up souls who have no idea what these feelings are.

"Fuck you, Ryder. What do you think, Prez?" My eyes take in the table and all my officers staring at me. And I have no idea what the fuck they've been saying. We've been cooped up in here all day. It stinks of cigarettes and stale liquor. One of the beer signs in the corner is going out. The fluorescent waterfall of beer is flashing like an annoying strobe light making me want to take my gun out and shoot it.

"Cash flow. How we gonna deal with it?" Axel chimes in as Edge and Ryder look at each other and down at their beers, both not even trying to hide their grins.

I sit up and grab my bottle of Budweiser. "The drug should be put to rest. I have no interest in bringing it back to life." Silence is all I hear, followed by Axel telling everyone how we need to stay quiet until this is final.

I glance at the clock—it's close to five, and I tune out the conversation about selling marijuana while we decide what's best.

"I want to deal with guns and that's it." Heaving myself up, my exhausted body starts to reject the lack of sleep. I toss the beer bottle in the trash can, hearing it shatter as I move the old brown filing cabinet so I can open the safe. The room goes quiet again minus the annoying hum from the sign. I don't care. I'm too tired to care. Moving money aside and a bunch of Glocks, I pull out my very first knife. It was my grandfather's. He brought it back with him from Vietnam. It's nothing special, just a standard hunting knife. But the old wooden handle has the Disciples logo branded on both sides. The brand is the same one that Eve has on her neck. I take it out and close the safe, moving the filing cabinet back in front of it.

No one speaks as I walk toward the door and kick an empty bottle of Jack Daniels to the corner as I stop next to Ryder.

"We're done. I need sleep."

Axel clears his voice. "O-kay, so you've decided?"

"Yeah, I've decided I want to fuck and sleep. Everything else can wait until tomorrow. Ryder?"

He glances up from the laptop he's been staring at all day. "Yeah, Prez?"

"Tell Amy to send up dinner for me and Eve." He grabs his phone and starts typing as I look around the room daring anyone to say anything.

His phone dings. "She says she already has it ready, Prez. You go get some rest. I'll know more tomorrow." He sets down his phone and goes back to his computer.

We found a couple of stupid bikers stalking around the Hemet lab site on one of the security cameras we planted in a tree on the property. They were not Disciples and they were dumb enough not to know we have serious surveillance equipment at all our businesses. It's only a matter of time until Ryder figures out who the two stupid fucks are. They basically smiled at the cameras, their tattoos visible. Obviously, it looks like Doc has been doing business on the side, another headache.

"Thanks, man." All my guys stand and if I wasn't so tired, I might smile at Axel who looks like his eyes are going to pop out of his head.

"Meeting adjourned until tomorrow. What time, Prez?"

"Later. I have something I need to take care of in the morning." I don't enlighten them that I'm too tired to take Eve tonight to see her old man. As I'm closing the conference room door, I see Amy carrying a huge tray of food. My stomach growls. "Amy, why don't you get one of the guys to help you?" I snap as I make her give me the large tray.

"They're all drunk or high. Besides, I don't trust them around Eve." She marches up the stairs with me.

I arch a brow. "What does that mean?" Instantly my body goes on alert. My heart starts to pound in my temple. "Has anyone bothered her?"

"Only Crystal." She smirks.

I reach the top of the stairs and give Amy my full attention. "Spit it out."

She smiles at me and I almost drop the tray. "Fine. You've been gone too much." Before I can respond, she cocks her head and I nod for her to continue. "Crystal's been trolling around and I heard her telling Eve that her time is almost up." She puts her hands on her chest. "Now I know that Eve is the one, but maybe it's time to let others know." She straightens her shirt.

"Trust me, word is spreading," I grunt as I walk toward my door.

"Good," she says over her shoulder and walks down the stairs as if she doesn't have a care in the world.

What the hell? Somehow without even trying, my little badass gypsy has everyone eating out of the palm of her hand. Well, all but Axel, but he doesn't trust women.

I adjust the tray and open the door and instantly breathe in her coconut scent. Her smell reminds me of sunshine and happiness.

Christ, I need sleep. I'm not even making sense to myself. Eve is sitting on the edge of the pool table dressed to kill, and a pang of guilt fills my head.

She looks up and drops her phone on the pool table. I absorb her very essence as she moves toward me.

I sigh. "Babe, I'm beat. Can I take you tomorrow to see your dad?"

Setting the tray down, I watch the different emotions play upon her face. Her dark sooty lashes blink back her disappointment. She shimmies out of her short, military-green jacket and drapes it on the back of the chair.

"Actually, tomorrow is better. He'll have more energy." She smiles and adrenaline floods my body. Smoothly, she moves to the bar area. If I thought she would be uncomfortable with this morning, I'm wrong. We both seem to fit and I like it.

"Do you want a beer?" Her raspy voice coats over me like caramel on an apple, and I drop my tired body in a chair, stretching my legs out.

"Or whiskey?" She picks up the bottle of Jack Daniels and gently shakes it. Her eyes sweep my form. I chuckle as her cheeks turn pink in seconds.

"I missed you today. Bring the bottle and come kiss me."

She cocks her head, a saucy grin on her face. "Jack it is." As she passes, she grabs two tumblers.

"Hi." She leans over me, her honey-streaked hair falling down my chest as I reach and bring her sweet lips to mine. She tastes like minty toothpaste and I deepen the kiss because I can.

When I finally let her up for air, she caresses my cheek, but there's a small frown in between her eyebrows. "You look so tired."

I lean back in my chair and reach for the bottle. Unscrewing it, I let the hot, spicy flavor burn and warm me up. "It's hard being king."

She stops for a second and cocks her head to look at me. It's like a caress really, her eyes soft as she slowly smiles and looks down at the tray. She bites her lip as if she's thinking of something and all I do is stare as she gracefully unwraps the aluminum foil that covers our dinner. The room instantly fills with the aroma of steak, carrots, and sautéed cauliflower.

"Oh my God... this smells so good. I hope you pay Amy a ton of money. Her cooking's amazing." She unwraps the bread, her eyes huge as she waves the baguette at me. "It's still warm."

It's physically impossible not to touch her. I reach out a hand and tug her into the chair next to me.

"Come here, beautiful. Sit."

She reaches for the napkins and silverware and arches a brow at me. "Are you okay?"

I chuckle. "Probably not. Drink with me." I pour two generous shots.

Eve leans over, elbows on the table. Her long, slender fingers wrap around the glass and I shift as my cock gets hard. Jesus Christ, I could fuck her ten times a day and it be wouldn't be enough.

"What's wrong?" her voice brings me back to her.

I shrug. Leaning forward, I place my hand on her leg. "I'm trying to figure out my next move. It would be nice if I don't have to kill anyone."

She doesn't even blink. If I've scared her, she does an amazing job of hiding it.

"This is what you deal with everyday? Always looking over your shoulder?"

Our eyes meet as she moves closer and her warm breath is mine to steal. Slowly I answer, "Yes, this is my life."

She swallows, her eyes huge as I caress her cheek and stare at her parted lips.

"I keep telling you I'm a bad guy, Angel." Our faces are inches apart, but I need her to believe this. Dropping my hand, I lean back and reach for my glass. "Don't get confused and think I'm some kind of hero."

LETHAL

A slow, sexy smile graces her lips and it hits me right in the chest. It's like she's a witch or a fairy that's cast a spell on me. And fuck if I care. I can't help myself as I lean forward again.

"You don't seem upset about that?"

"Because I'm not." She smiles. "What should we toast to?" her voice purrs into my lips.

I can't help but grin. "How about to bad guys?"

Pouting for a moment, she smiles. "How about... to bad guys and bad girls." That saucy stare goes right to my cock.

I clink her glass to mine. "I love it," I say, and shoot the whole glass. This time, the whiskey sends a soothing warmth down my throat.

She watches me. Her eyes narrow and she takes a dainty sip. I burst out laughing, grab her face, and kiss those plump red lips, which taste like bourbon and heaven, and I know in this moment, she might very well be my downfall. It takes all my willpower to stop kissing her before I can't look at myself in the mirror tomorrow.

I sit up and look around my room. Much as she's done with the bathroom, Eve has slowly become a part of my bedroom. Her gossip magazines litter the coffee table. Her shoes are under a chair. Trying not to think about why this doesn't bother me I say, "I'm hungry. Let's eat."

She looks down at her plate. Her long golden tresses fall over one shoulder. Again, I can't seem to stop this need to touch her as she cuts her steak.

"And if you finish all your food, I have a surprise for you," I tease, caressing the softness with my fingers. She stops eating for a moment and cocks her head. I wink and pop a sautéed carrot in my mouth. Her eyes drop to my mouth as I chew.

I chuckle and dig into my dinner. She gives me one of those smiles that goes straight to my chest then travels down to my cock. I sense her excitement and reach down into my boot to pull out the knife, setting it in front of her. She puts down her bread and her fingers glide over the knife stroking the wooden handle that sports the exact brand that's on her neck.

"It was my grandfather's." I lean back. "He brought it back with him from Vietnam."

Her big blue eyes focus on me. "This has sentimental value. Why would you give it to me?"

I lean over and start eating again.

"Jason?"

"Trust me... he would love for you to have it. He had a weakness for blondes with long legs."

She shakes her head and starts eating again. "You confuse me."

I take the last bite of steak and push the plate back. "He's the one who started the Disciples—well he and some other buddies. All they wanted to do was ride their bikes and do drugs. It wasn't until my dad came along that he figured out how much money he could make selling weed." Swirling my glass in front of me, I take a deep sip. "Then one day, my buddy and I were messing around in my dad's basement. Both of us thought we were the shit and we created a drug."

"And...?"

"It changed everything. It wasn't like crystal and it wasn't X, although the high you could get was better." As soon as my dad found us and the drug... it took us to a different league. The demons I keep at bay are there wanting to come out tonight. Or maybe I want her to truly know me.

"Jason? I'm here for you. You can trust me."

My eyes scan her face. The turmoil that is my life merges with the shit that is her life. I take another swig of whiskey, my eyes holding hers. I see that day so clearly. It was years ago, but if I close my eyes I can feel the sting of the rain hitting me in the face as a member of the military police informed me. Her hand touches my cheek making me blink and look away.

"Please don't shut me out," she whispers, causing me to look at her.

"My brother and old man died in that explosion. I didn't blame myself. They knew what they were doing." I reach for her hand. "I have a cousin, David. We were close. We're the same age. Fuck, babe, you don't want this shit." My eyes dart to the window. The inky blackness outside makes me pull away.

"Hey." Both her hands are on my face. Her blue eyes are pooled with tears but her voice is strong. "I want to hear and know everything about you."

Jesus Christ, I should not have gone here. I'm breaking my code, letting her in. My demons spill out like a child with a secret. "David had a girlfriend and a daughter. A fucking little girl with gold curls and she was with them when the explosion happened."

The truth fills the room. Eight years of agony has just been aired. This time I can't sit still. I don't want to see her face, so I lean my forehead against the cool window. Like the grim reaper, my past is coming to take me down.

"In one day, I lost them all—even the baby girl." My voice is gruff. I feel her hand on my back and don't give a shit. Right now, she's all I need. I turn and jerk her into my arms and bury my face in her hair and breathe.

"It's not your fault. Accidents happen. You're not to blame." She kisses my forehead, my cheeks; her hot tears drift onto me as I taste sorrow.

Lifting my head, I say, "That's where you're wrong. The day that baby girl died was the day I changed."

She shakes her head, tears streaming down her cheeks. "You weren't even there."

I pull back, suddenly disgusted at my weakness for letting this come out. "You don't get it?" My voice makes me sound like an ass. "I'm the one who created the drug. The lab blew up, and no one knows how or why. But it sure as fuck had to do with my drug.

Of that I can guarantee you." I'm done. I need to leave, sleep on one of the downstairs couches.

"You are not responsible." She grabs ahold of my arms, her nails attached, causing me to stop. "I don't know why horrible things happen to us. I don't know why some people seem to go through life with no tragedies." She lets go and snakes her arms around the back of my neck forcing me to connect with her. "You're not bad or good Jason. You're human."

I growl out my pain as I jerk her willing body tighter to mine. Her hands lace into my hair. I blink back all the horrible memories, nightmares I've had about what happened that day. But she's right. I wasn't there and I have no clue about who blew them up. And since David is gone—last I heard he was a junkie in New York—clearly, he's not in any condition to find out.

"You have to let the dead rest in peace." Her voice cracks and my neck is drenched in her tears. Exhaustion mentally and physically is taking me down. I pull back and start to frantically undress her then jerk off my shirt and pants. Reaching for the lights, I turn them off and guide her to our bed. I close my eyes and let her warm body merge into my cold one. I don't even want to fuck her right now... only hold her like this forever. Maybe for one night, I can be human.

NINETEEN

EVE

I smell coffee, but I'm too tired to open my eyes. My hands feel around for him but the bed is cold. I groan and roll over trying to open my eyes. They feel like small weights have been put on them. A mug of coffee sits on the nightstand along with the knife that belonged to Jason's grandfather. I reach out and touch the wooden base, the Disciples brand still clear. A little flutter of excitement runs through my chest. Jason gave me his grandfather's blade. It sounds crazy, but this is the most thoughtful gift anyone's ever given me and I stroke it lovingly. Hearing the shower, my mind travels back to last night. Jason told me things. He confided in me, he…"Shit." I bolt up. He's supposed to be taking me to see my dad. *Fuck that… he is* taking me to see my dad. I throw off the covers and instantly steady myself as a wave of dizziness takes over.

"What the hell?" I groan as I steady myself on the bed. My stomach does not feel good at all. We went to bed without finishing dinner, so the remains of last night's food fill my nose right now. I close my eyes and breathe through the nausea. *Relax, Eve. You need food*, I chant in my head over and over. The last thing I need to do is throw up. Jason will never take me to see my dad if he thinks I'm sick.

"Eve?" I jump and look up at the most beautiful man ever. My heart flutters and I have to remind myself not to be too obvious He stands above me in jeans and a gray T-shirt drinking coffee and frowning at me.

"I'm up." It's lame, and I cringe at how stupid I sound.

Jason cocks his head, his damn green eyes scanning my face. *Perfect.* I feel shy today, I don't want to look at him because if he's shut down like he usually is, I don't think I can handle it after last night. A warm gentle hand touches my chin forcing me to look at him.

"You tired, baby? You want to rest and go tomorrow?" It's caring and intimate and I'm so relieved that he's not pulling back that I'm almost self-conscious.

My hand goes up to my wild hair and I stand up smiling. "No, I'm fine." I swallow back the saliva.

He doesn't look convinced, but I'm saved by modern technology as his phone goes off, though his eyes narrow at me.

"What's up, Axel?" He walks toward the window, his muscled back rippling in the gray T-shirt.

He hasn't put on his cut yet and my eyes take in all of him before I enter the bathroom. Grasping the cool counter of the sink, I breathe in and out and feel like absolute shit. Maybe I shouldn't see my dad. God, what if I have the flu? I would hate to give it to him. Turning on the shower, I step in and sigh as the soothing hot water helps. See? I'm fine. A million times better.

Quickly I throw on some light makeup and look at myself. I'm presentable, but do I look fabulous? No, and I don't have time to go crazy trying to fix myself up. I switch off the light and scream as I almost plow straight into Jason who is frowning at me again.

"What?" I hate when I can tell he knows, like everything. "Why are you scowling at me?" I go around him and jerk open my underwear drawer and grab a black G-string and matching bra. His eyes are like lasers watching every move I make until I sigh and give in. "What, Jason?"

His stare starts at the top of my head and follows all the way to my bare feet and he looks me straight in the eyes. "Nothing... I'll be downstairs waiting."

I roll my eyes as I finish dressing then reach for my black UGGs, blowing my hair out of my face.

Grabbing my bag, I smirk as I wrap my new Disciples knife in one of Jason's T-shirts. As I roll my neck, I pull on my three-quarter-length jacket trying to shake this crappy feeling.

I don't even have to walk into the kitchen to know that my stomach is not going to like it at all. I smell rather than see the huge skillet that Amy is cooking bacon and sausages in.

"Shit." I stop and try to swallow back the bile rising up.

"Eve! You okay?" Amy's cool hands touch my fevered cheeks. Unfortunately she smells like bacon and I have to turn away as I sit on a barstool and reach for a napkin to cover my nose. Or maybe to help soothe me as I look at the offending pan sizzling and popping with grease.

"My stomach is not happy today," I say, looking around the room because I don't want to deal with Amy's knowing eyes. There're actually around six or seven bikers waiting for Amy's cooking. One's staring at me and I raise an eyebrow at him. He smirks and turns to a buddy to talk shit I'm sure. *Asshole*. A lot of these guys are creeps.

Blocking them out of my mind along with the massive amount of pork in the pan, I mumble, "Have you seen Jason?"

She says nothing and I have to look at her. Again this woman is rumored to be fiftyish and she looks thirtyish. She eyes me then goes into the refrigerator and pulls out a smartwater and a bottle of C Monster. "Hydrate." She hands me a banana too, and I want to hug her.

"Thank you."

Nodding, she and turns back to the disgusting bacon.

"And Jason's outside, Eve." It feels like I'm twelve and going off to school as I slink off the barstool, throwing all the beverages into my bag. I walk out toward the sunny porch where a group of guys are talking to Jason. They all get quiet as soon as I approach. I straighten my shoulders and peel my banana.

Axel looks like he wants to strangle me, so I flash him a big smile. His blue eyes narrow. Jason doesn't even stop talking and snakes his muscled arm around my shoulder while barking orders. Sighing, I nibble on my banana and glance around. The yard might as well be a motorcycle shop. There're parts strewn all over the gravel, and the smell of gasoline makes me gag. I turn my nose into Jason's spicy, clean smell. It seems to calm me.

"You ready, Angel?" his gravelly voice startles me.

"Yes." I clear my voice and toss the banana peel over on an old picnic table littered with trash, wiping my hands on my jeans. *Holy shit!* I'm going to see my father. The butterflies take over. Jason clasps our hands together as he guides me toward his bike. Crystal shoots me a horrible look as she breezes past us, her awful perfume making me want to puke. And for the first time since I heard about that woman, I don't feel threatened. Jason doesn't want her; he wants me and I intend to get him.

I smile as he completely ignores her. I'm not as nice. She's been giving me crap from day one. So I wave and have to bite my lip not to laugh at her reddening face and the loud slam of the door behind her.

"Stop it." He shakes his head.

I can't help it and start laughing. "It's not my fault you have horrible taste in girlfriends."

This time, he laughs. "Don't talk that way about yourself," he says and kisses me in front of everyone. There are snickers and whistling behind us.

"I wasn't talking about me," I speak into his mouth. It comes out breathless instead of sarcastic. He pulls away and shakes his head as he reaches for a shiny silver helmet hanging on the handlebar. A bright red Disciples logo is on the back. He moves to put it on my head and stops as our eyes connect. God, I'm hot, flushed. What is wrong with me?

"Who shares my bed?"

"Me."

He smiles and I blink back my tears... I don't even know why. Maybe because he's so hot and he wants me. And just like that I feel so much better. I move my purse to the back and climb on. He plops the helmet on and settles in his seat. Excitement tingles down my spine as his bike rumbles to life. I scoot as close to him as I can. He reaches back and his hand rests casually on my thigh as I wrap my arms around his waist. We take off, stirring up gravel and dust and causing the guys behind us to yell. I close my eyes and lay my helmet against his back as he maneuvers his bike. It seems as though we left seconds ago when we stop out of nowhere. I open my eyes as Jason turns on his right turn signal. I lift my head, trying to see exactly where we are. It's a nice neighborhood and the bike rumbles past a couple of houses with large green yards. We pull into a small parking lot. I take off my helmet and observe a large white building with a beautiful lawn. Roses and flowerpots are all over. An ambulance is parked in front with an oxygen tank truck behind it.

I pull the helmet off and stare at the newness of this place.

"Is this it?" I grab his arm as I get off the bike. It took like ten minutes. *Ten minutes* is how far away my dad is from me. Hot tears sting my eyes already. I grab ahold of Jason's strong, tan hand as he guides me through the large sliding glass doors. A girl with dark brown hair and glasses is at the front desk. Her eyes widen as we approach.

"Hey Blade, welcome back." She smiles at Jason and here comes the nausea again.

"Don't tell me—Ashley, right?" Jason grins and my hand tightens on his. He looks down at me.

"Yes, that's me." She rubs her hands on her dress. Visions of me punching her dance in my head. She glances over at me, and her smile promptly fades as her gaze follows down to our hands.

She clears her throat. "Go ahead and sign in."

Jason lets go of my hand as he quickly signs his name. It's hard to ignore the way my heart is pounding. My cheeks are likely flushed.

"Ashley, this is my girlfriend Eve. She's James's daughter." I look over at the girl who sits up and pushes her glasses back.

"Oh, he'll be so happy to see you. He talks about you and your brother all the time."

"Thanks," I croak, feeling like a bitch. This girl is actually nice and she likes my dad. God, what is wrong with me today?

Jason places his hand at the base of my back as he guides me toward a door. Glancing around, I smile at how pretty and peaceful this place is. It's all cream and celery-green walls along with hardwood floors. Large coffee-colored leather chairs sit by a fireplace.

"Thanks, Ash," he says over his shoulder. I'm in shock at how clean and homey this place looks. As we walk down the hallway, I notice pictures of what I'm assuming are staff on one wall and flowers and landscapes on the other.

We stop at room 104 where Jason knocks and swings open the door. And there's my beloved father sitting in a shiny new scooter-type chair with his oxygen tanks strapped to the back. He's dressed in dark slacks and a navy sweater, and for a second, I have to blink to make sure it's him. I look down at my dark jeans with their designer-cut holes and my bright mauve T-shirt that shows off a slight bit of my flat tummy and wish I had worn a dress or something. Even with his oxygen tube, he looks so clean and elegant I can't help but let a sob out as I run to him. For a moment, he jumps in his seat. His thin shoulders are caved in as he sits hunched over. I stop and let him whirl his scooter around.

"Evie?" His once-strong voice is gone now and nothing but a hiss.

I nod. "It's me, Daddy." I lean over to hug him, vaguely aware that I'm sobbing on his downy-fresh sweater.

I pull back to look him in the eyes. "I'm here, it's me." He wheezes and starts to cough, his thin body shaking.

"Oh my God, Jason." I look over at him for help. He stands watching us, his eyes alert.

"James? Do you need a nurse?" My father straightens up and waves away the offer. He watches me. I drop my hand, and I guess reach for Jason. I feel like a bad teenager who stayed out past her curfew.

"Daddy, I think you need more oxygen." I reach for his cold hand, which makes him look like he's eighty when he hasn't even made it to fifty. He pulls out a smartphone from a small pouch to his right and adjusts the oxygen. Jason has done all of this. My eyes are blurry with tears and when I look up at him, it's hard to see him. But he wasn't lying. My dad has been getting the best care and it doesn't matter that Jason's a bad guy. I don't care that he may even kill people. All that matters is he's mine.

"You brought me my baby girl," he hisses out.

I rub his hand trying to get him to focus on me. He's wheezing and his eyes are watering, but his hand squeezes mine. "Oh, Daddy, I missed you. Is there... do you need anything?"

"I need to take care of some things. I'll be back." Jason reaches for me and I hesitate. It's one thing to kiss in front of disgusting bikers and another with my father in the room.

"Eve?" I look up at him then my dad who looks confused.

"Angel, your father's not stupid. He knows I fuck you." I freeze. Holy shit he did not just say that, did he?

"I need to make some phone calls. I'll let you two catch up." I stand and nod.

"Christ." Jason reaches for me and his warm lips find mine. It's tender and tears well in my eyes again. He breaks away. "I'll be back shortly." Then he looks at my poor dad, whose eyes are huge and fists are clenched. "You look good, James."

My father hisses out what sounds like "fuck you." Jason grins and looks at me. "Call me if you need me." I nod and sink into a leather chair watching him leave, then turn to smile at my dad. He stares at the closed door. Sighing, I get up and pull the chair close to him so I can face him. It smells like Lysol in here and I flash to Amy constantly spraying the clubhouse. His room has a large, beautiful window that faces the backyard of this place. The yellow walls and green lawn and flowers make it look like a picture.

"Daddy, are they treating you good?" He is still looking at the door and turns his blue eyes on me.

"Don't tell me you are with him."

"I don't want to talk about Jason. How are they trea—"

"Jason?" he gasps out. "That's Blade. He got that name because he cuts people up." His hands shake as he wipes the side of his nose, which is running because of the oxygen.

"Okay... Blade. Let's not get all worked up." I try to soothe him.

He sits and looks at me. "You think you're in love?"

Instantly, my cheeks turn pink. Shit, this is not good. My dad is all upset. Maybe I should lie.

I go to open my mouth and he turns away. "The thought of you whoring yourself makes me sick."

Speechless, I'm also paranoid Jason will walk in. "Daddy, you don't know him," I hiss under my breath. "He's different with me."

He reaches into his pocket and brings out a Kleenex. "You aren't nothing but a plaything for him, Evie. I thought you were strong."

I lean forward and take his clammy hand. "I am strong. And you have nothing to worry about. All you need to do is get better and—"

"I ain't getting better, Evie. I'm dying. No matter how much money Blade spends, it's not going to change that I'm dying and you're sleeping with a man who will never put you first or a ring on that finger." He slumps back, but he's glaring at me like if he had the strength he would paddle my butt. "He's a killer and he took you," he rasps.

"Yeah, well we can thank Benny for that." I stand up. The room is light and airy but it's warm and I need some space.

"He's your brother."

"He sacrificed both of us." I look out his window. This place is unbelievable with all the grass and flowers, not to mention the professional landscaping. That's what the compound needs: some flowers. Maybe it wouldn't always smell of gasoline and oil. I spin toward my dad. "I'm working on taking care of you." He looks from me to the door.

"He tossing you out?"

"No... and I'm working on making sure he is going to keep me."

"You are my pride. Don't give him your heart. You've got plenty of time to find the right man."

I look up at the ceiling wondering if I should tell him the truth. Before I can say anything Jason strides in along with a doctor. I pull my T-shirt down, hoping I don't look trashy. The middle-aged doctor smiles at my dad and me.

"You must be Evie." He holds out his hand. I reluctantly shake it. I hate shaking hands—it always seems so phony. "Your father talks about you all the time." He looks smart, meaning he has salt-and-pepper hair with dark thick-rimmed glasses.

"Um... yes, that's me." I look at Jason who stands next to the doctor, his eyes unreadable. With his arms crossed, I can't help but glance at his biceps.

"Well, we are happy that we are keeping your father as comfortable as we can."

I stare at the doctor. "What does that mean?" It comes out harsh and I hear my dad wheeze harder.

"Excuse me." The doctor moves to my father and looks at his eyes then at Jason. I guess he's forgotten I'm here.

"I'm going to give him something to help relax him. This has been a busy day." The doctor goes to the door, and I move to stop him but Jason takes my arm.

"It's okay, Angel. Let him help your dad," he whispers in my ear, and I sag into him. Tears, fucking wretched tears, are threatening to fall again.

"James, we're gonna let you rest. Eve will be back tomorrow to visit if you would like."

I look at him. Green eyes swirl in front of me and I almost feel as if I might be lightheaded.

"Really? I can come back?"

Jason looks aggravated but stays quiet with a nod.

"Daddy, I'll be back tomorrow." He nods and starts the very same coughing that gives me nightmares.

"Daddy?" Jason holds me as a nurse barges in with a syringe that she injects into a tube on his wrist.

I watch my father's eyes roll back and his head falls forward as if it's too heavy for his neck. But the coughing stops. I must make a sound because Jason holds me tight in his arms and the nurse looks confused. "He's fine," she says. "Trust me, we are taking great care of him."

I want to scream. He's not doing fine—he's dying. Instead I focus on Jason's hands as he takes charge.

"Thank you, Harper. This is Eve, his daughter. She'll be coming and going."

If I wasn't trying to pull myself together I would roll my eyes. Because Harper the nurse looks at Jason like he's a god or something. He is, but he's mine.

"We'll let you take care of him." He laces our fingers as he gently walks us out and nods at the doctor as we pass by.

Jason pushes open the side door and I scrounge around in my bag for my sunglasses. I'm wired yet tired. My heart feels like it's racing and Jason stops and turns toward me. He's so tall his body blocks the sun for me as his warm hand tilts my chin up, and I almost choke on how absolutely perfect he is. Suddenly I want him. Like it's almost primal. His thumbs caress away my tears and he leans down and licks my lips and his spicy, smoky scent envelops me.

"I'm sorry." His mouth is on my forehead.

"He's dying?" I can't believe I said that. Of course he's dying—has been for years. "I don't know why, but I thought you could save him."

"I'm not God, Angel. And he's not dead today, so stop crying." His gravelly voice makes my skin hot and butterflies of excitement snake all the way down to my sex. I look at him and he either feels the same way or it's all over my face because I'm burning.

"Fuck." He looks around the parking lot, which is packed but certainly not deserted. He grabs my arm. "I can't lean you over my bike to fuck you right now, so stop looking at me like that," he says, his voice gruff.

"I need you." It's the most honest, vulnerable thing to come out of my mouth. And for a brief time, I let myself acknowledge that he can take away this sadness and make me feel better. I shift, the wetness of my need already making me flushed. His green eyes change, his nostrils flare as if he can smell my want. Suddenly he's urging me back toward the nursing home. Instead of entering, he pulls me around to the side and up against the warm wall. Then his mouth is on mine as a growl rises from deep in his throat. Our tongues touch and it's as though the world, maybe even the universe, has stopped existing. People, staff, nature vanish as I cling to him, his strong arms holding me up. His hand unbuttons my jeans and I hear myself make a sound I didn't know existed inside me as he starts to rub my clit with two fingers.

"I'm going to rub this plump clit until you scream, and then I'm going to take you home and fuck you."

His fingers are like magic. "Oh God." I roll my head and look at him. My fingers dig into his chest, the cotton a slight barrier as my nails latch onto him. "I need this... I don't know why..."

"Look at me." He pulls back and my eyes lock on his. "That's it... Now come, Eve."

"How do you do this that quickly? Holy shit, I'm coming."

His strong fingers thrust inside me as I clench around them and see stars, white light, and him. Death, despair, sadness vanish as I orgasm.

His voice rumbles in my ear. "Jesus, that's it. Squeeze my fingers." He kisses my forehead as he leans toward me. "I've been neglecting you, haven't I?" He kisses my tearstained eyes and I shudder. Slowly, almost reluctantly, he pulls his fingers out and shoves them into my mouth, his eyes like green fire.

"Suck."

My tongue licks his wet fingers and he smirks as he dips his head to plunder my tongue with his as we both suck and kiss. I taste myself and him and almost want to shove his wet fingers back down my pants to match him in naughtiness.

He kisses the tip of my nose. "Feel better? Less needy?" He grins as he kisses me again.

"No, but you take the pain away." His face is almost too pretty to belong in the life he lives.

"Such a fierce little badass." He gently brushes my lips then zips me up. Taking my hand, he brings us back to his Harley.

"Here, babe." He hands me the helmet.

"Thank you," I say, clearing my voice, which is raspy from all my crying. I look down because if he sees me right now, I'm sure he... well I'm not sure what he would do if he knew I was falling for him. But he doesn't need to know that yet. I pull my blond hair out of my eyes and put the helmet on, watching his muscled legs grip the bike as he waits for me. I hop on and wrap my arms around him. My father's words replay in my mind, yet all they do is make me squeeze and hold on to him tighter.

TWENTY

BLADE/JASON

"Does this look good?" Eve steps out of our bathroom. I'm on the phone with an arms dealer in Moscow; otherwise I would send her back in to change. Which is why she twirls in front of me happily and my heart starts to thump. When I frown, she stops, puts her hands on her hips, and rolls her eyes before flouncing down in a chair with her phone as she waits.

"Sergei, I need an answer. I'm done negotiating," I shout into the phone. He's going to try to pretend he doesn't understand English right now. That's what he does whenever he wants to drag out negotiating, but I'm sick of it.

"Nyet—"

I cut him off. "Shut up, Sergei. We've spent numerous times getting drunk off vodka and caviar. I know you understand me. Do you want the guns or not?"

My eyes drift to my Angel whose long legs seem to go on forever in that yellow dress she's wearing. She crosses them and rolls her head. I watch as her golden tresses fall across her shoulders like caramel slides down ice cream. She's been busy the last two weeks with her dad. I've assigned Dewey as her bodyguard slash spy. He gets up every day, proudly takes her to the home, then brings her back and tells me everything. I stare at her and a surge of possessiveness takes ahold of me. Her skin is glowing; her blue eyes sparkle like the clearest blue ocean. She seems peaceful and happy, which should scare me, but I'm growing used to it. Absently I wonder if I'm reprogramming my brain. Or maybe she's doing it. I should stop asking her questions. I don't need to know what her favorite color is, but for some reason I do. As soon as I found out it was yellow, I had a dozen yellow roses delivered to her and her father at his home. I almost stabbed Edge when he snickered walking by me as I placed the order.

She sighs and sets down her phone, closing her eyes as if she's tired.

"Wait, did you actually just try to tell me you want me to give you these guns for that price?" I scream into the phone, causing Eve to jump and her eyes to pop open. I can't help but smirk. When I demand things from others, it turns her on. And sure enough, her mouth opens a little as she licks her lips. I turn toward my window, gazing down at the pool, and wonder why this girl seems to be it for me. The excuse that she's new and fresh and mine sounds shallow and juvenile. It's going on almost five months since I rode into her carnival. I rub my neck as I absently hear Sergei trying to backpedal.

Ignoring his ramble, I think about two nights ago. I got drunk with Axel and Ryder and confessed that I've only had Eve's pussy all these months. For the first time in my life, I'm monogamous. Axel actually got up and left the room. Ryder put his hand on my shoulder as if I needed support. Nodding his giant dark head, he said that it happens to the best of us.

Christ. I force myself back to the conversation. "I'm done. I have given you a fair price. You know my stuff is the best, so decide. I have an appointment and have no intention of being any later," I grumble into the burner phone. When I'm done, I'll throw it away. Silence is all I hear—that and some slight static and a long dramatic sigh.

"Da, I want you to know that I'm getting the worst end of the deal this time, so next time, please make it up to me."

I snort. "Sure, I'll have my guys be in touch," I say then hang up and turn to my addiction, who sits and stares at me with a small, proud smile. I lean down to cage her in.

"It turns you on watching me, doesn't it?" She nods slowly as her tongue comes out to lick her bottom lip.

"It turns me on knowing that." I lean in farther to kiss her. I already fucked her in the shower less than an hour ago, but the thought of turning her over the chair with her ass in the air almost makes me forget that I promised her a date tonight. Jesus, she's going to kill me.

"Pack a bag. We might be gone for a couple of days." I've been thinking about this all day and I guess I finally made my decision.

She jumps up. "But... what about my father? He may need me."

"We're not going far," I say over my shoulder. "I need to tell one of my guys what's going on." I chuckle at her stunned look.

I make my way down the stairs and enter our office. Edge is sitting behind an old beat-up desk, typing on his laptop. The desk has definitely seen better days. It's old and dark wood. My grandfather probably put notches on it every time he fucked someone on it, so not only is it beat-up and ugly, but also for family history alone, I can't get rid of it.

"Hey, man." I open up the cabinet for the keys to one of my cars.

He looks over at me, says, "Blade," and returns to his computer.

I stand twirling the keys and take in his wrinkled clothes and dark circles. "What's up, Edge? I'm sick of all your dark shit."

He leans back rubbing his hands over his face and sips his beer. "I don't know what you want me to say." He takes another drink. "Dolly. Dolly hates the Disciples. So... my life sucks."

I nod and look around this small room that holds a safe, some filing cabinets, and the beat-up desk. "I didn't know you guys were back together."

He snorts and lays his head back on the chair. "We're not, Jason. She wants me to leave the Disciples, man. How can I leave my family? And why would she want me to? It's not like she wasn't raised in it too." He looks at me.

I don't know what to say. Unlike a lot of the guys, Edge and I share something. His old man was with my dad. Died of cancer years ago and the Disciples is all Edge has ever known. He's never left, so Dolly's demand for him to leave for her is a mistake.

"I'm thinking about taking Eve to my house, get away—"

"She's the one, Jason. I'd say don't fuck it up, but if you're taking her to your house, you're obviously serious." The pain in his eyes makes me uncomfortable. He looks at the beer bottle then slams it on the desk and types on his laptop again.

"You know where to find me." I start to walk out.

"Hey Prez?" I turn. "You look awfully fancy, man. Where you going?"

I look down at my clothes. I'm in dark jeans and a tight, long-sleeved, green waffle T-shirt.

"I'm taking Eve out to dinner."

His lips twitch. "I want to laugh, but since you're the Prez and all, I won't. Have fun. This is like your first date in years, right?"

I stare at him.

"What? It's an honest question."

"You know I haven't gone on a date in probably ten years." I twirl the keys again, daring him to say anything else. He doesn't but smiles and takes another sip of beer.

"I'll be sure to let Axel know."

I nod, and for a few seconds, I feel like a dick. *What the hell am I doing?* Then a pair of long legs descends the stairs.

"Good, do that," I say, trying to reason that it's no big deal that I'm doing all this. But it is a big deal—this is something I've never done.

I reach for her bag. "You ready? Got everything?"

"I think so." I guide her, my hand at her lower back, unable to stop from caressing her ass. She swirls around and dazzles me with a white smile. I open the door to my black Dodge Viper watching how she gracefully sinks into my leather seat. Her big eyes light up as she looks around. "You know, I was never in a new car before I got with you. I love the smell. This is new, right?" She sniffs and wiggles into the buttery black leather seats.

"It's pretty new. I don't drive it as much as a car like this deserves." I start up the engine and it rumbles to a perfect purr as we take off. I reach for her leg resting my hand on it. She's happily looking out the window as her hand reaches down to hold mine. I take a breath at the sheer intimacy of it. Simply holding hands while I drive makes me have those emotions I'm ashamed of having. She makes me weak and I despise it. But the farther I get from the compound, the more I can breathe. It's me and Eve, and I want to immerse myself in her tonight.

"So..." I push the volume down on the steering wheel. She turns sideways to face me.

"What do you feel like? Sushi? Want to try?" I wink at her, and she cocks her head and smiles.

"No, raw fish doesn't sound good right now." She wrinkles her nose and I grip the steering wheel tighter.

"Italian it is." I know an incredible mom-and-pop restaurant that has the most fantastic Italian food. My phone starts ringing and I push the answer button.

"Speak, Axel, and Eve is with me, so if it's not urgent I want to enjoy my dinner." The line is silent then I hear in the background,

"Pay up, motherfucka. I told you I wasn't lying." Loud catcalls and cheering fill the background.

"I'll talk to you when you get back. I don't want to ruin your... date." He kind of trips over the date part, but in this instance, I get it. If it were reversed, I wouldn't believe it either.

"I'm going to take her to my house. If you need me, I'll be there." I hang up because I don't want to hear anything he's going to say. Axel knows that besides my mother, no woman has ever entered my house. I turn left onto Ventura Boulevard then pull up to the side of the little red-and-green Italian restaurant and let the valet take over. A small group of people stand outside waiting, but I know I'll get a table. I reach for my phone and watch as a douchebag probably around Eve's age opens the door for her. He's blond and seems to want me to beat him up since he can't stop looking at her. At last, he glances at me and slinks away. I take the valet ticket and reach for Eve's hand. Walking straight past the group, we both blink at the darkness as we enter. I scoot her forward to the hostess while our eyes adjust to the room. It's painted in a wine red with a shot of Sophia Loren and her famous pout, her cleavage hanging front and center. A signed movie poster of *The Godfather* hangs nearby. The floor tiles are painted different colors giving the atmosphere a sense of fun. It's one of the reasons I picked this place. Not only is the food amazing, Eve will be comfortable. Frank Sinatra is singing and I have to fight a grin thinking of the last time we heard Frank. I hope this night ends better than that one.

Before I even get to ask for him, Gino appears.

"Blade, my friend, welcome." His big smile almost rivals his huge stomach.

I've known Gino for years. When he needed money to start this place up, I floated him some. He paid me back in no time and has brought over a bunch of cousins from Italy to help him. His place is legit. The guys and I come here when we want exceptional food and to get away from shit.

"My God." He covers his heart dramatically. "Who is this enchanting creature?" He holds out his hand and I watch, amused as Eve looks at me with an eyebrow raised and allows Gino to kiss her hand.

"I have been around the world and I swear I have never seen such beauty." He keeps holding her hand as he brings us to a table in the corner. The white tablecloth and candle make it look romantic.

For a moment I falter, wondering if I'm tempting fate. With all the shitty things I've done in my life, why would I ever think I could have this? And yet as she smiles at me and sits in to the offered chair, I wonder, why not?

"Thank you." Her voice does it for me. Shit, everything about her does it for me.

"Shall I bring some of my special stuff?" He waggles his eyebrows at me, and I can't not chuckle.

"Please, Gino, we'd love it." He spins around and I'm always amazed at how well he can get around. He's not a thin man. I turn to Eve and take her hand, I guess because I can't stop touching her.

"What are you feeling tonight?"

She inhales and peeks around, then clears her voice. "Whatever you think is good." Her hand shakes a little and I frown. I want her to enjoy this not be nervous.

"Angel?" Her big blue eyes shyly find mine. "You are exquisite. Every woman wants to be you and every man wants to fuck what's mine. You order anything you want." I watch as she swallows, her thin neck almost beckoning my thumb to find my mark. I reach up and pull her hair back over her soft shoulder, lightly running my thumb over the Disciples brand. I should feel guilty, but fuck that. This turns me on more than I will ever admit. It means I'm keeping her.

"Here we are." Gino returns and I reluctantly move back a little so he can set down the menus. The waitress places the flutes filled with Gino's family's prosecco. He has an uncle in Italy who makes it. Another waiter brings bread.

"Thanks, Gino."

He claps his hands together. "I'll be back. Tell me if you have any questions on the menu, my beauty."

I chuckle at Eve's wide-eyed stare. "Gino, this is my girlfriend Eve." Her mouth opens and she gasps slightly. It's all I can do not to reach over and kiss her ruby lips.

"Oh my... of course she would be blessed with that name. I'm Gino, and you need anything, you let me know."

Again, I laugh. "Thanks, man. We'll let you know." He stands smiling down at Eve until I have to clear my throat.

"Yes, sorry, I'm gonna send Eve out some of my mama's favorite specials." He turns and marches back to the kitchen area.

I hand her one of the thick red menus. Reluctantly she takes it in, her eyes staring at the picture of Sophia Loren.

"Eve?" She doesn't look at me but reaches for her crystal water glass. "Eve!" This time I'm demanding and her eyes dart to mine.

"What's wrong?" I've never seen her like this. In a way, it's adorable; in another, it aggravates me to see her this insecure.

She sighs and leans forward. "I... I was so excited and now I'm nervous."

I blink at her, my eyes caressing her face, and I see the truth: she feels inferior.

"What do you want to eat?" It comes out harsh but I want to know before I dive into this.

She slams shut the menu with a thud. "That's just it. I have no idea what this menu says. So why am I looking at it? I have never had Italian food unless Pizza Hut and Dominos count." Her big eyes pool with tears.

I set the menu aside as I take her chin, forcing her to look at me.

"You are beautiful. Not because of the way you look on the outside but because of what's inside. All this is just for fun." I indicate our surroundings with my eyes. A small tear glides slowly down her cheek as she tries to shake her head no.

"It's true. I'm doing this because I want to spoil you. The whole way over here I thought, I don't deserve to feel like this, or that I've done a lot of bad things, which means I can't have you." I lean forward to inhale her soft sweet breath and suck it in like I need it to live. "But I do, Eve." Her eyes light up with surprise and I kiss her. "Now, can you read?"

She goes to pull away, but I hold her. "Yes, but I don't understand a lot of the words." It's a whisper but I hear it clearly. And that protective instinct I have with her doubles if that's possible. I want to be her everything, her mate, her soul, her very life. Releasing her chin, I let the realization that I'm fucked sink in. That I have somehow fallen in love with Eve. Thank God I'm already sitting because I'm not sure what would happen had I figured this out standing.

"Here we go." Gino appears, his hands loaded with tiny dishes filled with pasta, cheeses, and small meatballs. Eve leans back and looks up at the ceiling trying to stop her tears and I reach for the stupid flute of prosecco, downing it in two sips.

"Ahh, I will bring more." He signals for a waitress to refill my glass. I want to order whiskey, but I don't want to insult him.

"We're ready, Gino. My Angel will have some of your mother's famous baked ziti and I'm gonna have the gnocchi."

"Wonderful, you are going to love the ziti. I will bring more samples." Before I can stop him, he's gone. The silence becomes like foreplay; it's thick and stifling and I wish dinner was over as I wait to see what she is going to do. She doesn't disappoint and sits up, straightens her shoulders, and reaches for some bread.

"I'm not stupid. I know you think I am, and just because I didn't get to go to school doesn't mean—"

"I know you're not stupid." I watch her chew. Again, that feeling that I'm falling into something I might never recover from slams me in the chest. "I'm not letting you go," I snap at her. Her eyes widen as I see confusion on her face.

"I think you should know that I won't be letting you go." She stares, almost frozen. "If you had any thoughts that I would, forget them." Even to myself that sounds crazy. It's not her fault I'm a bad person. I don't even know if a man like me can be in love. But if looking at this woman and never wanting her to leave my side is any indication, maybe I'm not as damaged as I thought.

She glances around the restaurant and I notice for the first time how crowded it is. People are laughing which is what I wanted to do. I want to introduce her to all things. Instead I'm being an ass.

"Look, Eve." I rub the back of my neck then reach for her cold hands. "I'm in uncharted territory here. All I want to do is take you to dinner, then I want to show you my house. No one but my mother and a few of the guys even know it exists."

She gulps down the bread. "I... need to use the bathroom." She stands and tosses her napkin on the table.

I lean back. "Fucking fantastic," I mumble as her slender form bolts toward the restroom. Two guys in suits sitting at the small bar area over by the bathrooms stare at my girl as her sexy walk and stunning face lure them to her.

I want to jump up and pound my chest that she's mine. Fuck, I already have my brand on her neck, but I want her wearing my vest, saying "Property of President." The visual alone gets my dick hard. Grabbing some bread, I wait for her. Gino brings out our dinner and still, I wait. As I start to worry, she emerges. She glides back to the table and I almost stand up so that the douches at the bar can see who she belongs to.

"Sorry, I'm tired." Her glow from earlier is gone. She looks pale.

"Eat something and we'll go home and sleep." She places the napkin back on her lap and takes a small bite. Our eyes lock. She blinks and I rub her soft cheek with my tatted hand.

"Eat, Angel." She looks down and starts to eat.

"Well? Do you like it?"

She nods. "I love it." She takes a sip of water. "Jason?"

"Yeah?" I can't help but smile at her and how good my gnocchi is. I hold a bite to her, my dick twitching as I watch her wrap her mouth around it. "It melts in your mouth, huh?"

"God," she moans. "It does." She smiles. "I need to tell you something."

I lean back. "Okay."

She reaches for her water again and I watch her swallow before she sets the glass down.

Our eyes meet and she says the words I've been thinking. "I want you to not let me go..." She reaches for the water again and the top of her cheeks are flushed.

I exhale and smile back. "Good, baby. Because I'm going to make an announcement when we get back to the clubhouse."

A loud commotion is happening at the bar with the drunk asses that were staring at Eve.

"Finish up, babe. I'm ready to get out of here." She takes a couple more bites and looks drastically better. Obviously, she needed food and maybe wanted to say what neither of us want to admit.

"You need to eat more. Your job is to please me, Eve. When it's us, alone, we are us, together. In front of my men, I need you to understand if I make you my old lady, you'll need to behave accordingly and that means being healthy."

She puts down her water glass with a thud. Small drops of water land on my hand. "You want me to be your wife?" Her voice sounds excited.

"It's not a formal wedding, but you'll wear my vest." I pull her close, my mouth next to hers. "We'll see how you handle it. My mom was great until my dad started moving his whores into the clubhouse."

She pulls back. "Oh God, that's awful. Your poor mom." She shakes her head as her eyes widen. "Wait, you're not saying that because you are going to do that, right?"

Setting my napkin down, I already sense the blood pumping in my ears. "Eve, you don't have a choice if you're my old lady." I sneer. "You need to know who's in charge and back your man." Monogamy is not in my genes. My dad, grandfather, and brother fucked their way through the clubhouse and anywhere else they went. I've never been monogamous and the fact that Eve has held my interest and satisfies my needs is a fucking miracle. So I slam it home as I lean forward. "If I want someone to suck me off, even if it's in front of you, you will shut up and watch like the good old lady you are."

She looks like I've slapped her and like she might be sick and she covers her mouth, her head shaking. Her big eyes stare at me like I'm not human, and I almost relent and tell her I have no intention of doing that. But the truth is that as the president of the club I can do anything I want. I'm motherfucking king and if she wants to be my queen she needs to shut her mouth.

Placing her napkin on her plate, she scoots back. "I can't, I won't." She stands up and looks around as if someone might actually help her. Her incredible golden locks fall around her bare shoulders in a wild, sexy way. "You can't honestly think that I would tolerate that." Her voice catches and her hands tremble as she reaches for her bag.

I bolt up not caring that my chair tips over. Taking out my wallet, I drop a couple hundred and grab her arm as she pulls away.

"Fuck off," she hisses, jerking her hand free. A couple sitting next to us gasps and I almost see red. In all my years, I have never been told to fuck off by a woman. *It. Has. Never. Happened. Ever.*

She breezes past the tables, her head held high like she's in a god damn beauty pageant. I shove the valet ticket to the punk.

He must feel the vibe that I might kill him if he even looks at Eve because he nods and gets the keys. I take them from him and grab her.

"Here." I toss a fifty at him. She tries to jerk free, but there's no fucking way. I pull her to my Viper and toss her in.

"Hey man, thanks," the valet calls out, staring at the fifty.

I don't respond and shut my door and start the engine. The loud click of me locking the doors should alert her that I'm beyond pissed. She crosses her arms and stares out the window.

"I warned you," I say through gritted teeth. It's all I trust myself to say at the moment. My hands grip the steering wheel so tight my knuckles crack. The pure anger that she still defies me pumps through me like a heart pumps blood. I actually feel high with it and accelerate down Ventura Boulevard, taking a fast left and gunning it up toward the hills that lead to my house. I bought this house as soon as I became president. It's in the hills of Sherman Oaks, the view is incredible, and it's close enough to the clubhouse that I can be there in no time. I let the Viper have its way with the twists and turns up the hill. Eve sways with the movement, her arms are crossed and that pisses me off more. Her eyes are focused on the scenery, but with it getting dark, she won't get much until the morning. I pull into a cul-de-sac that I share with three other houses and push the remote for the garage to open.

Suddenly she turns. "I want to go back to the clubhouse." I almost laugh. It wasn't a plea; it was a demand and if I wasn't so angry, I'd give her credit. Unfortunately for her, she brings out the most intense emotions in me. Her cheeks are flushed and her breathing is coming in short gasps. I guess it's dawned on her that for the first time ever, we're completely alone.

"No, Angel. It's time you learn what your future is."

"What the fuck does that mean?" she screams at my back as I exit and slam the door. She swings hers open and steps out. Our gazes lock and I stare as her chin comes up and her hand tightens around her purse. *Badass* floats through my brain and I sincerely hope for her sake she doesn't pull her blade on me. I narrow my eyes almost daring her.

"I'd think about this, Angel." My voice is soft, almost coaxing. She stands, frozen, her chest coming in fast deep breaths, eyes blazing with frustration and hurt.

"For your sake, beautiful, I'd do everything I demand tonight." She sniffs back her tears. "Fuck you, Jason," she hisses softly. "Jesus Christ."

I reach for her and she yells, "I don't want you to fuck around… I can't handle it." Her eyes are almost wild and her pain fuels my need for her. She will submit; she will be everything I want her to be. Clenching my jaw so hard it aches, I pull her in and toss her over my shoulder. Instead of feeling guilty, I'm relieved. Gone are all the soft feelings. All the shit I've been struggling with clouding my true nature. In one quick snap, the confusion is erased. Now I let my power pump through my blood, my dick so hard it's almost painful.

Fuck you. I keep hearing it replay in my brain. She's struggling and I slap her ass hard and she screams. Then she growls; it's almost animalistic. I recognize that sound, that kind of energy.

It's rage.

I'm taking away her power, sucking the last bit of her independence because after tonight, Eve will be tied to me body and soul. Bursting through the door, I bypass the kitchen and head straight for my bedroom where I throw her on my king-size bed.

She scrambles back like a caged beast and licks her lips. Her eyes darts around the room, which is nothing but large glass windows and the bright lights of LA at night.

"Strip," I growl as I jerk off my vest and pull off my shirt. She's panting and on her knees as if she's looking for an escape.

"I said *strip*. So help me, Eve, if you make me do it, tonight will be a nightmare you will never forget." Her eyes swing to mine and she must see I'm dead serious. She hesitates as if she's actually going to test me. Then she reaches for the bottom of her dress and pulls it gracefully over her curves. Her body has gone from too skinny to awe-inspiring. Now that Amy forces her to eat nothing but organic meals at least three times a day, she has curves. She's glowing with health, her stomach flat, waist small, yet her fucking tits have grown. Reaching down, I unbutton my jeans and kick them off.

"Come here and kneel." She hesitates then moves quickly, lowering herself back on her heels until she's eye level with my leaking cock. I reach down and roughly pinch her rock-hard, dusty rose nipples and she lets out a small whimper. Like the addict I am, I fill myself up with my medicine. My hands cup and roughly fondle her breasts and I almost grab her hair and lift her so that I can suck on them, but I'll suck later.

"Open." Her eyes flash blue fire and I reach for her hair and jerk her angrily forward.

"Make it good, Eve, if you don't want someone else's lips wrapped around my cock," I snarl as I shove myself into her mouth. My unapologetic anger and frustration make me thrust deeper as I hear her gag. "Fuck that feels good," I grunt as I loosen my grip slightly. After all, she does need to breathe. She surprises me by opening her mouth wider. "That's it, Angel, breathe through your nose." Aggravated, I wonder if that sounded encouraging rather than demanding.

She reaches up and cups my hard balls, and I hiss as she starts to lick and suck forcefully on my tip. Pleasure at seeing her blond head and puffy lips wrap around my cock makes me breathe loudly. Pleasure zings through my entire body—I even feel it in my toes. As I let my gypsy pleasure me, her legs rub together and the flush across her chest tells me she's aroused. I wrap my hand tight in her hair and jerk her off me with a pop.

"You're going to deep throat me and then I'm going to come." Before she can respond I shove my shaft down her throat and she gags again. "Jesus... yeah." Holding her tightly, I move her head up and down as my body tenses with pleasure. Without taking my eyes off her, I watch her mouth, transfixed.

"I'm going to come and not one drop better leak out of these lips." I grunt and let up a little. Her eyes are oozing tears, but I'm not sure if she's crying or if it's her gag reflex. One more deep thrust and my balls tighten along with my stomach muscles as I groan out her name in agonizing pleasure. I don't blink as I watch her neck move and she swallows every single drop. And my body and mind start to calm. Gently, she pulls back and looks up at me and I have never seen her look more magnificent. She's flushed; her lips are ridiculously red and swollen, and her eyes are at war. Whether it's with me or with herself, I don't care. I lift her up and carry her to the bed. She lies back and my eyes take in all that's mine.

"This body"—I reach my hand over her full breast—"is mine. You will listen, you will submit. And if you ever tell me to fuck off again..." She leaps from the bed.

"Jason, I don't feel good." Her flushed cheeks are suddenly pale.

"Jason..." Her eyes plead and I literally pick her up and take her to the bathroom.

"Christ, Angel." I lean her head over the toilet as she dry heaves.

"You're kidding me." I snarl but gently hold her hair and wrap my arm around her waist to steady her as she clings to me.

"I don't know what's wrong with me." She looks up and for the first time since she told me to fuck off, I have that god damn flutter again and wonder if I'm losing my mind. A moan and "Oh God" snap me back to her as her body unloads this time. She pukes up her dinner in pitiful, heaving gasps.

"I got you, baby." I caress her back, now sweaty from the effort. She finally stops and her thin hand flushes the toilet. My

Angel sinks back into my arms, and her perspired head rests on my chest as I hold her from behind.

"Better?" I kiss her temple.

She nods, then turns and wraps her arms around me and cries. This is not the first time I've made Eve cry and I'm positive it's not the last. But it's the first time I'm worried about her. I hold her tight as I start the shower. "Come on, babe, step out of your panties." I manage to detach myself enough to pull them down because Eve is like a rag doll. I gently bring her in with me and hold her as she continues to hiccup and cry. I cup her cheeks and make her look at me, my back facing the water. She blinks and shudders in some air. Both of us are caught in the steam and energy that is us. I rub my thumbs over her lips and back her up to the wall.

The hot water beats down on us. I take the soap and start to lather her as she leans against the pearly white-and-black-checkered tile and I wash her. Reaching for my toothbrush and loading it up with toothpaste, I hand it to her unable to avert my eyes from her boobs as they move with her brushing. My thumb rubs one nipple. Her breasts are definitely fuller. I take the toothbrush from her and put it back in the caddy that holds all the soap and shampoo. I do a quick wash of myself and reach for a fluffy white towel as I turn off the water. Wrapping her up, I carry her back to my bed and sit down with her. I pull open the towel and look at her, like really look at her.

"You told me you can't get pregnant, so why are you throwing up?"

She sits up and frowns. "You shoved your cock down my throat, not to mention, I swallowed a shitload of come and you're wondering why I threw up?"

Relief surges through me, which is pathetic. If I was normal, I'd be insulted that she got sick off my jizz, but the alternative—being pregnant—is not one I can handle.

"So, there's no way? I have nothing to worry about?"

She climbs under my sheets with quick jerky movements. "Only if you are God and I'm Mary because I already told you I can't get pregnant!" Her voice trembles and I've had enough drama tonight.

"Good." I reach over and turn off the light and slide into bed pulling Eve's warm body next to mine.

TWENTY-ONE

EVE

I wake to large windows and the most peaceful view I have ever seen. Blinking, I take in my environment, my mind still fuzzy from deep sleep. The sound of the shower must have woken me. Steam and spice waft out of the cracked bathroom door. I snuggle into the comforter and wonder how I ever survived sleeping on the floor with a rat-infested mattress for eighteen years. It seems almost like a dream. I've started to block out the bad smells and years of dirt and cramped living in that beat-up trailer. Only my dad cared for me. He tried even though I had nothing unless I stole it. The water turns off and I blink. It brings everything into focus. From what I can see all the walls are white with nothing on them. I barely move as I take a hesitant swallow. Nausea makes my mouth water and I close my eyes and try to breathe through it. I can't throw up. Jason will know I'm sick.

Don't throw up, don't throw up, you're so close, I chant in my head as I breathe in Jason's spicy scent. For some weird reason, over the last couple of weeks it calms my stomach when nothing else does. Opening my eyes, I look out the windows and exhale. Nothing but green trees and brush cover the hillside all the way down to what I'm guessing is the Valley.

Jason's house has a view that I can't help think people have to pay a lot of money to see.

"God," I mumble as I remember last night. I'm pissed at myself for thinking he was going to propose to me. Instead he wants me to wear his stupid vest and be his whore.

Un. Fucking. Believable.

The need for him to love me, cherish me has become my goal. Call it never having any stability in my life, and Jason provides that.

None of this is enough. Having him admit that I'm his and he's never letting me go is cheap without a rock on my finger. Sighing I throw a hand over my eyes as I try to reason with myself. I'm obsessed with him, but that doesn't mean he feels the same way. I mean, what the hell? I hate how they call their women ole ladies! That's not me. Now if I could feel better, I'd be able to do more to entice him. Instead all I want is for him to come out of the shower and hold me and tell me he loves me.

Groaning, I swallow back the bile. *I'm so stupid! Stupid, stupid girl.*

"You okay, Angel?"

Caught up in the pity rant in my head, I drop my hand almost screaming. "Yes," I whisper swallowing and trying not to bolt to the toilet.

He stands, glistening wet with a white towel wrapped low around his waist.

"You're so hot." It comes out raspy, and his eyes change.

He grins. "You going to be a good girl today?" And his words go straight to my wet core. God, I'm pathetic, but fuck it—I need him to fuck me.

"Yes." I nod and pull the sheet down so he can see my breasts. I can't help but bite my lip to stop smiling as his cock swells and the white towel moves along with it.

He lets the towel drop to the floor, his green eyes like emeralds as he stands in all his six-foot-four Greek god glory.

I lick my lips. He is truly magnificent. I want him and intend to have him. My legs rub together and I'm flushed all over. Maybe I'm dying? He hasn't even touched me and I'm feverish.

"Jason..." I'm breathless.

He puts a knee on the bed as he stalks me. And all I can think is I love this man, want him, need him.

"Yes, baby? Tell me what you need." He leans over me and my body heat bounces off his. We melt together.

"You. I need you."

Again he grins. "Open your legs. Let's see how much."

I don't even hesitate. He leans back and all I hear is my harsh breathing. His nostrils flare and he looks at me. Time stops. I'm captured, ensnared by the fierce want, maybe even need in his gaze.

"What do we have here, Angel?" His thumb brushes my sensitive clit and I moan loudly.

"Fuck, look at you—you're slick and wet." He gently rubs my swollen bud. "Yeah... Angel I love how your cunt drips for me when I haven't even touched it yet."

"Oh God," I groan as he inserts two fingers. At his hiss, I reach for him, our lips seeking each other's as he attacks my mouth with his strong tongue. His thick erection stands proudly by his stomach and I grab for its velvety hardness and pump it like he's taught me.

"So good, baby." He latches onto my neck and sucks, his hand pumping and rubbing.

"Holy shit... Jason," I scream, 'literally scream' as I come so hard the wetness pours out.

"Yeah that's it." He rubs it all over my swollen clit. I must have dropped his cock because I'm clinging to his wrist as my body jerks.

"Who owns this body?" He kisses me almost gently as he removes his fingers.

"You," I breathe out as his hand fondles my breast. His eyes turn darker as he watches me. His fingers pinch my nipple and I hiss and moan.

"They're sore aren't they?" His eyes search my face, causing me to shiver as adrenaline spikes through my head all the way to my throbbing clit.

"They're sensitive."

He leans down and takes my bottom lip to suck as his hand massages my tender breast.

"I need to suck on these ripe titties," he says, lowering his head so his tongue and teeth can tease one of my hard nipples while his other hand rubs and squeezes the other. I almost scream again when he starts sucking on the nipple almost as if he thinks he's going to milk it and the pain slash pleasure makes my core contract.

"They're full, red, and juicy." He reaches for the other one to suck on. "Are you ever going to sass me again?"

"No," I rasp as he takes his thick cock in his hand and starts to rub it up and down my slit. A growl of pleasure flows through me as I drop my hands with a loud thump and grab ahold of the sheet, arching my hips.

"Spread your legs, Angel," he demands and I do.

"Watch," he says and I look down at my legs spread open and his beautiful hard mushroomed head rubbing my bud.

His eyes are slits, pleasure all over his beautiful face as he rubs my plump clit with his tip.

"Jason... I'm going to come again," I whimper as my core starts to pulse and I shut my eyes as the pleasure makes my heart skip.

"Eve?" Jason is staring at me as I open my eyes to his beautiful face.

And instead of answering him with "what" I say, "I love you."

His eyes darken and a ghost of a smile is on his lips as he lifts my legs and lines up his rock-hard cock. Slowly he thrusts into me.

"Oh my God," I cry out and arch my back off the bed. He is so huge and I love everything about the way he makes me feel.

"Say it—I want to hear it and see your face while I'm inside you." He's so strong and terrifyingly powerful I don't hesitate.

"I love you, I'm yours." I stare at him as he moves inside me and our eyes meet.

"That's right, Angel. I'll kill anyone who touches you," he grunts into my mouth, our bodies moving together like a composer with his music.

"I know."

"You better." His kisses are so rough I'm positive my lips will be puffy for days. I cling to him tightly as our tongues tangle and I quiver.

"Touch yourself. I want you coming when I shoot my seed inside you."

I reach down and moan at how swollen my clit is as I circle it.

"That's it, Angel. Get all that slick wetness and rub your clit while I fuck you." My core clenches on his cock and together we come. My fingernails grind into his back as I hear, "Fuck" and he jerks filling me up with his hot semen.

He lowers his forehead to mine, his face almost pained as I try to catch my breath. Never feeling so free, I sigh and wrap my arms tighter around him. Gone is my sickness. It's only Jason and me.

"Angel, look at me." He kisses the side of my mouth as he pulls out yet keeps me caged in. I'm still catching my breath as I lock eyes with him.

"When was your last period?"

"What?" I whisper.

"When was it?" He rubs his nose with mine and all of a sudden, I know he knows.

I push for him to get away from me. He takes my hands and holds them on top of my head. "Take a shower. I have a doctor coming in an hour." He releases me and gets up.

"A month ago," I lie. It sounds desperate and guilty. After a deep breath, I say, "I had my period a month ago," pulling the sheet up around me.

"Then we have nothing to worry about." He reaches for his cigarettes watching me as he lights up. I have to turn my head. Smoke makes me sick.

"You're wasting your money," I snip, almost choking on my words. My mind spins but at this second, my main priority is not puking again. "I'm not pregnant, but... I may be sick." I cover my mouth fighting back the gag that is threatening. He inhales deeply and looks down at me. "Let's hear it, Angel. Tell me how you're sick."

I inch back until I feel the cool metal of the headboard. Reaching for one of the pillows like it can shield me, he inhales and blows smoke out and I close my eyes.

"What? Don't like the smell of it, do you?" His smoky hand grabs my chin. "Speak. I want to hear what you think you have. I mean that's only fair, right? After all, I'm the one who's going to foot the bill. *Tell me.*" He rubs his thumb across my lips, back and forth almost like he's pulling it out of me.

"I... think I might have cancer." My eyes fill with tears. He drops his hand and runs his other through his hair as he takes a deep drag and moves to the ashtray sitting on the windowsill. I watch almost trancelike as his long, muscular legs and ass move. He's so perfect it's almost not fair. God, he's even been blessed with a thick, giant penis.

"Cancer?" he says slowly, smoke escaping his mouth as he blows it out. "Cancer?" It's as if he's testing the word. "Huh... I guess it's a good thing that I have doctors ready and willing to make house calls. You should have told me earlier, Angel. Cancer is nothing to fool around with." He's using that tone that I hate. It's the tone he uses with people he's getting ready to demolish.

Swallowing, I look around and try not to panic.

"Go take a shower. The sooner we get this out in the open, the sooner we can move on." He jerks open a drawer and pulls on some dark jeans. His chest still glistens with drops of moisture from the shower and I stare wide-eyed at his tattoo. The wings reach from one shoulder to the other, the long blade almost piercing his solid, ripped eight-pack. My face heats up as I realize he's talking and I have completely zoned out. Admiring his body and face is so much better than my reality.

"Go, Eve." I jump up. His eyes follow me as I walk to the bathroom. His room is big and airy. Almost cold-looking, it barely has any furniture; its only warmth is the sunlight that fills the large windows leading to the view. Two large doors look like the opening to a wooden deck. This place is incredible. Why would he not fill it up and live here? I shut the bathroom door and look around. It's white and spotless. I thought the clubhouse was clean, but this bathroom puts it to shame. The tile is white except for the shower, which looks to be black-and-white tile. The towels are large and so snowy white I almost don't want to mess them up. Jason's used towel is on the floor. The smell of fresh spice lingers in the air.

Tentatively I use the toilet and notice the hardware is bronze. With a turn of the faucet, I almost jump back as the shower releases a sudden blast and water jets out at me. I step in and close my eyes, terrified. If this turns out bad, my father and I might be fucked. Absently I realize that I have completely become dependent on Jason. He's made it so that I am. Taking my time, I let the hot water caress me as I try to think.

If I have something horrible, but curable, hopefully I can convince him to at least let me stay until I have more money saved. If it's really bad, I have to be ready for the worst. I reach for the soap and instantly recognize it as Irish Spring, then have to use his AXE shampoo. Turning off the water, I step out and wrap the towel around me. The sound of a woman's voice makes me freeze.

"Let me get this straight. You got your girlfriend pregnant? How is that possible? You are always so careful." The woman's voice is strong and clipped. She sounds like a bitch.

"Hilary, she assured me that she was sterile. Her appendix burst when she was a kid and they said the bacteria spread to her tubes causing her not to be able to get pregnant," Jason snaps.

Hilary? Not doctor something, but Hilary? Tossing aside my towel, I reach for one of the dresses in my bag. It's powder blue and matches my eyes. I slip on some panties and go braless since it has a racerback. Tentatively I follow the voices.

"Whatever you need to tell yourself. I've known you since you were a kid. You never trust anyone. All the club sluts want to trap you." I wince at her horrible, direct approach. Tiptoeing, I take a look at his house. It's fucking amazing, like I never want to leave amazing. At the end of the small hallway, I gaze at the huge open floor plan. The house sits so that you have a view of the Valley and some palm trees. The morning traffic looks like ants crawling along the highway. Again, there's barely anything in the house other than the view and a cherry-colored wooden deck. And one L-shaped black leather couch with a large flat screen. The hardwood floors are so clean and shiny I can see my reflection.

"She's not a club slut." He sighs. "Just find out for sure and don't say anything until I decide what I'm doing."

They must be in the kitchen because I don't see them as I toss my wet hair back and walk into the great room. A large fireplace on the side of the room sends a tingle of excitement through me at the thought of sitting next to Jason watching the flames. I've never actually seen a real fireplace much less felt one, but that's what it looks like on TV.

With a sigh, I turn and gasp, my stomach fluttering as I stare at a pair of piercing green eyes. His arms are crossed and he wears one of his dark T-shirts. My eyes travel down his body to his bare feet and I have to close my eyes so he doesn't see how much he affects me.

"Hilary? Come meet Eve," he bellows.

A dark-haired woman in her forties, I guess—although it's hard to tell given her striking looks—steps forward. Tall and stylish, she wears a blouse with dark trousers and high-heeled pumps. Her hair is in a bun and she sports stylish librarian glasses. Everything about her reeks self-confidence and wealth.

We both stare at each other. As she drinks a cup of coffee, her gaze travels the length of me and back.

"Well." She takes another sip, then sets it down. "I'm Dr. Hilary Gordon and I'm here to see why you haven't been feeling well."

I lift my head and straighten my shoulders as I watch Dr. Hilary smile and shake her head at Jason.

"So, tell me everything." She turns toward the kitchen, her heels echoing on the hardwood floors.

I cross my arms and snap, "I'm not pregnant." My face is on fire as I spin toward Jason. "I can't have children. Sorry to disappoint you, but you're not going to be a father." The woman walks back in carrying a cup and a plastic-looking stick, wand, *whatever*.

"Yes, Jason was telling me that. Your appendix burst at what age?"

"Twelve." I roll my eyes and walk over to the window and look out at the city.

"I need you to pee in this cup." She hands it to me and I see her wrist bearing the Disciples brand. My eyes jerk up to hers. *What the fuck?* If she notices, she doesn't show it. In fact her pretty face is all business. I take the cup. Her perfume smells like flowers and I instantly back away.

"Where's the bathroom? Or do you want me to squat?" That gets a finely waxed eyebrow raised at me and a snort from Jason.

"Angel, before you use the second door to your right, why don't you tell the doctor what you think it is." He's behind me and heat radiates from his body into mine. He sweeps my hair onto my shoulder, his thumb lightly stroking my brand. He does this a lot. Whenever he feels I, or anyone else, need to be reminded.

I lean into him and his smell makes my stomach calm rather than churn.

"I'm worried it might be cancer," I spit it out, hating that it sounds hollow and slightly echoes in the large empty white room.

Suddenly his arms are around me, pulling my back to his chest. His strong hands lie on my stomach.

"Yes, she thinks it might be that serious. So maybe you should take blood?" The doctor looks from me to him and rolls her eyes.

"The test is good enough, Jason, but sure, if you want one hundred percent..." She spins on her heels and goes back into the kitchen.

"How you holding up?" His mouth is at my ear and I shiver for numerous reasons. First, he's scaring me with his attitude and somewhat robotic king-like behavior and second, he's being condescending again.

"Go pee in the cup, baby, then she'll take your blood and we'll know which doctor you need to see." He kisses the top of my head and pulls me toward the bathroom.

I shut the door, sit on the toilet seat, and want to cry, which I hate—I've never been a crying girl and actually prided myself on never shedding a tear. But it's all changed since I've gotten with Jason—or Blade because that's who he is right now. Jason vanished after he came inside me this morning. Blade emerged right after. I wish I had my knife on me, although what I would do with it is anyone's guess. A bang on the door makes me jump.

"Are you done?" Blade's voice leaks in. He's not yelling, but he doesn't have to. Power bleeds out of him.

"Almost." I lift the toilet seat and quickly pee in the cup, wash my hands, and open the door to a waiting Blade. His eyes sweep me and then his bathroom. Like I'm hiding someone in there to pee for me.

"Here." I shove the cup of piss at him. He doesn't take it and his full lips smile as he moves aside so I can exit.

"Hilary? She's ready," he yells. Dr. Hilary walks out talking on her phone and motions for me to give her the cup. Which I do, somewhat fascinated that she doesn't miss a beat in the conversation as she rips open the stick and dunks it in my pee then whirls around for her large designer bag.

"Hold on, George." She looks at me. "Sit." She sets the pee on the coffee table as she goes back to her phone and George I guess. Suddenly her cold hands are efficiently wrapping a rubber band around my arm and our eyes lock for a moment. Hers dark, mine light, but she looks rather impressed or maybe I'm crazy and seeing things. The needle goes into my vein as she continues to talk. Blade strokes my hair as she fills two vials with my dark red blood. Straightening, she sticks them in a plastic bag and tells George goodbye before reaching for the pee and the stick.

I think I might have stopped breathing because she looks at me and up at Blade.

"Well? Is she dying?" It's a sneer and I instantly stand.

"No, she's pregnant. I have to go. I'll have the bloodwork back in a couple of hours." She grabs her bag, reaches for her keys, and nods at us.

"I'll show myself out." Her highs heels click and she's gone before I can laugh in her face. Gone before I can scream, "That's impossible!" Gone and I'm left with a man who hasn't uttered a sound. And I think for the second time in my life Blade might kill me.

TWENTY-TWO

BLADE/JASON

She lied.

I take in her pale appearance and wait to see how this is going to play out. Her breasts, which are already twice their normal size, heave. She licks her lips as if she's thirsty.

I'd like to say I'm shocked, but then I'd be a liar. I suspected as soon as Axel said she threw up at the club. It's finally happened—I knocked someone up. For some strange reason that I won't dive into right now, I'm kind of the opposite of upset and I almost smile. But I don't need my little gypsy rat to know that her con has worked. I was already going to make her my queen but now I'm gonna lock her down forever.

"Blade," she whispers, and I cock my head. It's been a long time since I've heard that name from her perfect lips. She shakes her blond head—her golden tresses fill my house with color.

"I swear I can't get pregnant. There has to be a mistake." She looks as though she might faint, so I reach for her and drag her into my kitchen, dump her in a chair, and pour her some orange juice. Slamming it down in front of her, I flinch as she shrieks and tears pool in her eyes.

"I... it can't be—"

"Shut up, Eve. I know you." I grasp the side of the table, leaning into her. "You can try to lie your way out of this, but it's pointless. I've knocked you up. Deal with it. I was already making you my ole lady. Now you'll be my baby momma too." Pushing off the table, all I want her to do is acknowledge that she trapped me. She stares out the window almost lost and wide-eyed.

"Are you... I mean, I thought you didn't want children." Her voice is shaky. "Because I would never... I swear I don't know how it's possible. You need to believe me." She looks up at me, and her big blue eyes blink at me with fear and sincerity.

Such a smart, conniving liar. I've come to know her: what makes her tick, how she thinks, what makes her scared, and what she wants more than anything. And that's security. She craves it like a baby needs milk. She wants me to take care of her dad and she wants me.

And what's more, I know, *know* in my heart she knew exactly what she was doing. But hey, I have to give it to her. No other woman has ever gotten me so crazy with desire that I lost sight of what I was doing like wrapping up my dick. I took her word and truly believed she was perfect since I never wanted kids and she can't—well, couldn't—have them. I've killed men for looking at me wrong, yet I have to hold back a smile at her. She sits so dejected I can't wait to hear what she says next. It's almost laughable, except that she's right—I don't want kids. They don't fit into my life.

"So, you want it?" Her cheeks are flushed pink and her hands slightly shake as she brings the juice to her lips.

"No. I can't stand kids actually. I mean some are cool, but I'm not father material. You did this, so you'll be raising him. I'll stop in and say hello on birthdays and shit, but other than that—"

She jumps up and grips the table as if to steady herself. "Are you telling me that you're dumping me with your kid to raise on my own?" Her voice cracks.

I move directly in front of her and look her straight in those baby blues. "I'm saying exactly that. I. don't. want. kids! I'm the president of a motorcycle club, Eve. Grow the fuck up. You did this. Now you get to deal with it."

Her breathing is harsh as the tears slide down her cheeks. She looks up at the ceiling and back at me.

"I thought... I lov..." She swallows and clears her throat, all signs of the tears gone. "I thought you needed me. But all you are is a scared, pathetic thug who kills and sells drugs."

Badass. She stares at me, her eyes swimming with tears but almost glowing with an *I want to kill you* look. My eyes narrow and I rub the back of my neck. My head is throbbing. She needs to know the truth. I can't have her as a liability. I'll make her my ole lady, move her in here, and that's where it ends.

"Oh my God." She spins in her pretty dress and flip-flops and runs back toward my bedroom. The door slamming makes my heart squeeze and I hate it. I look at her chair where she sat seconds ago and at her barely touched juice. For a second I have to force myself to stay strong. "Fuck." I reach for my cigarettes and call Axel.

"Yeah?" he grunts into the phone. Axel thinks phones are evil, so he always sounds like a dick.

"Eve's pregnant."

Silence then a long sigh. "I knew it, I told you..."

"Meet me at the—" Suddenly I stop. I'm not actually going to leave Eve alone and pregnant. I'm a dick but not that much of a dick. "I need to go check on her."

"Blade?"

"Yeah?" Glancing around my empty house, I wonder what it would look like with a family.

"I know I'm not her biggest fan, but I think she's good for you. It's only a matter of time before we find our other halves, and she's yours, man. And if you tell anyone I said that I'll deny it."

I look down at my bare feet and take a breath. "She lied. I know she's lying, and for some fucked-up reason that turns me on."

Axel chuckles. "Yeah, you're fucked. Make it work, man. I don't want your job."

Silence surrounds me as I let his words sink in. He doesn't want it, I don't want it, but in a way I do. It's my birthright and my father, brother, and grandfather deserve more than a pussy-ass dumbass running from his shit.

"I'll be back tomorrow. I might leave Eve here."

"Whatever you need to do, man. And hey..."

"What?"

"Congratulations."

I don't say anything and hang up. Axel will get it. This is all fucked and I need to think. Ripping open my wooden cabinets, I grab a bottle of whiskey, unscrew it, and take a guzzle. Lack of food and the fact that it's barely noon make me put it back. I pick up the phone and order a pizza and some hot wings, and then tell the guy to make sure the pizza is well done, since that's the way Eve likes it. I go outside and smoke again and try to figure out what to say to her. She said she loved me. *Loves me.* Can either one of us truly love? I take a long drag and hold it. The warmth of the liquor and this cigarette have helped. My phone vibrates in my back pocket. I pull it out. "Well?" I say to Hilary.

"She's pregnant. I've emailed you names of a couple of incredible ob-gyns. I'm at the hospital. I have to go."

"Thanks, Hilary."

"Your old man would be over the moon to be a grandfather. Congratulations."

"Too bad us McCormick men can't seem to live to be older than fifty, huh?" I say and hang up. Hilary got with my old man when... shit I don't even think she was seventeen. He put her through school and even paid for her to become a surgeon. She always held out hope that he would one day do what he promised her and leave my mom. She's a good doctor and has stitched me and my boys up more times than I care to admit. I pay her a shit ton of money and she does what my dad spent a fortune on getting her trained to do. Other than that, I get sick of her thinking because she fucked my old man for years she's like a second mom and shit. I have my mom, and she's not perfect, but I think she is. So I tend to only use Hilary when absolutely needed. Today I wanted a female, since I needed Eve to feel comfortable.

The doorbell rings and I toss my cigarette in an ashtray, making a mental note to order some more outdoor furniture. The grass and view are peaceful. Eve will like it.

I pay for the pizza and wings and seriously consider bringing in the bottle of whiskey I was drinking from. Instead I stand outside my own bedroom door hands full of food, wondering how best to deal with my life.

"Fuck it." I throw open the door. She sits on the edge of the bed. She's changed from the dress to gray jeans with holes in the knees and a tight white T-shirt that says *Groovy* across her tits. And she's frantically typing on her phone. Other than her fingers gliding over the phone like a pianist, she seems calm, which of course puts me on alert. I look around.

"I need furniture," I say.

I have no choice but to put the pizza on my bed—it's either that or the floor. She crosses her legs and gives me her back.

What the fuck? A half an hour ago she was weeping and now she acts like I'm beneath her, not even acknowledging me. My neck clenches and I roll it hearing it crack.

"Eat," I demand. She still types, but this time she looks at me. Her eyes are puffy but her cheeks are pink and her lips are dark red. She's so beautiful for a moment I hope we have a girl: a little girl who looks like her mommy.

"I'm assuming I can get a second opinion?" She snaps and stands. My eyes dip to her chest—her tits are nothing short of amazing.

"Don't worry. You'll be seeing the best tomorrow morning." I flip open up the box of pizza. The aroma of sausage and pepperoni permeates the room.

"You need to eat." I pull out a piece of gooey pizza. She stares at me then turns and looks out the window.

"Eve, it wasn't an invitation. You will eat." Chewing the spicy sausage and pepperoni, I use my pants as a napkin. She stares at me as if I'm the disappointment in her life, which I should not care about. Instead I swallow my mouthful and say, "Fine. Don't eat. I guess I can call—"

"Stop." She holds her hands over her ears. "I can't handle you torturing me about my father. Or that I trapped you," she screams in my face, her voice trembling as she holds back the tears that want to spill down her flushed cheeks. Jesus Christ, she's like a fierce little lion cub and my dick instantly gets hard.

"Eve." I rub my chest almost as if I'm trying to block my heart from her. "I need you to be honest. It's done. You won, Angel. I'm going to support you and your father forever, okay?"

She stares at me then bites her bottom lip as she looks at the ceiling. "You honestly think I wanted to trap you?" The accusation in her eyes makes me lose it.

"I don't give a fuck," I yell. "Christ, it was bound to happen sometime." Her face pales and it's like I can't help hurting her since for some reason her lack of joy, or not doing what I want, makes me angry. I shrug. "I'm sure this one won't be my last accident."

She looks like I've slapped her, and I guess I have. That was a shit thing to say since I don't want anyone but her. Jesus, I have no control around her.

I need to get away from her. She stands tall, her shoulders back, but the pain my words inflicted makes me want to grab her and kiss away all our demons.

"Eat, Eve." I turn, leaving her standing with a pale face and eyes glistening with tears. *What the fuck is happening?* I swing open the cabinet in the kitchen and reach for the bottle.

"Jason?" I don't look at her and take a swig.

"What?"

"This is where I'll stay. That way you can fuck whoever you want at the club house!" She spits it out, venom dripping with every word. If she didn't have a slight tremble I would believe that she was done. I lean my head down as I grip the counter.

"That's perfect. You can decorate... and see the doctor." I take another swig looking out the kitchen window, seeing nothing but my Angel. "Yeah, that's best." I lift my head and turn to her. Our eyes lock and time stops as my heart aches. I take a step toward her.

Her big eyes are filled with an emotion I don't know or understand, but it's something I want. In a second, her eyes change and it's gone. She turns and walks back into the bedroom and shuts the door. Grabbing the bottle, I slink onto my couch and turn on the TV absently thinking I should order another pizza because there is no way I'm going into that bedroom.

TWENTY-THREE

EVE

I wake up and stare out the window. Alone, I can't fight the tears forming in my eyes. Dejected. That's what comes to mind as I stare out at the gloomy morning. Turning onto my back, I look up at the ceiling. How is this even possible? I have become everything I swore I wouldn't.

"Oh God," I groan, laying my hand over my forehead as I wait for my stomach to reject what little I put into my mouth yesterday. Somewhat in awe, I touch my flat stomach. Since the age of twelve, I've been told I could never have this. Jason left early this morning. I heard the door close and lock behind him, the click reminding me I'm a prisoner. Why did I have to be so weak and fall in love with a dick? I sigh, loud and dramatic. It bounces off the white walls. Sitting up, I look at the fantastic room. With the right furniture and maybe some paint, it could be spectacular. I haven't seen the whole house yet, but if it's anything like the rooms I've seen, I might actually enjoy decorating. My mind is already conjuring up a pleasing green that would look great in here.

Stretching, I stand *annnd* here it comes. "Christ." I sit back down as the dizziness and horrible nausea that strike anytime come roaring back. It's always bad the first hour or so after I wake.

"God this sucks," I groan, but at least I'm not dying, so there's that. I take another deep breath and my phone dings. Reaching over for it, I see three messages. One's from Dolly, with *OMG!* Then there's a gif of a pregnant woman and hula hoop going around her stomach. I texted her yesterday after Jason told me that I was basically his slave and that he has no responsibility to his baby. Instead of being outraged or even sad for me, if her gif is any indication, she seems excited, like all of this is rainbows and unicorns.

The last message is from Jason the asshole telling me that Dewey will be picking me up in an hour for a doctor appointment.

"Whatever," I mumble as I push on Dolly's number.

It doesn't get more than one ring when she screams, "Holy shit! We're dying over here." Loud music blasts through the phone.

Clearly she's at the salon and I hear Doug's voice in the background. "Is that our queen? Hand it over."

"Knock it off, Doug. Me first. I can't stand it... I mean, I couldn't understand your text yesterday. You hate him, you love him. You want to fuck him." She starts giggling at that last comment. "You were all over the place." She squeals and I have to pull the phone away.

"Dolly, stop screaming. I'm already nauseous. There's not a lot of time. I have to go to the doctor." Loud shushing makes me roll my eyes again.

"Okay, I'm putting you on speaker. Don't worry—it's only us." Her nervous energy sinks straight into my gut causing my breath to hitch. I stand up and look out the window, ultimately deciding to open the adorable farm-style door, which has glass on the top and wood on the bottom. I pull it open and step onto the redwood deck.

"Wow," I mumble looking at his backyard. Nothing but green grass and a view. The deck has been glossed so much you could probably skate on it if you wore socks.

"What? Eve go tell us everything. How did you do the unbelievable?"

"You're set, baby girl. Mission accomplished. You know that, right?" Doug starts in and Dolly steamrolls over him. She and Doug talk about how I'm so lucky. Jason is going to be a great dad and our kid is going to be *so* beautiful.

"Guys," I yell over the gushing on the sex of said unborn heir. "He's not happy. He thinks I'm trapping him and he's making me stay at his house so he can stay at the clubhouse to fuck other women." My voice is getting louder and higher until I have to stop and gasp in some air.

Silence ensues and they start laughing. I roll my eyes again.

"You both suck."

"All right, let's break this down." It's Doug speaking in a calm, soothing voice much better than Dolly's excited energy.

"First, Jason says stupid stuff. He's completely obsessed, so don't worry about the fucking of the skanks. Second, he's going to fall in love with the baby, so he'll be around too much and third... he has a house? I didn't know he has a house, did you?"

And they're off again carrying on their own conversation. I walk back into the bedroom and lock the door, putting them on speaker as I go into the bathroom. Apparently Dolly knew he had a house but has never been here before. So I tell them both I'll need help decorating, which makes them both scream and I can't help but smile. Somehow their excitement and complete support make me feel drastically better.

"Okay, you two, I have to get ready. I'll call soon."

"Yeah, we need to go too. Customers and all that. Congrats! Love you!" Dolly chirps and the phone tells me the call has ended.

I start the shower and decide that maybe they are right. Jason talks the talk yet he didn't abandon me. He didn't come in and sleep with me last night, but he didn't leave either. My mind goes over all my options as I shower quickly. Suddenly I decide to play this out. The phone call with Dolly and Doug ate up a lot more time than I thought. Throwing on a pink tube dress and some light makeup, I decide I look pretty good. My skin has a healthy glow thanks to all the veggies Amy shoves down my throat. Either that or my body likes being pregnant because besides the morning sickness, I look fantastic. Emerging from the bathroom, I look at the box of pizza. I love cold pizza, so I flip it open and grab a slice as the doorbell rings. My heart goes to my stomach until I remember it's not Jason. He wouldn't ring the bell.

Throwing on some ballet flats, I open the door and smile at happy Dewey.

"You ready?" He's practically beaming. Jason wouldn't have told everybody, would he?

I grab my bag. "Um, I don't have a key, so—"

"Don't worry. Prez gave me one." He proudly pulls it out of his pocket and grins when I step out and allow him to lock the door. I hold out my hand, but he puts it back in his pocket.

"Wait, that's not my key?" My voice gets louder as I see the gloom starting to burn off and the warm sun coming out. I take in his neighborhood. Last night was dark so I couldn't see the two neighboring houses up here. They're beyond nice. I almost feel like I'm in a dream. I mean, who would ever think I'd end up in this neighborhood and pregnant a year ago?

Dewey opens the Tahoe door for me.

"Nope, Prez says you'll get one when he says so."

As he slides into the driver side, I say, "You know, you don't always have to drive me. I can drive if you're tired or…"

His brows knit and he frowns. "Girls don't drive." He starts the truck and pulls out.

"Dewey, I hate to break it to you, but I've been driving since I was thirteen."

Again, he frowns as if I'm ruining his fantasy. Whatever, it's not his fault he was raised the way he was. My baby won't be raised like these guys or like me for that matter. My baby is going to have everything I never had. I can't wait to tell my dad. This might be exactly the inspiration he needs.

TWENTY-FOUR

BLADE/JASON

"Hey Prez, you want another one?" Ryder yells from inside. I'm out by the pool trying to decide this very second if I'm going to go down the rabbit hole tonight. The pool glistens like sparkling diamonds. I blink at the glare only to have Crystal's big fake tits dripping water on me as she tries to straddle me. I lay back and close my eyes as she slithers up my chest, rubbing her fake breasts all over me. All I see is Eve.

Eve!

"God damn it." I sit up and gently but forcefully scoot her off me.

"What the hell, Blade?" she whines, making me stand up. I'm not even hard. *Christ*, I might be fucked, like *fucked* fucked. Like karma's a bitch fucked. I run my hands through my hair, looking at Crystal's hurt face.

"Yeah Ryder, I need another one," I yell. He nods and comes out of the house. I shake my head still needing a moment to get used to his new look. He shaved his beard and head the other day. Now every time I look at him, I think of Drax in the *Guardians of the Galaxy* movies.

"It's her, isn't it?" Crystal brings my attention back to her. Her shoulders slump as she sits on the edge of the cushion. Thankfully the backyard and pool area are packed with drunk brothers and club whores. Someone turns the music up as Eminem pumps through my chest. It's so loud that Crystal's fake tits are bouncing to the beat. I lift her chin and feel a pang of remorse. I led her on, even going as far as having Edge make sure she was off at the club so that she could be here today. She was so happy that I asked for her. We've been drinking all day and now I'm done. The sun and stale beer are starting to aggravate me, along with the fact that I have no balls anymore. Ryder walks up with a bottle of Jack. He looks from me to Crystal and lights a cigarette.

"Hey darlin, I need a moment with the Prez."Crystal looks up at me, her face slightly burned and black mascara running down her cheeks.

"Jesus. She's a mess." Ryder glances back at her then me.

"Crystal, go clean up," I demand. She tries to stand, but she's so sloppy drunk she sinks back into the cushions sobbing.

"I'm done." My eyes meet Ryder's.

He nods. "I'll take care of her. I was coming to let you know Dewey's back." He takes her arm. She starts to argue then stumbles with him as he walks her toward the house.

Those are the magic words. I scan the yard littered with drunk brothers and naked girls and it's not even night yet. A bonfire is being set up a few feet away, the smell of lighter fluid permeating the air. I scan the yard spotting Dewey immediately. He's the only one dressed in jeans and a T-shirt along with his cut. He's talking to Axel. The hair on my arms stands up.

"What happened today?" I snap. Dewey jumps and looks at Axel who instantly lights up a joint. He inhales and hands it to Dewey.

"What happened? Before you party, you tell me everything."

He drops his hand from taking the joint. "It was so cool." His whole face seems to light up like he's almost hopeful.

Axel snorts and Dewey shakes his head. "No, Eve was awesome. And her new doctor loved her, like he couldn't take his eyes off her. Even saying she was his new favorite patient."

"What the fuck are you talking about *he*?" Suddenly the rancid smell of the weed along with the massive amount of sweaty bodies makes me look away and up at the sky.

"Dewey?" I demand.

"Her doctor is a man."

I blink at him.

"And she's almost three months, can you believe it? She couldn't." He chuckles. "She kept saying 'Are you sure?' to the doc."

He looks at me then Axel, a huge excited smile on his face. "I heard the baby's heartbeat!" Excited, he rubs his hands up and down his legs, and for the first time ever I want to take Dewey out. Like lay him flat. I take a breath and sense Axel's strong hand on my chest, pushing me back.

"Take it easy, Prez."

Dewey's eyes widen. "I did what you told me. I was with her the whole time."

Axel pushes me back some more. "Let's take this inside and you can tell Blade all about it where it's quiet."

Throwing his hand off me, I storm into the clubhouse, ignoring the crap that's going on inside. Drugs are everywhere, but I couldn't give two shits. Adrenaline pulses through me. It's that same feeling I get when I use my blade or gun. My mind keeps repeating *heartbeat*.

Dewey heard my baby's heartbeat. I don't know how I haven't broken a tooth at how hard I'm clenching my jaw. I throw open the door to the meeting room, my breathing harsh. Christ, I'm like two seconds from doing something I'll regret. But I can't stop it, so I growl, "Now. How the fuck did this happen?"

Axel clears his voice as he moves to the refrigerator in the corner. "Anyone want anything?"

I glare at him.

"Christ, Blade, leave it alone." He snaps the cap off the beer bottle and tosses it in a trash can. "If you really wanted to hear the heartbeat, you would have taken your pregnant girlfriend instead of getting fucked up with Crystal and humiliating her and Eve." He looks me straight in the eyes with that shit. Suddenly all I hear is my heartbeat as I move to stand face-to-face with my best friend.

"The fuck you say to me?" I spit.

Axel's eyes narrow on mine. "You told me this morning that she was nothing special. That this baby wasn't changing you, that you weren't cut out for father shit."

I hiss out of my nose. "Fuck you."

"Man. The. Fuck. Up. You want Eve. *Be with her*," he yells and Dewey slinks back. "You knocked her up. Your kid deserves a dad." He gets in my face. "Stop lying to yourself. It's fucking disgraceful. You'll be lucky if Eve will even let you near her or your kid."

That's it. I literally see red as I charge him. He's ready and goes straight for my stomach, but rage is a powerful thing. I don't feel the hit in my jaw. In fact it makes me smile as we both beat the shit out of each other. The room is silent even as we tumble on chairs and knock over glasses.

"Jesus Christ, what the hell?" Edge yells.

I shake my head as I grit out, "Fuck." Edge and Ryder pull me off of Axel. I look down at Axel, his face a bloody mess, but he has a big-ass smile.

"You're my brother." He sits up and spits blood on the floor. "But you are completely addicted to this girl, and if you don't acknowledge it, it's going to destroy you." Dewey tries to help him up, but he knocks away his hand.

"Motherfucker." I go toward him, but Ryder is stronger.

"Prez. It's gonna be okay, man. I told you my dream. Why are you fighting it?"

I jerk out of his grasp and ignore his fucking comment. My eyes zero in on Dewey. "Did you take her home?" I spit it out as I take small breaths in.

He shakes his head. "No, she wanted to stay the night with her father. We were having the party, and I thought that would be nice since you were going to be occupied."

I hear Axel snort and mumble, "That's a joke. His dick is owned."

I straighten and hear my neck and shoulder crack. I wipe my mouth as I taste blood.

"Give me the keys to the Tahoe," I demand.

"Prez, why don't we all calm down. You've been drinking and both you and Axel are bleeding."

"Are you my fucking mother?" I turn to Ox. "Do I need your permission? *No.*" I turn back to Dewey. "Give them to me."

"I'll take you." Edge announces and holds out his hand for the keys. Dewey reluctantly hands them over. Nodding, I'm too tired and pissed to argue. As I walk by Axel, I stop to inspect the damage: his right eye is split and already swollen shut.

"You feel better?" He holds his ribs with one hand and reaches for a bottle of tequila with the other.

I nod not bothering to answer. My throat is raw and I grind out, "I'll be back in the morning."

No one says anything as we walk to the Tahoe. Either they're too fucked up to care or my face says it all as I throw open the door and get into the passenger seat.

Edge stays quiet most of the way to the nursing home. It's not until he puts the Tahoe in park that he turns toward me.

"You going to be okay in there? The last thing she needs is you going crazy, Prez." He rubs his hands on his face.

"Edge, you have no clue what's going on. Dewey heard my baby's heartbeat."

I must sound insane because he frowns and says, "What?"

"My baby. He got to hear its heartbeat before me."

"Why?"

I look over at him and say nothing because what am I going to say? I think I'm in love with Eve and that scares me? So I made Dewey go with her?

He glances over at me and opens the door. "It's hard to be king."

"Well, I am." I grunt as I move my sore jaw around. "I need to work this shit out."

I barge into the lobby. The poor woman behind the counter is so stunned she stares with her mouth open.

"We're here to see James Smith." Edge sighs as he signs us in.

She nods. "Um... is he, are you okay?"

I turn as we start walking toward James's room. "Never better, why?" She stares again and I throw open the door to James's room not even bothering to knock.

Eve sits with her dad at the round table. They must have recently finished dinner because the room reeks of mashed potatoes and garlic. They both glance over surprised, and for a man who is dying, he doesn't look any worse. If anything, he looks better than the last time I saw him. At least his eyes are alive. I grin because he looks like he wants to kill me. Not that I blame him.

"Let's go," I demand. Her nose goes up and her eyes take in my face and shift down to my ripped-up hands.

She tosses her honey waves off her shoulder and reaches for her dad's skinny, blue-veined hand and strokes it. "I guess I'll be back tomorrow." She stands up and kisses his forehead, and even drunk, I still look away. She's gonna be a fucking mess when he kicks it and now she's pregnant.

"Come on, Angel." I reach a bloody-knuckled hand at her. She stiffens and James starts to hiss, but she obeys.

"I thought you were at the clubhouse sleeping with whores," she whispers as I drag her out of the room.

Edge, who was waiting at the door, falls in behind as I literally pull her with me. The poor woman behind the reception desk stands up but sits when she sees me glare.

"I'm not in the mood for your mouth." I open the truck's door and Eve gives me a look. I'm drunk enough to laugh at how she's trying to actually be fierce.

"Well, I'm not in the mood to be jerked around and unless you want me to puke on you, I'd stop any fast movements."

Edge coughs as he grins. Looking away, he gets into the driver's seat. I stop and take in this woman who has addicted my mind. She's beautiful, but it's more than that. For whatever reason, she's what I crave.

I lock eyes with her and can't help but smirk. "Come on, my little badass. In the truck... *please.*"

She huffs and frowns but does get in. Crossing her arms and legs, she turns her head away. I almost laugh at her nerve. If she was a man she'd probably be dead. Clearly, she's delusional if she thinks I'll tolerate her ignoring me. I reach for her arm. She glares, but I ignore it as I slide her warm body next to me. The tingle of touching her almost buzzes with energy. It's uncanny; I need her, want her, she's mine, and I'm sick of being in turmoil over her.

"I heard about our baby's heartbeat," I whisper against her forehead. That gets her attention.

She looks up at me. "What?"

"Dewey told me." Her eyes travel my face, which probably looks a mess. I didn't check if any blood remained on me from earlier. I haven't tasted any, so hopefully I look better than I feel.

"Jason... you didn't hurt him, did you?" Her blue eyes are so sincere and full of concern a wave of jealousy takes hold followed by anger that she would think I would hurt Dewey.

"If you think I'd ever hurt Dewey, you don't know me at all."

She looks down at her hands then back at me, her eyes shiny with tears. Sniffing, she looks out the window at nothing but darkness and street lights.

"I thought you were staying at the clubhouse." Her voice catches at the end. I stretch my legs out sideways and pull her so that she has no choice but to rest on my chest.

"Shh, I'm tired."

"Yeah, you look like you've been busy today." I stay silent. How else am I going to defend myself. "Whatever," she mumbles but stays quiet as I hold her.

Edge turns up my road and she feels so good in my arms I almost tell him to keep driving. Her even breathing makes me squeeze her. For whatever reason, everything about Eve does it for me. I want to take care of her. Christ, I want her so bad that I'm not even upset she's pregnant. The Tahoe stops and Edge turns to face me.

"You want me to pick you up in the morning, Prez?" His eyes are filled with understanding, almost longing.

"Yeah, get me in the morning." I open the door and lift her into my arms. How the hell has she become my life? Holding her tight, I walk to the front door and wait for Edge to unlock it and punch the alarm.

"I'm happy for you, man," he says.

Before I can say anything, he's shut the door. Eve stirs. Her dark, sooty eyelashes blink open as she looks confused for a moment.

"I got you, Angel. Go back to sleep," I murmur as I walk us to our bedroom.

"I fell asleep?" She seems alarmed.

"You're pregnant. It's normal." It sounds foreign to me. Pregnant. Eve and I are going to have a baby. Suddenly I want to hear everything from her. I need a shower—anything to erase what I did earlier.

As I start the shower, I watch her take off her clothes in the walk-in closet. I wash quickly, the need to be with her so strong it's like I'm possessed or an alien has taken over my body. But instead of a little outer space man it's a woman with long golden hair and eyes that are so blue I get lost in them. I finish and wrap a towel around my waist. Eve is already in bed with the covers up so high all I can see are her slender arms and hair spread out on the pillow. Turning off the light, I look out my window. The lights of the city twinkle and glow. Usually I close the blinds so that it's pitch black, but tonight I want the moonlight along with the city below. Tossing my towel, I climb into bed and reach for my Angel. She goes willingly, and her coconut-scented hair wraps around me like smoke at a campfire. She sighs and says something about French fries. I grin as I kiss her forehead. Eve talks in her sleep. So far, it's usually about food. Only once did she call out for her mother when having a nightmare. Christ, we're both so scarred and fucked up, how is this even possible we're having a kid?

"Eve, baby?" My anger has vanished. She's all I need even if it's only tonight. I want to be a real person. Not the president of the Disciples, not Blade.

I want to be Jason. Inhaling her, I let my mind drift. Maybe I didn't have the best upbringing. My mother tried the best she could for my brother and me. But when your husband is the Prez, you're fucked. My dad was taking us to the clubhouse when we were way too young. I remember the first time I actually held a gun. I was maybe six. One of my dad's officers had passed out and I picked it up and it went off. Thankfully it didn't kill anyone. Instead of scolding me, he gave me an atta boy. Had the officer whose gun I picked up circle it with red paint. It's like a rare picture in the clubhouse. Then he took me outside and taught me how to properly shoot a gun.

Eve blinks and looks up at me. Our gazes lock and I lower my lips to her sweetness. It's slow and almost painful when I lift my head.

"Tell me about our baby."

She smiles, and I finally acknowledge it. I love her. Fuck! I don't care if she did this to trap me. I don't care if she did it for security. All I care is that she makes me feel alive. That if she ever left me, I might not survive. Jesus, I'm like a caveman with his mate. I want to drag her by her hair twenty-four seven.

"It was amazing, Jason." Her voice cracks and her blue eyes are full of emotion.

"Yeah?" I reach up and my thumb rubs her rose-colored lips. "I'm sorry, Angel. I should have been there."

She blinks as if she doesn't understand. I love her like this. She's always easier to read when she's not quite awake—when her guard isn't up and it's only us. So I take advantage of it by rolling over and caging her in as I look at her beautiful face.

"I want you, and I want us." Before she can speak, I take her lips and groan as they part for me. It's like the glow of the moon has cast some spell on us as I pull my T-shirt off her. Her skin, so soft and flawless, calls to me and I lick her, lips moving down to her neck and finally to her fucking tits. She moans as I latch onto one hard nipple and arches up so I can suck harder.

"Jason," she whispers, turning her head into the pillow.

"Open your eyes, Angel." My cock is leaking with need to get into her silken walls. My mind swims as my body takes over and both of us growl and pant our pleasure as I enter her.

She's whimpering as I brace myself on my elbows. I need to see everything she feels.

"Fuck... It's so good with us." I thrust into her.

She reaches for my face. Her hands are warm and I inhale her scent. I'm inside her. She's wrapped her soul around mine and I never want this feeling to end.

"Angel." I lean into her beautiful lips. Her breath is sweet and I take it from her and breathe mine back into her mouth. Our eyes lock, the moonlight casting the right amount of light to make this whole night almost unreal. Then she tells me with words what my heart already knows.

"I love you." Strong and confident, her words caress us. And for one moment, it almost spills out of my own mouth that I love her too. Instead I hold her gaze as I move deeper inside her. I watch her and hear her breath become labored. She's close.

"Angel, my Angel." Her eyes narrow and her nails latch onto my back and scratch down as her core pulses and contracts, milking my cock in ecstasy. My balls tighten, my stomach muscles jerk, and the pleasure seeps out of me snaking down to my toes as I shoot my seed deep inside her.

"Jesus Christ," I grunt as the world and room spin. I've never experienced anything like that. Rolling over, I bring her with me. The intensity that I share with this woman is consuming me. She's becoming my need, salvation, life.

"Jason?"

I'm caressing her back as we catch our breaths.

"What, baby?"

"I really do love you." She leans up on her elbow, her cheek resting on her arm.

"Yeah?" I move her hair off her shoulder.

"Yeah," she purrs as she brushes my lips. "And I know how you feel about me." Her voice is raspy and dipped with honey and my dick twitches.

"How do I feel about you?" I can't help but grin at her. She's a mixture of goddess and fallen angel.

"You love me too." She flops back onto the pillow and my heart squeezes. I say nothing but turn toward her on my side and grab her, pulling her snugly into my arms.

"Go to sleep, baby."

TWENTY-FIVE

EVE

There's a buzzing, a sort of annoying bee around my head. I'm warm and safe. Why won't that buzzing go away? I blink my eyes open and I'm being held tightly by a muscular, tattooed arm. His phone is buzzing and vibrating on the floor.

"Jason." I wiggle around so that we're nose to nose and last night comes happily back to me. We made love, and it was amazing. I told him I love him and I know he'll tell me the same soon. No one can feel the way we do and not love each other. "Jason, your phone."

He grunts and rolls to his back, bringing me with him. "I hear it—I want a few more minutes with you."

His gravelly morning voice is my favorite, but did he insinuate that he's leaving again? No, he wouldn't. We made love last night. This is a beginning for us.

"Umm, I need to pee." My voice sounds unsure.

He opens his pretty green eyes and I can't help but smile at him. We stare at each other and I watch the wall come down over his eyes. In seconds, he goes from Jason to Blade. I turn and get out of bed, reaching down to get his phone and tossing it to him. After I bolt into the bathroom, I lock the door.

"Shit." I drop to my knees as I try to silently puke. My mind races at the fact that I laid myself out like an open book. Standing, I groan and reach for my toothbrush. He didn't say shit. I said everything.

"Eve." Jason bangs on the door causing me to almost drop my toothbrush.

"I have shit that's going down," he yells as the door handle jiggles. "Unlock the door."

I glance at myself and sigh. I've definitely looked better, but at least I'm naked and my tits look spectacular. Unlocking the door, I'm greeted with Jason staring at his phone, his tatted arm leaning on the side of the bathroom doorway. "I have to go."

"Okay." My voice cracks and I clear it because there is no way I'm going to start crying. *No fucking way!*

He finally looks up from his phone and for a split second his eyes soften and almost caress my face, moving down my body. Then he pushes off the wall and reaches for my chin. His warm hands smell like smoke. He must have had a quick cigarette.

"You need anything, you call me. You want to go anywhere, you call me." His eyes are so indifferent I almost take a step back in confusion.

"I want to see my dad." Then I want to take my nails and claw his chest or better yet his bruised lip. If only I could lean over and—

"I'll have Dewey take you." His warm hands leave my face as he turns and grabs his gun out of the nightstand.

"No doctor appointments without me."

Like I'm a pet, an object. What the fuck was I thinking telling him I loved him? I stare, almost frozen, as my stomach flips and his tall form moves away, the slamming of the door a loud reminder that I'm an idiot. He doesn't love me. I'm some stupid girl who is going to be his baby momma. Sinking to the bed, I look around. His room is so white it almost makes me nervous. Like the shows on TV where the lead character gets locked in the psych ward and goes crazy.

"God." I cover my face with my hands, groaning as I remember every single thing I said to him last night. "Why, Eve?" I drop my hands with a loud dramatic thud. I should go back to bed. I look down at his clean black sheets, his spicy scent wrapping around me like the smoke that he exhales from one of his cigarettes. Maybe I'll wake up and everything I said to him will be a bad dream. Snorting at my delusional and pathetic thoughts, I force myself to stand and make my way into the bathroom. Swallowing back my gag, I almost retch again at the lingering smell of my vomit.

Quickly, I start the shower. The hot water is so fast, I never seem to get used to it.

I close my eyes and let the soothing hot water caress my skin. My mind clears as I formulate a plan. One, never tell Jason I love him again. He doesn't deserve it and it's mine to cherish. Two, I need to go steal something. Actually, it's not even a need; it's a must, a sense of myself that I have to bring back to life. I need the high. *Control.* I need control of my life. I turn off the shower with a new strength I haven't felt in weeks and step out. Wrapping a towel around me, I look at the fogged-up mirror. I don't need to see myself to know I'm back. I straighten my shoulders and dry off. The clean sink counter is white and empty.

"Damn it." This is why I always, *always* made sure I had all my stuff in my bag. Hand lotion, makeup I always had everything. But lately I've been slipping. I mean why carry around all that shit when I have plenty at home? *Home.* I snort in disgust. Am I actually thinking of the club house as home? Rolling my eyes, I turn to take in the whole bathroom. It's all white and clean—I swear you could eat off this white-tiled floor. *What the hell?* In the corner is an attractive French country white cabinet.

"Perfect." My eyes take in the objects. "What the fuck?" I pick up a bar of some fancy rose-smelling soap. "That dick." I start to grab all kinds of women's shit. Olay face cream, Bath & Body Works coconut hand cream, and gold and pink bubble bath beads.

He lied.

Of course, he lied. Why would he tell me the truth? I'm nothing to him. Slamming the cabinet, I toss my towel on the floor and go to get dressed. "Never brought a woman to this house, huh?" Everything he says I believe. I almost want to take all that shit from the cabinet and dump it on his side of the bed. But that would make it obvious that I care and I've already humiliated myself enough by telling him I love him.

Groaning at the thought, I pull on a pair of tight white jeans and a pink T-shirt along with some white Converse sneakers. Absently I shake my head. I'm getting spoiled… soft even. First no hand lotion in my bag and now clean sneakers. I'm a shell of my former self. That stops today. I have a baby to think about and my dad. I reach behind me as a wave of dizziness—maybe a serious dose of reality—hits me and almost brings me to my knees. *I'm pregnant.* I'm actually pregnant. I never thought I would have this, and even though Blade doesn't want it, I do. In fact, I'm thrilled. He or she will rule the world. With my brains and its father's guts, nothing will be able to stop it.

Twirling around, I reach for my bag, making sure my knife is still there. I do this every day. Even though I've grown soft, I'm not stupid. For a split second I worried Jason might take it from me, but it's still here. I grab my phone and text Dewey that I'm ready to get out of here. I should probably get something to eat. Not that I'm hungry, but I'm sure my baby is. Smiling at that thought, I make my way to the kitchen. I need to go shopping if I'm staying here. This is crazy. Everything in this house is perfect. It's clean and white and smells like bleach. Wrinkling my nose I wonder, is it Pine-Sol? A large glass fruit bowl is in the middle of the wooden butcher block island and I take a banana. A couple of French doors overlook the deck and the view of the Valley below.

Opening them, I step out and close my eyes. Only for a moment, I let the heat from the morning sun warm my face. For a moment, I actually allow myself the luxury of listening to the birds chirping. I can smell cut grass, and a lawn mower roars across the street. For the first time in my life, I like where I am. Jason's house is amazing even with its white walls. I sigh and open my eyes to peel the banana and take a bite.

"Wow, even his bananas are perfect." I can't help but snicker. Seriously, it's ripe and not mushy, firm and delicious. Kind of like his thick hard cock. My cheeks burn as I visualize his dick, fingers, lips, and I rub my legs together. *Great, now my panties feel wet and gooey.*

A buzz in my bag makes me come out of my dream land. Digging into it, I pop the last of the banana into my mouth. Absently I wonder if I should put on a clean pair of panties. I look at my phone: it's a text from Dewey. Of course all it says is *Outside* and a smiley emoji.

"God, Dewey." I roll my eyes and dump my phone back into my bag. Sometimes I wish I was Dewey. He's always so... happy, never letting things get to him. Actually, the only time I've ever seen him upset is when I stabbed him. That nagging guilt starts to make me second-guess myself. Pushing my hair back I reason with myself. Dewey is fine. He's not going to get hurt because Jason is not going to find out. I need to be smart, on my toes, and no one will be the wiser. And I will have a nice little nest egg just in case. *Just in case...* what? Just in case Blade really does only show up for birthdays and holidays? I almost laugh at how silly I was to even let that bother me. I'm gambling on the hope that he can't stay away. He wants me. He may not love me, but he wants me.

Putting my sunglasses on, I'm almost ready. Thank God I didn't act like a child throwing all that girl shit on the bed. "I need to be calculating if I want him." *And I do want him.*

"Want who?"

I spin toward the door and gasp out "Holy shit you scared me."

Dewey smiles and stands in the kitchen—a grown man with happy child eyes.

"Dewey! You can't let yourself in like that. You scared me."

He looks confused. "But I texted you and you didn't come." He shakes his head. "It's my job to watch over you."

I grit my teeth at the reminder that he's right. Jason doesn't trust me. Not I that I can blame him. I'm all over the place in the emotions department right now.

"Well, next time knock." I wave my hand at the door.

"Sorry. I was worried." His brown eyes are sincere. And again, I have that sensation that's hard to express, almost like… compassion or responsibility. I don't know, but I hate it so I push it away.

He nods and holds the door open as I step outside. I look back and have to glance away before I steal Dewey's keys. I'll have my own set soon enough. That's if I play my cards right.

"Are you hungry? I'm supposed to make sure you eat." He opens up the Tahoe door for me.

"Actually, I'm starving. Why don't we go to that bagel shop over by Dolly's salon and I can get my dad some bagels."

"Um, that's kind of the wrong direction."

"I know, but I should probably stop by and see Dolly anyway. You know how I need to stay waxed and all that."

Dewey's face turns red as he clears his voice. "Prez said to feed you and take you to your dad's but… I guess a bagel is food."

I bite back a smile. Like tampons, anything to do with the vagina makes men stupid. "Sorry, Dewey. I'm only trying to keep Blade happy."

He coughs into his shoulder and cracks his neck like Jason does.

"Hey, no problem." He pushes the button for the window to go down and turns on the radio. I almost groan out loud at the country music he seems to love. Instead, I look at the narrow street and its incredible houses. I'm fascinated at all this. Jason has a house in a neighborhood that appears to be wealthy. People are jogging and walking their dogs.

"How long has Jason had this place?"

He shrugs and keeps his eyes on the road. I always forget that Dewey needs to focus way harder than most. I'm beginning to recognize the shops and restaurants on Ventura Boulevard. We pass a huge CVS and I almost scream for him to stop. But come on, I need to be thinking about diamonds, not hand lotion. Speaking of diamonds, there's a pawn shop across the street from Dolly's place. Not that it does me any good. Pawn shops are filled with cameras and everything is locked up with super thick glass. Yeah, the way you can rip them off is if you take a hammer and smash the glass. Grab whatever you can, praying you don't get shot. I don't work that way. The guy who ran the fun house at the carnival had a son who did that. He took a long wrench and tried to rob a pawn shop in Arizona. He's still in jail I think. Anyway it's desperate, sloppy, and stupid. I'm not stupid.

"So, do you want a plain bagel? Might be good for you and your dad's stomachs? You always get the everything bagel and I don't know..." Dewey has parked the car and is preparing to get out.

"Oh, um." Jesus, how long have I been in my head? I had no idea he even stopped.

"Yes, plain bagels." I hop out and head over to Dolly's salon, calling over my shoulder, "And something sweet if they have it. My dad loves anything sweet."

He nods and looks at his boots as he shuffles to the bagel shop. This is it. Holy shit, I'm free. Adrenaline pumps through me all the way to my fingertips and I have to breathe for a second. It's been way too long. I'm not Eve anymore. I'm a dirty-haired blond girl who used to be able to pick people's pockets in seconds. I turn and make sure I'm alone and enter a small boutique. Incense hits me as soon as I enter and a small bell alerts that I'm here. A woman in her late forties sits behind the desk on the phone as I nod and quickly scan the place for cameras. I find one pointing toward the shop. God, it's almost too easy. Like stealing candy from a baby.

I brazenly walk over to the racks of actually pretty dresses and start to grab a bunch. I hear the woman say she has a customer and has to go.

I'm making my way over to the jacket section when I hear her say, "Can I put all of that in a room for you?" Her eyes are sharp and alert and I smile my sweet smile.

"Yes." I dump my pile into her outstretched arms and watch as she turns and walks over to a tall, amber-colored curtain. I guess that's the changing room? Whatever. I don't have time to ponder. I reach over and take a couple rings sitting on the counter. It's actually a cool-looking display with different-colored sand. The rings are placed in the sand or on a black lava rock.

"Thanks." I wander over to the curtain noticing how the wood floor has flowers painted on it.

"If you need anything else let me know. Maybe a belt to go with the dresses?"

She needs to dye her hair. Now that I'm up close to her, it's dark brown with an inch of gray roots. I almost tell her that she should go see Dolly or Doug, but then that would be horribly rude. Also, I'm pressing it on time here. If there's a line at the bagel place, I probably have a few more minutes. If not, Dewey is going to panic if I'm not at Dolly's. Shutting the curtains with a swift whoosh, I get to business, grab my phone, and go to settings and ringtones, pick the opening tone and let it ring. And it's on... "Hello... Wait, what? I can't hear you. Great. I'm shopping. What about Dad? Oh shit, okay calm down. I'll be there soon." The whole time I'm having this fake conversation I'm wishing I had more time to try this stuff on. Some of it is super cute, but I don't, so I stuff black overalls that are ridiculously priced at $399 and a cut white T-shirt to go with them in my bag. Now here's the deal. I can't see any device on them, which leads me to believe she is relying on the mirrors and camera. Or they are sewn in and she deactivates them at the check-out. Whatever. I'm not sticking around long enough to figure it out. Actually, judging from her hair, Dolly's salon is the perfect place to hide. I smile as I slip the rings on my fingers, the clothes safely in my bag, and step out looking every inch the distraught girl that I am.

"Oh my God, here." I dump the pile of clothes on her glass counter. Looking her in the eye I say, "My sister said my dad fell. I'll be back. I love your stuff," I say, waving my hand with her rings on my fingers. She nods. "Of course. I hope all is well, dear."

This is it... my blood is pumping. I'm so charged that I sense every little sound and smell. It's alive and tingly and I don't want this feeling to end. Reaching for the door, I step out and the alarm goes off. I turn and look at the woman, rolling my eyes like it's her fault.

"Listen, sorry, but I have to go. Jesus, I didn't even buy anything. Is that thing going off on me?" I'm completely playing dumb.

My eyes start to fill with tears. "What? God can this day get any worse?" I lift up my hands and start walking. She doesn't follow and I make myself not run. The adrenaline is flowing through my bloodstream like hot lava runs down a volcano. *Breathe, Eve.* I stop and wait for a large black SUV to turn but it doesn't. Instead it pulls up in front of me.

"Christ!" I almost pound on the hood. The doors open and out steps some Hispanic guy.

"Eve Smith?" I look at the man. He's in a dark suit and all of a sudden, my stomach lurches. The blood flows to my face and I close my eyes. *Holy shit, I've been set up.*

TWENTY-SIX

BLADE/JASON

"You okay, man?" I'm staring out the window. The morning gloom has burned off to a sunny day. The driveway is littered with Harleys, the chrome catching the sun perfectly to make me blink and turn away. I'm on edge. I don't know if it's the fight last night or Eve saying she loves me. The baby? I turn to stare at Axel. His blue eyes reflect concern. Besides one being black and purple he doesn't look bad.

"I'm fucked, I think." My eyes take in our conference room. It has the usual shit going on. Drinking, drugs, and arguing and I'm not in the mood for it today. "Everyone out but my officers," I bark.

The room goes quiet and I don't turn to watch them murmur and leave.

"Take it easy, Blade." Axel looks at me then down at his phone, which is vibrating. "Shit," he hisses, looks at me, then turns and answers. Time and noise stop. It's the same thing that happened right before my dad and brother died. Everything stops, and I know the shit in my life is going to come crashing down on me. I blink as I watch Axel talk animatedly into the phone, then look over to Ryder. My enforcer, the rock of my club, looks as though he might burst into tears.

"Get me our lawyers." I say this without even hearing what's happening, but I don't need to.

"On it." His fingers are already tapping at his screen.

"Stay there. Ox is on his way," Axel shouts into the phone and I wait to hear what I know is going to be the game changer.

He looks up. "Eve got picked up by the Feds for shoplifting." He rubs the back of his neck. "She won't talk, right?" Which is code for *do you want me to put a fucking bullet in her head?* Because we don't allow traitors and we certainly don't need any more shit.

"I take it by the look you are giving me that's a no," he says.

I breathe in and out and look at my brothers. "This is my woman. She's my responsibility. I need you guys to protect her." All of them nod, their eyes trained on me.

Ryder looks up from his phone. "Rodney is on his way to Burbank PD."

Phones are vibrating as texts are coming in. "We're on lockdown. Everything that happens does not leave this room. *Fuck.*" My phone vibrates as I look down to see Doc's number come up. I roll my neck and prepare myself.

"What?" I snarl because he's the cause of all this heat. And now I have to protect Eve, all because his wife's a fucking junkie and he's worthless. Rage takes over my brain and for a few moments, I don't comprehend that it's not Doc speaking but a woman. She's screeching and weeping on the end of the wire.

"Sandy?" I reach for my blade and stab the wooden table. "You're going to have to stop that crying," I command.

"You did this, Blade! It's all your fault… If you would… If he could have made the drug… this wouldn't have happened. He would have left us alone." Her sobbing and slurring words are almost hard for even me to understand and I'm a god damn pro dealing with drug addicts.

"Sandy, what the fuck are you talking about?" I look down at my forearm. It's covered in goose bumps as I stab the table again. This time, the force is so great a bottle smashes to the floor.

"Um… I think he needs an ambulance… Doc?" She's gone into sounding like a child. "He can't be… did you kill him?"

My pulse beats in my temples. "Who are you talking to?" Her breathing is labored and I definitely hear a man in the background. "Sandy? Is that Doc?" I scream into the phone, but it's eerily silent.

"Fuck." Looking around the room, I see all my guys are ready, eyes alert. I push on Doc's name, but it goes straight to voice mail. "Christ! Something's gone down with Doc and Sandy." I breathe out before I look up.

"She killed him, right?" Edge speaks as he pockets his phone and checks his Glock. He looks up, eyes eerily calm, quiet, deadly. It's one of his strong suits. Edge never loses it.

"I have no idea… It sounded like someone is with her. Jesus Christ." I look at Axel who is pale and anything but calm. "Axel, you come with me and Ox to get Eve."

I look straight at Edge. "Go take care of it." He nods. "Ryder go with… if it's out of control…"

"We got this." Ryder goes to the safe and hands Edge another Glock along with a bunch of bullets and another two burner phones.

I look down at my phone and hear my teeth grinding. "Talk to me, Roddy. This day has been nothing but fucked. Tell me my girl is safe." I motion for Axel and Ox to move.

An unsettling foreboding is pumping through my blood like venom from a snakebite. Axel barks orders to the guys playing pool as we pass and Ox beeps open the Tahoe.

There's static and then Rodney's voice. "Stay calm, Jason. I'm here and Eve is with me. I got here in time. They haven't interrogated her yet. They tried but she said nothing." The breath that I've been holding for hours slowly slips out.

"According to one of the cops, she was mute except to ask for water."

Slamming the Tahoe door shut, I nod at Ox to start driving. "I'm on my way."

"Don't come in, Jason. I will call you when we I have her released."

"I'm not stupid, Rodney," I snap, getting ready to go off on him. Instead I need him, so I swallow back my scathing remarks. "I know not to come. We'll wait for her outside."

"Hold, please." If all this wasn't so morbid I would laugh at my lawyer's polite manners. He's mumbling something to someone.

"Sorry, Jason, they are being difficult, saying that the clothing she happened to accidentally have in her bag is reason enough to hold her. I've informed them that the outfit was planted and she has no priors. So please, one thing at a time. Let me take care of Eve." He hangs up. The line goes dead and I look down at my fists, which are red and swollen from last night and also because I've been clenching them so tight they actually ache.

"Axel?" I know I'm snarling but I have a bad feeling that something is going to happen that I might not ever recover from. "When was the last time you saw Doc?"

He says nothing and stares out the window.

"Brother, I need you now. Shit's going down."

He turns and I lower my head into my hands. "What? What happened to make you look like this?" Rubbing my face, I lean back and wait for my best friend to speak his sins.

"Doc came by last night... late after you left. He was nervous and acting paranoid." He laughs as he glances out the window. "He wanted money, said someone was after Sandy and that he would pay me back as soon as he started cooking again."

I take a deep breath and let it out. "Did you tell him that we had voted on not dealing anymore?"

Axel looks over at me then down at my phone, which is vibrating in my hand.

tears. "And now he's dead and I feel like shit." He slams the door and walks in the opposite direction from the station.

Ox clears his throat and looks back at me. "Let him walk it off, Prez. He'll be fine."

I look over at him as I take a long drag of nicotine into my throat. "Doc was working with the Feds. Sandy's involved and whoever she was talking to killed Doc." I swallow the smoke and feel it burn all the way down my throat. I need to pick up Eve and get to a safe place. I feel like I'm high. My head is buzzing almost as if I'm in a tunnel and a bee is next to my ear. The doors open and I see my lawyer Rodney emerge, his dark suit out of place on this warm day. He has his arm around Eve as he ushers her out. My heart does this tightening thing.

"Stay here and keep the engine running." It comes out as a growl. My whole body says, *Get to her.* Maybe it's all the crazy training I've been through. But something's wrong. I feel it, know it.

"You bitch! This is all your fault. Your fucking brother ruined everything, then Blade ruins everything." Sandy stands two feet from Eve, her eyes darting around like a wild, caged animal's.

I'm moving as I fast as I can because this can't be happening. We're in the middle of the Burbank Police Department. Sandy continues to scream at a shocked Rodney and Eve. Her greasy hair and fucked-up skin almost look like she's been dipped in oil. I can smell her as she looks over at me either because I'm calling for Eve or Eve is calling for me. In slow motion I watch her hand go straight for her dirty backpack and I know what this insane bitch is thinking.

All my mind is saying over and over is *get to her.* It's like blinking Christmas lights.

I'm so close. Why can't Rodney take her inside? Why aren't there any police? I'm screaming, but so is Sandy. No one but Eve seems to hear me. My eyes find hers and everything in me is in her. She has somehow become my reason for breathing. And at this very moment, I know what I need to do. What I will always do if I'm lucky enough to be able to spend more time with her.

    I've had these moments in my life where my mind stops and focuses on the events that are happening. I see Eve's beautiful blue eyes wide and defiant at Sandy. My whole body's on alert. I don't know how I know that Sandy is going to do the unforgivable but I do. For the first time in my life, I literally take a bullet for someone. The noises are muted now. And I'm falling. All I feel are cool hands on my hot face as I fall to the concrete. I have never minded dying. With all the shit I've done in my life, I certainly can't be surprised. I close my eyes and I see a blond-haired boy who looks up at me with eyes so blue they can't be real. He has to be mythical, a magical being because he smiles and calls me daddy. Then everything goes black.

TWENTY-SEVEN

EVE

I'm on the ground. Jason's warm body has cushioned my fall. It takes me a moment to get my bearings. The smell of copper—or is it metal?—is all around me. I blink as I look at his beautiful face. His green eyes are almost black and I reach up to touch his face. Vaguely I hear the ravings of the woman who shot Jason.

Shot.

Jason.

I squirm as he tells me to stay still but I can feel warm wetness that I know is his blood flowing onto my belly. The woman screams like a caged beast, but all I can do is focus on Jason.

"Eve, Angel, you're okay?" He hasn't moved—it's as if he can't. Fear takes hold of my whole body and I realize I'm clinging to him and yelling.

His eyes blink and he lays his full lips, which always are warm, on my forehead, but this time, they're cold.

"Jason… don't you dare close your eyes." I force myself to look around at the commotion. Cops are everywhere, guns are drawn, and that crazy bitch is restrained. Dirt and smoke cause me to choke or maybe it's only my own tears.

"Eve? Are you hurt?" He grunts it out.

"No." I grab his face with two hands. "She shot you." Then I look over at Ox who is struggling to get to us and I hear Rodney tell me I need to let go of Jason, that the paramedics must get to him. I nod and Jason grunts again. But his lips are still on my fevered skin.

"It's a boy, Angel. I see him."

"Jason? What the fuck? Someone help me." I look up as Axel screams and two police taser him. Someone lifts Jason off me and I watch in muted slow motion as they give him oxygen and suddenly I'm in the ambulance with him along with Rodney.

"Eve? When we get to the hospital, I want you checked out." I don't talk as I watch him talk on his cell. I stare at the guy in blue scrubs as he tends to this man who has become my life. I reach out and touch his hand, the one with the tattoo. It's warm and I clutch at his strength.

"He's okay." My voice sounds calm and strong. The guy looks at me with a strange expression.

"I need to cut off his shirt. Is that okay?" He looks at Rodney who is getting loud and agitated to whoever he's talking to.

"It's fine."

The paramedic hesitates then cuts his T-shirt off. After inserting some needles he turns to me. "He's lost a lot of blood. Do you know his blood type?"

I shake my head no as I stare at his beautiful chest. A bloody bruised hole has pierced his side.

"You're his wife, right? I mean this guy, he's like the real deal." He's says this as he starts to hook him up to some fluid.

I lick my dry lips then sit up straight and look him in the eyes. "It's fine. Fix him."

"He's stable."

Leaning back, I rest my head on the back of the ambulance, close my eyes, and try to steady my breath and stomach. Jason saved my life. He threw himself in front of me. My ears are still ringing with that woman's terrible shrieks and the gunshot.

"You okay?" I jump at the man's voice. His brown eyes are focused on me and my white pants, which are covered in Jason's bright red blood. My pink shirt is drying, stuck to my stomach. I hold up my hand to rub my forehead. "I'm fine."

His eyes narrow and he gives me a curt look. "Make sure someone checks you out."

I lurch a little as the ambulance turns and glides into the ER entrance. The doors fly open and I blink as the sunlight pours into the ambulance. Hospital staff are pulling Jason out. Rodney jumps down and tosses his phone into his bloody suit jacket.

"Come on, Eve. We need to get you situated." He holds out his hand for me. We pretty much run next to Jason. His eyes keep fluttering open as they wheel him away.

"Wait, he's waking up." I move to go around the woman attending to him.

"Sorry, we can take it from here." She's tall and her hair is held in a tight bun. The shade might be red but the bun's so tight, for all I know it's brown.

"But he needs me." I must sound crazy because she pats my shoulder as she gently walks me in another direction.

"Are you his wife?"

"Yes." It just comes out.

"Okay, we will send his doctor out to tell you everything as soon as they have any information. But let's concentrate on you right now. Okay?" She's talking slowly and so calmly I almost don't like her.

The woman lightly touches my arm. "Let's check you out." She smiles kindly and I nod.

"Wait, where is my Rodn—where is the man I came in here with?"

"I'll find him and send him to your area." She guides me through some doors and into the main ER area. "Here." She hands me some grayish towels. "In case you want to wash up. A doctor will be in soon to examine you." She shuts the curtain and it's at that moment that I start to shake. The fear and need to be with Jason almost make me push back the curtains and run. But I have no idea where he is and my whole body is shaking so badly my teeth are chattering. I grasp the aluminum sink and turn on the water as a new nurse says, "Knock, knock." The curtain opens and a friendly, fit Asian guy in purple scrubs enters.

"Oh, man... I heard about what happened to you. Can I get you some blankets? You're shaking."

I turn the hot water on and let it sting my bloody hands. Red blood, which looks like paint, spins and swirls down the sink. He's at the computer asking me questions, half of which I have no idea how to answer. Have I had all my vaccines? My mother's and father's medical histories?

What the fuck?

"Are you all right?" He looks at me then the water, which I completely forgot was running. He reaches over and turns it off.

"I think you're in shock. Please sit." I look at my hands—they're clean but bright red. As he glides me to sit at the end of a hospital bed, my hands feel as though someone is taking a needle and poking it all over my fingers and the top part of my hands

He looks at me and smiles. Reaching into a cabinet, he hands me a couple of grayish white sheet-type covers.

"Thank you."

He's back on his screen, glancing over his shoulder. "Are you on any medications?"

"No, but I'm pregnant." The poor guy's fingers freeze.

"You're pregnant? You should have told us this first. Let me get a doctor."

I look around as he leaves. I'm miserable and the shaking hasn't gotten any better. I'm full-on borderline convulsing. I need Jason. The fear of the unknown is not my friend. Can't fall apart now—I have to hold it together.

"Eve?" I hear Rodney's frazzled voice.

"Over here. I'm... here." I stand and open the curtain. This ER is busy. Nurses, firemen, paramedics fill the nurses' area and I wave at a frazzled-looking Rodney. He rushes over and grabs my arm, pulling the curtain shut.

"Christ, I'm getting ready to check myself in." He runs a hand through his light brown hair. His dark blue dress shirt is splattered with blood. His black suit pants are wrinkled and smudged with dirt. I have no idea what happened to his jacket. "Are you okay? Where's the doctor? My God, you look awful."

I almost burst out laughing because after all the horror we have been through I was thinking the same thing about him. "I'm a little cold."

"You're in shock, Eve." He looks down at his buzzing phone. "I talked to one of the doctors treating Jason. He's fine. The bullet missed all organs. They cleaned it and stitched it. They gave him a blood transfusion." I feel my knees literally start to give out and lower myself into the chair to my right.

His phone rings again. "I need to take this. It's about security. Also..." He pushes the button on his phone. "Hold on a second," he tells the caller. "I think it's best if you stay with my wife." I open my mouth to say no way but he turns his back so that he can rattle off lawyer stuff.

I hear myself exhale. *Jason is fine. He's okay...* And I burst into tears.

"Shit, let me call you back." Rodney hangs up and awkwardly pats my shoulder. "Eve, sweetheart, it's going to be fine. Unfortunately, these things happen and we deal with them."

I glance up at him and hiccup back something between a sob and a laugh. *These things happen?* I want to tell him that these things rarely happen, and what the fuck?

Before I can speak, a doctor walks in. I wipe my eyes so that I can see him. He's African American with a kind smile and eyes that twinkle with compassion. He instantly starts asking me questions about the shooting and wants to know how many months along I am. Moving aside, he allows a nurse to wheel in a machine. I lie back, close my eyes, and let them do what they need to do.

Half an hour later and I've been checked out. They did a blood test and ultrasound before the doctor allowed me to be discharged. Thankfully the baby seems fine. I've stopped shaking, and now I'm tired. I need a shower and Jason. Rodney and I are waiting to get our stupid passes. He's on his phone again, so I'm left waiting.

The sound of heels clicking makes me look over at a woman. She's walking fast, something that always amazes me. How can women in heels do that? If I'm not in like a wedge heel or boot, I have trouble. She walks like she was born in them. Her long blond hair hangs down her back, and her giant black sunglasses cover most of her face. She turns and seems to look at me as she pushes the elevator button. When I look away and back again, she seems to be frowning at us. The sunglasses are hiding half her face so I could be imagining it. I peer down at my hands, which are still slightly pink, and then at the older woman behind the information desk trying to confirm my pass. She types the info into her computer at a snail's pace.

I try not to sigh, but I can't seem to help it. She throws me a disapproving look and hands me the passes. Rodney takes them and grabs my arm to guide me. I want to tell him I can walk, but I'm too tired to care. He pushes the button and turns to me.

"I have to ask you this because the FBI will be here soon." The ding of the elevator arriving makes me jump. I glance at my reflection in the mirrored elevator, somewhat shocked at my reflection. Jesus, I can't believe I'm even allowed in here. No wonder everyone is looking at us. I look so bad it's like I'm in a Halloween costume and Freddie Kruger has gotten ahold of me.

"What?" I take my rubber band from my wrist and pull my hair off my face into a messy bun.

The elevator opens and we stand aside as a couple and a doctor exit. As the door dings closed behind us, Rodney shows me his phone and a mug shot of my brother stares at me.

"It's... Benny." I breathe out and search Rodney's tired face.

He turns off the screen and puts his phone back into the pocket of his suit trousers. "This is who Sandy is saying killed Doc and made her go crazy."

I reach for the handrail behind me and shake my head. "What are you talking about? My brother has been gone for almost a year. And who's Doc?" I must look unsteady because he reaches a hand out to steady me.

"Sandy is the wife of Doc. Doc is or was part of the Disciples." He clears his throat. "He um, it has been rumored that he and Jason hypothetically made a street drug."

I shake my head, my mind spinning. "I don't know anything about that."

"Good, so when they interview you, you say exactly that." I almost roll my eyes, but I'm too tired and can only stare at him.

"From what I'm getting from one of my guys inside the Burbank PD, Sandy is saying that Benny killed Doc. That he was threatening them and when Doc didn't do what he wanted, he killed him." The elevator slowly opens and Rodney takes my arm again. My eyes dart around as my mind spins like a hamster going around its wheel.

"I don't understand. This woman is *insane*! She shot Jason! I hope she dies a painful death at the hands of one of Jason's gang."

Rodney stops and stares at me like *I'm* insane and maybe I am. But that bitch almost took my life, and that, I won't ever forgive. He coughs and escorts me past the nurses' station where they all stare at us.

"Please, keep that last part to yourself, Eve. Stick to you know nothing and haven't seen or heard from your brother in close to a year."

"Whatever," I mumble. "My head hurts and I need some clothes. I'm staying with Jason. Who do I talk to that about?"

We stop at room C49 and Rodney turns to me. "Eve, I honestly feel that you will be safer staying with me and Sarah. She'll love having you." He smiles and even though he looks like he wants to drop from exhaustion his eyes are shiny and kind. But I don't need kind; I need Jason.

"Thank you, Rodney." He smiles a little wider. "But I intend on staying here until Jason gets released." I pat his shoulder and brush past him to the door. A large window greets me. The sun is casting a pretty glow on the two blond heads. I stop for a moment, causing Rodney to propel right into me.

"Oh, excuse us," Rodney says to the tall blond woman from before. She sits on the edge of the bed, crying. Jason is propped up with an IV.

I must make a noise because they both turn and I'm lost in the most incredible green eyes. They're bloodshot but he's awake and alive and everything stops for me. I breathe in his breath from across the space. My love for this man consumes me, overpowers me. He is my everything. I don't care that we're not alone in the room or that this woman is staring at me. I run to him and he smiles as I throw myself at him. He grunts but laughs.

"I'm fine, Angel." He strokes my back since I seem to have latched onto his chest. The smell of disinfectant makes me slightly nauseous and I bury my face in his neck. He touches my cheek. I stay still and listen to the strong beat of his heart and enjoy the warmth of his skin.

"Eve... baby, sit up. I want you to meet my mother."

His mother? I bolt up to look at the blond woman staring at us in what looks like shock if her open mouth is any indication.

"Um... hi." All of a sudden I'm shy. I mean, I've never met anyone's mother. She stands peering at me with the same green eyes as her son—one of those women you can tell used to be beautiful but sun and whatever else life has thrown at her has made her age. She's tall and thin, but her skin is almost too tan and the lines around her red lips tell me that she smokes. Her long blond hair is almost down to her butt.

"Jason?" She looks at me then her son, her voice so raspy it reminds me of Emma Stone's.

He holds my hand, probably because he senses my neediness. It's obvious: I can't seem to stop touching him.

"Mom, this is Eve. She's my girlfriend." He knows I hate being called an "ole lady" and smiles. "And the mother of my children." The room is all of a sudden warm and I plop down on the chair next to him. Did he say *children*? I grip the arms so tightly my nails leave marks.

"Oh my God." His mom covers her mouth and shakes her head. "Well, that settles it. You need to step down. After what happened today… for Christ's sake, Jason, you have a baby to look after." She reaches for some Kleenex and almost violently pulls one out.

"Mom, this is not the first time I've been shot." He sits up and I'm instantly on my feet making sure… I don't even know what I'm making sure. It's like we are bonded together now. His blood is still on me and his baby grows in my womb, but what he did today made me his in a way I can't fully understand yet.

"I'm not stepping down. Eve and the baby will be protected. Don't worry about that *ever*." His words make my belly flutter and core clench. "Angel?"

I look at him, so beautiful even sitting in a blue hospital gown with an IV in his arm. His face is bruised and his coloring is off, but he still radiates energy, a magnetism that makes my heart beat faster.

She sniffs into the Kleenex and I look down at myself. "I need a shower." It sounds crazy, but at this point, I don't care. Jason likes me and that's all that matters.

"You're not leaving," he snaps. "And Mom, please stop crying. The bullet went all the way through me. I lost a lot of blood is all." He reaches for my hand and surprisingly pulls me to the side of his bed.

"Go take a shower. I'll get Mom to go and buy you something from the boutique. I need to talk to Rodney anyway."

Rodney turns around, his phone in his hand. "Yes, you need to be filled in." He points at him, smiling. "I'm also charging you double for today." He grins as Jason groans. Rodney is a good man and an even better lawyer if his phone time is any indication.

"Go get cleaned up, baby." I watch as he pushes a button for either more pain medication or a nurse. Either way, he wants me to stay and I intend to. As I turn on the bathroom light, the adrenaline that has kept me going and hunger hit me like someone has thrown a rock at my belly. A loud growl and acid burn their way up my stomach to my neck. Partly scared at what I'll find, I avoid my reflection and instead strip the now dry and stiff bloody clothes off me and start the water for a shower.

As I lather up, I take stock of my injuries. I have a skinned knee that's super sore. My elbow is scratched up, but other than that I'm fine. Jason saved my life. He's sitting in that hospital bed because he threw himself in front of me. Lifting my face to the spray of the showerhead, I allow myself to digest the truth that my brother is either a completely insane sociopath or the bitch who shot Jason is crazy. Reaching for the mini shampoo, I wash my hair, trying to decide if Benny could really be a killer and do I really care? He wasn't perfect and he changed with the drugs... but a coldblooded killer? And why would he even be hanging out with Doc and Sandy, knowing that the Disciples would be watching? That's plain stupid.

Turning off the water, I wish everyone was gone and I could climb into bed with Jason and sleep for days. I wrap the cheap white towel around me and peek out. Rodney and Ryder are talking to Jason. His mom is sitting in the corner vaping an e-cig. I'm pretty sure that's not allowed but it's not my place to say anything. A plastic bag sits next to her. I clear my throat and she and Ryder look up. His brown eyes are on alert as he nods and goes back to Jason.

"Oh... here, I hope it fits." She looks at me from the bottom of my feet up to my wet, dripping hair. "I got you a dress."

"Thank you." My face heats up. The pressure of wanting this woman to like me is so important I drop the bag. I sneak a glance at Jason. Whatever they're telling him must be bad because he's got that look in his eyes. I'm sure it's about Benny and I almost want to say something to defend him, but I think better of it. God, I remember when I first got taken to pay the debt. I hated Benny. Now... I think he's a selfish dick and a drug addict. And let's be honest—if he offed Paul, well, the world is a better place without pieces off shit like that creep roaming around. Karma's a bitch. I reach down and pick up the gift shop bag and pull a pink halter dress out.

"It's so pretty. Thank you." I smile and she stands holding her e-cig, her eyes taking me in. Finally, she says, "Get changed. I'd like to buy you dinner at the cafeteria, Eve."

I blink then move as fast as my bare feet can carry me to the bathroom. Quickly I drop the towel and pull the dress on, my hands shaking. This is absurd. Why am I so nervous? Sighing, I assess myself in the mirror. The dress is cute. The color makes me look fresh, happy. After all the hot water and scrubbing of my skin, I have a healthy, pink glow.

"It's going to be great. You're having his baby, and she's going to be nice," I say to the girl in the mirror. I switch off the light and open the door going straight for my bag. I pull out a brush and try to detangle my hair then sweep it back with a rubber band at my neck. Throwing on some lip gloss, I glance down and stare in disgust at my bloody sneakers.

"Here." Jason's mom hands me some bright pink flip-flops. I look over at him. He holds up his hand for Ryder to stop.

"You okay?" His gravelly voice makes my face flush hotter, his green eyes taking in every single detail. I must pass because his full lips smile slightly.

And I want to die right there. Instead I say, "Yes."

His mom reaches for her purse. "I'm going to take her to get some food. Take care of business." She reaches down to kiss Jason.

"Good." His eyes find mine. "Come right back."

I nod. "I will."

Ryder smirks and Rodney starts to argue that I should stay with him and his wife.

"She stays with me."

Rodney opens and closes his mouth, running his hand up and down his tie. "Fine, but—"

"No." One word and I smile with confidence.

"I'll be back. Do you want me to bring you anything?" I walk up to him and again, as soon as our eyes lock I get this warm sensation like the first bite of a hot fudge sundae: that delicious warmth of the fudge followed by the sweetness of ice cream that makes you happy. We stare at each other until Jason grins again and reaches for me bringing my lips to his.

"No, Angel. Go eat a good dinner."

I can't breathe. He's robbed me of myself and all I hear coming out of my mouth is the truth. "I love you."

Someone coughs and I look up for a moment and back at him, his green eyes so alive with what I know has to be love.

"Ryder?" He releases me. "Send someone with Eve and my mother."

I hear her huff. "God, here we go. Come on, Eve. The secret service will keep us safe." She rolls her eyes dramatically at Jason.

"It's not up for discussion, Mom." He leans back farther into the pillows and grimaces for a second in pain.

"Jason? You need more pain medication." She softens instantly and for a second, I long for my own mother. I blink back the tears.

"Don't worry, Mom, I got this." She nods and we walk to the door. Ryder follows and five Disciples stand when they see us.

"Sean, go with them." He nods at him and that seems to be all Sean needs because he looks at us and I blink in shock. He's like cliché bad biker guy. Medium height, dark hair that needs to be cut, and tan, weathered skin.

"You women ready?"

Jason's mom rolls her eyes. "Come on, Eve. We need to talk." She loops her arm with mine as she kind of glides me through the nurses' station and into the elevator. Sean pushes the lobby button.

"Jason didn't introduce us properly. I'm Leah."

It's as though I'm in a weird state of I don't know what. Like my head is nodding and I'm talking, but everything is slightly muted and a little off.

"It's nice to meet you." There. I sound normal. The elevator opens with a ding. Leah once again loops her arm with mine. I'm actually grateful—it's nice to have someone guiding you when you feel lost.

"I wish I could say this is the first time I've been to this hospital." We enter the large cafeteria that's surprisingly empty.

"Hey you," Leah yells over to a Hispanic guy dishing out hot food.

"What the hell? You just love me, don't you?" He grins at her. "Your usual, Leah?"

"Yes, of course." Leah turns to me. "José, this is my son's fiancée Eve." Ashamed at how my heart skips a beat when she says it, I almost choke. I clear my throat and give him a smile.

"Well, he sure is luu-cky." He winks at me. "What can I get for you, Eve?"

My stomach rumbles as I look at everything. "Can I have two slices of cheese pizza?"

"Absolutely." He turns to grab a plate. "So, who's it this time, Leah?"

She sighs and wraps her arm around my waist as if she's helping me stand, but I think I might be helping her. "My son." She takes a breath. "He got shot earlier, but thank God he's fine." She puts her hand on my arm.

"José, please no pizza for Eve." She waves her hand dramatically. "Make her plate like mine, thank you." She smiles at him and looks ten years younger. I almost say something, but I want her to like me so I stop myself. Also, José is doing her bidding. I guess it doesn't matter what I want.

"I'm going to be frank, and I hope you don't mind." She moves us toward a cooler full of beverages. I nod and swallow as I reach for a can of Coke. She doesn't even stop but casually takes the can out of my hand as though I'm three and replaces it with a bottle of water. I bite my lip, because come on, this is almost comical. If Jason wasn't in a hospital bed recovering from being shot, it would be hilarious.

José places our trays in front of us and I look down at boneless chicken and I think spinach? Not positive but it's dark green with chunks of garlic so I'm betting on that.

"Thank you, José." She smiles again and I follow with my tray like a lost puppy.

"I'll grab us a salad and—"

"Bread," I interrupt before she pays. "Please, I need bread." Her green eyes twinkle looking way too much like Jason's.

She sighs. "Fine. Grab some rolls and butter." I quickly grab a plate and load it with four rolls and butter before she changes her mind.

"Okay, I'm ready." I sigh as if I just scored. Again, absurd considering I met this woman an hour ago.

She pays and we slide into a hard plastic booth. She places her napkin on her lap and I mimic her. She looks up and her eyes seem tired and sad.

"So, Eve... tell me, how old are you?"

I reach for my cold bottle of water and twist the top open. "Nineteen." I take a sip, the coolness making my hot mouth and tongue almost yearn for me to guzzle it. I should feel bad about lying, but I'm almost nineteen and the way she's looking at me makes me think lying is best.

"Hmm." She picks up her knife and fork and starts cutting her chicken. "I was even younger when I met Jason's father. He was the most beautiful man I have ever seen." She grins. "Well, besides my son. The thing is... I thought I was in love. But I wasn't." She takes a bite and I take a breath. How do I answer any of this? *Sorry?*

"Anyway..." She waves her fork in the air. "He was the president. It became obvious that the club came first, his bike second, the kids third, and then maybe one of his whores or me."

I almost choke on my swig of water. "That's awful," I wheeze out.

"Yes, it was. This life they live is like their own world and he was king." She looks down at her lap. "He killed Chuckie."

"What? He killed his own son?" I'm completely shocked. You'd think someone would have mentioned that.

"It was his lab. He made Chuckie go with him that night. I hated him before, but after the accident..." She looks up at me, her green eyes swimming with tears. "After Chuckie and David's girlfriend and baby died in that explosion, well, it was good he got blown up too because I would have murdered him." She sets down her fork and reaches for her water, letting her words circle around us.

"I had no idea." Well, I had a little idea, but it seems right to let her talk. "Jason doesn't talk about his past." I almost reach across the table for her hand, but I don't.

"They were close, Jason and Chuckie, but Jason was away in the Navy. He was never supposed to be the president. Never," she hisses as tears run down her face. This time I do reach for her hand as tears start to cascade down my cheeks too.

"I'm sorry." She pulls her hand away. Sitting up straighter, she reaches into her purse and puts on her dark sunglasses then starts to cut her food again. I look down at my food and slowly start eating.

"I gave up everything for that man and all it did was give me heartache. Are you sure that's what you want?"

I drop my fork with a loud clatter and look her in the eyes. "I love Jason, and yes, he is exactly what I want."

She stares at me so long I start to squirm in the hard plastic booth. I'm about to say something, but she beats me to it.

"I think... Eve, I think you will be perfect as his queen." The corners of her mouth turn up into a small smile.

My eyes blink back what feel like tears as I digest her words and find myself truly smiling at her. For the first time ever, I have a woman in my life who looks at me with respect and something close to admiration and I like it.

"Did you know that both my boys are named after horror movies?" It's completely off subject and yet absolutely perfect as we laugh at her stories and I bask in her glowing approval.

TWENTY-EIGHT

BLADE/JASON

I'm staring at this woman who has literally stolen my soul. She's dripping wet as she comes out of our shower. Holding out the large white towel, I wrap her in it. Eve is almost seven months pregnant and I'm in awe. I mean that literally. I'm. In. Awe.

Her body is pink where the water has hit her creamy back. I can't help but drop to my knees as I start to towel her dry, her laughter making my cock harden as I caress her stomach. Our baby instantly kicks my hand. Dark to light, that's how my tan hand looks on her pale swollen belly.

Tossing the towel aside, I reach for her ass and pull her tightly to me, kissing her stomach as I lick the remaining drops off her. I had no idea I would feel this way. Every day I grow more in love with our baby and our life. She drops her head to the side as her beautiful eyes slant down at me. Her dark lashes look like fans.

"I love you, Jason," she moans as I gently move her legs open. I don't answer her and never have even though the words are burning to get out.

"Sit on the edge of the tub, Angel." For a second her eyes reflect hurt as if she thought this would be the moment I tell her.

But then it's gone as she obeys and perches herself on the edge of the tub, legs open. Her pussy is pink and glossy already and I groan as I lower my head to feast.

You see, this is how I show her I love her. As I eat her and suck on her delicious clit, I breathe into my nose and stroke my hard, aching cock. It's leaking, allowing me a nice lubricant as I feel Eve contract and come in my mouth.

I pull back to take in all her golden glory. She's magnificent and I need to be inside her. She smiles and gracefully turns so that her beautifully arched back teases me. I rub my hand up and down its smoothness then grip her hips as I sink slowly, almost tortuously into her silken walls.

I hold in my groan until I'm so deep inside her I can't not let it out. She's dripping for me and I lower my chest to her back so that I can wrap my arms around her.

"Oh God... you're deep." Her voice catches as her strong arms tighten and her fingers turn white with the grip.

"Yeah, so good." I pull back and thrust into her. In and out, our rhythm almost so in tune that my stomach muscles tighten. The pleasure zings straight to my tight balls and down to my toes as I grab her hips and hit her G-spot to send my Angel soaring.

"Yes... yes," she moans into her arm, her long hair swinging with every deep thrust.

"Yeah baby. I can feel it." I reach down and grab her hands as I go deep. My other hand seeks her clit, and in seconds, she's screaming my name.

"Fuck." I can't stop it—the pleasure's too intense. My body jerks as I empty my seed deep inside her. We stay together as our breathing slows and I gradually pull out.

"Hmm... I needed that," she murmurs as she turns and wraps her arms around my neck.

I reach down and pick her up as I take her to our bed. It's late. I've got a busy day tomorrow and I'm fucking tired. I set her down and go to turn off the light barely recognizing the transformation in my bedroom. Gone is the white wall. A deep burnt red wall is by our bed surrounded by pale yellow walls where black-and-white photos of my bikes hang. Long, gauzy curtains blow in the breeze. I walk over and shut the French doors. Climbing into bed, I reach for her again. She purrs and my heart thuds. Again the words she has been wanting, needing almost come out. But until I find her junkie piece of shit brother, I keep them locked inside me.

Getting shot wasn't what bothered me. Almost losing Eve made me acknowledge the truth. I need her, I love her. She is my world and because of that I will do whatever it takes to keep her safe. Safe. I almost didn't get there in time. That day haunts me. I've never had nightmares of any of the things I've done. But the thought of not getting there in time to save Eve will cause me to wake up reaching for her. I rub her arm and she snuggles closer to me. Two months and I will be a father. Along with decorating and shopping with Doug and Dolly, Eve has become extremely close to my mother. A better role model I can't find. Most of the time we stay at our house, but sometimes we stay at the clubhouse and my beautiful golden queen makes me look good.

One of our phones vibrates and I frown—it's Eve's. The clock on the end table reads close to midnight. I know who and what it is. With a sigh, I close my eyes. The phone stops and moments later, a ding alerts that a message has been left. Eve is so peaceful in sleep; her sweet breath lightly kisses my neck as she moves her nose into me. I reach up and hold her head to me. I give up and let go. What has happened is going to change her and I hope it doesn't damage her.

Again, I close my eyes as my mind retraces the last four months. After the shooting, all hell broke loose. I completely put all drug selling to a halt. It weeded out the brothers who truly are family and want to be here from the guys who want to look tough and have free drugs and pussy. I'm done dealing drugs and I'm getting too old to risk prison. Eve groans as she rolls to her back and I instantly turn to my side, my hand on her large stomach caressing our baby. I do this a lot. I had wanted to find out the sex, but Eve insisted that it would be more fun to be surprised. But I know the truth: it was yet another carrot for her to dangle in front of her father. *Look, Daddy, if you want to know the sex, you better not die on me.*

Every day I drop her off and she spends hours with him. Talking to him. Christ, half the time she watches him sleep. Sometimes I go with her, help him go outside, but I always feel James's animosity. He may have accepted me, but he certainly makes it clear I'm not good enough for his baby girl. He's right—Eve deserves better, but fuck it, some people win the shit lottery. The truth is it's been a miracle that James Smith has made it this far.

"Fuck." I sit up and reach for a cigarette and grab Eve's phone, slipping out the French doors to my deck. It's fucking freezing out, but there is no way I'll smoke in front of Eve.

As I glance down at her phone, there it is like a rock has been thrown at my chest because I know what's coming. "Christ." I enter her code to unlock then push on the button to the nursing home.

"Dove's Grey Nursing Home."

I exhale and my smoke dances in front of my face as it swirls upward.

"This is Jason Mc—"

"Oh hey, Blade, it's me Sarah." Her tone gives it away before I even have to ask. "He just passed away." I look up at the stars. The cool air seems to wake up every cell in my body. "June said he was peaceful."

June is the nighttime nurse. "Thank you. Did the mortuary come get him?"

She clears her voice. "They are on their way. I'm sorry. He was kind of like our miracle patient. And Blade?"

"Yeah?" I smother my cigarette and lean against the wooden railing.

"Tell Eve that we all are sorry."

"I will. Thank you, Sarah." I hang up. My life is about to change. The last months have been something I had no idea existed. I certainly haven't seen it. My parents didn't have it. My brothers don't have it. So to feel this happy, this content... well, it's changed me. I have a mate, a partner, and she loves and accepts me. I want it all with her, everything. But first we need to get through this. Fuck, taking a bullet for her was easier than what I'm about to do. I open up the door and the warmth of my room cocoons me and I breathe in the scent. It's coconut, vanilla, and Eve and I could bathe in it and still want more. I stare down at my Angel. Her hair is spread onto my pillow like spun gold as it shines in the moonlight, her stunning face so peaceful, so god damn happy. Tears sting my eyes.

This is going to be bad. I almost slide into bed and put it off. Instead I turn on the light and pull on some jeans. Then I sit next to her on the bed. Her long, dark lashes flutter open and she smiles and closes them again as her hand reaches for mine. She's come so far these last months. Made it through the trial like a champ and all I had to pay was a hefty fine. The FBI has been quiet since they are charging Sandy with the murder of Doc. Her trial is set later this year. She swears it was Benny, Eve's brother, who killed him. But without Benny, Sandy is left with all her prints and crazy confessions. The bitch tried to shoot Eve. I don't give a shit that she was out of her mind on drugs. I do not forgive. She can fucking rot in jail for all I care.

I reach over and stroke her cheek. "Eve, baby?" My voice is gravelly with pent-up emotion, my mind on alert. The hairs on the back of my neck are standing up. *This is going to be bad, so fucking bad.*

"Babe."

Her eyes jerk open and she sits up, or at least she tries to sit up. Eve is all stomach.

She looks at me almost wild, and I know she knows, so I don't say anything.

"No," she croaks.

"Baby, it's okay." I reach for her, but she slaps my hand away.

"No." She throws her legs over and stands. Her pregnant belly and beautiful breasts make me realize that I should have told her I love her. She was brave enough to tell me. Hell, she tells me all the time.

"No." This time she screams. "Just no!" She goes toward the bathroom and I know her. She's going to lock herself in and crawl into a corner. I won't allow it. Not now—not ever.

I grab her arm and bring her to my chest cradling her head as the hot, wet tears run down my chest.

"He can't be gone... he's all I have," she sobs out, and for a moment, I almost shake her. How dare she say that?

"He died peacefully and you're never alone. I'll be with you until one of us buries the other." She pulls back, her beautiful blue eyes swimming in tears. I cup her face. "I'm here and I'm never letting you go." My thumb wipes her cheek as she shakes her head and backs up.

"You... You were supposed to keep him alive." She lifts a finger at me. "You promised me. You promised!" Her hands are in fists and her long golden hair is wild.

"You need to calm down. You don't want to hurt the baby." I walk toward her and she snorts and attacks me. Her long nails go straight for my face and chest, and there's a stinging sensation as she rips her nails down my chest.

"What the fuck?" Grabbing her wrist before she can get my face, I hold her hand back.

"You promised... you don't love me."

"I'm not God, Eve. I know you thought I was keeping him alive. But it was you, Eve. He fought to the end for you." My voice is calm and I marvel at how well I'm keeping it together.

"What am I to do?" Her body shakes with her anguish coming in loud, stuttering gasps.

"Stop it." I shake her.

"Fuck you, *Blade*. You don't scare me. I gave you everything. I've done everything to make you love me, but you don't love me." She takes a small gasp. "I'm alone. Don't you see? He *was it*. I thought you and I, well... I thought that you and I were..." She stops as if she's too tired to hold herself up. I reach for her. Her nails dig into my forearm. "And the one person in this world who loved me is dead. Oh my God." She jerks a hand free and puts it over her mouth. "What am I to do? I'm nothing but a whore."

"Enough. You're making yourself sick. You're mine—that's all you need to know."

She shakes her head, the sobs making her stomach jiggle. "I'm not yours! You don't love me," she snarls in my face.

"If you can't settle down, I'll take you to the hospital."

"I don't care." She laughs. Her eyes search the room. "I'm done, and I want to see my father. You can take me or I'll walk because if you try to stop me..."

I don't move.

"If you try... and stop me..." Her voice sounds confused. Then she sort of crumbles as I catch her. Lifting her into my arms, I carry her to our bed, her loud sobs making my heart bleed. I've killed men and felt remorse, yet watching my girl's pain is unbearable. I turn her so that I can spoon her tightly letting her cry and hiccup into the sheet. Finally, the tears stop and she whispers, "I'm sorry."

"Why? Because you loved your father? You're devastated. Don't apologize." I snuggle my nose deeper into her neck. Her hands are warm as they cling to me and her coconut smell weaves around me.

"No, because I said those things to you," she stutters out. "I want you to love me, but I can't make you and—"

I turn her face to mine and cup her chin. Her cheeks are splotchy and her lips and eyes are red, but to me she's never looked more beautiful. "Who took a bullet for you?" My voice is gravelly as I stroke both sides of her face. "Who?"

Her eyes well up with tears. "You."

I bend to kiss her swollen lips. "I took a bullet for you because I don't want to live without you." I look at her, deep into her eyes seeing everything, and I want it all. I don't give a shit if she likes to steal or needs a marriage certificate to feel loved. I like everything about her.

"I took a bullet, Eve, because I love you more than I love myself and if you're not by my side..." Her eyes are spilling hot tears and I reach down to lick and kiss them up. "Then my life, my reason for being is gone."

She lifts her hand and traces my lips. "Really? You love me?"

I nip at her fingers. "I don't know what more I can do to prove that to you. I've loved you the moment I saw you at sixteen, with legs to die for and a mouth to kiss."

She closes her eyes and shivers as I reach down and pull up the covers. "You won't ever be alone. I'm not going anywhere without you."

She grabs my hand and places it on her swollen belly. Our baby kicks. "I thought you could save him." She shakes her head. "I know it sounds crazy, but I did."

I pull her tightly against me, my pants a barrier I wish was gone, but her hands cling to me. "I know you did, baby, but he lived way longer than anyone ever believed he would. He's at peace. The way he was living... wasn't living."

Shaking her head, she whispers, "I know, but I miss him. Who am I going to talk to? He wasn't even that old."

I pull away yet she reaches for me. "I'm going to turn off the light and take off my jeans," I say. "We're gonna be okay, Angel."

As I turn off the light, she sniffs and sighs and I slip back into bed, the cool sheets underneath me a cruel reminder that I will always be looking over my shoulder. Always worried about my children and Eve.

"Sleep, babe. You need all the rest you can get."

She sighs into my arms and drifts off as I stare up at the dark ceiling wondering how I'm going to keep her calm. Christ, she was so sure he was going to be able to see his grandchild. I close my eyes and try to sleep, knowing the next few days are going to be hell.

TWENTY-NINE

EVE

I'm in a white room—at least I think it's a room. It's all white and I'm alone, which bothers me because I've hated being alone lately. "Jason?" I yell, but he doesn't answer me.

"Hey, baby girl."

I turn. "Daddy?" He stands right in front of me and he's cured. Strong and handsome, he smiles at me and I throw myself into his arms. I guess I'm crying, which is silly because he's not sick anymore and he's not dead, so why am I crying?

"Oh God, I thought you died, and I didn't know how to go on without you." I laugh, but it comes out a sob.

"You listen to me, Evie. You take that baby boy of yours and you raise him to be strong and fierce."

Shaking my head, I look up at his beloved face. "I don't understand."

"You do." He nods and backs up, a frown on his face like he's aggravated. "You stop mourning me, and get on with livin'. You love that man of yours. He loves you. Together you both will be unstoppable. I have to go now. Let me go in peace." Smelling like cigarettes, he moves forward and hugs me again. "I need you to believe in your brother too. I know he's done some bad things, but he's your blood, baby girl."

"He's killed people, Daddy." He pulls back and starts to walk away again. "Wait!" I try to move but can't. Why can't I move? "Wait, Daddy, please... don't go. I need you."

He turns and waves. "You're my pride. I love you."

"Eve... Baby... wake up." My eyes bolt open as I gasp for air and sit up. Jason is next to me, his warm strong hands caressing my hair as if I'm a wild creature he doesn't want to spook.

"You're okay... you're dreaming." Taking a breath, I look at him and around the room.

"My dad just came to me, like it was him." Suddenly hot, I throw the sheet off and sit up.

"I'm serious, he came to me, Jason."

"Okay... that's good, Eve." He lifts my chin to give me a kiss. "We need to get up and get ready anyway." He's using that tone again—the one I've come to hate.

"Stop talking to me like you think I'm crazy." I jerk away and stand. "I hate you talking to me like I'm insane or... fragile." Hands on my hips, I stare at him. "*I hate it.*"

He looks confused and at a loss. Momentary guilt runs through me and I sigh.

"I don't think you're crazy," he says. "You were having a dream, Eve. That's it."

I shake my head. "No, he came to me." I wave my hands, his eyes following my movements as he frowns. "He asked me to let him go and to live... be happy with you. Oh my God it was so real."

Suddenly I'm encircled in warm arms and his lips are on my temple. He lets out a deep sigh. "Well, then you better do what he says."

I pull back to look at him. "So you believe me?" I don't know why this is important, but it is.

He looks down at me and our eyes lock. Time stands still. "Of course."

I sag into his chest as I rest my forehead on him. "Thank you."

He kisses the top of my head telling me to get ready for my father's funeral. It's today. Jason is having him buried in the same cemetery where his father and brother are laid to rest. I'm numb. I've cried so much that I don't remember fixing myself up. A flutter and sharp kick in my stomach bring me back to the present. Gazing down at my large stomach, I straighten my black dress, which Dolly brought over yesterday while I was taking a nap. I miss Dolly and Doug and haven't seen anyone but the funeral director, Amy, and Jason. All the decisions: What color flowers? Does he have a suit that he wanted to be buried in? All of it has been overwhelming especially since I have no idea what I should answer. I finally told Amy to do what she thought everyone would enjoy foodwise for the gathering after the funeral.

We're at the clubhouse today. It's easier to answer all the questions while Jason is nearby. I lean over the sink to get a good look at my face. Despite the black circles, I seem okay. My father's voice drifts over me. *He loves you. Let me go.* I shudder because that dream was so real. It had to be my dad coming to me. I touch my stomach. Jason and I need to start discussing names.

"You ready, babe?"

"What?"

He walks over to me and pushes my hair off my shoulder. "I asked if you were ready. It's time to go."

I nod and look at him. "Are you allowed to wear that?" My heart flutters as I admire the man standing in front of me. Jesus, he's wearing a suit. It's black with a white shirt and I want to die he's so gorgeous.

"That's the great thing about being the president—I can do anything I want." He winks and opens his suit jacket so I can see his black leather Disciples vest underneath.

"You're so handsome." I reach up to stroke his honey-colored hair. He catches my hand. Bringing it to his lips, he sucks on my finger.

My breath catches. "Jason." It comes out in a whisper.

He smiles and lightly bites me. "And you're stunning. Let's go."

Jason helps me into my coat and takes my hand. Warmth from his hand transfers to my cold hand making all of today seem more bearable as we go downstairs. The sound of chairs being moved and feet shuffling make me take notice: all the men have come to their feet. My eyes sting as I nod. Somehow I've become part of this crazy family of tatted men.

Amy comes out of the kitchen, teary-eyed yet smiling. As we walk by, every single man says they're sorry. It's surreal, like I'm truly their queen. Jason's expression is serious. He gets like this every time we go out. I guess being shot will do that to you.

"Eve?" I jump. Jason is frowning.

"Sorry, I'm fine. Please stop looking at me like that," I snip.

"I hate that I can't take away your pain. It makes me feel helpless and that's an unacceptable emotion for me." He kisses my forehead as I slide into the back of a dark Cadillac SUV and Jason follows. Ox waits for us, smoking a cigarette. After a deep breath, I close my eyes. They sting from days of crying.

"I love the way a new car smells." Opening my eyes, I blink away more hot tears so I can hold Jason's hand again.

"I guess I'll have to make sure I get a new car for us every six months."

"My dad probably never smelled a new car before." I reach for his hand and pull my bag close as I look out the window, the tears spilling onto my cheeks.

The scenery goes by. I don't notice or maybe I don't care. It's winter but still sunny. My father would like that. At one point I wanted to bury him next to my mom. The sad thing is I don't remember where she is. Maybe Minnesota. When I used to ask my dad, he would get that faraway look and change the subject. I blink back the tears. That part of my life is over, done. Jason, my baby, and I guess the Disciples are my future. I blink, forcing my tears away now that we're pulling into the cemetery.

"Prez, I've got men everywhere." Ox shuts off the Cadillac and turns to glance at us.

"Good." Jason looks at me, his eyes caressing my face. "Let's go." We step outside and a gust of wind whips my hair back as I inspect the graveyard. It's beautiful, calm, and has green grass. My dad would never believe he'd be buried in such a beautiful place. One time, he told Benny and me to leave him at the hospital and have them deal with his remains.

A tall man, maybe Ryder's size, except probably a hundred pounds lighter, stands in a black suit talking to Leah. The funeral director notices us and nods our way. Leah hurries over. Hugging me, she says to Jason, "He's nervous so please put him at ease, Jason."

She wasn't kidding. The poor man is sweating—not that I blame him. This quiet graveyard of beauty and tranquility is being taken over by bikers. The rumble of their bikes causes me to look at the entrance.

"Prez, the Devil's Aces are here from San Francisco. So are the Demons from Arizona to pay respects."

Jason looks around. Actually Jason is gone. It's Blade who stands before me. He grabs my arm and I shiver at his touch. There's something exciting when Jason becomes Blade, yet I'm disgusted with myself. I shouldn't be thinking like that. I'm getting ready to say my final farewell to my father. "Give me a second." I watch as he shakes the funeral director's hand and turns back toward us. I suck in my breath at his physical beauty.

"I did good, didn't I?" Leah has a small smile as she watches her son come back to us.

"You did, Leah, you definitely did," I whisper as Blade takes my hand.

"Let's go." He walks us down a path—not too fast since both Leah and I are in heels. I cling to his arm as we get closer to the burial spot. White chairs have been set out and Leah squeezes my hand as she sits in one. It's truly happening. I'm at my father's funeral. There are flowers everywhere and the sweet scent floats through the air.

"Who are all these people?" My voice cracks as my eyes take in all the different arrangements. I spy Edge and Dolly in the parking lot. They look like they are arguing and I feel like a bad friend. I haven't even talked to her this week.

"It's respect, Angel. Stay right by me or by Axel's side." The noise level is growing loud as Harleys arrive in an awe-inspiring line. Looking down at the grave, which has already been dug, for a moment I want to run, hide even. Then maybe I won't have to go through this.

"Prez, you ready?" Ryder walks up in dark dress pants, a dark shirt, and his cut. For a moment, I wonder if my imagination's in overdrive.

"Hold on." Jason tilts my face up and rubs away my hot tears. "You ready?"

I shake my head yes because if I talk it's all over. The anger, the loss, all the shitty things that happened to me and my dad. All of that and more might come out.

"Let's start, Ryder," he announces without taking his eyes off me. "It's getting too crowded and we can't control things if it gets bigger." Ryder nods and gets on his phone.

I look around, my eyes swimming with tears again. This is insane. There are bikers everywhere—at least over a hundred. The frazzled funeral director rushes over and I watch Blade take over. Then a gun goes off and I jump. The funeral director looks as though he might faint and wisely steps behind Jason and me as I watch in agony as Edge, Ox, Dewey, and three other Disciples carry my father's dark silver casket by us and place it on the pedestal that will lower him to the ground.

"Breathe, Eve, I mean it." Jason pulls me closer and a whoosh of air fills me as I obey him. The priest I picked walks up carrying a bible and starts talking.

"Why?" I ask Jason, not caring if anyone hears.

"Better to cover all the bases." He pulls me into his arms and a strange giggle starts to escape. Am I losing it? I mean, what the hell was I thinking getting a priest? My father wasn't religious or even a good person. I loved him, but he did a lot of bad things. I stare straight ahead and pretend to listen. The wind blows, reminding me that I do feel. I feel Jason. His strength radiates into me as his thumb caresses my palm. I stare at my feet. They're aching and I feel that too.

"Angel?" I look up at him and gasp. He's so magnificent, like a fierce, sleek lion.

A boy... My dad had said we are having a boy. Jason looks down at me and our eyes meet, and everything I will ever need is in his look. He's mine. I don't even worry about the club sluts anymore. Jason only has eyes for me. I lean back into him as he lays his large hands on my belly. Finally, the priest finishes. I have to give it to the bikers—they have way more patience than I do. Another two minutes and I was going to tell Jason to remove him. I roll my head to the side and freeze. Over in the parking lot, my brother stands, leaning against a car.

Benny!

The adrenaline spikes all the way up to my face. Even my ears are hot and burning.

What the fuck! Is he suicidal? There are at least a hundred Disciples here and God knows about the others. But he stands there, staring at me. He doesn't move and bikers are walking around him. He's dressed in black and my eyes dart around at the many blank faces around me. Maybe they think he's here for another funeral?

Holy shit. What do I do? I should tell Jason, maybe even Axel... definitely not Ryder. Ryder is Blade's enforcer.

As all this is spinning through my head, I stare back at him. He nods and I take a deep breath. This is where I need to say something. He's a murderer, or at least that's what they say. Instead I nod back. He slowly turns and disappears from my sight.

"You're shaking. Are you okay?" I jump at Jason's yummy breath at my ear.

"I... Jason." I swallow and stare at him.

I need you to believe in your brother. I hear my father's voice loud and clear. I'll tell Jason tonight. I owe at least this to my father. I mean, how tacky would that be to have Jason's guys kill my brother while they bury our dad. I shake off my guilt. After all, this isn't the first time I've lied to him. But that stops today. I lean back into Jason's secure warmth. I did what I had to survive and to get where I need to be. So I've told some white lies like the not being able to get pregnant bit. I might have stretched the truth on that one. My appendix did burst at age twelve and it did get infected. But the doctors never actually said I couldn't get pregnant; they said it might be difficult. See, white lie and I needed this baby. How else was I ever going to make sure I didn't lose him? He's everything to me.

"You ready to say goodbye, Angel?"

For a split second I suspect he knows, but that's me being paranoid. "Do you need me to go with you?" His green eyes search mine.

"Yes... I always need you," I breathe out.

"Then we'll say goodbye together." He walks me to the casket where I lay my hands on the cool metal and I know I made the right decision. I'm in love with the leader of one of the most notorious motorcycle clubs. I close my eyes so I can tell my dad what needs to be said. *Today I have to say goodbye to you, Daddy. You will live on, through me, my baby, and even Benny.*

I sigh and open my eyes to stare into the greenest, most magnificent eyes. They narrow as if he knows everything I am.

Yet he can't. Some secrets are mine. He holds out his hand for me. I take it and move to his side as everyone else lines up to pay their respects. I look around at the numerous men and smile up at Jason. "I love you."

THIRTY

BLADE/JASON

I reach for her chin and gaze at her. She's glowing. Even the death of her father can't take that away. Her eyes meet mine as she blinks away her guilt. I gently lower my head and brush her glossed lips to mine. "I love you," I murmur into them.

Her eyes narrow as she pulls back to look at me. "Jason." Her voice is soft, almost breathless. In my peripheral vision, I see Axel. I want to smirk at how clean-cut he looks. The guy could pass for a model. When he shaves and puts on a suit, he's a whole new man.

He nods and the sun catches his mirrored aviators. I move behind Eve and slip my hands around her, bringing her back hard against my chest. As I lean down, my nose goes straight for her neck and I inhale her scent. Her breath catches and her hands tighten around mine and we both feel our baby kick as if he's happy we're both touching.

"I know about Benny, Eve." She stiffens slightly but does not turn to face me and simply stares straight ahead. I have to fight my smile. She's such a badass. I caress her hair before I say, "I saw him, babe." Her nails are clawing into my forearm. That's the only sign that it even bothers her.

"I let him go and thought you should know."

This time she does turn her head toward me. Her big blue eyes stare up at me. The conflicting emotions she so desperately wants to hide are all over her face. "Thank you." It's honest and I almost forget that she chose not to say anything about her junkie, murdering brother to me.

Knowing she needs to hear this, I sigh. "You don't have to thank me—you're my life."

Some of the Demons clan walk by to pay their respects to the man in the casket and both of us nod. I glance around at the green grounds and over to the parking lot where Benny was. The sky darkens as a cloud covers the sun. Benny's got some balls on him. Either that or he's an arrogant ass. Maybe both. I should have had Axel put a bullet in his head, but then again, he knew I wouldn't. See, I'm beginning to think that much like his sister, there's way more to Benny than I once thought. Never underestimate a man who's willing to sacrifice his own blood to survive. I look down at my gypsy. Yeah, he's not stupid. He knows what my weakness is.

Eve turns and stares straight at me. The clouds part and the sun kisses her face making her truly look like an angel.

"I'm a bad guy, but even I can't kill your brother today."

"Jason... my father wants me to be open-minded, so that's why I didn't say anything," she whispers, her eyes darting around, her cheeks growing pink.

"I don't care." I stare at her, almost wanting to shake her because she needs to understand this. "I love you no matter what. Do you honestly think I don't get you?"

Her breaths are coming short and fast as her eyes go to her stomach. "You don't... I well... I'm not what you—"

"You are exactly what I think." That makes her jerk her eyes to mine again. She's so beautiful and I want her. Fuck, I want her forever.

"None of it matters, Angel. You're my queen and I love every single thing about you. I want you to know you can tell me everything, but if it makes you feel good to think you have secrets, then that's okay too." She's startled, almost as if she didn't hear me. I glance around. My mom lifts her eyebrow at me reminding me that we are standing next to her father's casket and it's hardly the time and place to have this conversation. But then again, maybe it's perfect. She can't run and hide. I nod at everyone as they pass by murmuring their condolences.

"What are you even saying, Jason?" she hisses. My little badass wants to run. I can feel it like I can feel all her thoughts.

I take her elbow and bring her a few feet away, then force her to look at me. "Everything. I know everything, and if you think I don't, you're kidding yourself."

I grin at the wide-eyed, stunned look on her face and reach down to stroke her cheek. "I. Don't. Care."

She sighs and shakes her head, her hands coming to rest on my chest. "You know how you always say you're a bad guy? Well, I'm a bad girl." She licks her lips as she looks at me. "I am. I steal and I lie to get what I need." She goes to turn, but I grab her wrist and hold her still.

"Are you hearing me? I'm not what you think." She huffs, her eyes darting around.

I grab her chin. "Eve. I know all of it, and I love all of you, especially those parts."

She frowns as her eyes slowly change and the truth of my words finally sinks in.

"Why?" She looks confused.

"Why do you love me? Why do you accept me? Because you truly love me. It doesn't *matter*." I lean into her lips stealing her breath.

She looks back at the people who are starting to thin out. The rumble of bikes starting up makes her cock her head. "How did you know?" Her voice is low.

"Which one? The one that you lied about not being able to get pregnant?" She blinks those long, sooty lashes spiked with tears.

"I'm not stupid, Angel."

She looks up at the sky, her eyes closed in pain; her tresses slide like golden honey down her back. "So, you're saying that you like everything about me, even that I'm a bad girl?"

I have to bite back my laugh. After all, we're in the middle of her father's funeral. But it's almost like he's giving me his approval because the weight I've been holding is draining into the very ground I'm standing on.

I pull her close, not giving a shit what anyone thinks. "I'm saying I love that you're *my* bad girl."

When I take in her stunning face, her eyes are sad but hopeful. This time, I can't help but laugh as I whisper in her ear, "You want the ring, don't you, Eve? You honestly believe that people like us can have a happily ever after?"

She pulls back and holds my face tightly. "I know we can have the happily ever after."

I lift her up so that she's eye level. "You're my life. If I make you my queen legally, will that make you happy?"

Her eyes, the first thing that drew me to her, are pooling with tears.

"Yes." She sniffs, then before she can respond, I kiss her and all the world melts away. She's all I need... she's all I'll ever need.

THIRTY-ONE

BLADE/JASON

"Oh God," Eve moans, or whimpers, maybe both. Wisps of her golden hair wet with sweat stick to her forehead and cheeks.

"You're doing great, Angel." I caress her damp forehead and her eyes blink blue fire at me.

"Are you fucking kidding me?" She moans again. "I'm dying."

My heart literally drops to the pit of my stomach and darts to the nurse who stands to the other side looking at the monitor. They have some belt wrapped around Eve's stomach alerting us if our baby's heart goes into distress.

"She's not dying," the older woman replies. "She's in labor." A small twitch ghosts her wrinkled mouth. Her clothes have a faint smell of smoke and I would give a thousand dollars for a cigarette. But that would require me to leave Eve, which is not an option. Instead I inhale the smoke that clings to her.

"You're not dying," I repeat her words. My voice doesn't even sound like mine. *What the fuck?* I stare at the room we're in. It's bright with a large window showing the Hollywood hills perfectly. The white walls are typical hospital. One picture of flowers and butterflies is bolted to the wall, a huge flat screen on the other. My head is about to burst. Lack of sleep, nicotine withdrawal, and true mental agony at having to witness Eve's pain make my head pound.

"Listen to me." She pants, not from exertion because we haven't even gotten to the push part yet. Eve's late, like over a week past her due date. She's swollen, uncomfortable, and nervous. After taking her to her last doctor's appointment, I suggested it might be time to do something. Wisely her ob-gyn agreed, and she started getting induced at five this morning.

Another moan then, "I need Blade." It's clipped and strong. "Do you get me?" Her blue eyes blink at me like I'm not right in the head.

"O-kay," I say, not getting her.

"No, you don't." She grits her teeth as more sweat forms on her upper lip. "No Jason right now. I need you to be Blade and get me some fucking drugs."

I stare at this woman who has aged me in the last few hours. The nurse informed us that the hospital had only one anesthesiologist on right now. C-sections come first, so Eve has to wait. This is not my forte. Watching my very reason for breathing endure so much pain that she's not even screaming makes me want to punch the wall. *Christ,* this isn't like the movies or TV at all. A nerve-racking, heart-pounding amount of excitement courses down my neck. Blade gets shit done. I look up slowly at the nurse who freezes and slightly and frowns at me then takes a step back.

"I assure you she and the baby are doing great." She sniffs and moves around me to pull up the ugly blue robe Eve is in so that she can make sure the heart monitor belt is still in place. "Yep. stil—" I cock my head and my hands fist.

Her eyes travel to my face, then my hands, and back to my face. "I'll go see how much longer for the anesthesiologist," she says, a disapproving frown on her face.

"Thank you," Eve moans into the crappy plastic pillow. I don't know who she's thanking, maybe both of us. Even being incredibly nervous and in agony, she's been remarkably nice to all the nurses. "I want this over with. All I want is a healthy baby." Her beautiful blue eyes focus on me. They shine with pain, and again my heart beats so hard my temples throb.

"He's coming and he's healthy." She blinks as she hisses a moan but a small smile twists her lips.

"Sometimes I really love Blade."

I grin and lean down to kiss her when the door swings open and a young Asian woman in a white doctor jacket bursts in with the old nurse behind her.

"Okay," she says. "Let's do this."

Suddenly it's as if I'm not in the room. I'm still next to her, still holding her hand, yet that's all I can process. My brain seems unable to digest that I'm watching the love of my life take a needle. A fucking long needle injected into her back.

"You okay?" The anesthesiologist looks at me. "You're pale. If you're going to pass out, sit first. Or do I need to have a nurse get you some orange juice?"

I grumble something. It must work because she nods and goes back to Eve and announces, "She's dilated. I'll get her doctor." I almost grab the woman and shake her to tell me what the fuck that means? But Eve has my hand as she starts to lift up and push. That old feeling of time stopping caresses my numb body and I stare mesmerized.

"You're my everything." It comes out harsh, causing her doctor to smile encouragingly at me. I blink because when did her ob-gyn come in? I don't even know if Eve hears me since she is fucking busy doing exactly what the doctor says like the badass she is. The hypnotizing beeps and sounds of the hospital are all mingling together. What I'm witnessing is nothing short of a miracle or fucking mayhem. Either way, it's calming me. I'm used to chaos.

For the rest of my life, I know I will remember the moment my son took his first breath. And it's not because someone says, "It's a boy," or by his angry wail, announcing himself. It's because the moment he takes his first breath, I feel it inside me.

"Jason? Are you okay?" My vision clears enough for me to see my Angel.

"Taking a bullet for you is nothing compared to how I feel right now with you."

She nods, her eyes red with tears. "I know."

Both my arms grab ahold of the bed railing. "I don't know if you do." I brush her swollen red lips.

"Mr. McCormick?" The doctor clears her throat and for the first time in hours the room comes back into focus. She's younger than I thought. Her smile is genuine. "Would you like to hold your baby?"

I look around at the room. I take in everything as if I'm reborn. Snickering, in a way I am. "Yes."

She nods and moves aside allowing the nurse to place the fierce red-faced baby in my arms. *Badass just like his mother!* My eyes blur at this child and one lone tear lands on his cheek startling him to stop his angry rant. He blinks and our eyes meet. Time, the universe stops as my son bonds with me. A bond that will never be broken. I know this like I knew his mother was my mate. He's the most incredible thing I've ever seen. I almost throw my head back and laugh. Guns, knives, drugs, torture—none of those things can bring me to my knees. This... this child, my woman, this very moment has taken away the biker, stripped the king, and allowed the man to be let out.

I'm a mere mortal who's in love with his family—a family that is more than a gang of brothers and bikes. This is who I am. I breathe in and out. I will move heaven and earth to make sure they are protected and loved until the day I die.

"Jason?" Eve turns her head so that she can fully see me. Her cheeks are flushed, her eyes tired. I know she just gave birth but she has never been more stunning to me than right now.

I move to her and give her our son. She opens her gown, the nurse urging her to try to breastfeed. He latches right on like the fucking heir he is. My eyes lock on Eve's; hers are pooled with tears. Love pours out of her like lava spilling out of a volcano. So I say the only thing that's left to be said. "Thank you."

EPILOGUE

BLADE/JASON - Twelve months later

I stare at the compound and shake my head. It's a fucking zoo, and I mean that literally. Eve hired a wrangler to bring animals to our son's one-year birthday party.

"Go ahead and tell me I'm a genius." Eve happily stands in front of me, hands on her hips, blond hair twisted up into a messy bun, her face fresh and happy. My mouth twitches as I reach for her. She squeals as I start to back her up to the side of the house.

"Jason, stop it. You're going to step on my geraniums." She laughs, her eyes full of blue fire.

I look down and she's right—I'm stepping on some of the flowers she and a bunch of old ladies planted around the compound. Apparently, she was sick of seeing only gravel, trucks, and bikes.

"Let's go upstairs while my mom is watching James," I growl into her ear.

"Jason, we can't it's—" My mouth stops hers from telling me anything but yes and my tongue makes her moan.

"Come on. I want to be inside you in two minutes."

"But..." Her eyes are closed as she leans into me.

"Upstairs," I demand as I pull her with me.

"Wait." Her eyes pop open. "We need to tell your mom."

A pony neighs and James, our son who's being held by Axel, laughs with glee. His chubby hands move happily as he pounds lightly on the pony's nose.

I gesture toward my best friend and son. "Even better. Axel has him. You know he'll be safe." I reach for her other hand and place it on my throbbing cock. "I need you."

"Jason," she hisses and tries to pull away, which is stupid because I'll never leave her alone. Although I do let go of her hand and yell at Axel.

"I need a moment with my old lady. Watch my kid." He and half the party turn toward us. Axel looks at me like I'm insane and turns his attention back to my son. I shake my head. "He needs a kid of his own."

"Don't be jealous. It's not his fault he's like the baby whisperer."

"I'm not jealous," I grumble as I bring her into the house.

Amy comes around the corner with tortilla chips in one hand and a large bowl of her famous guacamole in the other. She stops and rolls her eyes at us. I wink at her and drag Eve up the stairs. I hear her mumbling that it won't be long before Eve is knocked up again. The thought of my Angel having another baby makes my cock grow harder. I'd love it, but she wants to wait. I throw open the door to our room and immediately start pulling down her shorts, not stopping until I reach my goal.

I look at her as a slow smile spreads across my lips "Your cunt's wet, Angel. Get on the bed and let me eat you."

"God, Jason," she moans and steps out of her shorts and panties. She climbs onto the bed and slowly opens her legs. I inhale her fucking scent as I pull off my vest, T-shirt, and pants then kneel as I jerk her forward. "You can scream as loud as you want, babe. We don't have to worry about waking the baby." I rub her juicy clit with my thumb and watch her eyes flutter shut.

"Oh. My. God... Jason that feels good," she moans into our thick down comforter.

Leaning forward, I put my tongue where my thumb was and hear her moan and arch deep into my mouth as I lick and suck her.

"Yes..." she hisses as I lift my head and pull her to the end of the bed, pushing her knees up. When I go straight for her sweet, tight rosette hole, her eyes fly open as my tongue licks it. She tries to lower her legs.

"Don't you dare," I murmur as I dip two fingers inside her honey core and the slick wetness makes me rub my throbbing cock on the side of the bed.

"Don't come yet." I pull out my wet fingers and replace my middle one at her small entrance and rub.

"Jason... oh God." I hold her right leg. As soon as I insert my finger in her sweet ass, she's going to tighten up.

"Look at me, Eve." Slowly, I insert my finger in her sweet hot hole. *Fuck* I love to watch her face—it always displays a mixture of confusion and wild passion.

"Yeah, that's my girl..." She's already contracting on my finger and I've barely started to finger her tight hole. I drop her leg over my shoulder and lower my head to suck on her clit as her pussy and ass clench my tongue and finger tight. I slowly pull my finger out and roll her on top of me making her straddle me. "Fuck me hard."

Her lips look bee stung and her face has a slight dewy sheen to it. She grabs ahold of my thick cock and slowly lowers herself onto me.

"Jesus," I breathe out. The pleasure is intense and my muscles tighten as I fight the desire to come already. Her hair has fallen down around her breasts in a golden mess. I watch as she arches her back to take me deeper. "Yeah, that's it, Angel." Her eyes are slits as she starts to lift herself up and down on me. And I'm consumed, being carried away as we both ride the exquisite wonderment of the feelings we create together. I can't take my eyes off her. Every expression, every moan makes my balls grow fuller as she throws back her head in ecstasy.

"That's it, baby... fuck me." My voice is harsh as I grab her ass and jerk her hard onto me. She grinds her pussy on me, her full breasts moving with her. "Jesus," I groan, "you're beautiful." I grab her hips to guide her as I thrust. "Fuck... your cunt is hot and slick." My stomach muscles tighten as I continue to grind her on me.

"Yeah, just like that." Her nails are latched onto my chest and her pussy jerks my cock off as she screams her orgasm. "Christ!" I let the pleasure take over transporting me to a different dimension. A place where only she exists. My body jerks as I see spots, my seed shooting deep inside her. She collapses on top of me, our breathing labored.

"Oh my God," she says, her voice raspy, her sweet lips peppering me with kisses all over my face. "You're so hot." She bites the bottom of my lip.

I grin. "Angel, don't call me hot. I'm bad, rough, not hot." I slap her ass holding her still as we look at each other.

Her eyes narrow. "And... I told you not to go near my... you know." She whispers the last part.

It's impossible not to laugh. "Your ass! It's okay, babe. It's only us—you can use your grown-up words." She gasps and tries to get off me. I hold her still to see her face grow pink. Eve gets shy about anal play. For a moment, I gently grasp her face with my hands so I can gaze at her. She's my favorite thing to look at, besides my son. I grin and my thumb moves to her puffy lips as I rub them. "You love it."

"Jason... I do not." She huffs and jerks away. This time, I let her go and reach over her for my cigarettes on the nightstand. Our faces are inches apart.

"You do. It's okay to like it." Her eyes change and I full-on laugh this time.

"You're such a jerk." She pushes me back as she stands and stretches. "I need a quick shower. Do you think James is fine?"

I sit back on the wrought iron bed frame and light up. My eyes travel up and down her, stopping as I admire her full breasts. She drops her hands to her hips.

"Focus." She snaps one finger in my face. "Our son... we need to get back to him."

"He's fine. Why don't you come back to bed?"

I reach for her, but she squeals and sashays into the bathroom, calling over her shoulder, "We need to get back down to the party. I've got a balloon guy coming." She shuts the bathroom door. The water instantly goes on and I close my eyes and enjoy my cancer stick. I should rinse off too, but I love the smell of Eve and sex on me. I take one more deep drag on the cigarette and put it out. Reluctantly, I get up and pull on my jeans. Since James's birth, I've cut my smoking back to the point that I hardly miss it. So, if I get a chance to sneak one, I do. I push open the bathroom door and there on the counter of the sink is a pregnancy stick.

Eve is humming in the shower and my stomach flips. *Shit, do I look?* I should wait for her... but it's right there. The shower turns off and I look over at my wife in all her wet glory and my dick hardens. Crossing my arms, I say, "Something you want to tell me?" I can't help but smile.

She laughs. "You tell me. It's obvious you looked." She rolls her eyes at me. "I took it because I'm late and my boobs hurt. But since I just stopped breast—"

"It's got two bright pink lines." I show her.

She purses her lips as she towels herself off and my heart thuds in my chest. To say I'm excited is to put it mildly. I want a bunch of kids with Eve.

"Babe? Talk to me. What's going on in that beautiful head?"

She sighs and folds the towel, hanging it up. "Are you happy? Do you want another baby so soon?"

I nod. "I'm thrilled, but if you're not ready..." I lean on the cool dark rock of my shower and look at this wild, beautiful gypsy who has captured my soul.

She walks up and wraps her arms around my neck, her warm, sweet-smelling body pressed into mine, and I groan as I jerk her as tight as I can into my arms. My nose is instantly in her neck as I breathe in her scent and hear the words I need to hear.

"I'm thrilled."

"Get dressed, Angel, and let's go tell everyone. My mom is going to be ecstatic."

Then I give her another kiss because I can't seem to stop. With reluctance, I let her go. She twirls around and graces me with a smile that makes my chest hurt at how much I love her.

"I'll only be a second." She pulls on a black tube dress. We rarely have a babysitter so I'm debating if I should turn her around and fuck her again... as a celebration, you know? I'm reaching for her when a loud knock makes me pull Eve behind me. She's clutching one Converse to her chest.

"What?" I snap.

"Um, Prez... we got a situation." Ryder's voice booms through the wood.

Eve's hand goes to her throat, the thud of her shoe falling a loud reminder that this is my life. *Every day,* the stress of something happening to my woman or boy makes me weak. And now Eve's pregnant again.

"Is it anything with my boy?"

"No." He chuckles and I sense Eve's whole body relax. "James Dean is having a blast with Axel... it's a family matter."

She sinks down onto our bed and reaches for her shoe. "Jesus Christ, can't we have one day without a situation?" she snaps as she reaches for her sneaker and slips it on.

"Apparently not." I look down at her flushed face. "You okay?"

She stands and pulls down her dress then flips her hair over her shoulder. "I feel like a hundred dollars." She reaches up on her tiptoes to brush my lips. "I'll see you downstairs."

She swings open the door to Ryder lounging in the doorway. She pats his arm as she grabs her bag, then flashes me a saucy smirk. "Hurry up, you two. Cake is happening soon."

My heart beats faster. I would die a thousand times for her. I rub my hands over my face and inhale. The smell of my Eve calms me. I drop my hands and face Ryder.

"What?"

"He's in the conference room." I arch a brow at him then shake my head as I walk past.

"By your cryptic message, I'm assuming this is going to make me unhappy on my son's birthday and make us late for cake?"

He lifts up his hands like I have a gun pointed at him. "I didn't say that. Actually it's about time he came back and finished what needs to be done."

"Eve is pregnant again." He stares at me and for a little bit, that horrible slither of dread causes the hair to stand up on my arms.

"Eve's a fighter. She'll be fine. It's time, brother."

I let his words swim around my head knowing Ryder's right. This has been a long time coming. I barely acknowledge anyone as we pass the loud game room. Bikers are playing pool and doing shots, but there are no drugs in sight. This is a family party. That means no weapons, no drugs. If they can't follow the rules, they're gone. I have no tolerance for any shit of any kind. My kid is not growing up like me. Eve and I are on the same page when it comes to parenting. Translation—we both do the opposite of what our parents did. I stop at the door.

"Revenge needs to happen, Prez. People need to atone," Ryder hisses. I look at him for a second and wonder how bloody this is going to get.

"I got your back, man. We ain't going down this time."

I grin because Ryder is one scary motherfucker when he wants to be. I nod and jerk open the door. His back is to me. I can't not snort at his dark suit that stinks up the room with money.

He turns and I lock eyes with his silver ones. The room is quiet, and the sun pours in casting a shadow across half the floor, almost as if it's warning us.

Fuck it. Ryder's right. It's time to find whoever is responsible and make them pay.

So, I step inside and say, "Hello, David…"

THE END

CONNECT

Website: http://www.cassandrafayerobbins.com
Facebook: http://www.facebook.com/cassandrafayerobbins/
Twitter: https://twitter.com/CassFayeRobbins | @CassFayeRobbins
Instagram: www.instagram.com/cassandrafayerobbins/ | @CassandraFayeRobbins
Goodreads: http://bit.ly/CassandraRobbins
Newsletter: www.cassandrafayerobbins.com
BookBub: https://bit.ly/2KIOeqB
Book+Main: https://bit.ly/2HZdc7D
Personal Facebook Group:
https://www.facebook.com/groups/cassiessassycrew/

ALSO BY CASSANDRA ROBBINS

Rock God Series

Rise
https://amzn.to/3k66VXE

The Entitled Duet

The Entitled
https://www.amazon.com/dp/B07HKZGWG7

The Enlightened
https://www.amazon.com/dp/B07KFQY1FG

The Disciples Series

Lethal
https://www.amazon.com/dp/B07Q3C9L5M

Atone
https://www.amazon.com/dp/B07YQM4GPW

Repent
https://www.amazon.com/dp/B0887NJ2CT

The Entitled

People say you can't find your soul mate at eight years old. I did.

I found Reed and loved him more than I loved myself.

We were young... beautiful... *entitled*.

Money and private schools, our families' lavish parties and posh New York City apartments—it was all mere window dressing. What was real was our obsessive love, which grew right along with us as we moved toward adulthood. It consumed me, and only in his arms did I feel wanted and safe.

But I have a secret. It's big and to some, unforgivable. And it's why I let Reed destroy me, or maybe I destroyed us. Either way, I'm worse than broke—I'm broken.

Once upon a time, we were happy...Yet privilege has an ugly underside and in the blink of an eye, my world crashed down around me.

I don't feel *entitled* anymore.

The Entitled is first in *The Entitled* duet. Their story concludes in *The Enlightened*.

ACKNOWLEDGEMENTS

First and always, to my husband and my two beautiful children. Their patience when I'm trying to figure out how to do this self-publishing journey is amazing. I love you guys more than you can imagine.

My brother Chris and his wife Dahlia, my baby brother, Duke, and cousin Jake, I'm so lucky to have you. My dad and Susie, my Minnesota family, thank you for all your support.

To my editor Nikki Busch: not only are you the best at what you do, you are also a good friend.

To my incredibly talented cover designer Michele Catalano Creative. You amaze me at how you understand my vision and bring it to life. Michelle Clay and Annette Brignac, I'm beyond grateful and thankful to have you two and Book Nerd Services. You both have the golden touch and I'm honored to call you both my dear friends. Thank you. Elaine York, you're a master at making the inside of my books look fantastic. To Hayfaah Sumtally, you make the most beautiful teasers. I adore you.

My betas Michelle, Annette, Ann Marie, and Annie, thank you from the bottom of my heart.

I have been lucky enough to have some truly incredible, talented friends in my corner and they need to know how much I appreciate them. Auden Dar, my soul sister. You're literally one of the most positive, supportive people I know. I owe you more than I can ever say in words. Tempi Lark, you're my kindred spirit and also one of my best friends. Your help and support have been beyond expected. Also, your trailers literally brought Blade and Eve to life. Bex Dane, you have been my friend from the very beginning and your knowledge continues to inspire me. Leigh

Lennon, Trilina Pucci, Naomi Springthorpe, Leslie McAdam, and Nelle L'Amour: all of these women are so talented and I am so thankful they are in my life.

Monica, Kelly, Frances, your friendship and support mean the world to me.

Lastly, and most importantly, I thank you, my readers. You're what matters. I hope you enjoyed Blade and Eve's story. I can't wait to continue on with these naughty Disciples boys!

ABOUT THE AUTHOR

Cassandra Robbins is a *USA Today,* Amazon Top 100, KDP All-Star, and international bestselling author. She threatened to write a romance novel for years and finally let the voices take over with her debut novel, *The Entitled.* She's a self-proclaimed hopeless romantic driven to create obsessive, angst-filled characters who have to fight for their happily ever after. Cassandra resides in Los Angeles with her hot husband, two beautiful children, and a fluffy Samoyed, Stanley. Her family and friends are her lifeline but writing is her passion.

Made in United States
Orlando, FL
06 July 2022